PRAISE FOR *WE*

"The swoony banter, the hilarious travel mishaps, the close proximity—*Wedding Dashers* has it all. I was hooked from the very first page!"

—Lynn Painter, *New York Times* bestselling author of *Happily Never After*

"Heather McBreen weaves complicated, flawed, lovable characters into this joyride of a rom-com. *Wedding Dashers* is a total winner."

—Annabel Monaghan, national bestselling author of *Summer Romance*

"*Wedding Dashers* has everything I look for in a romantic comedy: whip-smart banter, sizzling chemistry, and two incredibly compelling leads I fell for right from the very first page. I cheered so loudly when Jack and Ada finally found their way to each other it could probably be heard from space. Heather McBreen is a rom-com author to watch!"

—Jenna Levine, *USA Today* bestselling author of *My Vampire Plus One*

"Did Heather McBreen write *Wedding Dashers* for me specifically? This book has everything my heart desires in a travel rom-com—plans gone awry, perfect banter, and multiple instances of only one bed. It's funny, heartfelt, and hot as heck; I couldn't decide whether to laugh, swoon, or fan myself. A true delight!"

—Sarah Adler, *USA Today* bestselling author of *Happy Medium*

"*Wedding Dashers* is road trip romance at its best! A non-stop adventure filled with hilarious detours, scorching hot chemistry, witty banter, and emotional growth and self-discovery. I loved every second of Ada and Jack's journey!"

—Naina Kumar, *USA Today* bestselling author of *Say You'll Be Mine*

"This book! I can't stop thinking about it. *Wedding Dashers* gave me everything I want in a road trip romance: a case of "anyone but you," travel shenanigans, only one bed, and the best *Leap Year* vibes. Sign me up for anything Heather McBreen writes after this because I'm now a forever fan."

—Jo Segura, *USA Today* bestselling author of *Temple of Swoon*

"Heather McBreen's romantic romp of a debut is the exact sort of funny, dreamy journey I always want to get lost in! *Wedding Dashers* is a perfect companion for anyone who loves to find the joy in taking the unexpected route."

—Courtney Preiss, *USA Today* bestselling author of *Welcome Home, Caroline Klein*

"Heather McBreen brings all the fun, all the feels, and all the chemistry with her debut *Wedding Dashers*, a rom-com in its truest form that kept a smile on my face from the first page to the last. Ada and Jack's mishap travel adventures are side-splittingly funny and the tender moments in this book will stop you in your tracks. This is a book you'll want to read again and again."

—Meredith Schorr, author of *As Seen on TV* and *Someone Just Like You*

Wedding Dashers

HEATHER McBREEN

Berkley Romance
New York

BERKLEY ROMANCE
Published by Berkley
An imprint of Penguin Random House LLC
penguinrandomhouse.com

Book design by Daniel Brount

Library of Congress Cataloging-in-Publication Data

Names: McBreen, Heather, author.
Title: Wedding dashers / Heather McBreen.
Description: First edition. | New York : Berkley Romance, 2025.
Identifiers: LCCN 2024017706 (print) | LCCN 2024017707 (ebook) |
ISBN 9780593817629 (trade paperback) | ISBN 9780593817636 (ebook)
Subjects: LCGFT: Romance fiction. | Novels.
Classification: LCC PS3613.C2758 W43 2025 (print) |
LCC PS3613.C2758 (ebook) | DDC 813/.6—dc23/eng/20240510
LC record available at https://lccn.loc.gov/2024017706
LC ebook record available at https://lccn.loc.gov/2024017707

First Edition: January 2025

Printed in the United States of America
1st Printing

To Alex, I'm all in

Author's Note

This book involves alcohol consumption, divorce, death of a parent (not on page, but referred to), and an abusive romantic relationship (not on page, but referred to). If any of these are potentially sensitive topics for you, please read with care.

Wedding Dashers

Chapter 1

83 HOURS UNTIL THE WEDDING

I stare at the flight display, weighing the likelihood that I'm currently experiencing some kind of jet lag–induced delirium, or if my connecting flight from London to Belfast really is canceled. I blink a few times just to be sure, but in angry red letters the word *canceled* continues to flash aggressively across the screen.

The remnants of a partially digested bag of airline pretzels churn inside my stomach and for a brief moment I wonder if they're about to make a reappearance.

How could this be happening? I double-, no, *triple*-checked the departure schedule before I left. But apparently sometime while I was flying over the Atlantic, the universe—or more specifically the shady budget airline I booked last minute—conspired to ruin my life.

But of course this happened. Because this is just one more ill-fated domino in a series of unfortunate events. Perhaps I ought to just accept my fate as a serially unlucky person. Throw in the towel now and resign myself to the life of a quirky heroine in an early 2000s chick flick . . . *before* she gets the makeover.

I wipe clammy hands against my jeans and try to focus. There must be a solution. Maybe there's an open seat on another flight. Or maybe I could ride in the cockpit. They let people do that, right? I mean I'm sure if I explain the situation . . .

But the longer I stare at the display screen, the more my chest feels like a hollowed-out pumpkin.

If I don't make it to this wedding on time, Allison is going to kill me. Not in a hyperbolic sense—my sister is literally going to murder me and ask her soon-to-be husband, Collin, to help her bury my body, and I'll end up as the subject of one of those murder podcasts Gen Z is obsessed with.

And not because she can't bear to get married without me, her beloved older sister, by her side. It's because I am carrying precious cargo. The veil. And not just any veil, but a one-of-a-kind Demi Karina *custom* veil.

Allison would have carried it herself, but with seventeen dresses, ten pairs of heels (one might break!), more makeup than a fully stocked Sephora, and enough cans of hair spray to single-handedly destroy the ozone, I, as the maid of honor, got tasked with transporting the veil. Which doesn't feel like an honor so much as a death wish.

I cast the garment bag under my left arm a scathing look as though it were the veil's fault we're in this mess. But I know perfectly well the real culprit in this shitstorm sandwich is the castle. The overpriced, out-of-budget, embarrassingly extravagant castle.

Why couldn't Allison get married in a chic barn like everyone else in the Greater Seattle area? Somewhere rustic yet tasteful. Somewhere *not* six thousand miles away.

But no. It *had* to be a castle. And not just any castle—a castle in abso-freaking-lutely-nowhere Ireland. Inconvenience to others be damned.

So now I'm trapped on the wrong island with no clue how I *or* this veil will make it to this wedding.

So much for traveling to the land of luck.

Shoulders slouched, I make my way to the customer service desk clinging to my last shred of optimism that this is all just a silly misunderstanding and I'll be on the next flight to Ireland in no time.

But it's not.

"There's been a staffing mix-up with the airline," the clerk tells me, tone strained, like it might be the three hundredth time she's recited that line today. "All flights on this route have been canceled."

My stomach dips. A mix-up? I'm about to miss my little sister's wedding and be cursed for all eternity because of something as random and arbitrary as a staffing *mix-up*?

"Please," I plead. "My sister is getting married. I *have* to be on that flight."

"Is your final destination Belfast?" the clerk asks.

"Yes," I tell her. *And it's gonna be six feet under if I don't get there on time.*

The clerk shakes her head. "I'm sorry. I don't have anything. But in the meantime, please take a seat and I'll let you know if something opens up."

If.

The single syllable sends a new jolt of anxiety hurtling through me.

I want to ask her what happens if she doesn't find anything. What then? Will I have to rent a boat? Swim to Ireland? Flirt my way onto a rich person's private jet? I shoot a quick glance over my shoulder, halfway hoping there might be some such person, until

I remember that the kind of people who own private jets usually aren't hanging around the customer service desks of obscure budget airlines that offer major discounts on both prices and legroom.

I force a smile and thank the clerk before slumping into the only available plastic seat, which—as luck would have it—is beside a young couple who is making out like the world is burning down around them. *Really?*

I don't know whether to hate or envy that a canceled flight and an airport full of disgruntled travelers does nothing to curb their passion. Must be nice.

Trying to distract myself, I connect to wi-fi and check my email. I expect the usual slew of Bed Bath & Beyond coupons and lengthy newsletters I've been meaning to unsubscribe from. Instead, there's only one email, from a design firm I interviewed with weeks ago. My heartbeat ratchets up, and my fingers scramble to open the email.

> Dear Miss Ada Gallman,
>
> Thank you so much for taking the time to interview with Hewitt & Goldstein. We had many incredibly qualified applicants for the role of graphic designer, and unfortunately . . .

I don't finish reading. Instead, I close my email tab and try to ignore the impending sense of doom that's settled in my gut ever since the tattoo studio I opened—Sleeve It to Me—went under nine months ago. But like an old injury, I can ignore it for a little while, until the reality that I'm twenty-eight, unemployed, broke, steeped in business loan debt, and sleeping on my parents' couch flares up once more.

I sigh and slump lower in my seat, halfway hoping the cold, unforgiving plastic might just swallow me whole, when my phone vibrates, announcing all the texts I missed while I was flying over the Atlantic.

2:17pm **MOM**
Have you landed? What time will you be here?

2:17pm **MOM**
Watch out for pickpockets! Did you bring that money belt I told you to?

2:18pm **MOM**
Check out this apartment listing on Zillow!

5:06pm **ALLISON**
You have the veil, right?

5:08pm **ALLISON**
Tell me you have the veil???

5:09pm **ALLISON**
When are you getting here?

5:29pm **ALLISON**
Mom is being so annoying. I swear if she asks me about the seating chart one more time I'm gonna lose it.

5:37pm **ALLISON**
FYI Mom is considering applying for you to be on The Bachelor. I told her it was weird that one guy dates thirty-two women simultaneously, but she won't drop it. She thinks you're gonna die alone.

6:47pm **MOM**
I heard Dan's company is hiring. Have you thought about doing interior design? That's kind of the same thing, right?

6:53pm **MOM**
Remember Karen and Scott's son? The engineer? He'll be at the wedding! And he's still single!

I don't think my mom pitching the neighbor's son as *still single*—like he's a bargain bin closeout item marked down to its *lowest sale price yet*—is the rave review she thinks it is, but I don't respond. I'm too focused on another text. One from him.

1:37pm **CARTER**
Let me know when you've made it safely to Belfast. Hope you have a great trip. x

I stare at the *x*. It's mocking me. What does that *x* mean? That he thinks it was a huge mistake to take a break and we should get back together? Or a platonic kiss on the cheek? Short for ex-boyfriend? A typo? Solve for *x*?

I wish I knew. But apparently even after eight years together, I still don't know him well enough to know what that *x* means.

But what I do know is that just because a guy says he loves you and wants to be with you forever, does *not* in fact mean that he truly desires any of those things. In fact, what he might actually want is *some space* and to *take a break* for three months to *see how we feel about things.*

And now he apparently has the audacity to hope I *have a great trip*. Like he's not the one who ruined it. Like it's not his fault that I'm attending my little sister's wedding alone. Like it wasn't *him* who broke *my* heart.

I got the text from Carter right before I boarded my flight to London, and I've since had nine hours to think of the perfect funny/sexy/you suck response. But I've still got nothing.

I type out: There's a couple sitting next to me who I'm pretty sure is going to join the mile high club. Could have been us. Your loss.

I frown and delete it. Trying too hard.

How about . . .

I'm having a great time WITHOUT you. Never better. In fact, let's stay on a break for three MORE months. P.S. I never liked your friends.

I immediately press the backspace, then release a long sigh before imagining what I wish I could say. What I really feel.

I miss you.

But I can't tell him that. I can't tell anybody that.

"Miss?"

I look up to see the clerk beckoning me back to the desk and my chest seizes with hope.

"Looks like we might be able to put you on a flight first thing tomorrow morning. Does that work?" the clerk asks, frowning at her screen.

I mentally review the schedule. The rehearsal dinner is in two days, but Allison has all these pre-wedding events planned: a spa day, high tea, a pub crawl.

"Are there any earlier flights?" I ask.

"I'm sorry, this is all I have available." Her eyes drift to the growing line of people behind me. "But this seat will go fast, so I suggest you take it," she says, lowering her voice to a whisper.

I risk a glance over my shoulder at the gaggle of bloodthirsty travelers, each ready to pounce on the ticket in the event I don't take it. I turn back to the clerk.

"I'll take it." I guess the pub crawl will have to crawl on without me.

She nods and punches something into her computer. "Come

back at six a.m. tomorrow to this same gate. Since the airline is at fault, we can give you a hotel voucher as well."

Relief swarms my chest.

The last-minute flight wiped out my bank account along with the three-hundred-dollar bridesmaid dress that makes me look like a leprechaun. Green really isn't my color. It totally clashes with my faded lilac hair—an unfortunate remnant of a post-break self-makeover that I can't afford to have fixed at a salon. But the point is it certainly isn't in my budget to pay for an extra night in a hotel.

"Thanks," I tell her. "A hotel voucher would be great."

The clerk nods and a printer under the desk buzzes to life. A second later she hands me a voucher for a hotel nearby and instructs me on how to take the courtesy bus from the terminal.

I thank her and steer my suitcase toward the exit, rollers clip-clopping behind me.

Once on the bus, I press my nose to the glass, searching for evidence that I'm somewhere new and exciting—after all, I've never been to England before—but apart from driving on the other side of the road and the bus driver saying "cheers" when I come aboard, there's nothing particularly exotic about the industrial buildings surrounding the airport. Though now that I think about it, I don't know what I expected. For us to deplane right in front of Big Ben?

When I arrive at the hotel—a no-frills chain—I take my place at the end of the check-in line and try to think of something positive.

Maybe this hotel has robes. I love robes. And maybe I'll finally get some much-needed alone time . . . I think of my pink vibrator tucked into my suitcase. Since I've been sleeping on my parents' couch, I haven't exactly gotten much *me time*. Maybe tonight won't be so bad after all.

I sigh as the line shifts forward.

Also, the plane didn't crash. I guess that's something. And I didn't lose my luggage. Or the veil. Though I suppose if I had to choose between wearing the same pair of underwear for thirty-six hours or losing Allison's custom veil, I'd choose dirty underwear in a heartbeat.

I'm next in line when my phone buzzes from my pocket. I feverishly yank it out, wondering if it might be Carter again. But it's Allison telling me to make sure the veil is hung in an upright position.

I groan and shove my phone back in my pocket without answering her.

I'm the older sister. Aren't I supposed to be the bossy one? But I guess this is what happens when you get married in a castle. You start thinking you're royalty.

And yet, annoying as my sister can be, I know it's not really the veil, or even the castle that bothers me. None of that is a surprise. Allison's always been a little over-the-top. The kind of person to throw her dog a Barbie-themed birthday party *just because*. No, the part that really stings is that we aren't close anymore. Not since Collin's been in the picture. And everything about this wedding is another reminder of that.

The next available staff member waves me forward and I put the voucher on the desk.

The receptionist examines it, frowns, then hands it back to me.

"Madam, this is for last night," she says in a clipped British accent. "It's expired."

"What? No, it's for tonight," I insist, jabbing my finger at the paper voucher.

She shakes her head. "I'm sorry, but it says right here. See? We cannot accept this."

I take back the voucher. My stomach bottoms out. She's right.

Now what am I supposed to do? Sleep on the street? Go back to the airport? Beg?

I run a hand through my hair, unnerved. "Is there something you can do? Please?"

"Madam, I'm terribly sorry, but unless you have a voucher for tonight, there is nothing I can do." Her tone is nice enough, but her blank expression makes me think *sorry* probably isn't an emotion she's currently experiencing.

"Can I call the airline?" I ask, desperation stretching my voice thin. "They'll explain it's all a mistake."

The receptionist looks like she'd really rather not, but she nods tightly, and I pull out my phone and call the 1-800 number for the airline. It rings. And rings . . . *and rings.*

"I'm sure the line is just busy," I whisper, but she doesn't look convinced.

The phone rings for what feels like three whole lifetimes before the call gets unceremoniously dropped.

Shit.

"If you don't have a voucher for tonight, I'm afraid I can't help you."

"Please, can't I just call another—" But it is in this moment that I realize my life must be one giant case study in Murphy's Law, because the strap on my purse snaps and the contents—including, but not limited to, three tampons, a lucky rabbit's foot I purchased from a very promising internet retailer, and approximately twenty dollars' worth of change—spill out onto the floor, hitting the linoleum with a resounding clang.

Everyone in the vicinity goes silent, watching me like I'm a gruesome car accident they can't look away from.

I take it back. I wish the plane had crashed.

Cheeks aflame, I duck to collect my stuff and what's left of my tattered dignity. My fingers are closing around a stray tampon when an outstretched hand holds out the lucky (unlucky?) rabbit's foot. I follow the arm up to a tall man with dark hair, warm eyes, and a perfect five-o'clock shadow.

He's about my age or older—it's hard to tell with the facial hair—and sexy in that tall-dark-and-handsome sort of way that feels almost fake. Do people like this really exist? And we just let them walk around? Unsupervised? I feel like that kind of hotness ought to come with a warning label. And maybe an instruction manual. *Step one: don't totally humiliate yourself in their presence.*

Heat fans across my skin as I accept the rabbit's foot. "Thanks," I tell him just as the receptionist's voice draws me back.

"I'm afraid that you're holding up the queue," she says, now visibly annoyed. "So if you don't have a voucher for tonight, I'm going to have to ask you to please step aside."

Humiliation churns inside me. What am I supposed to do now? Cut my losses and leave? Go back to the airport? Demand to speak with a manager?

But I've never been a speak-to-the-manager type of gal. In fact, I'm much more likely to pretend to enjoy the beef tartare I totally didn't order. So I grab my luggage, mutter a begrudging *thanks,* and walk away.

I don't have a plan. I don't even know where I'm going. But I start walking, hoping to maintain my composure for three more seconds until I can find somewhere to cry.

But three seconds is a tad optimistic.

Hot tears prick my eyes and I shut them tight. *Don't cry. Don't cry.* I'm a grown adult woman. I can figure this out without crying.

But panic and more than a little self-pity flood my body in hot torrents. I'm in a foreign country with nowhere to sleep. It's getting late. I'm exhausted. I haven't eaten anything in hours. My face is totally breaking out. And worst of all, I don't even want to go to this wedding.

Before I can stop them, two fat tears roll down my cheek.

Chapter 2

82 HOURS UNTIL THE WEDDING

Crying in public is the worst.

It's gotta be a top five Most Embarrassing Thing. Just behind accidentally calling your teacher *mom* and clogging the toilet at your boyfriend's house. Both of which have happened to me. So, in a way, this is very on brand.

I cover my face, pretending to suffer from allergies—hay fever if anyone asks—when I notice there's someone standing behind me.

Great. They're going to offer me a tissue or something. Can't they just let me be a hot mess in peace?

"Excuse me?"

"I'm fine," I start to say just as I look up to see it's the same man from before. Mr. Tall-Dark-and-Handsome.

His gaze meets mine and his eyes widen, clearly embarrassed. "Oh, uh, sorry, I . . ." His voice stops then restarts. "Are you okay?"

"I'm fine," I say again, but the second *fine* is even less convincing than the first. I wonder if he's coming to return another stray tampon. Which is nice and all, but, sir, please read the room.

"I didn't drop another tampon, did I?" I ask.

"What?" His brow furrows with genuine confusion before shaking his head *no*. "Actually." He clears his throat, gaze skirting to my luggage. "You took my suitcase . . . by mistake, I think," he adds, like he's weighing the possibility I arranged that entire spectacle just so I could steal his luggage. "So if I could get it back that'd be great."

I frown, eyes darting down to my own suitcase . . . which is, in fact, *not* mine. It's the same black with silver buttons, but this one is much nicer. It has leather accents and a plated luggage tag.

My face warms. "Oh, sorry. My bad." I roll the suitcase toward him, and he hands me mine. "I guess I was distracted," I say, tilting my chin toward the reception desk.

"No worries. I assumed it might throw a wrench in your travel plans when you discovered the twenty pounds of cocaine in there."

I freeze. "W-what?"

His expression expands into a grin. "Kidding."

I try to laugh, but it comes out more like a cross between a squeak and a sputter.

"Well, thanks," I say, gesturing to the suitcase. "And sorry again."

I expect him to leave, but he just stands there, studying me with a mix of pity and intrigue until he says, "I couldn't help but overhear what happened. Sorry about the room."

"Me too."

"Do you have anywhere else to go?"

"Not really."

He nods then glances away, and I follow his gaze to the window where it's now pouring rain. Because of course it is.

"Fuck," I mutter under my breath. "This is *really* not my day."

"Could be worse."

My eyebrows shoot up. "Could it?"

He looks me over with calculated interest and an unexpected rush of heat diffuses across my skin. "I mean, at least you won't have to wear my clothes for the next week," he says. "I don't think your tiny frame would fit into anything of mine."

"Well, I could say the same to you. There's a green dress in there that I'm positive you don't have the legs for."

He lets out a surprised laugh and I notice he has dimples. Just like Carter. But while Carter is firmly in the cute category, Mr. Tall-Dark-and-Handsome is distinctly hot.

He has eyes that remind me of spilled ink and a sharp jawline dotted with meticulous stubble, the kind that probably requires fancy shaving products and an extra thirty minutes in front of the mirror.

If I were sketching him, I'd use sharp strokes for the angle of his jaw and softer lines for the creases under his eyes. I'd smudge my charcoal pencil to darken his gaze and lightly shadow the hollow in his throat. *If* I still sketched, that is, something I haven't done since Carter and I went on a break.

"Can I buy you a drink at the bar?" he asks after a beat.

My eyes widen, caught off guard. "You want to buy me a drink?"

"It seems like the least I can do after . . ." He gestures vaguely toward the reception desk.

"I'm the one who took your luggage. Shouldn't I be the one buying *you* a drink?"

His mouth quirks. "Are you offering?"

My stomach gives a traitorous flutter and I bite my lip, letting my gaze trail back toward the door. "I sort of have to find somewhere to sleep. Also," I say, shooting him a conspiratorial look, "I don't usually drink with strange men I don't know in foreign countries."

He considers me a moment before sticking out his hand. "I can't do anything about the foreign country part, but I'm Jack. My last meal on death row would be pizza. Boxers, not briefs. And I once cheated on a high school history test and was so consumed by guilt that I told the teacher and got ten weeks of detention." His face ripens into a smile. "See? Now you know everything about me."

"That's everything?"

"Well, not *everything*. I've graciously left a few topics out so that we'll have something to talk about later."

I look down at his outstretched hand, considering it before giving it a firm shake. "Ada," I say. "And I'm *not* telling you which kind of underwear I prefer."

He coughs out a laugh.

Not going to lie, he has a nice laugh. It's deep and full-bodied, and something inside me stirs at the sound of it. I want to make him laugh again.

"So, one beer?" he asks.

I can't say I'm not tempted. He's attractive and charming-ish, and it's not like I have anywhere else to go. Besides, after the day I've had, I could do with a free beer. In fact, maybe this is my consolation prize for World's Shittiest Day. I get to have a drink with a hunk before sleeping on the cold plastic of an airport bench.

"Why not?" I say with a shrug. "It's not like this day could get any worse."

"Ahh, very good. I'm glad you're keeping your expectations low," he says, nodding sagely.

I follow Jack to a sparsely decorated hotel bar with leather booths and dim mood lighting. We pick an empty booth and Jack orders us both lagers.

The drinks arrive and I take a sip. It's bitter and I wince as I swallow.

"So, where are you from? Seattle?" he asks.

My gaze narrows. "How can you tell?"

His lips curl upward, halfway between a smirk and a smile. "You're wearing a University of Washington sweatshirt. It was worth a guess."

I look down at the purple and gold logo on my front. "Right. Yeah, I'm from Seattle."

"I grew up near Seattle. They have . . ." He looks me up and down, gaze lingering just a beat too long on my lips. "Nice trees."

I blush. Is he hitting on me?

"Really?" I ask. "Nice trees?"

The corners of his mouth twitch with thinly veiled amusement. "It's the first thing that came to mind."

"And where do you live now if not Seattle?"

"Portland."

"I hear they also have . . ." I drag my eyes up his tall frame, pausing to let my gaze linger the same way his did. "Nice trees."

He laughs, then sets his elbows on the table, propping his chin up with his hands. "Is this your first time in London?"

"First time out of the country if you don't count spring break in Cancun," I tell him.

"London is a great city. Fun nightlife. Amazing food." He pauses, brows scrunching like he's just realized something. "Not many trees though."

I laugh. "I thought British food was supposed to suck. Isn't it all boiled potatoes and mushy peas?"

"British food can be good if you know where to look, but the international food scene here is amazing."

I haven't eaten in hours, not since the bag of airplane pretzels

I had mid-flight, and the thought of any food is enough to make my mouth water. Right on cue, my stomach growls.

Jack's eyebrows lift. "You should feed that thing. You want a burger?"

"I'm fine," I lie. He's already been nice enough; he doesn't need to feed me too.

"I'm hungry too. We should eat," he says with a decisive dip of the chin before ordering us both burgers and *chips*.

"Thanks, you're *really* nice." I pause, frowning. "You're not gonna try to kidnap me like in that Liam Neeson movie, are you?"

His eyes flash and he cracks out a laugh. "I don't think you'd have agreed to have a beer with me if you thought I was going to try to sell you into an international sex trafficking ring."

I give a conciliatory nod. "True. I'm just wondering *why* you're being so nice to me."

"I felt bad about the hotel situation, and well . . ." Jack's eyes lift to meet mine. "I thought you were pretty cute."

I freeze, beer halfway to my lips. "You thought I was cute? Which part? The tears? Or the overall demeanor of pathetic-ness?"

"The purple hair actually."

I laugh, then run a self-conscious hand over my head as though just realizing it's there.

"It doesn't normally look like this," I tell him.

"I figured you didn't come out of the womb with purple hair."

"I just mean it's a new look for me."

He looks me over and my skin prickles under the full attention of his gaze. "I like it," he says after a pause. "Very *sexy mermaid*."

My cheeks sizzle.

Now I know he's flirting with me. But I'm sort of okay with it. He's nice, and attractive. Why shouldn't a nice, attractive guy flirt with me? After all, Carter and I are on a break.

And yet, as flattering as it is to think about a handsome stranger showing interest in me, flirting is about my limit. I don't want to *see other people.* Or *explore my options.* I don't want to work out my frustrations in the curves of a stranger's body. Or whatever it is people do on breaks. I just want things with Carter and me to go back to normal.

Once the food arrives, I reach for the saltshaker. I pour a little pile into my palm and toss it over my left shoulder. Jack stares at me, eyes wide.

"What was that?" he asks.

"To ward off the bad luck."

"You're superstitious?"

"I prefer *proactively cautious.*"

I never used to consider myself a superstitious person. I'm much more inclined to see "luck" as a matter of perception rather than the work of nefarious forces in the universe, but after my credit card got stolen three times last month, I got much more *proactively cautious* about things. I saged my car. I bought a rabbit's foot. I even started meditating. But a whole lot of good that's done me.

"Is that why you had the rabbit's foot in your purse?" Jack asks. "For luck?"

"I just figure that if there's something I can do to change my luck, I should at least give it a try, right?"

"And you believe that will work?"

"I'm getting a free dinner right now, aren't I?"

He cracks a smile. It's a nice smile, the kind that fills his whole face.

"So, where are you headed?" he asks, popping a fry into his mouth.

"My sister's wedding."

"Alone?"

I smack my forehead with my palm. "Shit! I knew I forgot something! A date!"

He laughs. "I mean, if you're going to your sister's wedding, why aren't you traveling with your family?"

"I was supposed to." I pluck a fry from my plate. "But I realized too late that my passport expired and had to expedite a new one that didn't arrive until yesterday."

"Shit. You really do have bad luck."

"It's honestly a miracle I haven't been struck by lightning."

"Better stay away from metal rods to be safe."

Our eyes catch, twin grins snaking across our mouths.

"I'm going to a wedding too." He gestures to the garment bag perched atop his suitcase. "I'm the best man."

"I'm sorry."

He reaches for his beer, frowning. "Why?"

"Because anyone who would make all their friends and family fly halfway around the world to take part in ritualized self-aggrandizement is seriously disturbed."

Jack's eyes widen and I can tell what sounded like a joke in my head, did in fact *not* sound like one out loud.

"Sorry," I say, wincing. "Did that sound as bitter as I think it did?"

He tilts his chin, eyes flickering between amusement and curiosity. "Is it the *ritualized self-aggrandizement* that bothers you, or this particular wedding?"

I fidget with my napkin. "I don't usually have a problem with weddings, but . . ."

"But you're not looking forward to this wedding?" he finishes for me.

"Not exactly."

Jack's eyes dance to my ring finger, then back to me.

I do the same to him. No ring.

"Bad breakup?" he asks.

"That obvious?"

He laughs in confirmation. "Let me guess. He was supposed to be your date to the wedding?"

I arch an eyebrow, impressed. "You're good."

He sits back in his seat, perusing me with interest. "So what happened?"

I pick up my fork, then set it back down again. "You really want to know about my boyfriend?"

"Take it from me, there's no one better to vent to about your personal problems than a stranger at a bar."

"But I thought you weren't a stranger anymore? After all, I know what kind of underwear you're wearing."

The corners of his mouth curl upward. "Go on, tell me about the jerk."

"He's not a jerk," I say quickly. "He's a great guy."

"But he isn't here?"

"No, he's not."

"Why not?"

I hesitate, not sure I want to spill my guts to this guy I just met. But then again, who cares if I tell him? It's not like I'll ever see him again. He's the burner account equivalent of a person. Right?

"We've been together eight years," I say, reaching for another fry. "And I thought we were going to get married. Instead, he suggested we take a break for three months so we can reevaluate *where we stand*."

Jack's eyes widen. "*Eight years*?"

"We met sophomore year of college."

"Damn. That's like, what? A third of your life with the same guy?"

I look away, not meeting his eye. "Something like that."

"Did you know he was having doubts?"

"Not really," I say, feeling the familiar churning sensation, like my insides are turning to cheese curds as we speak.

The truth is I'd known things weren't perfect between us. Especially in the months since Sleeve It to Me closed when I didn't feel like doing anything that wasn't sitting on the couch, binging Netflix, and feeling sorry for myself.

After the business closed, Carter was understanding, but over time that understanding started to wane. And I got it. I wasn't exactly a delight to be around. But I assumed it was just a rough patch. Certainly something we could move past, until one night we were making dinner and Carter came out of nowhere and asked to take a break.

He said something about wanting to have other experiences. That since my business went under, things had been strained. That he wasn't happy.

Now I'm not sure what I want anymore, he'd finally said. But all I'd heard was that he wasn't sure about *me* anymore. About *us*.

At first, I was angry. How could he do this to me? To us? After everything?

I moved to New York for him when he got accepted into Parson's for photography. Then back to Seattle nine months later when he decided it *wasn't for him.* I supported him through every career change, transition, and switch, from marine biology to architecture. But my business failing was a bridge too far for us? So much so that he needed to completely reevaluate our entire relationship?

I was pissed, and more than a little betrayed. But I also didn't want to break up.

It was hard enough losing the business and my relationship with my sister. I didn't think I could handle losing Carter too. Not when my life already felt so unstable. So I agreed to the break, hoping that in a few weeks, when it's time to talk again, Carter will want to get back together and everything will go back to the way it was. Like none of this ever happened.

"So how long has it been since the break started?" Jack asks, voice drawing me back.

I dunk a fry in some ketchup and twirl it around. "Two and a half months."

"Do you think you'll . . . ?"

"Get back together?" I finish for him before popping the fry in my mouth.

He nods.

That's the thing. I'm not sure what Carter is going to say when the three months are up. Will he want to get back together? Or will he want to break up for good? The question swims inside me like I've swallowed something wriggly.

"I don't know," I admit. "But the waiting sucks. Like being stuck in some kind of relationship purgatory. Shouldn't he know if he wants to be with me by now?"

I search Jack's face, like maybe the answers to the questions that have plagued me for weeks might be printed across this stranger's forehead.

"I'm not really a good person to come to for relationship advice," he says.

"But you're a guy."

"I am," he confirms.

"So how long would it take you to know if someone was *the one*? Would eight years not be enough?"

Jack's expression molds into a pensive frown. "I guess it depends on the person . . . and if you believe in things like *the one*."

I nod, considering his point. Because I do believe in *the one*.

And I always thought Carter was it. My first kiss. My first love. My first *everything*. And I assumed that a white dress and a fancy dinner with a choice of chicken or salmon would be in our future.

Carter and I have always been *that couple*. The couple everyone assumed would end up together. Friends would ask how I wanted Carter to propose or if Carter and I wanted kids someday, like our future together was guaranteed. A matter of *when* not *if*. And why wouldn't it be? We'd been together forever. We even lived together. Wasn't marriage the obvious trajectory? But four years together turned into six, and six turned into eight, and still no ring.

I told myself it was because we were busy, that life was hectic and weddings were expensive, and when the time was right, he'd propose. But whenever we were alone and the *m* word came up, Carter would dodge questions or say things like, *I like how things are*, or *Why do we need that figured out right now?*

I tried not to let it bother me. After all, things with Carter were good. We had a nice life together. He bought me roses on Valentine's Day and held my hand at parties. Who cared if we didn't have a ring and a date yet?

But deep down I did care.

Not just because I wanted the ring and the dress and the party, but because I wanted the certainty. The security. The promise of *forever*. I wanted to know that Carter and I were endgame. That the last eight years meant something. Something that fit into the sparkly movie version of our relationship in my head.

A version where Carter and I end up together. Where in two weeks, when the three months are up, he tells me I'm the love of his life and it was all a mistake. A version where he pulls out a little box and begs me to marry him and everyone *oohs* and *awws* and says, *Yes, of course, we always knew you two were meant to be together.*

Despite everything that's happened, it's a version I still want to believe in, because without it, I'm not sure what else I have.

"It just sucks," I say, picking at my food. "I know I'm supposed to be happy for my sister, but it's hard not to feel resentful when the guy I was dating for eight years wants to take a break, while she's marrying someone she hardly knows."

Jack's eyes thrum with interest. "Your sister doesn't know the guy she's marrying?"

"Sort of. It's not like an arranged marriage or anything," I say quickly. "But they got engaged really fast. Like Pam and Tommy fast. And I'm pretty sure the whole thing is going to blow up in her face."

"You don't think he's *the one*?" Jack asks.

"I mean . . ." I scrunch up my face. "Let's just say that if my sister is a Godiva truffle, this guy is the two-year-old, unwrapped Hershey's Kiss you find under the seat of your car."

Jack's dark eyes crinkle with laughter. "Ouch. That's harsh."

"This is my baby sister we're talking about. No one is good enough," I tell him. "Except for maybe Tom Holland. Or Harry Styles."

"Fair enough. Harry Styles can wear the hell out of a wide-legged trouser."

"Damn right he can," I say with a firm nod.

"So, this Mr. Unwrapped Hershey's Kiss—" He pauses. "God, that sounded dirty, didn't it?"

"A little bit," I say, pinching my thumb and forefinger together.

"So, your sister's fiancé," he tries again. "How well do you know this guy?"

"Not well, considering they practically just met."

The first time I heard about Collin, he was some guy my sister was casually texting, and the next thing I know, *BAM*, they're picking out monogrammed hand towels, preparing to mold their lives together in holy matrimony. All in the space of three months.

"But you know you don't like him?" Jack asks.

"I know enough," I say stiffly.

I only know two things about Collin, my sister's husband-to-be:

1) He's almost ten years older than her. Thirty-three to her twenty-four, and

2) He's a cosmetic plastic surgeon, aka breast implants, which somehow doesn't feel like a real doctor to me. If he's ever on a plane and someone shouts, *Is there a doctor on board?* what's he gonna do? Say, *Sorry, I can't save her life, but she'd look great with double Ds?*

"But maybe once you get to know him, you'll like him," Jack says.

"Doubtful." I dunk another fry. "There are too many red flags. Like, apparently, the guy who's his best man is a total pig."

"And is he?"

"No clue, never met him," I say, thankful I haven't yet had to make the acquaintance of Collin's best friend, Houghton. "But my sister says he's some kind of player who's turned more tricks than Houdini, and you know what they say about the company you keep." I give Jack a knowing look.

Jack picks up his beer, considers it, then sets it down again. "You seem to be making a lot of assumptions about people you don't know very well."

"Trust me, you'd understand if you'd seen the guys she's brought home over the years."

When Allison was nineteen she dated a twenty-five-year-old with questionable piercings and a felony. A few years later she dropped out of college to go on tour with her then–drummer boyfriend whom she eventually caught with another girl on the tour bus. Then there was Bradley, the guy I still can't think about without wanting to punch a wall.

I'd say Allison has bad luck with men, except this is a pattern with her. Always the same thing. Instant attraction. Big declarations. A short fuse that burns out a little too quickly followed by a messy, explosive breakup. Which is when I usually step in to pick up the pieces. Like I always have.

"But they've spent a shit ton of money on the whole thing," I continue. "So now I have no choice but to put on the hideous green bridesmaid dress that totally gives me a uni-boob and pretend to be happy for them, I guess."

Jack's left eyebrow arches into a parenthesis. "A uni-boob?"

"Yeah, like it looks like I have one giant glob of boob instead of two."

"A giant glob of boob," he repeats as though it were a fascinating scientific discovery. "So, what are you gonna do?"

"About the uni-boob? I don't know, but with the right bra—"

"No, I mean about the wedding."

I go back to playing with my food, no longer feeling hungry. "There's nothing to do," I tell him. "It's my little sister's wedding, I have to suck it up and plaster on a smile."

"But have you told her any of your concerns? I'm sure she'd want to hear what you think."

I push my food to one side of my plate, then back again. "Trust me, she doesn't care what I think."

"I doubt that. You're her sister."

My eyes dip into my lap. That's the problem. I *did* tell Allison what I thought. I told her I thought she was rushing into things, that she was making a mistake.

But we're in love, she'd said, exasperated. *You don't understand.*

But I *did* understand. I understand that she's been *in love* with every loser, asshole, cheater, and liar she's ever dated. I also understand that Collin's not some flavor of the month that she can easily discard when she gets bored or things go south. She's actually *marrying* this guy. And when the whole thing undoubtedly blows up in her face, it won't just be another breakup. It will be divorce. A very *expensive* divorce.

But Allison doesn't care what I think. Something she made clear when she told me that if I wasn't going to support her and Collin, I might as well not show up to the wedding.

The memory feels heavy in my gut, like I've been drinking cement instead of beer.

"So, what's the couple like at the wedding you're going to?" I ask, eager to change the subject. "Do you think they'll last?"

"Not sure. The bride's sort of . . ." Jack frowns, like he's trying to make up his mind in real time. "Intense," he decides on. "And very judgmental. But my friend says he loves her, so . . ." His voice trails off and he gives me a look like *whatcha gonna do?*

"What did you get them as a gift?" I ask, thinking of the incredibly lackluster set of wineglasses currently being shipped to Allison and Collin's condo.

"A gift card," he says.

"Wow, so thoughtful," I tease. "I'm sure they'll cherish it for generations to come."

"Call me cynical, but I'd rather buy them a gift card than an overpriced Crock-Pot that outlives their marriage."

My eyes double in size. "And I thought *I* was pessimistic. I'm at least rooting for my sister and her groom to work out." I pause, making a face. "But I suppose some of that can be chalked up to selfish intentions. I *so* don't want to have to do this again for her second marriage."

That earns me a laugh. "For your sake, I hope they make it work."

"I'll cheers to that." I reach for my beer.

He grins then reaches for his own.

"We have to make eye contact, you know," he says, glass hovering midair.

"Why?"

"If we don't, we'll be destined for seven years of bad sex."

"Did you just make that up?"

"It's a real thing, I swear."

"Well, in that case, we'd better not risk it."

"Better safe than sorry," he agrees, holding my gaze—an unmistakable heat behind his eyes.

"To making it work," I say, lifting my glass higher.

"And beating the odds."

Eyes locked, we clink our glasses and drink.

I'm not sure if it's the half a glass of beer I've consumed or the dim bar lighting hitting his jaw just right, but somehow Jack's gotten even more attractive. All strong-boned and honey-eyed, like someone's placed an Instagram filter over his face.

I sit back in my seat, putting a finger to my chin.

"What?" he asks.

"I can't decide if you're a rom-com hero or the villain in a Lifetime movie," I say.

Jack hums with laughter. "Depends on who you ask."

"That's so not what I want to hear from the random stranger I've just told all my secrets to."

"All your secrets?"

"Well, not *all* my secrets."

He props his elbows up on the table, shirtsleeves rolled up, and I find my gaze lingering a beat too long on the network of veins in his forearms.

"I'm sure we're all the villain in someone's Lifetime movie," he says.

"Damn. Really makes you think." I reach for my beer. "If I'm the villain, I at least hope I'm the Miranda Priestly–style villain with great shoes and a Manhattan brownstone."

He laughs and takes a swig of his own beer. A small line of foam clings to his upper lip and he wipes it away with the back of his hand.

"This might sound weird," I say, setting my glass back down with a *clang*. "But this is like the best thing that's happened to me all week."

"Must have been a shitty week."

I grin. He's not wrong.

"Mine hasn't been too great either." He pauses, eyes lingering like I'm a Renaissance painting he could look at for hours and still find new details in. "But tonight isn't too bad."

I blush. Even if he's just a stranger I'll never see again, it feels nice to be seen. Noticed. I can't remember the last time Carter looked at me like that.

We slip into an easy silence, and I look past Jack to the window where it's raining harder than ever. And getting dark. I should probably figure out where I'm going to stay tonight, but it's warm and cozy in here and I'm not quite ready to face my fate yet.

Jack follows my gaze. "It hasn't let up, has it?"

"No, it hasn't."

"So where are you planning to sleep?"

"I'll figure something out," I say, waving my hand like I'm swatting away an invisible fly.

Jack's shoulders stiffen, and I can feel him trying and hesitating to respond. Finally, he says, "I hope I'm not being too forward, but if you want, you can stay in my room tonight."

My eyes widen at the offer.

I shouldn't. I'm a girl traveling alone. It's a bad idea.

But I also don't want to sleep on a plastic bench.

I drum my nails against the tabletop, thinking. "I don't know . . ."

"Is it because I'm a stranger?" he asks.

"I mean, *yeah*," I say with a nervous laugh. "I've seen *Dateline*."

"I promise I'm not a creep."

"Which is exactly what a creep would say," I point out.

"Do you want to see my ID or something?" Jack reaches into his pocket and pulls out his wallet, but I put out a hand to stop him.

"No, it's fine," I say, heat creeping into my cheeks. I'm being silly. It's not like he's a serial killer. I mean *probably* not, anyway.

I take a long sip of my beer, stalling while I weigh the wisdom of accepting the offer.

On the one hand, he's a stranger. But on the other hand, if I sleep in his room, I can take a hot shower and presumably sleep in a real bed.

Besides, he's totally respectful. And fit. And as Elle Woods famously noted, exercise gives you endorphins, and endorphins make you happy, and *happy people just don't murder their husbands!*

Maybe it's the beer, or the warmth hovering behind his eyes, or simply that I'm starved for a little bit of kindness, but I feel like I can trust him.

"Okay," I say after a beat. "And here I was just trying to get a free drink."

The corners of his mouth lift. "Happy to be of service."

"You know, I'm really glad I met you tonight," I tell him.

He smiles. "Me too."

I wonder if my luck is finally starting to turn.

Chapter 3

81 HOURS UNTIL THE WEDDING

When Jack and I step into the elevator we stand close enough that I can smell his cologne. It's musky and tangy with a hint of something sweet—a far cry from the fresh, earth scent I'm used to Carter wearing, but in a good way, and I discreetly lean closer trying to catch another whiff.

When we reach Jack's floor, he pulls out a key card and swipes it on the first door to my right. The lock clicks and he holds the door open for me as I roll my suitcase into a generic-looking hotel room with beige carpet, beige curtains, beige walls, and a beige bed. *One* beige bed.

Maybe this was a bad idea after all.

What if he snores? Or worse, has morning wood?

Should I offer to sleep on the floor? Or was that the plan all along and I was just being wildly optimistic that I'd be sleeping in a bed tonight?

I search Jack's face, waiting for clues, but either he doesn't care about sharing a bed, or he hasn't yet realized the predicament as he tosses his garment bag over a chair and heads straight to the minibar.

"How about another drink?" he asks, reaching for the ice bucket.

"Uh . . ." I'm still a little tipsy and drinking any more probably isn't a good idea. "How about we just talk?" I try.

A question mark hovers behind Jack's gaze, but he blinks and it's gone. "Sure. Let's talk." He sits on the edge of the bed and pats the spot next to him.

As I sit beside him, our thighs touch and a zing of electricity awakens in my gut. But I can't tell if it's a good zing or a bad zing.

Everything downstairs felt so fun and chill, but now I'm hyperaware that I'm alone in a hotel room with a stranger.

Was I naive to come up here? What if he really is a Lifetime movie villain?

My eyes skate from the window to the door, assessing how quickly I could make it out of here if I had to.

I'm probably being paranoid. But maybe I should update my location on Snapchat? Or punch the emergency number into my phone? Just in case? Except, we're in England and I don't even know what the emergency number is. Which is probably something I should have thought of before I came up here.

Why didn't I?

Oh yeah. The charming stranger.

I notice he's shifted closer, close enough that I can make out the tiny shaving scar on his chin and the subtle flecks of red in his otherwise dark beard. I also notice that his gaze keeps dropping to my mouth. A shiver of awareness runs down my spine.

He clears his throat, eyes hooking back up to meet mine. "So, Ada, before anything else happens, I wanted to let you know that I've been tested recently and I'm all clear."

Tested?

The last time I took any kind of a "test," it was a Buzzfeed quiz to find out what kind of hotdog I am (Seattle dog with cream cheese). But something tells me that's not what he means.

I sit back, searching his face. "Tested?"

He flashes a faulty grin. "I know it's not exactly a fun conversation to have. But better safe than sorry, right?"

Better safe than sorry? My brain whirs to action. He's not . . . ? No . . . He can't possibly mean . . . *STD testing*?

I shuffle backward across the bed, putting as much space between us as the queen mattress will allow. "What are you talking about?"

"Aren't we gonna . . . ?" Jack's voice trails off and his brows knit together.

I sit up, body jolting to attention. "Gonna *what*?" I demand.

His frown deepens. "Isn't that why you came up here? To have sex?"

I freeze.

Sex? He thinks I came here to have sex? As in *sexual intercourse*?

I try to swallow, but my throat's coated in sandpaper. And the churning is back in my stomach. But for a different reason entirely.

Suddenly the top blanket on the bed is too scratchy, my jeans too tight. *Everything* is too much as I scramble up and off the bed, nearly tripping over myself in the process.

But I'm too anxious to be embarrassed. All I can think about is how I need to leave. Stat.

Beer sloshes around inside me as I jump up and grab my purse, eyes already zeroing in on the door. If I can just—

"Ada, wait!" He stands up, too, but I take a giant step back.

"I have pepper spray!" I cry.

I don't. It's a lie, but he doesn't know that as I reach into my purse.

He puts up his hands in a sign of surrender. "There's no need for pepper spray," he says in a low, calm hum, like he's trying to talk down a horse that spooks easily. "I'm sorry. I just thought . . ." He clicks his tongue and gestures between us.

"You thought *what* exactly?"

"That we were on the same page that this was a . . . you know . . ." He makes a face. "A hookup."

A litany of *no*'s spill out under my breath.

Have I really been out of the dating scene so long that I didn't realize this was supposed to be a one-night stand? Not that I've ever had a one-night stand. But I at least thought I'd recognize an invitation if I got one.

Did I give some kind of unintentional hint I'm not aware of? Was it the cheers? Teasing him about what kind of underwear he's wearing?

But just as I replay everything that happened downstairs, searching for some kind of pattern, my thoughts come to a screeching halt. Why am I blaming myself here? Clearly this is his fault.

Sure, there might have been some harmless flirting. But that's all it was. *Harmless*. Besides, I told him about Carter, my long-term boyfriend whom I clearly want to get back together with. Not exactly an invitation to jump into bed with me. If anything, he misread the signs. Not me.

My gaze sharpens on him as embarrassment bleeds into indignation. "Why didn't you say something?" I ask.

Jack's forehead creases. "I thought I did when I asked if you wanted to come back to my room."

I make a noise somewhere between a snort and a gasp. "How was I supposed to know that meant you wanted to have sex? You should have used precise language! Like maybe, 'Hey, Ada, wanna go upstairs and have sexual intercourse?' That might have been a good start!"

"Okay, okay." He puts his hands up, voice even and measured.

"I'm sorry, I just thought we were kinda . . . having a moment down there," he says.

My eyes skitter away. He's right. We were definitely having some kind of *moment*. But it doesn't mean I wanted to have sex with the guy.

"Listen, you're attractive, don't get me wrong." All kinds of warning bells go off in my head, each of them blaring, *Shut up! Shut up right now!* "But what I mean is *no*, nothing was going to happen," I say tightly. "I have a boyfriend, remember?"

"I thought you were on a break?"

"But it doesn't mean I want to sleep with someone else," I shoot back.

His mouth twists like he might argue, but I don't give him time to as I spin on my heel toward the door. This is now painfully awkward. I need to leave.

But go where exactly?

I think of having to shell out hundreds of dollars on a hotel and remember that my bank account is basically in a race to zero.

Shit, shit, shit . . .

I sit on the edge of the bed and put my head in my hands. Jack looks like he might sit next to me, but I shoot him a scowl and he backs away.

"What am I going to do?" I whine.

"Maybe you could go back down to reception?" he tries. "See if they've had a cancellation?"

Even if there was a room available, I couldn't afford it. But that doesn't matter right now. The only thing that matters is that I get out of here.

"Right, good idea," I tell him, standing up and grabbing my luggage.

"Do you want me to walk you downstairs?" he asks.

"No. I'm fine."

I got myself into this mess. I can get myself out.

Jack shoves his hands in his pockets, mouth bending into a pensive frown. "Well, good luck," he says after a beat.

"Thanks." I swallow thickly. "You too."

It feels like there's something else we ought to say, but I'm not sure what. This doesn't exactly seem like a *nice meeting you* type of situation.

"Well, bye," I finally say.

He rubs the back of his neck. "Bye, Ada."

We share one more cursory look, then I move toward the door. My hand is hovering over the handle when my phone buzzes from inside my pocket. I probably would ignore it if it weren't for the fact that Jack's phone buzzes at exactly the same time.

We share a look of surprise before reaching for our respective devices. But as soon as I see my screen, I almost wish I hadn't.

I have one new email notification telling me I've been bumped off tomorrow morning's flight to Belfast.

Great. So much for the luck of the Irish.

"Shit," Jack mutters under his breath. "I just got bumped off my flight."

I look up, eyes meeting his. "Me too. What do you think happened?"

"No idea." His brows hook down into a scowl. "But it looks like there aren't any flights to Belfast for a few days."

My stomach jolts, the panic inside me swiftly replaced with a different kind of panic.

Belfast?

Jack's going to Belfast?

But didn't he say he was going to . . . ? I rack my brain, trying to remember. I swear I would have remembered if he'd said Belfast. I mean how many weddings are there in Belfast this weekend? What if . . . ?

Oh no.

"The wedding you're going to is in Belfast too?" I ask, hoping he'll correct me and say no, he's just passing through on his way to somewhere else. Somewhere like Reykjavík! Or Timbuktu!

But as soon as I ask, I already know the answer. I can see it in the visceral look of panic that starts in his eyes, then sweeps lower into the downward curl of his mouth, finally settling into a frown.

Slowly, he nods. "My best friend, Collin, is getting married in a castle outside Belfast."

Collin?

My insides jumble. Because holy shit. *Holy shit.*

Jack and I are going to the same wedding. And if he is the best man then that means . . .

I jump back as though knocked off-balance by the realization. "*You're* Houghton?"

There's a brief moment of surprise, like he's shocked to hear his name on my lips, but he almost instantly swallows it back. "Houghton's my last name, but most people call me Jack. Except Collin, the 'unwrapped Hershey's Kiss,'" he adds with a heavy look.

Panic swarms my body in hot torrents, brain zipping from one incriminating detail to the next like a game of spin the wheel. But instead of cash prizes and tropical vacations, it's bone-numbing embarrassment.

Congratulations, brain, you now have a new scenario to remind me of when I'm trying to fall asleep!

I expect Jack to share in the embarrassment, to look as mortified as I feel. Instead, he shakes his head, fighting back silent laughter.

"It's not funny!" I cry.

"You have to admit, it's sort of funny. It's like a Shakespearean misunderstanding."

I fold my arms over my chest. "Did you know?"

"Know what? That you're Allison's sister? Of course not. You didn't even say where you were going."

"But how did you not realize? I told you plenty of details!"

His jaw ticks, expression filtering from amused to annoyed. "I'm sorry, I was a little distracted."

"With what? Trying to get laid?"

His lips set into a grimace. "Why didn't *you* put it together, Nancy Drew?"

I open my mouth to argue, but he's sort of right. Why didn't I figure it out? He told me he was going to a wedding. But he hadn't said where. Though, perhaps I should have asked instead of word vomiting about Carter and Allison.

For a long moment neither of us speaks. We just stare with increasing hostility like either one of us is moments away from declaring *this town ain't big enough for the two of us.*

Finally, I ask, "You do realize what this means, right?"

"That you called me a pig downstairs?"

"No. I mean, *yes,* I did say that, but I didn't know it was *you* when I said it," I say, brows scrunching in frustration. "But I was right, considering you just tried to spring your dick on me!"

"I didn't try to *spring my dick* on you. I was trying to have an adult conversation about STDs," he says. "*I* was being responsible."

"Yeah, well, the responsible thing to do would have been to make it clear you wanted to have sex in the first place."

"I thought I did!"

"Well, not clearly enough."

He shoves his hands in his pockets. "I'm sorry, okay? I thought you were into it. How many more times do you need me to apologize?"

"At least three more times and maybe some groveling wouldn't hurt."

The ditch between his brows deepens. "Shouldn't you be the one apologizing to me? You're the one who referred to my best friend as an 'unwrapped Hershey's Kiss.'"

"You called my sister intense! And judgmental!"

"And now I see where she gets it from."

Fire builds in my stomach. What is wrong with this guy? And why on earth did I find him charming? Clearly that had been the beer.

He sighs, shoulders deflating. "Listen, I get that this is weird—"

"Weird is an understatement!"

"*But*"—he holds up a hand to stop me—"I think it's lucky we ran into one another."

I flick one eyebrow upward. "And please enlighten me as to why on earth I ought to feel lucky to have run into you?"

He bites his lower lip, which would be sexy if I wasn't so pissed off right now.

"Given the flight situation, it's better if we stick together," he says. "Would you rather be stranded in London alone?"

Flight situation. London. Alone. His words hurtle through me, reminding me why we're even having this conversation in the first place.

"Wait, so there aren't any flights to Belfast tomorrow?" I ask.

He shakes his head. "Everything's booked. There aren't any more available flights until next week."

Next week? The rehearsal dinner is in two days. And the wedding is in three. There's no way we're going to make it.

If whoever is running *The Truman Show* could please give me a better plotline, now would be a great time!

I sit on the edge of the bed and flop back on the mattress. "This is terrible," I say to the ceiling. "I can't miss the wedding. My sister will kill me, if my mom doesn't get to me first. Fuck . . . *fuck.*"

"Relax. It's gonna be fine," Jack says.

"How? Unless you can charter a private jet, we aren't gonna make it." I pause, gripped by the idea. "Wait, can we do that?"

"I'm working on a plan, okay?"

I sit up. "What about a train? A boat? A car?"

His jaw clenches. "Will you calm down?"

"How can I calm down at a time like this! I'm the maid of honor! I'm supposed to bring the veil! I can't miss my little sister's wedding!"

"We're not gonna miss it. I told you, I'm working on it."

I stand up and begin to pace the length of the hotel room. This is bad. I'm trapped in a foreign country with a stranger (Is he still a stranger?) and no way to get to Allison's wedding.

"She's gonna kill us both, you know," I say. "She'll probably kill you first because she hates you. But if you're lucky it will be quick and painless. But me? God, she'll probably torture me for hours. Something really sick and twisted." I shiver, physically disturbed. "She'll—"

"Ada, will you stop? You're not making anything better. Now come here and look." He gestures to his phone. "Tomorrow morning we can take the train to Liverpool and from there we can take the ferry to Belfast."

My heart begins to steady. "We can?"

He nods.

"How fast can we get there?" I ask, trying to calculate how many hours a cross-country road trip might take.

"Three hours to Liverpool . . ." He pauses as he scrolls through his phone. "And eight hours from Liverpool to Belfast."

"Eight hours?" My eyes widen. "On a ferry?"

"Unless you want to swim?"

I violently shake my head. "I get really bad seasickness. I. Will. Die. Like, vomit *everywhere*." I spread my hands to demonstrate the volume of vomit Jack might expect. "Trust me, it won't be pretty."

"All right, all right," he says, putting up a hand to stop me. "I'll see if there's something else. I'm *not* holding your hair while you puke." Jack turns back to his phone, forehead creased in concentration. After a beat, he says, "We can take the train to Scotland, then the ferry to Belfast."

"Scotland?" I ask.

"You know, the place with the Loch Ness Monster and the kilts?"

I glare at him. "I know what Scotland is."

"The ferry from Scotland to Belfast is only two hours."

I nod, digesting this new information. "I can do two. Two hours on the high seas is very different from eight."

"So it's settled, we'll go to Scotland tomorrow," he says, eyes snagging mine in confirmation. "See? Everything's fine."

But everything's not fine.

A few minutes ago I thought I was never gonna see Jack again. He would be nothing more than a footnote in this disastrous trip. Now, not only is his best friend marrying my sister, but I'm going to have to go on a cross-country road trip with him?

My brain takes a lap around this new development, assessing for impediments—of which I'm sure there are many—before snagging on one crucial detail.

"Wait. How much is all of this going to cost?" I ask.

Jack's brow furrows in thought. "We need to get to the wedding, right? So does it really matter how much?"

"It definitely matters to me considering I'm sort of broke," I admit.

"Broke?" he asks, like he's never heard the word before.

"Yes, *broke*," I repeat, exasperated. "It's what happens to some millennials when they spend too much money on avocado toast."

His face twists with confusion. Clearly he doesn't have to check his account balance before buying cereal. Must be nice.

"My business went under a few months ago," I clarify. "So I'm not exactly flush with cash at the moment."

"Can you borrow the money from someone?" he asks.

I think about calling my mom and stepdad and explaining the situation, but they're already letting me crash on their couch while I look for a job and I really don't want to have to ask for money too. Not when I'm supposed to be the daughter who has her shit together. The one who fixes things, not breaks them.

When Allison forgot she had a presentation at school, I went to get poster board at eleven p.m. And when mom had to work late and couldn't make Allison's choir concert, I showed up with flowers and took her for ice cream after. I was the one who could always be counted upon to take care of things—the *responsible one*. The *fixer*.

But now I'm the one who is penniless, unemployed, and crashing on my parents' couch, and I can't help but feel like my circumstances are more than just temporary setbacks. They're the result of failure. Because *I'm* a failure. And I don't want to be more of a burden to anyone than I already am.

"No," I say after a minute. "I can't borrow the money."

Jack runs a hand through his perfectly coiffed facial hair, eyes sharpening, like there's an invisible math problem he's trying to work out in his head. Finally, he says, "I'll pay."

My eyes stretch wide. "You'll *what*?"

"You can pay me back," he says offhandedly, like it's the last stick of gum, not an offer to bankroll a whole-ass trip.

"I can't let you do that," I tell him.

"Why not?"

"Um, because it's a lot of money," I say, mentally tallying up what this little adventure will cost. "And I don't like owing people things."

"I get that, but I don't think either of us has a choice. Either I pay, or you miss your sister's wedding." He tilts his chin, giving me a knowing look. "Besides, I thought you're supposed to bring the veil?"

My stomach climbs into my chest. He's right. I have no choice.

"Fine," I reluctantly agree. "But I swear I'll pay you back. Every penny! With interest!"

"It's fine," he says, giving me an insistent look. "And just a little business tip, don't offer to pay interest."

I ignore the dig and we shake on it.

Wonderful. Just wonderful. Not only do I still not have anywhere to sleep, but now I'm in debt. Well, *more* debt.

"Okay, so . . ." I reach for my suitcase and make my way to the door. "I'll see you tomorrow then?"

Tension creases his forehead. "Where are you going to sleep tonight?"

"I don't know. Maybe the train station."

It's not exactly a warm, cozy hotel bed, but hey, maybe the rats are friendly?

"I'll figure it out," I tell him.

I move toward the door, suitcase in tow, when he calls after me.

"Ada, wait."

When I turn back to face him, his arms are crossed over his chest, brows narrowed. Finally he says, "You can stay. If you want."

"As appealing as that sounds, I can't."

"Why not?"

"Because . . ." My eyes zip around the room like the reason I can't stay might pop out at me, but of course I don't have a very good reason, and he knows it too.

"Listen," he says, gaze latching on to mine. "I get that you think I'm a sleaze right now, but I'm not gonna let you go sleep outside or at a train station or whatever it was you planned on doing."

"You're not *letting* me do anything," I tell him.

He sighs, frustrated. "That's not what I meant. Just that it doesn't make sense for you to leave. Not when there's a perfectly good, very large bed right here." He gestures toward the bed. "Besides, I'm not exactly a stranger anymore, right?"

Part of me is already mentally slamming the door, racing toward the elevator and away from this nightmare. But another part of me—the rational, practical part—is wholly aware of the constraints of my predicament and knows I should at least consider the offer.

My eyes trail toward the bed then back to him. It's not exactly the night of reality TV and *me time* with my vibrator I'd envisioned, but it's certainly better than sleeping on a bench at a train station. Besides, as he pointed out, he's no longer a stranger, so it wouldn't be *that* weird, right?

I hook my eyes back to his. "Are you sure?"

"I mean, yeah . . ." He frowns like he's reconsidering. "But you're not going to tell Allison about the whole, uh—"

"Sex incident?"

"I was going to say *misunderstanding*."

"And have to suffer that humiliation? No thanks."

"Ada." He gives me what I imagine is his attempt at a meaningful look. "It was an honest mistake. And I wouldn't have invited you upstairs if I didn't think you were into it."

I sigh. As much as I'd like to hold on to my annoyance, it's not like I haven't misread signs before. Like the time I thought Carter was proposing, but really he just wanted to tell me he'd enrolled in culinary school. The point is Jack's right. It was all a misunderstanding, and if we're going to travel together for the next few days it's better to forgive and forget, right?

"I guess it's all just fodder for my tell-all," I say, rolling my suitcase back into the room.

"So you're staying?"

"Looks like I am, *roomie*."

For a minute we just look at one another, trading suspicious glances until finally I sigh and plop down on the bed. "And I should probably say thanks for saving my ass three times in one night," I tell him.

His dark eyes flash like he's not sure whether to say *you're welcome* before finally saying, "Looks like it was your lucky day when you took my suitcase by mistake."

I grimace, but only because he's right.

Chapter 4

79 HOURS UNTIL THE WEDDING

After we agree on tomorrow's plan to catch the train to Glasgow, it's time for a scalding, center-of-the-sun-hot shower.

I adjust the temperature until Satan himself pours out of the faucet and seductively licks my back. *Perfect.* I lean into the stream, relishing in what feels like the first moment of privacy all day.

As I lather shampoo into my hair, my thoughts stray to Carter.

Part of me is angry at him for not being here. For putting me in this situation. For asking for the break in the first place. But behind the anger looms a bone-crushing, ache-in-the-pit-of-my-stomach loneliness. The kind that feels like a brutal hangover that just won't go away.

I don't just miss him, I miss our life together.

I miss making pancakes on Saturdays and our apartment with the busted drain and the lumpy couch we've had since college. I miss going to parties together and having my hand held in a crowd full of people. I miss sex.

Shortly after the break started, Carter and I hooked up once. I didn't plan for it to happen, it just did. Probably because there was a part of me that hoped he would say we should get back together—clearly we were still attracted to each other—but he didn't. Which was somehow worse. Like being rejected all over again.

Now I don't know what's next. Only that I miss the familiarity of our relationship. Of knowing where my next orgasm is coming from and that his toothbrush will always be on the left side of the sink. I miss all the tiny layers of certainty insulating me from the swells and storms of life. Certainty I no longer have.

After I get out of the shower, I pull on pajama pants and a ratty old college T-shirt. Not exactly the type of outfit I'd like to be seen in—especially not by Jack—but it's not like I'd planned on spending the night with anyone.

When I emerge from the steam-filled bathroom, Jack is sitting on the edge of the bed, still fully dressed. His eyes stay glued to his phone until I approach the bed and pull back the covers. "Let me just say, I'm feeling more and more thankful I didn't end up with your luggage," he says.

"What's that supposed to mean?"

He gives me an impertinent look and I follow his gaze down the length of my body, landing on my pajama bottoms. *Oh.*

They have cartoon cats on them and are sporting several holes and definitely fall into the category of *alternative birth control.*

"They were a gag gift," I say sharply. "I wasn't *intending* for anyone to see them."

"I wish I hadn't."

I glare at him, then lie back against the pillow and shut my eyes. Though I'm not sure how I'm gonna fall asleep.

The mattress creaks as Jack gets up and begins unbuttoning his shirt. I follow his movements like a cat following a laser pointer.

"What are you doing?"

"Changing for bed."

"I thought we went over this. Keep. Your. Clothes. On."

"Relax," he says as he pulls his belt out of its loop. "I'm not getting naked or anything."

I'm about to tell him to at least keep his shirt on when—

Holy. Cow.

Jack is *jacked.*

He's not bulky exactly, but he clearly spends time at the gym—time well spent, I might add.

And to think I almost had sex with *that.*

Not that I would have. But still.

My eyes travel from his defined abs to his chiseled biceps, and I can't help but wonder what would it be like to be thrown down on a bed by *those.* The thought sends unwanted tendrils of heat snaking through my body.

"We can still have sex," he says, deep voice cutting through my less-than-wholesome thoughts. "If you changed your mind, that is."

I jerk back, blood rising in my cheeks. "Excuse me?"

"Offer's still on the table," he says with a shrug. *A shrug!* Like he just asked me for my drink order, not whether I wanted to get naked with him!

"You *cannot* be serious," I chide.

"Well, you were just checking me out."

"No, I wasn't!" I say a little too defensively. "And if you're worried about me looking at you, maybe don't prance around half naked!"

I wait for a bruised look, or at least a whiff of embarrassment. Instead, his smirk only deepens. "So you admit you *were* checking me out?"

My God. The nerve of this man. His ego must have its own zip code.

"Is this how you usually do things?" I snap.

"Do *what?*"

"This!" I gesture wildly between us. "You assume I'll want to have sex with you because you're—" My eyes pause on his pecs and his smirk intensifies.

"Because I'm—?"

A frustrated groan rumbles in the back of my throat. "You're not even trying to seduce me!"

"Did you want me to?" He gives me a look like he already has several strategies in mind.

Heat licks my neck, crawling straight into my cheeks. "No," I say tightly. "My point is that women want effort, not to be told *offer's still on the table.*"

"Effort," he repeats, pretending to jot it down in an invisible notebook. "Great sex tip. Thanks."

"Yes, *effort.* Maybe you can try that out next time you pick up a girl at the bar."

"I did buy you dinner first. Does that count?"

"Trust me, if I had to do it again, I would have said no."

"And you'd rather sleep outside tonight?"

I fold my arms over my chest. "Maybe."

"You know you can go if you want. I'm not keeping you hostage or anything."

I squirm and I can tell he sees my bluff.

"Well, it's too late for that now," I tell him. "And if you don't mind, I'm going to sleep." I roll over, facing away from him, and flick the light off.

The room goes dark, extinguishing Jack from view, but the sounds of him undressing fill in the gaps. His belt hits the floor with a thud. Followed by the rumpling of jeans as they slide down legs. Then the pad of bare feet across the carpet. The bathroom door opens and shuts, then the toilet flushes and the sink turns on. When he comes back, his shadowy outline hovers over the bed.

"Should I make a barrier?" he asks.

"A *what?*"

"You know, stack the pillows in the middle like a barrier," he says, motioning between us. "So we don't have to touch."

The thought of us touching sends a whoosh of curiosity through my stomach, swiftly followed by annoyance for not being more immune to whatever the hell kind of voodoo Jack is apparently deploying.

"No, it's fine," I say stiffly.

"You sure? I wouldn't want to offend your *delicate sensibilities* with an accidental toe graze."

"It's fine," I say again, determined not to be affected by him.

He gives me one last look before sliding under the covers beside me. "Well, we're practically like family anyway."

I wrinkle my nose. "Not really."

"I mean not by blood, but I imagine we will be seeing a whole lot of each other in the future, considering your sister is marrying my best friend."

"Doubtful."

"We may even be spending Thanksgivings together from now on," he goes on.

My nose crinkles with confusion. "Why on earth would we spend Thanksgiving with you?"

"Collin's family always invites me to Thanksgiving, so I'll probably be asking you to pass the stuffing soon enough."

My mouth pinches. "That's nice, but I'm sure you can find someone else to mooch off of."

He laughs and the bed vibrates under us. "You know, you were much nicer downstairs," he says.

"So were you."

Jack pulls back the covers before reaching into his bag and retrieving a zebra print sleeping mask. A cackle spurts out of me.

"You're kidding, right?"

He squints at me through the dark. "What?"

"You made fun of my pajamas, but you're wearing a zebra sleeping mask to bed?"

"I can't sleep without it."

"Are you seriously telling me that if we'd, uh—" I gesture vaguely.

"Had sex?"

"—you would have whipped that thing out after?" I ask.

"I'm gonna try to ignore the part where you said *whip that thing out*. And no. I would have rolled over, said something macho like, *Good work, kid*, then fallen asleep naked," he says. "But if I'm not getting laid, I'd rather get a good night's rest."

"Wow. And to think I missed out on getting called *kid* postcoitus. How will I live with the regret?"

Jack snorts as he pulls the mask down over his eyes.

We grow silent and the rumble of airplanes taking off overhead fills the void.

I nestle into the covers, trying to get comfortable. But I have no idea how I'm supposed to fall asleep when there's an attractive half-naked man lying next to me. A half-naked man that I spilled my guts to because I thought I was never going to see him again.

I guess a stranger at the bar just isn't what it used to be. From now on, I'm keeping a journal. No more telling anyone anything.

"Hey . . . can we forget all the stuff I said downstairs?" I ask, voice cutting through the darkness.

"You mean how you don't think Allison and Collin will last,

you dislike my best friend in the whole world, and you don't want to go to the wedding? *That* stuff?"

I wince. "Yes. *That* stuff. I don't want it getting back to Allison. So if you could please keep your mouth shut, that'd be great."

"Fine. I'll try not to mention any of that to Allison, but on one condition."

"So you're blackmailing me now?"

"It's not blackmail, it's more . . ." He searches for the words. "Mutually assured destruction."

"*Mutually assured destruction*? Please tell me this is the first time you've said those words in bed?"

He barks out a laugh and the bed rattles. "How about I won't tell Allison what happened—"

"You mean what *didn't* happen," I interject.

"How about I keep our little misunderstanding a secret if you don't tell Allison that I said their marriage won't outlast a Crock-Pot? As you so eloquently put it, Allison doesn't exactly like me, and I'd rather not add fuel to the fire if she and Collin are actually going to do this." He says *do this* like he means walking over hot coals or electrocution, not marriage.

I purse my lips, considering. As much as I'd love to use what Jack said as further proof for why this wedding is a bad idea, things with Allison and me are already strained, and I don't want to make it worse by Jack tattling on me.

"Fine," I say at last. "But if I find out anything that puts Allison at risk, I'll tell her everything."

"So I assume this is a bad time to tell you we're going to a strip club for Collin's stag night?"

A low groan vibrates in the back of my throat. "*A strip club?* Are you trying to make it harder for me to like you?"

"It's a classic bachelor party activity you can thank P. T. Barnum's grandson for."

"The circus guy?"

"The very same one."

"You know, I don't understand the appeal of a bunch of dudes going to a strip club together. Like why would you and all your straight bros want to get boners at the same time?"

He laughs and despite every ounce of protest in my body, the sound runs warm and liquidlike in my ears. "It's not for me, it's for Collin."

"Well, it's gross. And disrespectful to my sister." I shift my weight, trying and failing to get comfortable. "She's going to kill you."

He pulls the sleeping mask off and turns to face me. "No she won't, because she's not going to find out."

A sliver of light filters in past the curtains, catching an unmistakable glint in his eyes. I can tell he's challenging me, testing our flimsy bargain to see how much weight it can bear.

But as much as I hate the idea of Collin treating his stag night like some kind of last night of freedom, it's not worth the headache of Allison finding out about Jack and me.

I need this wedding weekend to go well, not just for her, but for me too. It's the only shot I have at repairing our fragile relationship.

"Fine, I won't tell her, but I won't need to tell her. Allison *will* find out," I warn.

"How?"

"Because she's a snoop. It's like her superpower," I say.

Jack nods, considering this new information. "Can I confess something?" he asks.

"As long as it's sufficiently embarrassing for you, then yes."

"I've always been scared of your sister. She gets this look in her eye like she's judging everything about you," he says. "It's terrifying."

"Oh, you mean this look?" I make a face like I'm supremely disappointed in every life choice he's ever made.

Jack laughs and it's like the sound has its own gravity, each vibration pulling me a little closer. "Yes! That one!"

"I know that look well," I tell him. "I've been seeing it since she was two."

He props his elbow up and rests his head in the crook of his palm. "You know, I didn't even know that Allison had a sister until Collin said something a week ago."

"Great. So nice to hear that she speaks so highly of me."

"Hey, at least she didn't call you a pig."

"True," I tell him, though I'm not sure obscurity is much of an upgrade.

"So what else did your sister tell you about me?" he asks. "Or do I even want to know?"

I think back to when Allison first mentioned Jack, trying to reconcile the faceless groomsman I'd heard about while licking stamps for save the dates with the half-naked man now beside me in bed.

"Hmmm. Where do I start?" I put a finger to my chin. "The Slovenian Olympic figure skaters you hooked up with? Or that you allegedly had sex in a glass elevator?"

"Okay, that's not true."

"Which part?"

"They were Slovakian, not Slovenian."

"Should I take that as confirmation of an exhibitionist streak?"

"You'll have to wait and see."

"I certainly hope not."

Jack rolls onto his back and the mattress squeaks. I flinch as his feet graze mine. They're cold as ice.

"Ada, can I ask you something?"

"You just did."

"What's the deal with the purple hair?"

"I thought you said you liked it?"

"I was trying to sleep with you."

"So you lied to me?"

"It wasn't a lie per se, but I couldn't exactly say that I liked what your ass was doing in those jeans, could I?"

Unwanted heat fans across my skin. "This isn't helping me think more highly of you, you know."

Jack laughs and the corners of his eyes crinkle, a half-moon grin appearing through the dark. "So, why purple?" he asks. "I feel like there's a story there."

"When guys go through breakups do you ever just get the urge to chop off all your hair and move to South America?"

"Um, no."

"Then you wouldn't understand."

"I'm sure I wouldn't."

He flops over and I turn onto my side, facing away from him.

"We should get some sleep," I say, nestling into the covers. "I'm sure there will be plenty of time for you to mock my hair in the morning."

He rolls over again, silence stretching between us for a long moment before finally he says, "Good night, Ada."

"Good night," I say into the black.

Chapter 5

70 HOURS UNTIL THE WEDDING

I wake up to Carter's arm slung around my waist, heated skin pressing against my back. He feels solid and safe as I nuzzle into him, relishing in the warmth of his body. Except something's different. Carter usually doesn't smell so sweet. And unless he's been working out more, his chest isn't so hard . . . Wait a minute . . . My body jumps to attention, eyes flashing open.

Not only is it *not* Carter I'm cuddling with, but there's also something hard poking my lower back. A *big* something. Not that the size matters, but it makes the whole thing much more noticeable. Like being prodded by a water bottle. And not an Aquafina. We're talking a Smartwater here.

"Ahhhhh!" I shriek, scrambling to the other side of the bed.

Jack's eyes fly open. "Whatswrong?! Whassgoinon?" he asks, voice still muddled with sleep.

"Your dick is what's wrong!"

"My *what*—?" Jack looks down at the tent in his boxers, and I watch as awareness slogs through his expression.

He frowns and adjusts himself, not that it does much to hide the evidence of his erection.

Eventually he gives up and pulls the blanket over himself, thus hiding his lower half from view. "Morning wood is a perfectly normal and healthy bodily function," he says. "I offered to make a barrier last night."

"Great. And your excuse for cuddling me is . . . ?"

"Cuddling?" His lips crease into a frown. "I was *not* cuddling you."

"Unless that was some other dude in the bed with me, then, yeah, *your* arm was around *my* waist." I decide to leave out the fact that for a brief moment I'd cuddled him back. But that was only because I thought he was Carter. Obviously.

Jack's eyes stretch wide, and for a moment I think he might actually be embarrassed, but his expression reboots, shifting from discomfort to dour. "Whatever I did or didn't do, it was clearly an accident," he says stiffly.

I'm about to point out that *he's* the one who thought we were going to have sex last night, and these types of *accidents* appear to be a pattern for him, when my phone buzzes from the bedside table. I pick it up and see I have fourteen missed calls from Allison and twenty-nine unanswered texts.

The first few texts are polite, cordial even:

8:12pm **ALLISON**

Hey, where are you?

8:46pm **ALLISON**

Do you have an ETA?

9:18pm **ALLISON**

We are worried

All the way to the most recent:

6:38am **ALLISON**
Ada where the fuck are you?

8:49am **ALLISON**
Are you alive?

8:56am **ALLISON**
I swear to God if you miss my wedding . . .

9:02am **ALLISON**
Have you been sold into a sex trafficking ring?

9:13am **ALLISON**
If you can read this: I have a very particular set of skills. Skills I have acquired over a very long career. Skills that make me a nightmare for people like you.

My stomach grand jetés right into my throat. In all the craziness I forgot to let my family know what happened.

I hit redial and Allison answers on the first ring. "Where the fuck are you? Are you alive?"

"No, I'm dead and it's my ghost making this call. Yes, I'm alive," I deadpan.

Jack gives me a questioning look and I mouth, *Allison.*

She groans audibly into the receiver. "Don't bullshit me right now. Where are you? Do you have the veil?"

Unbelievable. I could be holed up in a Russian gulag right now and Allison's primary concern would still be whether the veil was okay.

"Yes, I have the veil," I say with the same forced composure as if I were negotiating a hostage scenario. "But my flight got canceled, so I had to stay in London last night."

"London?" she repeats. "You're in London?"

"Yes, but—"

"You're gonna make it, right?" she asks, a thread of discomfort in her voice that, if I didn't know better, I'd mistake for concern.

"Yes, of course," I tell her, sliding out of bed and going into the bathroom, where I shut the door for privacy. "We have a plan. We're going to be there in time."

"We? Who is *we*?"

I dance from foot to foot, bare feet stinging against the cool linoleum. "So you're never gonna believe this, but I ran into Jack Houghton last night. Turns out we were supposed to be on the same flight from London. He actually let me crash with him last night. Isn't that funny?"

My sister doesn't seem to think so.

"Houghton?" she asks, voice cracking like it always does when she's pissed. "You slept with Houghton?"

"No! I didn't sleep with him! I mean we slept in the same bed, but we didn't *sleep* together."

"So you're with him right now?"

"Yes, and we have a plan to get to Ireland," I tell her. "All the flights are booked for the next few days, but it's fine because we can take a train and then a boat. We'll be there as soon as we can."

But my sister doesn't seem to be absorbing any of this. She's still stuck on the Jack thing.

"You and Houghton are going to travel together?"

"It appears so," I say, looking toward the bathroom door when I can hear Jack moving around on the other side.

"Well, he's a total player," she says. "I'd watch out if I were you."

I know Jack is a major headache, but what does she think is going to happen? That he'll lure me into his unmarked white van with candy?

"Allison, trust me, I don't like him either—"

"You know my friend Ashley?" she asks, cutting me off. "The one who can't come to the wedding because she joined Greenpeace?"

I mentally sift through Allison's ever-growing roster of friends. "Yeah?"

"She and Jack hooked up and he totally ghosted her after."

I frown, annoyed but not surprised. "I'm not interested in—"

"And you know he told Collin not to marry me, right?"

That one gets me.

I know neither Jack nor I are particularly thrilled about this marriage—something we certainly voiced last night—but to hear that he point-blank told Collin not to marry my sister makes my gut twist with frustration. Who the hell does Jack think he is telling Collin not to marry Allison? Allison is a catch. *Anyone* would want to marry her. Which is precisely how she got in this mess in the first place!

"Jack's a total commitment-phobe," Allison goes on. "He told Collin that marriage was a trap. Frankly, I'm surprised he's even showing up to the wedding."

"Isn't he the best man?"

"Yeah, well, that wasn't my choice," Allison says, a clear edge to her voice. "And I know he can be all sweet and charming when he wants to be, but remember what I told you about the Slovenian figure skaters?"

"I heard they were Slovakian."

I can practically see Allison's icy glare through the receiver. "Ada, I'm serious. He probably has a disease."

I bite down on my lip, deciding it's probably best if I don't tell her he's, in fact, disease-free. Or that said disease-free penis woke me up this morning.

"You don't need to convince me. I'm not gonna sleep with him," I tell her. "Besides, I still have a boyfriend. Carter? Remember him?"

"I thought you were on a break."

"We are. Which isn't the same as broken up," I remind her.

"So are you Ross or Rachel in this situation?"

I purse my lips into a grimace, not particularly interested in her unsolicited commentary on my eight-year relationship when she hasn't been in a relationship that's lasted longer than six months.

"Very funny, but we're evaluating our relationship," I tell her.

Of course, it's Carter who is doing the evaluating, but *we're evaluating* sounds less humiliating than *my boyfriend of eight years isn't sure he wants to be with me anymore and now I'm in the midst of an identity crisis.*

"I don't get what there is to evaluate," Allison says. "You guys have been together *forever.* Why can't you just figure it out?"

I resist the urge to roll my eyes. "Because not all of us can get married after knowing someone for a few months. Some of us actually take commitment seriously."

"Collin and I *are* serious. Which is why we're getting married this weekend instead of dragging our feet for eight years."

Ouch.

Well, this is a little heated for—I check the time—nine a.m.

"I have to go," I tell her, glancing over my shoulder toward the door, where I can hear Jack's footsteps drawing nearer. "Jack is getting up. I'll check in with you later."

"Keep me updated. And *don't* let anything happen to the veil." Then she ends the call without saying bye.

As soon as the line goes dead there's a firm rap of knuckles on the door.

"Are you done? I need to shower," Jack yells.

"I'm in here!" I yell back.

"Are you peeing?"

"No."

"Then I'm coming in." And before I can protest, the bathroom door—which I must have forgotten to lock—creaks open. Jack peers through the gap in the door.

"Hey!" I cry. "I could have been naked in here!"

His left eyebrow pops upward. "Are you normally naked when you talk on the phone with your sister?"

"Just get out." I move to shut the door in his face, but he sidesteps me into the bathroom.

"I need to take a shower before we leave to catch our train in . . ." He checks his watch. "Thirty minutes. Which means you're welcome to keep standing there, but I'm gonna get naked in five . . . four . . . three—"

"Fine!" I inch out the doorway. "Just be quick."

"Of course, *your highness.*" He flicks his wrist with a flourish before slamming the door in my face.

But five minutes quickly turns into fifteen. I bang on the door. "Jack! Hurry up!"

No answer.

"Jack! I'm serious!"

Still no answer.

A groan rattles in the back of my throat. What is he doing in there? I thought guys just rubbed soap over their junk and called it good.

I'm casting furious glances at the clock, wondering if I'll even have time to brush my teeth, when an unfamiliar ringtone goes off. My eyes dart around the room before landing on the bedside table where Jack's phone hums. I pick up the phone and see someone named Doug Weston is calling.

"Jack! Someone is calling you!" I yell. "You better get out here and answer it!"

That must work because I hear the shower turn off. A moment later the bathroom door opens, and Jack emerges in a cloud of steam.

My throat instantly turns chalky.

Not only is there a towel wrapped suspiciously low around his waist, but a million tiny, crystalized water droplets glisten from the grooves in his abdominals as though hand-placed by a Hollywood art director for maximum hotness.

Good grief. It's like he's trying to annoy me and, spoiler alert, it's working.

I drag my eyes away, trying to pretend like his chiseled chest won't be permanently imprinted on my retinas for the rest of time.

"Someone named Doug is calling you," I say, tossing him the still-ringing phone.

Jack takes one look at the screen, ignores it, then scowls at me. "Don't touch my stuff."

"It was ringing!"

"I *said* don't touch my stuff."

I certainly don't care about Jack, or whoever the hell might be calling him, but something about the thinly contained frustration hiding behind his stiff jaw fills me with undefined discomfort, like I've just walked in on something I shouldn't have.

But whatever it is, I don't have time to worry about it.

I turn my back to Jack and run my toothbrush under the faucet. A moment later Jack appears by my side, doing the same thing.

"Allison gave me the scoop on you, you know," I say, through a mouthful of toothpaste. "And let's just say it didn't improve my opinion of you."

Something uneasy flickers in his eyes, but just as quickly, it's gone, replaced by an arched eyebrow and his usual smugness. "Oh, did she?"

I spit into the sink. "I know you tried to convince Collin to not get married."

"Yeah, well, marriage is a trap," he says with a shrug before spitting out his own mouthful of toothpaste. "I'm just looking out for my buddy."

My jaw drops, mouth widening into an *o* shape. "You can't say that!"

"I can't?"

I huff, reaching for a washcloth. "You are *so* not best man material."

"Last night you didn't seem to be a big fan of marriage either," he says, giving me a pointed look. "Maybe you're not maid of honor material either."

My solar plexus flares as white-hot annoyance shoots down my spine.

"First off," I say through gritted teeth, "I thought we weren't going to bring that up. Second, I'm a fan of marriage, just not this particular one. And third, I'm trying to look out for my sister. Meanwhile, you're trying to take your bro to a strip club. *We*"—I gesture between the two of us—"are *not* the same."

The brackets around his mouth deepen. "You know, you would think that since I'm paying for you to get to your sister's wedding, you might at least try to be cordial to me."

"I *am* being cordial."

"Then I'd hate to see you be rude." He cups his hands under the faucet, splashing his face. "Aren't you going to say thank you?"

"I said *thank you* last night."

"Well, I think I need to hear it again."

"Fine, *thank you*."

His eyes meet mine in challenge. "For what?"

"Really? You're making me do this?"

"Fine. I guess you can find your own way to Belfast, then," he says, scraping a washcloth down the side of his face and neck.

A groan tumbles out of me. But as much as I want to tell him exactly where he can shove a *thank you,* I'm aware that right now he's my only shot at making it to this wedding on time, so I pull myself up to my full height and say in my most dramatic, over-the-top voice, "Fine. *Thank you,* Jack, for saving me. You're the air that I breathe. The wind beneath my wings. The reason for my being. Happy?"

His lips curl upward, eyes flashing with amusement. "That was serviceable, but I think three more times and some groveling wouldn't hurt."

I draw my eyes on him like a weapon. "You know, I'd watch it if I were you. Otherwise I'll tell Allison that you tried to get in my pants last night."

"That's funny, because I'll tell her that you don't want to go to her wedding."

I step closer, close enough to smell the minty toothpaste on his mouth. "Then I'll tell her *you're* planning to take Collin to a strip club for his bachelor party."

"Fine. Then I'll tell her you think Collin's an unwrapped Hershey's Kiss."

"Well, I'll tell Allison you don't think their marriage is going to outlive a Crock-Pot!"

We glare at one another, eyes flaring, caught in a wordless standoff for two more beats, then I grab my things, march out of the bathroom, and slam the door behind me.

It's just a few days, then I never have to see him and his annoyingly attractive face ever again.

Chapter 6

69 HOURS UNTIL THE WEDDING

From the hotel we take the bus back to Heathrow Airport, where we board the Tube to central London.

When I heard the word *tube,* I envisioned one of those sleek bullet trains like in Japan, but instead I discover the Tube is actually a rickety underground train that smells of dust mites and urine. And the floor is suspiciously sticky.

A cool female voice reminds us to *mind the gap between the train and platform* as the automatic train doors close with a mechanic hiss behind us.

As soon as we settle into our seats, Jack pulls out his phone. But whatever he sees on his screen clearly pisses him off, because he makes a kind of low growl sound before promptly shoving his phone back into his pocket.

"Everything okay?" I ask.

He clears his throat. "Fine."

"Work?" I try.

"No."

I'm not exactly thrilled about traveling with Jack, but I suppose the least we can do is get to know the basics about one another.

"What kind of work do you do?" I ask.

"Environmental."

"Like what? Are you a conservationist? Or one of those people who prostrate themselves in front of buildings scheduled for demolition?"

"No."

"Was that Doug guy who called this morning from work?"

"No."

"Are you going to give me anything more than one-word answers?"

"No."

Great. Such a conversationalist. I wonder if Oprah has to put up with this kind of shit.

"You know, if we're going to travel together, we could at least get to know one another."

He sits up, narrowed eyes weaving across my face. "Why? You've already made up your mind about me. I'd hate to interfere with all your pious judgments."

"I don't think you need my help. Seems like you've been doing a great job proving me right all on your own."

He grimaces but doesn't answer, and I redirect my attention to the window, hoping to get what might be my only glimpse of London, but the train travels underground and the windows turn dark.

The smooth operator voice tells us that this train terminates somewhere called *Cockfosters*, and I slouch lower into the scratchy eighties upholstery before pulling out my own phone, where Carter's text stares back at me. The one I still haven't replied to.

I test out, Hey Carter, I thought about you in the shower last night. Do you ever think about me?

Too desperate? I erase it and try again.

Carter, I'm on my way to Ireland with the best man. I saw his abs and he could be Ryan Gosling's body double. Oh, and he wanted to have sex with me. Have a nice life.

I snort, then delete it.

"What are you doing?"

I jump in my seat, eyes darting up to meet Jack, who's watching me with interest.

"Nothing!" I press my phone to my chest so he can't see the screen.

Jack's brows scrunch with disbelief. "Are you trying to make him jealous?" he asks.

The space between my brows pinches. "Oh, so privacy only applies to you and your phone calls but not me and my texts?"

"Is that why you were in the shower so long last night?" he asks, ignoring the question. "Because you were thinking about your ex?"

"I was not!"

Okay, fine, I was, but not like *that*.

He gives me a knowing look. "It was a pretty long shower, Ada."

My inner fuse scorches right down the middle and I let out a huff of frustration. "Not that it's any of *your* business, but I wasn't going to send that."

"Then why did you type it?"

"It was a joke."

"A joke?"

"Yes, *a joke*," I say more firmly.

But he doesn't seem to buy it.

"I mean if you want to make him jealous, I'm sure we could think of something," he says, giving me a heated look that translates into a dozen crackling embers under my skin.

"I don't want to make him jealous. I just . . ." But I don't finish that sentence because what I really want is for Carter to show up with a boom box outside my window. Or for him to hijack a high school stadium and sing "Can't Take My Eyes Off You." I want him to tell me he's sorry, that he loves me and he made a mistake. But somehow, I don't think Mr. I-Don't-Believe-in-Marriage would understand.

After a beat, Jack asks, "Have you been with anyone else since the break?"

I sit up, body jolting into defense mode. "You can't ask me that."

He blinks. "I can't? I thought *you* wanted to get to know each other better?"

I glare at him, lips curling into a scowl. It's not his business, but there's a not-so-tiny part of me that wants to tell him the truth, if only to prove that things aren't over between Carter and me.

"No. I haven't been with anyone else," I say stiffly. "And neither has he."

"How do you know?"

"Because if he had, he would have told me. It's called trust."

I don't know that for sure, but I'd rather tell myself that's the case than imagine the alternative.

Jack studies me, dark eyes scanning with interest. "Have you thought about trying to get over him by getting under someone else?"

I snort. "You mean someone like you?"

"No, not me." He gives me a look. "I'm just saying. Could be a better alternative to moping around, sending cringey, desperate messages."

"I told you; I wasn't going to send that."

He puts his hands up in a sign of surrender and I shoot him one more glare before burying my gaze in my lap, skin burning with frustration.

Seriously?

What does Jack expect me to do? Forget about the guy? Pretend like the last eight years didn't happen?

Maybe that's what Jack would do, because he apparently has the emotional depth of a kiddie pool, but I'm not going to throw away everything Carter and I have built together for a meaningless hookup.

It's not just that I don't want to sleep with someone else, it's the idea of change, of losing the last puzzle piece in the rapidly crumbling picture of my life. It's the idea of giving up, not just on us, but on the future. The thing that was supposed to be certain.

When Carter and I got together in college, everything about our relationship seemed easy and carefree. Our biggest problems were deciding which parties to go to and if I could get into the accounting pre-req this quarter or next.

Then we graduated and real life set in. Suddenly we had jobs and commutes and bills and student loans and we were always tired. The shift was hard on both of us, but it hit Carter a little harder. I could see it in the slump of his shoulders and the way he didn't laugh as much. It felt a little bit like losing him, so when he told me he hated his cubicle job and wanted to quit, I supported him.

After that, he tried a whole slew of things. Marine biology, architecture, photography—always looking for something new, something exciting, something to stave off the unfulfilling monotony of adult life. And for a while it felt like an adventure. One we were on together. One where each new path was an opportunity to grow and deepen our bond. To prove that this stage of our relationship could be just as strong as it had been in college.

But now, almost three months into the break, I can't help but wonder if maybe *I* was just another stopover on Carter's endless pursuit for newness. If, while I've been clinging to visions of forever, Carter's still looking for that next adventure, this time without me.

AFTER CHANGING FROM THE PICCADILLY LINE TO THE NORTHERN LINE, WE arrive at Euston Station, where tourists and Londoners alike dart in and out of shops like they're all in fast-forward, suitcases trailing behind them, selfie sticks raised. A train whistle echoes in the distance and a muffled voice comes over a loudspeaker announcing that platform fourteen has been delayed.

Hopefully someday, under better circumstances, I'll be able to come back and see London properly, but for now, this is all I get, so I drink in as much as I can. The expansive skylight overhead, letting in beams of light. The signs that say TOILET instead of RESTROOM. Souvenir stalls selling T-shirts that say hokey things like *My aunt went to London and all I got was this T-shirt.* The unfamiliar stores that all have fancy-sounding names like Holland & Barrett and Marks & Spencer and Waitrose. The quiet hum of accented English and a dozen other languages I can't quite untangle.

"Are we near Buckingham Palace? That's where the king lives, right?" I ask, huffing as I try to keep up with Jack's long strides as we hurry toward our platform.

"I guess."

"And what about the tower where King Henry the Eighth beheaded his wives?"

"I think it was only the one wife."

"Are you sure?"

"Not really."

"I read something about how the king flies a different flag when he's home? Is that true?"

"No idea."

"I thought you said you'd been here before?"

"I have, but it wasn't on a Rick Steves tour."

"Didn't you do any sightseeing?"

"No, it was a business trip."

"Well, if *I* came for business, *I* would make time to see the city."

He shoots me a sideways look. "What is this? *60 Minutes*?"

"I'm just making conversation!"

"How about we focus on making it to our train on time, then you can continue your little interview. Okay?"

Annoyance balloons inside me and I stop in my tracks, arms roped over my chest. "What was it you were saying about being cordial earlier, because—"

Jack holds up his hand to stop me. "We're already late. So either you can keep up, or I can pick you up and carry you to the train. Your choice."

My skin flushes as I fight back an image of Jack tossing me over his shoulder, firm hands gripping the backs of my thighs. I'd hate it. *Obviously.* But unwanted heat gathers between my legs, blurring the line between anger and arousal.

"No," I say, voice tight. "That won't be necessary."

"Good."

Jack keeps walking, but as soon as his back is to me, I give him the finger. It's the little things.

When we arrive at our platform there's a small huddle of other passengers waiting for the train.

"See? We didn't miss it."

Jack checks the reader board hovering over the platform. "Barely. It's scheduled to arrive any minute. You have your ticket?" He looks me over like he's sure I've misplaced it in the three seconds since I scanned it to get through the ticket barrier.

I wave my ticket in front of his face. "You don't have to babysit me," I say just as our train rolls onto the platform and my voice is lost in the rumble of the tracks and cool intercom voice announcing that the train terminating at Glasgow Central has arrived at platform two.

The doors to car twenty-three slide open and we board the train along with the other passengers. Jack walks ahead of me and I do everything in my power to not look at his butt in those jeans.

I've never been a butt girl. I'm more into a firm chest. And those V-shaped things that no one knows what to call. But Jack has an objectively nice butt. Nice enough to possibly make a convert out of me.

"Top or bottom?" Jack asks as the train doors shut behind us with a smooth click.

I freeze. "W-what?"

"Where do you want to sit?" He gestures to a skinny set of stairs to the left of the doors. "The top level or the bottom?"

"Oh, right." I feel my face flush. "Up top sounds good."

As soon as he turns away, I release a shallow exhale.

Get a grip, pervert. And for the love of God, stop thinking about sex. Or Jack. Or his butt. *Definitely* his butt.

My mind travels to the vibrator stowed in my suitcase and how deeply unfair it is that I won't be able to use it until we arrive in Belfast.

At the top of the narrow staircase, we find two open seats.

I attempt to lift my suitcase into the overhead compartment, but apparently I have the upper body strength of a toddler, and my knees buckle under the weight.

I try again, but it slips, nearly colliding with the man in the seat in front of me.

Is this why people go to the gym? So they can avoid these embarrassing scenarios? Because if that's the case, I have a renewed interest in working out.

"You want help?" Jack asks from behind me.

"No. I've got it," I say, just as a poorly timed bead of sweat runs down the side of my neck.

"Here. I don't want you to hurt yourself," Jack says, leaning over and placing his hand on the suitcase.

"*Stop.* I don't need your help." I twist away from him, but Jack reaches around my waist, hands grazing the exposed skin between my jeans and the hem of my top.

"Come on. Just let me help you," he says with a huff. "You're gonna get hurt."

"What part of 'I've got it' don't you understand?"

Using the suitcase as leverage, I try to push him away, but he doesn't loosen his grip and we yank it back and forth like we're playing an overheated game of tug-of-war.

Out of the corner of my eye I notice an older woman watching us, eyes wide like she's worried there's about to be a domestic incident. I shoot her an apologetic look.

"Fine," I whisper, loosening my grip. "Just stop making a scene."

"Me? I'm not the one making a scene."

"*Yes,* you are."

"*No,* I'm not."

I shove my bag into his chest with aggravated force. "Here."

He winces, stumbling backward. "What's in this thing? Cinder blocks? The tears of children?"

I give him a dirty look and size up his small duffel bag. "Oh, yeah? And what's in yours? Cash to stuff in strippers' thongs?"

"At least cash doesn't weigh much."

I roll my eyes. It's so unfair how easy it is for men to pack light. All they need is a toothbrush, a pair of boxers, and one of those men's three-in-one products that can be used as shampoo, bodywash, and motor oil.

Despite his protestations, Jack lifts my bag with ease and tucks it into the overhead compartment like it's light as air. His biceps don't even flex. How annoying.

Once our luggage is stowed, I slide into the window seat and Jack takes the seat beside me. His thigh lingers against mine for a second before he readjusts himself.

"We should arrive in Glasgow later this evening, then we can take a bus to the ferry terminal tomorrow," he says, glancing at his watch. "If all goes according to plan, we'll get to the castle around midafternoon."

"That's a big *if* considering how this trip has gone so far."

I mentally review the schedule. That means we should get there just in time for the rehearsal dinner with stag and hen nights to follow.

I shoot Allison a quick text.

ADA

We're on our way. Is everything okay?

She texts back instantly.

ALLISON

It will be when you get here.

In another time and place I might have interpreted her text to mean she misses me, that she can't imagine this day without me by her side. But given how things have been between us lately, I know her tone is less *I need my big sister* and more *I'm pissed*. Like it's somehow *my* fault the flight got canceled. Like this is all some conspiracy to ruin her wedding.

I'm sure she's just stressed—an expensive, international wedding to a guy you hardly know will do that to you—but it hurts knowing it didn't used to be like this with us. That before Collin, Allison and I were really close.

Before my mom married my stepdad, she was a single mom, which meant that growing up, I spent a lot of time as Allison's primary caregiver. I was the one who helped with homework and got dinner ready and made sure she got to bed on time when mom worked late at the hospital. Then when we got older, I was the person Allison came to when she needed advice about friends or if she should get bangs (she shouldn't). It was my wardrobe she would raid when she needed a new outfit, and I was who she came to when she didn't know how to use a tampon.

I wasn't just her sister. I was *her person.* Her best friend. Her confidant. Her steady rock amid the swells of life.

Then Allison discovered boys. And they discovered her back. And with that discovery came heartbreak. Lots of it. Nights spent sobbing in my arms and midnight ice cream runs that eventually became wine runs. But one thing remained. Every time she had her heart broken, she came to me.

I was the one who stroked her hair and told her she was going to be okay, that Will or Zach or Fred or Josh or whoever the hell it was that week was a loser who didn't deserve her. Then we'd eat ice cream and watch *The Parent Trap.*

But not every breakup could be solved with Dennis Quaid and ice cream. Some breakups were messier, uglier. Some involved me driving to California in the middle of the night to pick her up when she called me in tears that she'd caught her boyfriend cheating. Others involved me filing police reports for stalking and hours spent with the phone company, getting her number changed.

Part of me admires my sister's endless optimism in love. Her steadfast assurance that despite heartbreak and betrayal and downright disappointment, happily ever after is just around the corner. But another part of me wishes I could lock my sister away in a tower, Mother Gothel–style, to keep her safe from all the jerks and assholes of the world.

Of course I'm frustrated that she's not heeding my advice when it comes to Collin and this wedding. That she's apparently decided to have amnesia regarding all her past relationships. *And* all the times I've swooped in and saved the day. But mostly I'm worried that this will be her biggest heartbreak yet.

And I won't be able to protect her from it.

Chapter 7

67 HOURS UNTIL THE WEDDING

As the train pulls out of London, I imagine how I might sketch the city skyline. Long, broad strokes for the towering skyscrapers. Shading where the tallest buildings cast their shadows. Unlike the Seattle skyline, which is compact, London seems to stretch on forever, blurring only where the edge of the city meets the gray sky.

Jack leans over and gestures to a pointy-looking building called the Shard, and something called the Gherkin, which he says is what British people call pickles. And he is right, the building totally looks like a giant pickle.

"Have you done a lot of traveling?" I ask, impressed by his knowledge of the city. Then again, the only other time I've left the country was a spring break trip to Cancun in college, and it's easy to be impressed when Señor Frog's is the extent of your international travel.

"I've been to Paris, Tokyo, Rio, Munich, and Rome," he says, ticking the cities off on his fingers.

"And where's your favorite?"

"Wherever I'm going next."

"And where's next?"

"After the wedding I'm going to Naples for a few days. I always try to stop by when I'm in Europe."

"Really? For business or pleasure?"

"Pizza, which definitely falls into the pleasure category," he says, a dreamy look befalling him.

My eyes widen, surprised. "You're going to Naples just for pizza?"

"I mean, yeah . . . ?" He looks at me like he can't believe I'd even ask. "The art of Neapolitan-style pizza making has granted Naples UNESCO World Heritage status. It's serious business."

"I admire how dedicated and informed you are about pizza," I tell him.

His mouth creaks out an uneven smile. "There's this amazing no-frills spot, Pizzeria Vergini, around the corner from Palazzo dello Spagnolo, that has the best pizza in the world. In my opinion."

"*The world*? How much pizza did you have to eat to come to that conclusion?"

His eyes snag to mine, mouth expanding into a conspiratorial grin. "A lot."

I release a wistful sigh and draw my knees up into my chest, feet balancing on the edge of my seat. "I wish I could do something like that, go somewhere just because I felt like it."

"Why can't you?" he asks.

"I told you, I'm sort of broke right now. Besides, I've got a lot going on."

I think about the mountain of boxes in my parents' garage and the single suitcase I've been living out of for the past two months, and how my life feels like one of those old IKEA commercials with the packages all haphazardly piled on top of the VW Bug, ready to come crashing down at any moment.

"What do you have going on?" Jack asks.

I shift my weight, eyes skipping toward the window, then back to Jack. "Stuff."

"Like?"

"My sister's wedding."

And waiting to see if Carter wants to get back together.

"Your sister's wedding will be over in four days," he says. "Doesn't exactly seem like a major barrier."

"But then I have to help with the thank-you cards and organizing the gifts," I explain. "Being the maid of honor is a lot more responsibility than the best man. All you have to do is make sure he's sober enough to get down the aisle, tell a few cringey jokes, and call it a day. Meanwhile, I've spent the last few months designing place cards and seating charts and planning the bachelorette party."

"Okay, first of all, my speech won't be cringey. And second, I had to plan the bachelor party. So, no, it hasn't all been a cakewalk."

"Oh, you mean going to a strip club? Yeah, sounds like a ton of effort."

Jack's eyes flash, mouth turning up, like he can't decide whether he's amused or annoyed with me. "All right, so after you finish your mountain of wedding duties, where would you want to go if you could go anywhere?" he asks.

"Paris," I say without hesitation.

His face lights up, interested. "Why Paris?"

I fidget with the tray table attached to the seat in front of me. "I've just always wanted to go."

"Then you should do it."

He says it with such ease, like traveling to Paris is as simple as breathing. But of course it's not.

When I was a junior in college, I got accepted to a study abroad program in Paris—ten magical weeks of art and language immersion in the heart of the French capital—but Carter told me he didn't want me to go. That it would be too much time apart and he wasn't sure our relationship could withstand the distance. I was disappointed, but things were starting to get serious with us. He'd just told me he loved me for the first time, and we'd already begun looking for an off-campus apartment together. It seemed like a bad time to jet off to France for two and half months, so I stayed in Seattle that quarter.

After we graduated from college, I tried to convince Carter that we should take a trip to Paris. We'd stay in cheap hostels, and picnic in the Luxembourg Gardens, and stroll through Musée d'Orsay, and linger over long lunches at Café de Flore. But not long after graduation, Carter got accepted to grad school, so we packed up everything we owned and moved to New York, where we spent nine months in a closet-sized apartment that cost more than a brand-new car, with neighbors who were absolutely selling drugs, while Carter studied photography at Parsons.

Carter lasted two semesters before deciding that the professors *didn't understand his art* and he *didn't want to be bound by capitalistic dictates of what was "good."* After that, we moved back to Seattle, where Carter landed a cushy office job at his parents' custom cabinetry company while he figured out what he wanted to do next.

I tried to love New York, but it was never my thing. It was too busy. Too crowded. Too expensive. Too far away from my family. But Carter had this infectious ability to make everything feel special and exciting. He was the life of every party—a human disco ball—and it was easy to get excited about whatever he was enthused by. It was part of why I first fell in love with him.

When he wasn't in school and I wasn't working whatever

temp corporate job I had that week, we spent weekends exploring the city: barhopping in Greenwich Village and gallery openings in Tribeca and watching the sunset from Brooklyn Bridge Park, passing cheap bottles of wine back and forth.

There'd been nights we felt infinite, like Carter and I were part of the same space-time continuum, and we'd always be together, in every possible timeline, past, present, and future. Like New York was the first big step for the two of us. A step toward forever.

I hadn't felt I needed Paris when we had each other.

But now, in light of the break, the same memories that once felt shiny and sparkly, proof of how great we were together, feel tainted, painted instead in shades of gray.

Now I wonder if I've been clinging to a distorted, Instagram-filter version of our relationship. A version where relationship nirvana was always one milestone away. If Carter and I could just move in together. Meet the parents. Go to New York. Get engaged. *Insert next thing here,* it would solidify our relationship and prove just how in love, and happy, and committed we were.

If I could just be exactly what Carter wanted, then everything would be okay.

But what if I've been chasing the wrong things? What if in my desire to secure a relationship with Carter, I've lost sight of myself, of what I want? If I've let opportunities and dreams and wants slip through the cracks, lost in the pursuit of a future that was never guaranteed?

The question tangles in my chest, a gnarled rope of unease, and I slide lower in my seat, only half paying attention as London passes by in a blur.

ONCE WE GET OUTSIDE OF CENTRAL LONDON, THE BUILDINGS BECOME SHABbier and more run-down. Then finally we leave London behind, and we are racing through wide expanses of green as far as the eye can see. Rolling fields and pastures continue for miles and miles, dotted by the occasional village crowned by a looming church spire.

Each village looks like the type of place where nothing bad happens, except for a murder that's conveniently solved by a nosy but brilliant older woman who never leaves home without her knitting needles.

After I've gotten my fill of passing scenery, I reach into my purse and pull out the book my mom gave me.

It's called *Finding Mr. Right* and features a stock photo of a Handsome Man™ on the cover.

Despite numerous explanations, my mom still doesn't understand the difference between Carter and me "taking a break" and "breaking up." Though it's hard to say if that's due to a generational disconnect, or because after eight years with the same guy and no ring, she's gotten desperate and decided to take matters into her own hands.

I didn't think I would actually read the book, but then I got bored on the flight and decided to give it a try. It's not bad though—mostly life advice about female empowerment and finding your own inner heroine. Something I suppose I could use some more of.

I flip open to my bookmark and resume where I left off. *Chapter Six: Reclaiming Your Feminine Energy.* This chapter is all about harnessing your femininity and discovering the power of your own sexual energy.

I'm just about to find out about the power of the female orgasm when I feel Jack's eyes on me.

"Have you found him yet?" he asks.

I look up. "Who?"

He gestures to the book in my lap. "*Mr. Right.*"

I purse my lips, one eyebrow flicking upward. "You're reading over my shoulder? Again?"

"I mean with a riveting title like *Finding Mr. Right*, how could I not?"

"My mom gave it to me," I tell him. "And don't get too excited, it's mostly self-help stuff."

"So you're not looking for a man?"

"No. There's actually a lot of good material in here about . . ." I shuffle through a few pages. "Female empowerment and feminine energy."

Jack's eyes take a skeptical lap around my face. "Feminine energy?"

"Yeah, like harnessing your inner goddess."

A laugh rattles in the back of his throat. "Your *inner goddess*? Come on, you don't believe that, do you?"

I frown. "What's wrong with that?"

"Trust me, if you want to attract a man you don't need to find your *inner goddess* or whatever."

"Okay, Mr. Guru. And what do you suggest?"

"Straight men are very simple," he says. "All you need to do is wear a push-up bra and look confused in Home Depot."

"Is that where you hang out when you're not picking up women in hotel lobbies?"

His mouth tilts up, clearly amused. "I've had great luck in the power tools section."

I snort. "As much as I appreciate your extremely regressive dating advice, I think I'd prefer to meet someone who is actually interested in *me*, not just using me as a prop for their own fragile male ego."

"I thought you weren't looking for a man?" he asks, catching my eye.

"I'm not."

"But if you were . . . ?"

I groan, sinking lower in my seat. "Can we go back to the part where you give me one-word answers and pretend I don't exist?"

"I thought *you* wanted to get to know one another?"

"I changed my mind."

He settles back, arms folded over his chest, perusing me with interest. After a beat, he says, "I've thought about it, and I think you're right. We should try getting to know one another. Especially considering I'll be attending your family's Thanksgiving from now on."

"First of all, you're not coming to my family's Thanksgiving because you're not invited. And second, I already told you we're not having sex."

Jack laughs. "I don't mean *know* each other in the biblical sense. I was thinking we could play a game."

I sit up a little straighter, eyes narrowing. "I don't know if I want to play the kinds of games you like to play. Something tells me you don't mean I Spy."

"How about I ask you a question, then you ask me one back," he says. "Like Twenty Questions."

"I haven't played that since high school. It was always the same questions. *Who do you have a crush on? Are you a virgin?*" I pause, twisting my mouth. "Though, now that I think about it, this sounds right up your alley."

A bitten-off grin stretches all the way from his mouth to his eyes. "I was going to ask you what your thoughts were on carbon-neutral tax incentives, but if you want to make this game more interesting, be my guest."

Playing any kind of game with Jack Houghton is probably a bad idea, but I can't say I'm not at least a little curious. Know your enemy and all that.

"I'll tell you if you tell me?" I try.

His grin widens. "Now who sounds like a high school boy?"

I look around the train car as though worried someone might overhear us before turning back and whispering, "You go first."

Jack's eyebrows lift toward his hairline. "Are you worried the elderly woman behind us might be scandalized by the story of you losing your virginity in a squeaky twin bed?"

Damn. He's good. How did he know?

"No," I say, straightening my shoulders. "But I believe it's *your* turn, Mr. Houghton."

He presses the tips of his fingers together, features growing serious like he's preparing to defend a thesis. After a pause, he says, "I was seventeen in Holly Paulson's basement. And as soon as we were done her super strict parents got home and I had to hide in the garage. Naked. With the condom still on."

I cup my palm over my mouth, smothering a laugh. "How romantic."

"Oh yeah, super romantic. Especially when her dad came into the garage looking for something in the freezer and I had to stay crouched behind a Weedwacker, clutching my dick."

"And was it worth it?" I ask.

"All two minutes of it."

"Glad to know I didn't waste my time last night," I say.

He doesn't respond, just gives me a heated look that all but screams, *You have no idea what you're missing out on,* which would normally annoy me, but for reasons that probably have to do with the lingering scent of his cologne and the insufferably sexy piece of hair that keeps falling into his eyes, my insides twist like a sponge being wrung out.

"All right, your turn," he says.

"I didn't lose my virginity until college," I tell him. "It was with Carter. We were each other's first."

I remember the night six months into our relationship when I'd arrived at his dorm room wearing a matching bra and panty set I'd spent hours picking out, along with a pocketful of different condom types because I wasn't sure if I should buy *ribbed for her pleasure*, lambskin, latex, or flavored.

We'd made out to the new Coldplay album before proceeding to do the deed in his lofted dorm bed where the mattress squeaked so bad I'm pretty sure the whole hall heard the cacophony of our inexperienced lovemaking. It wasn't exactly the rose-petal-strewn fantasy suite I'd pictured, but hey, no one's first time is perfect, right? And the sex had gotten better over time as we learned what we liked and how we liked it.

"So you've only ever slept with one guy?" Jack asks.

His tone isn't judgmental per se, but he's giving me a look like I've just told him I've never tried chocolate before.

"There's nothing wrong with that," I say stiffly. "And just so you know, the sex was good," I add, unable to help myself.

"How would you know if you've only been with one person?"

"Because I can tell."

"How?"

"What do you want? A detailed explanation of his oral technique?"

The corner of Jack's mouth twitches, like he's doing everything in his power to not laugh. "If so, would this be another sex tip I can put next to *effort*?"

"Ha ha. Funny." I glare at him. "I'm just saying. I don't have to fuck a bunch of dudes and compare notes to know when it's good." He opens his mouth, but I cut him off. "And before you say it, I know what I like, and I don't need some random Chad-Bro to come along and show me what I'm missing out on."

"I wasn't going to say that."

"But you were thinking it."

He angles his body toward mine, brows narrowed. "You sure like jumping to conclusions about people, don't you?"

Heat percolates under my skin, but I can't tell if it's because of what he's just said or the way he's looking at me, like there's something on my face he's trying to decode. I clear my throat, eager to change the subject. "Okay. My turn. What's your deal with marriage?"

Jack's jaw tenses. "I don't have a deal."

"Puh-lease. You told me marriage was a trap. So what gives?"

"I just don't think humans are meant to be with one person forever," he says. "People change and evolve, and it would be silly to think that your *soulmate* at age twenty will be the same person at age fifty."

"But isn't that the point of love?" I ask. "To change and evolve together?"

He shakes his head. "But that's my point, what if two people evolve apart? What then? You stay together because a piece of paper says so?"

"It's not just a piece of paper," I say. "It's a commitment. A promise."

"Well, promises get broken all the time," he says. "It's a setup for failure."

"So what? You're going to die alone?"

"I said I'm against marriage, not celibate," he says, eyes cutting across mine. "I'm just more into expiration dating."

"Expiration dating?" I ask.

"Like you see someone with the full knowledge that it has an expiration date," he says. "No endgame. No labels. No commitment bullshit. Just a good time."

I cough out a laugh. "Have you thought about writing love poems? Or Hallmark cards?"

"Have *you* ever considered that the idea of forced monogamy is a social construct?"

I lean across the gap between seats. "Is that what you told Ashley?"

He looks up and down the carriage like he's expecting someone to pop out. "Who's Ashley?"

I roll my eyes, exasperated. "Allison's friend whom you slept with and ghosted. Ring any bells?"

Awareness slips over his features before morphing into a scowl. "That was a one-night stand. What do you expect me to do? Write her a sonnet?"

I lean closer, pressing my thumb to his forehead, pretending to examine his skull.

"What are you doing?" he asks, shrinking away from me.

"Oh, I'm just curious if we could donate your brain to science. Do you think misanthropy is genetic? Or more of a nature versus nurture thing?"

"Very funny."

"One more question. *For science,*" I add. "Do you really not have a heart? Or did someone break it?"

"No broken hearts," he says tightly. "Mine is perfectly intact, thanks."

"Likely story."

The peak of his lip twitches. "What does that mean?"

"Oh, come on." I gesticulate vaguely. "I don't buy your little *I don't believe in love* routine. Someone broke your heart, didn't they?"

His posture stiffens and he looks away.

"Romance and *happily ever after* are just oral traditions that have become so ingrained into our collective psyche that we can't tell the difference between the big screen and reality anymore," he says after a beat. "We use romance, or its absence, as an explanation for everything, as a way to find meaning within the meaningless. It's just a story we've told ourselves as a coping mechanism."

"*Or* . . ." I shoot him a look. "Guys are so desperate to avoid vulnerability, they'll make up branches of psychology out of whole cloth just to explain their commitment-phobia. Exhibit A." I gesture to Jack. "And exhibit B, Jean-Paul Sartre, who I'm pretty sure you just paraphrased."

Jack frowns. "I'm not a commitment-phobe, I'm a realist."

"Isn't that sort of cliché?" I ask. "The guy who engages in meaningless hookups with women whose names he won't remember, professing he doesn't fall in love?"

Jack's mouth sets into a tense line, eyes drifting past me to the window where endless pastures pass in a blur. "If love is waiting for a guy you spent eight years with to text you back, I think I'll pass."

Discomfort roils under my skin and I open my mouth, ready to be angry, to tell him he's wrong, that he doesn't understand, but there's a slight crack at the end of his voice that catches me off guard, and I can't help but wonder if maybe the words aren't for me at all.

Chapter 8

64 HOURS UNTIL THE WEDDING

Dusk flickers on the horizon when the train rolls into Lancaster. I have no clue where that is, except that's what the flashing sign outside the station says.

Beside me, Jack has drifted off. The side of his face is smooshed into the seat, chest rising and falling in a heavy rhythm. He looks so soft and tender when he's asleep. Good thing I know better.

"Wake up," I hiss, jabbing him in the ribs.

Jack jolts up. "Huh?"

I point overhead as the train conductor's muffled voice comes over the loudspeaker. Apparently due to some kind of train strike we will be changing trains in Lancaster.

"I'm starving, let's find food while we wait," Jack says, handing me my bag from the overhead compartment.

"I don't know . . ." My eyes dart across the platform. "I don't want us to miss our train."

"We have forty-five minutes," he says. "That's plenty of time."

We collect our belongings and exit the train onto a small double-sided open-air platform.

"How about this?" I gesture to a small kiosk selling snacks and candies I've never heard of before. Smarties chocolate. Aero. Flake.

Jack shakes his head. "I need real food. Sustenance. Not candy. Aren't you hungry too?"

As if on cue with our arrival, my stomach roars to life, reminding me I haven't eaten anything today.

"Fine. But let's be fast," I say.

We exit the station and make our way down a high street lined with narrow stone buildings that bend with the curves in the road. At the end of the street is a medieval tower rising in the distance.

It looks like the type of place that's probably bustling with tourists in the high season. Unfortunately, the gray weather doesn't appear to be doing the local economy any favors, because the street is mostly empty.

We walk a few blocks until we find a takeaway place with the word *kebab* flashing in neon letters outside.

"Come on. Let's try here," Jack says, leading me inside the doorway. The bell on the door rings as we step inside.

"Table for two?" the man behind the counter asks.

"Just to-go please," I say.

The man shakes his head. "Sorry. No takeaway. Sit-down service only."

I check the time. We have thirty-five minutes.

"We can't," I whisper to Jack. "We don't have time for a sit-down meal."

"Yeah, but it will take time to walk and find somewhere else to eat," he whispers back. "I didn't see any other restaurants on this street."

I shift uneasily, eyes darting the length of the restaurant. On the one hand, I *really* don't want to miss our train. But on the other, Jack's got a point. It might take us just as long to find somewhere else to eat. Besides, as evidenced by my noisy stomach, I'm just as hungry as he is.

"Fine," I say. "Let's just be quick."

We take our seats and I order a chicken shawarma and chips, and Jack orders a lamb kebab and chips. The man behind the counter slices meat from a giant stick while I cast nervous glances toward the door.

"We're fine," Jack says, giving me an insistent look. "We've still got plenty of time."

"I don't want to be late."

"We won't."

Hmph. Easy for him to say when he doesn't have a sister who will kill him if we don't get to this wedding on time.

Fortunately, the food arrives quickly, and I dive into my hummus-slathered chicken with gusto.

We eat in silence until I ask, "So are you going to tell me what you do for work? Or am I going to have to guess? Because I'm either gonna go with hit man or evil Bond villain."

Jack looks up from his food. "I'm an environmental lawyer, though depending on who you ask they might say that's the same thing as evil Bond villain."

My eyes stretch wide. I can practically hear my mom now. *A lawyer? Is he single?*

"So you're, like, smart?" I ask.

"What? Like it's hard?" he says in a perfect impression of Elle Woods.

A cackle rips out of me and he smiles like he can't quite help it.

"Why environmental law?" I ask.

"I just think it's important to be good stewards of our planet," he says. "My job's mostly paperwork, but I like to think that in some small way I'm doing some good in the world."

"Do you yell at big corporations?" I ask, inexplicably hot at the thought of Jack, dressed in a well-tailored suit, taking on corporate America.

"Sometimes," he says, pushing his food back and forth with the back of his fork. "My last case was against a beauty company that claimed to be cruelty-free but experimented on rabbits. It was really horrific, so now I'm extra careful to do my due diligence as a consumer. I think it's really important to be discerning about what we put in our bodies."

"Oh, I agree," I say, nodding vigorously.

His eyes hook up, meeting mine. "You do?"

"For sure. That's why I didn't want to sleep with you last night."

For a moment Jack just blinks at me before erupting into a full-bodied boyish laugh. The sound crackles like electricity in the air between us.

"So if you're a lawyer, I don't feel so bad about you paying for me," I say, spearing a piece of chicken with my fork.

"Easy there, I'm in environmental law. The big bucks are in mergers and acquisitions."

"Whatever. I see the Rolex you're wearing," I say, pointing out the fancy hunk of metal on his wrist.

He looks down as though surprised to see it. "It was a gift from Collin's family after I graduated law school."

"Wow, that was really nice of them. When I graduated, all I got was a Target gift card and a big fucking student loan bill. You must be close with his family."

He swallows then nods. "They've always been really supportive of me." He says it with a smile, but I notice he shoves his hands under the table, putting the watch out of sight. "What about you?" he asks. "You said you had a business?"

"I did." I glance toward the door, not sure if this is a conversation I want to have right now. Losing the business was hard enough. But having to relive that pain every time someone asks about it? Agony.

"What was the business?" he asks.

"I owned a tattoo studio."

His eyes widen. "Really? That's awesome."

"Yeah, it was super awesome, until the bank took it after I couldn't pay my bills anymore," I say, pushing my food around on my plate.

Before Sleeve It to Me, I took safe jobs. Corporate roles with 401Ks and dental insurance. But opening the business was the first thing I ever did that was just for myself. Not Carter. Not my mom. Not Allison. Just for me. And I loved it.

Growing up, art was the one place where I felt like I could break the rules. Where I could draw outside the lines and try new things without consequence. I didn't have to be perfect or in control or responsible. I could just *be*.

So when I had the idea to open the shop, I naively thought it would be like *Field of Dreams*—all I'd have to do was build it and they would come. The only problem is that despite majoring in business, I hadn't known the first thing about running one.

Sure, I got a favorable review in a big-time blog and someone on Instagram called me *Michelangelo with a needle* (a quote I'd considered inking myself with), but it hadn't been enough. At least not in the traditionally measured definition of success. And after two years of working myself into the ground, I had to close shop.

Logically, I know that the business closed for financial reasons and not some kind of intrinsic, personal failing, or because I wasn't a good enough artist, but it's impossible not to single out the one thing I'd ever done for myself as my biggest failure. A reminder that my art is a cute little hobby, but it can't—*shouldn't*—be more than that.

"I'm sorry to hear that," Jack says, cutting through my memories.

I slip lower into my seat as though I'm hoping the upholstery might swallow me whole. "Me too."

"So why tattoos?" Jack asks. "How'd you get into that?"

I play with my fork, picking it up, then setting it back down again. Reliving the failure of my business isn't exactly a fun subject for me. But something about the sturdiness of his gaze and the softness of his mouth, like he's really, genuinely interested, coaxes the words free.

"I majored in business in college because it was *sensible*," I tell him, using air quotes around the word *sensible*. "But my favorite class was an elective art class. I loved it so much I took it every quarter all four years."

"What kind of art?" Jack asks.

"I was mostly into painting. Acrylics and stuff. Then I got into stick and pokes and everyone told me I'd be good at tattoos, so after I graduated I started an apprenticeship with a local artist. I totally fell in love with it. It was like painting, but instead of the work ending up on a wall or behind glass, it was out in the world, taking on a life of its own. I love the idea of the human body as a canvas. It's so much more active, so much more intimate," I explain, voice picking up with excitement, like the words are tapping into some long-forgotten enthusiasm.

Jack smiles and I can't help but admire the way it seems to catch fire across his whole face, a flicker burst forth into a flame.

"One of my dreams is to spot one of my designs in the wild," I go on. "Like I'm out and about, and *bam*, I'll spot something I did, and it will be this full circle moment of knowing that long after that client walked out of my shop, my art followed them for the rest of their lives. That it became part of their identity."

"Have you had that happen yet?" Jack asks.

I shake my head. "Not yet, but maybe someday."

Jack's eyes peruse mine like my face holds the answer key to a test he's been studying for. My skin prickles under the intensity of his gaze and I reach for my water glass, suddenly terribly thirsty.

"Do you still paint?" he asks.

"I haven't for a while," I admit. "Not since my boyfriend and I went on a break."

I look down at my hands. They used to be stained, pinks and reds and blues. Yellow crusted under my fingernails. A swipe of green on my knuckles. But these days my hands are about as blank as my canvas.

After the break, I wanted to focus, to create. I wanted to do something to make myself feel normal and in control while everything else was spinning out around me. But I couldn't. It was like all the creativity inside me just dried up and I was left with nothing but tumbleweeds blowing through the barren wasteland of my mind. Now it's been months since I've so much as doodled on a napkin.

"Do you have any examples of your work?" he asks.

I stiffen, taken aback by the request. "You want to see my art?"

"If you're open to sharing, that is."

It's not that I'm uncomfortable sharing my work. My clients literally walk around with my art on display for everyone to see. But showing my work to someone new—someone whose response I can't predict—is always a little nerve-racking.

I scroll through my phone until I find a photo of one of my favorite pieces: a naked woman being embraced by a skeleton. Their limbs are wound around one another in a way that makes it hard to tell where the woman's arm ends and the skeleton's bones begin. It's one of the last custom pieces I did. Inked onto a forearm at 1:8 scale, it's edgy and provocative, but also tender and quietly intimate.

I hand the phone to Jack and he spreads his thumb and index finger across the screen, zooming in. "Wow. This is very cool. It's so . . ." His eyes narrow in thought. "Detailed," he says at last.

"Thanks. Line work is my specialty, actually."

"You're obviously incredibly talented."

My skin warms. It's not the first time I've been called talented. But somehow, Jack's praise seems to carry a little more weight. Though perhaps that's because Jack doesn't strike me as the type of person to say something just to be nice. He means what he says.

Jack hands me my phone and I shove it back in my pocket. "So . . ." He pauses, gaze sweeping over my body. "Do *you* have any tattoos? I sort of expect someone who does tattoos for a living to be covered in ink."

"How do you know I'm not?"

"Well, from what I've seen—"

"Which isn't much," I point out.

His eyes crinkle with silent laughter. "So do you have any?" he asks again.

I chew on my bottom lip, letting a coy grin sweep across my mouth before I say, "I do have one."

He leans across the table. "Where?"

"None of your beeswax."

Jack's mouth rises in tandem with his eyebrow. "It's on your ass, isn't it?"

"Wouldn't you like to know."

His eyes flash with a mix of amusement and intrigue, and I let my eyes dip into my lap as I fight back an inconvenient grin.

Last year on her birthday, I gave Allison and myself matching tattoos at Sleeve It to Me—something we'd talked about doing for ages. She'd jumped up and down screaming as she hugged me, telling me over and over I was the best sister ever. Now the once sweet memory feels sour, another reminder of how far we've drifted apart.

"Do you think you'll ever go back into tattooing?" Jack asks, bringing a napkin to the corner of his lips.

"I don't know if that's a good idea," I tell him.

I think about all the nights I cried myself to sleep, tormented by thoughts of overdue bills and everyone I'd disappointed. It wasn't just about the money. It was the stench of failure that seemed to permeate everything around me, lingering like cigarette smoke in a couch cushion.

Growing up, teachers and parents were always telling my mom how proud she ought to be to have a daughter like me. Someone so mature for my age. Someone so *responsible.* Carter used to say the same thing. He'd tell me he loved how sensible I was. How reliable. So much so that he used to call me his North Star.

I clung to those compliments like little mental life rafts. Each one telling me where my value was. Who I was supposed to be. But then the business failed, and it wasn't just a crushing blow to my self-esteem, it was a devastating blow to my very identity. Who was I supposed to be if I wasn't the responsible, reliable one? How was I supposed to take care of the people around me if I couldn't be the person they counted on me to be?

"But why not try again?" Jack asks. "You're clearly talented and you have a passion for it."

I look at him, baffled. "Talent isn't enough, Jack. My credit score is fucked. The whole thing was a failure. *I'm* a failure."

"Just because something didn't work out the first time doesn't mean you're a failure," he says, giving me a pointed look. "Besides, you're young, you have lots of time to rebuild your credit score."

A hollow laugh rattles inside me. "You make me sound like I'm some young whippersnapper with all the time in the world."

He studies me. "What're you? Twenty-five?"

"Twenty-eight."

"In that case, yikes, better get it sorted. You practically have one foot already in the grave. Leonardo DiCaprio won't even date you."

I laugh, annoyed that he's actually being funny right now.

"If I have one foot in the grave, you must be long dead. What are you? Thirty-eight?" I ask, scanning the network of creases in his forehead.

He presses his palm against his chest like he's been mortally wounded. "Thirty-three, and easy there, you ought to respect your elders."

A breathy snort escapes me. "While I appreciate the enthusiasm for my business ventures, it's not a prudent financial move for me. At least not right now. Besides, the business was sort of a sore spot between Carter and me, and I'm afraid that if I reopen, it will mess everything up for us."

"Carter." Jack repeats the name like it's some kind of rare species he's never heard of before. "So this is about your ex?"

My insides shift like an internal alarm's been tripped. "No . . . well, *sort of*. But it's complicated."

And I mean it. It *is* complicated.

At first, Carter was supportive of the business. On the night of the grand opening, he bought a bottle of expensive champagne he totally couldn't afford, and we sat on the fire escape, drinking and talking until two a.m. I remember how light my chest felt, like I was full of hot air and fizz, drunk on possibility. But over time the business became a sort of wedge between us. Carter didn't like the long hours I put in, how much time I spent at the shop—time that used to be with him.

He never said it exactly, but I always wondered if maybe he was jealous. If he resented how passionate I was about my work, while he'd spent years waffling between careers, always looking for, but never finding, that thing that thrilled him the way tattooing did me.

I figured he would eventually get over it, that one day he'd find something he was just as excited about, and everything would be okay. But when things started to go downhill with the business, he withdrew. He got more distant. Like he could see the iceberg ahead. Meanwhile, I stayed aboard, listening to the band play its final songs.

Later, after everything crashed and burned, Carter told me, *Maybe it was for the best.* That I should probably get a *regular job.*

He hadn't meant it to be unkind. But the words still stung. Probably because I'd spent years supporting Carter in every side hustle and shiny new life plan, and it didn't seem fair that my support for him was a blank check, while his support for me came with limitations.

But deep down, I think what really bothers me is that maybe Carter's right. Maybe I'm not cut out to run a business and it's better if I move on and get a regular job. Something *sensible* and *reliable.*

After a beat, Jack says, "I get being scared to try again, but every choice comes with a cost, even the safe ones."

I frown, not sure whether to be alarmed or annoyed by how well he can read me. "It's not that simple," I tell him.

He tilts his chin, studying me. "Why not?"

I shift my weight, newly aware of just how sticky this leather seat is. How tight my jeans feel around my middle.

When I don't answer, Jack says, "The first time I took the bar exam, I failed. Which made me even more nervous to take it the second time. What if I failed again? What was I supposed to tell people? I'd be humiliated. Not to mention I'd have wasted three years of law school. But I pushed past that fear and took it anyways, and I'm glad I did. Otherwise I'd never be where I am now."

"You mean this fine establishment with your best friend's fiancée's sister that you tried to sleep with?" I say, gesturing to the Formica tables and plastic chairs around us.

His mouth quirks into a half smile. "Well technically that's true. Aren't my four-hundred-dollar-an-hour legal fees bankrolling this trip?"

I make a face, but no comeback, and we return to silence like actors exiting the stage after a vignette.

But as Jack goes back to his food and I go back to mine, my thoughts stay stuck on what he's just said.

It's easy for him to tell me to take the risk when he doesn't have to bear the consequences of it. When he doesn't have to worry about failure, or if Carter's going to get back together with him, or if he can pay off his debt. But all that aside, he sort of has a point. Every choice comes with a cost. I don't know if later down the road I'll regret not going after what I want, but I can't deny the ember of curiosity lingering in the back of my mind. The part of me that's still hungry to try again. Not just because I want to prove myself, but because I miss it, the thrill of making art, of taking an idea from inception to a sketch to a tattoo. I miss the power and wonder and awe of creating something special, and I don't want to lose that.

The realization makes my stomach lift into my throat, and suddenly I'm not so hungry anymore. I look at the time and see we have seven minutes until our train departs.

"I'm going to find the restroom," I tell him. "Watch my stuff."

Before he can answer, I stand up and walk away.

The toilet is tucked away in some back room that I have to walk through the kitchen to get to. Inside, the toilet water is rusty and the floor is coated in a thick layer of sludge. I hold my nose and hover over the toilet seat.

After I finish peeing, I wash my hands and flick them dry because there aren't any paper towels. Then I try to open the door, but it won't budge.

It's stuck.

Chapter 9

63 HOURS UNTIL THE WEDDING

Okay, don't panic. I'll call Jack and he'll come get me. But as soon as I reach into my pocket, I realize I left my phone at the table with the rest of my stuff.

Fuck.

Okay, now it's time to panic.

I bang on the door. "Hello? Is anyone out there?" But there's no answer.

This is so embarrassing. Who accidentally locks themselves in the bathroom?

"Hello?" I cry again.

When no one answers I begin to pace the length of the room like a lion held in captivity, trying to formulate a plan.

Maybe Jack will come looking for me. Surely he won't leave without me. Right? But as one minute turns into two and two into three, I become less certain.

This is bad. Really bad. What if Jack doesn't come looking for me? What if I die in here? What if it's *days* before anyone finds me? What if I've decomposed to the point where all that's left to identify me by is my teeth?

I lunge back toward the door, pounding my fists against the cold wood.

"Help! Someone help me!"

I'm getting ready to pound even harder, maybe even throw in a piercing scream, when I hear feet outside the door.

"Jack? Is that you?"

"Ada?"

Oh, thank God.

"Jack, help, I need you to unlock the door!"

"Is everything okay?" There's a nervousness to his voice as though he's afraid I'm going to say something about tampons or bodily fluids.

"I locked myself in."

"You *what*?"

"Just open the damn door," I yell back, not in the mood to be chastised.

The doorknob shakes, but stays firmly shut.

"Can you get it open?" I ask, pressing my ear to the door.

"I'm working on it!"

Again, he rattles the handle and the door wobbles so hard that for a minute I wonder if he's going to pull it off its hinges.

"Fuck. It's stuck," he says after a beat.

A small sense of validation flickers inside me. See?

"Stand away from the door," he calls. There's an edge to his voice as though he's announced, *Yes, we'll have to amputate.*

I step back, wondering what he's going to do. Break the door down? Can he even do that?

But I only have a second to wonder before—*wham!*—Jack bursts into the bathroom, shoulder first. Behind him, the door swings, hanging limply off its hinges.

I gape at him. I didn't know it was physically possible to ram a door down. I thought that was just something Jason Bourne did. And now I can't help but wonder what else he could *ram* down.

Jack looks me up and down, chest rising and falling as he catches his breath. "Are you okay?" he asks.

I hold out my arms, surveying them for signs of damage. "I think so." My eyes lift, meeting his. "What the actual fuck was that?"

"*That* was me breaking you out so we don't miss our train." Jack checks the time. "Come on. We still have four minutes." He turns on his heel, waving for me to follow him, and together we run back through the dining area.

"Sorry about the bathroom door!" Jack yells over his shoulder as we collect our things. "I left fifty pounds on the table! That should cover it!"

The man behind the counter shouts something in Farsi, but we keep moving until we're pushing open the door. Something catches, but Jack takes my hand, yanking me away before I can stop and see what it is.

My lungs are on fire, bones rattling inside me as we run down the street back toward the train station, but somehow, all I can think about is the weight of his hand in mine. How sturdy and secure he feels, like no matter what, we are going to be okay.

But we aren't.

We run onto the platform just as our train is pulling out of the station.

I wave my hands, running after it, but it's no use. It's already disappearing down the tracks without us.

Jack comes to a halt beside me, panting. "Just fucking great," he rasps. "Now what are we going to do?"

"I'm sure there's another train coming," I say, forcing some levity into my voice even though I have no idea whether there's another train coming.

Jack walks to the ticket kiosk and punches something into the touch screen. As soon as he turns around, I know it's bad news.

"There are no more trains to Glasgow today because of the strike," he says. "Looks like we're stuck here for the night."

My stomach plunges. We're stuck? Here? All night?

"There must be something else we can do," I say, panic bleeding through my voice.

Jack's scowl deepens. "Like what?"

"I don't know." I look around, frantically hoping a solution will magically present itself. "Can't we call an Uber or something? They have that here, right?"

Jack's eyebrows lift toward his hairline. "You want to pay for a two-hour Uber from here to Glasgow?"

"I thought you were a rich lawyer?"

"Not that rich."

I glance up and down the platform, hoping another train will come along. But when none do, we take our things and exit the station, back onto the street. Somehow in the few minutes since we were outside, darkness has descended, smothering everything in a thick curtain of black. I shiver against the evening breeze, all the more aware that not only are we in a totally foreign city with no place to stay, it's getting darker and darker by the minute.

If I didn't think I was plagued by bad luck before, now I know for sure.

I count out seven steps, stop, then take seven more. I read on the internet that doing things in groups of seven can amass good luck, and right now I'm willing to try anything.

"What are you doing?" Jack asks.

"I'm trying to change our luck."

"We don't need luck. We *need* somewhere to stay for the night."

"Of course we need luck," I insist. "Have you not noticed what's happened to us in the past twenty-four hours? At this point we're on track to be hit by a meteorite any minute!"

Jack releases a long, frustrated sigh. "That has nothing to do with bad luck, and everything to do with *you* making us miss our train."

"Me?" I balk at him. "*You're* the one who wanted to eat at that place!"

Jack's eyes flash. "Well, it would have been fine if you hadn't locked yourself in the bathroom."

"I needed to use the bathroom. What would you prefer? That I peed myself?"

"I shouldn't have let you out of my sight," he grumbles, shoving his hands in his pocket.

"You don't *let* me do anything! I'm an adult, not your ward."

"I thought you didn't even want to go to this wedding."

Seriously? Is he suggesting that I did this on purpose?

"That doesn't mean I'm actively trying to sabotage getting there if that's what you're accusing me of," I snap.

His eyes narrow, glowing red with indignation. "Yeah, well, this wouldn't have happened if you'd listened to me."

A hot flash of anger ripples inside me. I'd thought we were starting to get along, but I guess I was wrong.

"You know what? Maybe this whole thing isn't working out," I say.

He stops in his tracks, eyes sharpening. "What are you talking about?"

"Us!" I wave my hands between us. "Clearly us traveling together isn't working out. Maybe we should split up and find our own way to the wedding."

"You know that doesn't make any sense, Ada."

I put my hands on my hips. "Why not?"

"Well, for starters, you're broke."

"I'll call my sister," I say stiffly. "She'll loan me the money."

I grab my phone and look for Allison's number. But as my fingers hover over the call icon, I imagine how the conversation will go:

Hey Allison. I know we haven't been on the best terms, but I'm broke and my life is a certified hot mess. Can you spot me a couple hundred bucks to make it to the wedding so I don't have to travel with your fiancé's bestie?

My throat tightens at the thought. I'm the older sister. I'm supposed to be the one who has her life together. Not roaming from one catastrophe to another like the purveyor of misfortune I am.

Besides, it's getting late, I don't know where we are, and as much as I'd like to envision myself a strong, independent woman, I'd really rather not travel all the way to Ireland alone.

I stuff my phone back in my pocket and wait for Jack to call my bluff. Instead, he releases a long sigh, hot breath curling in the air like trails of smoke. Finally, he says, "Look, why don't we find a place to sleep tonight, then we can figure this out in the morning. Okay?"

He still looks annoyed, but there's a flicker of resignation hiding in the shadows of his expression, like he genuinely wants us to move past this.

"Fine," I say.

WE TRY TWO HOTELS AND A BED-AND-BREAKFAST, BUT EVERYTHING IS either closed for the season, under construction, or booked. Because of course it is.

Jack doesn't say anything, but I feel the heat of his eyes on me, judging me, like this is all my fault. Which only makes things worse. It would be nice if there was some sense of solidarity between us—after all, we're in this mess together—but apparently that would be asking too much of him.

After the third hotel turns us away, I sit on the curb and put my head in my hands.

Jack sits beside me, and I brace myself for the barrage of insults, for him to tell me I've fucked up. Hell, he might even just leave me here. And maybe that would be for the best. Maybe our brief moment of camaraderie on the train was just that, *brief*.

"If you're just going to berate me again, I'm not in the mood for—"

"I'm sorry," he says.

I lift my head, frowning. Did I hear that correctly? Did Jack just apologize? To me?

"I'm sorry I blamed you for missing our train," he says again, voice softer this time. "That was shitty of me."

I meet his eyes, searching for the trace of irony, but either it's too dark out here to see it, or he's serious.

The hot-blooded part of me wants to agree, to tell him off for being a jerk, but the more prudent part, the part that's all too aware of our current predicament, knows it'll only make matters worse.

I release a heavy sigh. "Listen, I get that you don't want to be here with me, and trust me, I'd rather not be stuck here with you, but let's just try to get through the next few days. After that we never have to see each other again. Okay?"

"I'm sure we'll have to see each other again," he says.

My inner fuse crackles once more, annoyed that he's clearly missing the point. "You know what, forget it." I stand to go, but he calls after me.

"Ada, wait."

I pause, then turn back around. "What?"

For a minute he doesn't speak, then he takes a deep breath, gaze steadying on an unclear horizon.

"Can I confess something?" he asks after a beat.

I freeze.

Now he's got me worried. What's he going to confess? A series of fears flash through my mind. He actually *is* a serial killer. This is all an elaborate scheme to steal my identity. Or worse. He told Allison everything I said at the bar.

"This isn't the part where you tell me you're not really Jack Houghton and our final destination isn't my sister's wedding, is it?" I ask with a shaky laugh.

His mouth slides into an unconvincing smile, before fading away entirely. "I just wanted to say that I'm not exactly looking forward to this wedding either."

"Pretty sure you already made that clear when you told Collin not to marry my sister."

He shakes his head. "It's not that."

Allison's words flash through my head. *Frankly, I'm surprised he's even showing up to the wedding.* At the time I'd assumed she meant that he didn't support their marriage, but now I can't help but wonder if there's something else, something he's not telling me.

"You can tell me," I try, my voice softer this time. "If you want." I try to catch Jack's eye, but he just stares ahead, gaze pinned on something I can't see.

"Just personal stuff. But it's not you." He licks his lips, swallowing before he says, "I guess what I'm trying to say is I'm sorry for being an ass."

Maybe it's the way the shadows from the streetlight hit his face, highlighting every fine line and wrinkle, but he looks tired.

Like a dog that's been kicked one too many times and no longer has the energy to bark back.

I consider pressing him on it, but the wilt of his expression makes it clear that whatever it is, he doesn't want to talk about it. And as curious as I am to know why he doesn't want to go to the wedding, I don't want to upset our delicate equilibrium. So instead, I sit back down on the curb beside him and say, "It's okay," before letting my eyes dip into my lap.

A breeze tousles our hair, and we simultaneously shiver. I inhale the cool night air, eyes nudging upward to the diorama of impossibly bright stars overhead. It's both comforting and overwhelming to think these are the same stars I see at home, six thousand miles away. It's also a good reminder that the world is a lot bigger than my mom's couch. Or a stack of bills. Or a text from Carter.

After a beat, I turn back to Jack. "I guess I should say *thanks*."

Twin grooves form between his brows. "For what?"

"For knocking down the door and rescuing me . . . *again*."

His features soften, mouth turning up. "Well, I wasn't going to be the one to tell Allison I left you to die in a gross bathroom. She would kill me."

"Oh, I see. You didn't rescue me because you were worried about me? You did it to save your own neck?"

"Exactly." He nods sagely. "It was purely selfish."

My lips curl upward into a bitten-off smile. "I still can't believe you broke down a literal door. Who even does that?"

"Someone who's *very* desperate to make their train."

I laugh and my body feels instantly lighter, like whatever tension was holding me captive drifts out with the sound of my voice.

"Speaking of missed trains, we should get going," he says, standing and brushing off the back of his jeans. "We're not going to find somewhere to stay sitting here on the sidewalk."

He holds his hand out to me, a silent peace offering, and I take it, letting him help me to my feet.

We walk in silence, but this time the silence feels easier, more comfortable.

At the end of the street is a small white house with blue shutters and a neon sign that says VACANCY.

My heart surges with relief.

Everything is going to be fine. I can feel it.

Chapter 10

61 HOURS UNTIL THE WEDDING

A bell jingles above the door and we are instantly welcomed by an overbearing aroma of rosemary and sage.

There's no one behind the desk, but my eyes are instantly drawn to the large crucifix draped in rosary beads and a portrait of the Virgin Mary surrounded by flickering votive candles in the corner.

Jack and I both exchange looks.

"Hello?" I say into the vacant room, aware a second too late that I sound exactly like the girl in a horror film who asks, *Who's there?* before being brutally murdered.

When there is no answer, Jack strides forward and rings the bell on the front desk.

A moment later, an older woman with salt-and-pepper hair appears.

"Hi," Jack says. "We're looking for a room."

Her face breaks into a smile. "Yes, I have a room," she says, nodding.

My chest loosens. "Great," I tell her. "We'll take it."

Her eyes dart between us, narrowing. "And you are married?" she asks. She has an accent of some kind, but I can't pinpoint it.

"Uh . . ." My gaze flickers uneasily to the rosary beads and the crucifix, then back to the woman.

Her expression sours. "I only rent rooms to married couple."

I swallow. Is that even legal?

"Oh, we aren't—" I start to say.

"We aren't planning to stay in town long," Jack finishes. "We are on our way to our honeymoon, actually," he adds with a shameless grin.

My mouth parts, lips pinching into a surprised *o* shape. He said *what*?

But it's not his words, or even the cavalier way he says them that catches me most off guard, it's the way Jack's arm wraps around my waist, pulling me to his side.

Shock, followed by whooshes of awareness, shoots through my body, and for a moment I am unable to compute anything except the heat of Jack's hand on the curve of my hip. Or the intimate way his fingers thread along the waistband of my jeans, dipping in and out of my belt loops like they have a right to be there.

Thankfully, my brain reboots just in time to realize that the woman is looking expectantly at me like I've been called on in class to answer a question. A question I clearly don't know the answer to.

I try to catch Jack's eye, but he shoots me a look that says, *Just go with it.*

I force a smile that I'm sure won't earn me any Oscars. "Yup, just two . . ." I search for the words. "Two lovebirds here." I give his chest an awkward pat. Damn, it's hard.

Her face breaks into a Cheshire cat grin and she clasps her hands together. "Oh, how wonderful. Such a *special* time," she adds with a knowing smile that makes my gut twist.

Ohmygod. This woman thinks we're gonna be up all night making love like rabbits.

I look helplessly to Jack, but he gives me a discreet shake of the head, followed by another possessive squeeze that momentarily renders both my limbs and my thinking faculties useless.

"And how did you two meet?" the woman asks, eyes shining. "I just love a good love story."

Yeah, *me too.* If only we had one to share.

"We met in church," he says.

Church? I nearly choke.

The woman's face stretches into a smile. "Good, good," she says, patting Jack's arm. "That is a good place to meet nice young girls." She casts me a glowing smile like I've descended from Heaven itself. "I will set up our finest guest room for you. Follow me." And with that, the woman waves for us to follow her as she waddles up a spindly staircase in the back of the room.

"*Church*?" I whisper once she's out of earshot. "We met in church?"

"Seems like that's what she wanted to hear," he whispers back. "Besides, it was better than the truth."

"Which is?"

"That we met in a bar where I tried to get in your pants."

Something between a laugh and a choke catches in my throat and I cough.

"Everything okay, babe?" Jack asks, giving me a pat on the back.

I wince as I swallow. "Yup, *babe.*"

At the top of the landing the woman beckons us to a blue door with the number thirteen painted on it.

My stomach somersaults. Thirteen? As in *unlucky* number thirteen?

"Uh, is there possibly another roo—" I start to ask, but Jack gives me a small kick.

"Looks great," Jack interrupts, forcing a smile.

She swings the door open and makes a sweeping gesture inside. "Our finest room. The honeymoon suite."

If this is the honeymoon suite, I'm afraid to know what the other rooms look like.

There's a questionable crack running the length of one of the walls and a single porthole window overlooking the dark street below. A naked bulb flickers angrily from the ceiling.

"You like?" she asks eagerly.

"Uh, yeah . . . it's great." *If you like lighting that makes you feel like you're in an interrogation cell.*

I shoot Jack a look, wondering if he'll say anything, but he loops his arm around my shoulder and says, "It's perfect."

The woman clasps her hands together, clearly delighted. "Wait here. I get special treat," she says before rushing off.

As soon as she's gone, I untangle my body from Jack's. "Quit touching me," I hiss. "You're not going to win the Oscar for Best Actor if that's what you're thinking, *babe*."

"I was trying to lean into the role, *babe*."

"Your hand was too close to my ass, *babe*."

The corners of his mouth pull up into the kind of grin that ought to be illegal. "Has it occurred to you that maybe I just like messing with you?" he asks.

"Hand. Off. Ass."

Jack backs away, putting his hands in the air just as the woman reappears, quilt in hand.

"My grandmother made this," she says, holding up an orange and brown chevron-patterned quilt.

I smile. That's nice of her. It *is* a bit chilly in here.

"This has been in my family for generations," she says, spreading it over the bed. "It will bless your union with many children. My husband and I sleep with this blanket, now we have fifty-two grandchildren."

My mouth hangs open. "Fifty-two?"

She nods proudly.

My throat thickens. There is *no way* we are sleeping with a blanket. We may not be having sex, but with those kinds of fertility stats (and my bad luck), that's a chance I'm simply not willing to take.

"Uh, no, thanks," I tell her. "We don't want any kids."

Her mouth sinks into a frown. "No kids? But marriage is for making babies," she insists. "It is the Lord's plan."

"Uh . . . I think He has a different plan for us," I try.

She seems to consider this for a minute before her eyes widen, recognition sliding over her features. "You poor thing, you are barren?"

My cheeks crowd with heat. "Who, me? Nope. Very fertile. *Super fertile.* I'm practically a bag of fertilizer over here," I say with an awkward laugh.

She places a hand on my stomach. "I will pray that you will be fruitful and multiply."

"Uh, no need! Really, we are fine," I say, moving to push her hand away just as Jack steps between us.

"You know, I think we are going to go to bed now," he says, a finality to his tone that makes it clear it's time for her to go. *Thank you, Jack! Finally making yourself useful!* "We have to get started on all that baby making," he adds.

I don't know much (anything) about black holes, but I'm fairly certain there's one in the room with us right now, sucking up all the air, making every particle collapse in on itself.

I look to Jack, horrified, but he winks—*winks!*—and I'm not sure what's worse: that Jack is totally fine with letting this woman believe we're going to bone one another's brains out tonight, or the insufferable, smug grin on his face that tells me he's enjoying this.

The woman nods profusely. "Yes, of course. I will leave you alone," she says, slowly backing toward the door. "Breakfast is at eight a.m. in the lobby, *if* you can manage to get out of bed," she adds with a wink, and with that she shuts the door behind her and scurries away.

As soon as she's gone, Jack is doubled over, fighting back shaky laughs. "You should see your face right now," he gasps.

"It's not funny!" I cry. "Why would you say that?"

"Me? You should have just taken the blanket!"

"I didn't want the blanket! Didn't you hear what she said? Fifty-two grandkids!"

He raises an inquisitive eyebrow. "I don't know if you know this, but you have to actually have sex to make a baby. And last I checked we're not having sex."

"Thanks for the biology lesson, but keep that thing away from me. I don't know the last time it's been washed," I say, casting the blanket a suspicious glance.

Jack pushes it toward me, but I shove it right back.

"Don't you dare!"

A low laugh rumbles in the back of his throat, deep and gravelly. "What do you think? Should I sleep with a condom on? Just in case?"

My cheeks heat up at the visual, and I look away, suddenly fascinated by the pile of old magazines on the bedside table.

When I look back at Jack, his eyes are trailing up and down my face, pausing, then starting again.

"What?" I ask.

"I'm trying to determine whether you look like you could be my wife."

I frown, taken aback. "What is that supposed to mean? Does your wife have to look a certain way?"

His eyes sweep over me, mouth scrunched in concentration before he says, "You're not really my type, you know."

"Let me guess, your type is miniskirts and push-up bras?"

"I'm more of a leggings man myself," he says. "Thank God for whoever decided leggings could be pants."

I roll my eyes and flop backward on the bed (careful to keep my distance from *the blanket*). My foot accidentally grazes his and I expect him to move, but he doesn't.

"So what's your type then?" I say to the ceiling. I don't know what makes me ask it, but I find myself wanting to know.

"You really want to know?"

"*Yes, Jack*. I think I can handle hearing about the other women you've lured to hotel rooms."

"Oh, you know I only reserve that for you, *babe*."

I place my hand over my heart. "I'm honored, really."

A laugh breaks in the back of his throat and the sound crackles between us like an electric current.

I roll onto my side so I'm facing him and prop my head up on my elbow. "Just tell me. Or am I going to have to guess? Because I'm struggling with which Kardashian I'd pick for you."

"Kris. Obviously."

I give him a look and his grin stretches wider, consuming his whole face.

"Fine. You know *The Addams Family*?"

"Yeah . . . ?"

A streak of pink catches in his cheeks. "Well, I always had a thing for Morticia."

My face breaks into an open-mouthed gawk. "You're kidding."

"I'm not. She was sexy without really trying, you know? And her long black hair." A guttural groan forms in the back of his throat. "Oh my God, *that hair.* I think that was my sexual awakening."

I burst into stomach-pinching laughter and the bed vibrates underneath us. "I'm honestly shocked. I never would have guessed you like witchy vibes." I pause to shake my head in disbelief. "That's sort of kinky, isn't it?"

His brow lifts. "You're not kink-shaming me, are you?"

My cheeks flush with heat at the thought of what kinds of kinks Jack might have. I wonder if—? *Nope! Don't go there!*

"Of course not," I tell him.

He chews on his bottom lip, gaze tracking my expression, before he asks, "What about you?"

A nervous laugh rattles in my throat. "You want to know my kinks?"

"As intrigued as I am to hear about you and Carter experimenting with butt plugs, I meant *what's your type?*"

I nearly choke. "Did you seriously just say *butt plugs*?"

He shrugs. "I just thought that's what couples did after they've been together forever and wanted to keep things spicy. Isn't it usually around year three when those come into play?"

"And how would you know what year three of a relationship looks like?" I shoot back. "What's your longest relationship? Seven to ten business days?"

He laughs—and maybe I imagine it—but behind his eyes there's a shadow. It's there for just a second. Then he blinks and it's gone.

"So is that a *yes* or a *no* on the butt plugs?" he asks.

I give his arm a playful whack. "Like I'd tell you, perv."

"So . . . ? Your type?" he tries again. "Or are you going to make me guess? Because I'm definitely going to say a firefighter who not only rescues puppies from burning buildings and takes his grandmother to church on Sundays, but also isn't afraid to cry at *Marley & Me*."

"That is oddly specific . . . but no. It's Carter," I say. "He's perfect." The words come out in a rush, almost like I've read them from a cue card for a speech I've been memorizing.

"Perfect?" Jack repeats as though unsure if I'm serious. "No guy is perfect. You know that, right?"

I sit back on my elbows, body sinking into the mattress. "I mean, obviously," I say, making a big show of rolling my eyes. "Carter just . . ." But I let my words trail off, not sure how to finish that statement. Because as much as I miss the comfortable familiarity of our life together, I know things weren't perfect. Hence I'm on my way to Ireland with Jack and not Carter right now. And yet, I don't know who I am without Carter, without our life and our plans and the future I thought—*hoped*—was inevitable.

It's not just the big things like marriage and family and the future. It's all the tiny pieces that have made up the last eight years, pieces I expected to make up the rest of my life.

Without Carter, who will I spend Valentine's and Christmas and New Year's with? Who will I text, *Want anything?* when I'm at the grocery store. Who will binge-watch TV shows with me when I feel a cold coming on?

Our life might not have been perfect, but it was our life, and the thought of losing him feels a little bit like losing myself.

When I look back up, Jack's gazing at me intently, like there's some kind of puzzle on my face he's trying to work out. "You all right?" he asks.

I force a tight smile. "Fine." But the heat drains from my face as twin aches of confusion and anxiety flood my stomach. I try to shrug the feeling off, but the discomfort sits inside me, thick and heavy like undigested food.

Chapter 11

60 HOURS UNTIL THE WEDDING

Jack and I retreat to opposite sides of the bed—him frowning at his phone and me mindlessly flipping through the five-year-old copy of *Tatler* someone left on the end table—until I hear footsteps on the landing followed by a knock on the door. *Rap, rap, rap.* "Hello? Mr. and Mrs. Houghton? I brought you some extra sheets," our host says through the door.

Neither Jack nor I move. We both stay frozen in place, eyes darting to the door and back. I can practically hear the crackle of unsaid words firing off between us like electric currents.

What should we do?

I don't know, but do something!

Me? Why don't you you *do something?*

"Make her go away!" I whisper. But Jack doesn't move or say anything. For a moment I think maybe he didn't hear me, then he starts rocking the headboard back and forth, slowly at first, then faster, picking up tempo. The legs of the bed scrape against the floorboards. *Creeaaaak.* Followed by *eeeee uhhh eeeee uhhh.*

What on earth is he doing?

He's not . . . ?

Oh, but he is.

"Jack, stop!"

"Just trust me," he whispers, continuing to shake the bed. "She'll get the hint."

"I don't want her to get *that* hint!" I grab his arm, attempting to yank him away from the headboard, but the bed squeaks even louder under my movement.

"Hello?" she calls again. "Mr. and Mrs. Houghton?"

Seriously?

I'm deliberating if now is the time to tell her to go away like grown-ups, when Jack opens his mouth and—to my horror—lets out a litany of porno-worthy moans.

"Mmmmm, baby, you feel so good." His voice is ragged, carnal, like he's somewhere between agony and ecstasy.

The black hole is back, and this time I wish it would just take me with it.

"Jack! Stop!" I hiss.

But apparently the snappy *mom voice* I used to use with Allison when we were kids does nothing to curb the way his eyes flare, eyebrows raised in challenge.

"Come on," he whispers back. "She's still there."

My eyes zigzag to the door, then back to Jack, now watching me with calculated interest like I'm the wild card cast member on an unhinged reality show, and he's waiting to see what I'll do next.

I basically have two choices. I can answer the door and tell her to please leave us alone. Or I can follow Jack's lead and make a total and complete ass of myself. Either way she already thinks we're boning thanks to Jack and his . . . *sound effects.*

Before I can weigh the wisdom of what I'm about to do—because if I do, I'll chicken out—I let out a spine-tingling cry.

"Oh, Jack! Mmmmm. Yes! Right there!" My voice pierces the air, reverberating between us. Then for emphasis I smack the wall and the whole room shakes. A decorative picture frame falls to the floor with a crash.

Jack covers his face in silent laughter, and I do the same, fighting back my own unhinged gasps until our breaths harmonize in a cacophony of strangled, wheezing rasps.

Once we regain control of our breath, we freeze, listening as she mutters something about coming back later, followed by footsteps retreating back down the hall.

As soon as she's gone Jack raises his hand for a high five, and even though it's got to be the weirdest context for a high five of all time, it feels oddly deserved, and I smack my palm against his before collapsing against the bed, convulsing with laughter.

"I can't believe you did that!" I cry, clutching my stomach.

"You told me to make her go away!"

"I didn't mean by making *sex noises*!"

"It worked, didn't it?"

"You think she bought it?" I ask.

"With those porn star screams? No question."

A laugh breaks in my chest. "Can't that lady take a hint?"

"Maybe she's secretly a pervert?"

"She did listen for a long time," I concede.

Jack gets off the bed and picks up the fallen picture. Thankfully, the glass is still intact. Now *that* would be bad luck.

"Nice touch, by the way." He hangs the picture back on the hook. "Nothing says, *Don't bother us, we're having mind-blowing honeymoon sex* like breaking furniture."

"Thanks. I was inspired by *Twilight*."

He looks over his shoulder, eyes twinkling. "Very convincing."

Jack comes back toward the bed, and I scoot over, careful to avoid the special blanket to my left.

"Please tell me you don't really sound like that in bed?" I ask. "There was so much grunting, I wasn't sure if you were orgasming or constipated."

"I could say the same for you." His lips twist into a devious grin. "Are you really a screamer?"

Static waves flash across my skin as my pulse ramps up, making me newly aware of how close we're sitting, how his knee keeps brushing mine. I scoot back.

"I'm still not having sex with you, you know," I say. "So don't get any ideas."

"You know, for someone who was very adamant that they didn't want to have sex last night, you sure do bring it up a lot." He tilts his chin, considering me. "That's not a Freudian slip, is it?"

I pull a face, hoping to mask the fact that it feels like a cartoon-style anvil has just plummeted into my stomach.

"No, Jack. Believe it or not, I don't want your dick."

"Good. Because that offer has expired," he says.

I let out a humorless guffaw. "I didn't realize your generous offer of meaningless sex came with an expiration date."

I expect him to brush me off with a joke or one of his usual comebacks. Instead, his eyes search mine before saying in a low, almost cautious voice, "It's just . . . better if nothing happens between us, right?"

I'm not sure what catches me more off guard—the change in his tone, or the way the question dangles in the air, almost like he's waiting to see if I'll counter it.

And for one wild moment it's like my brain and my body separate and I let myself imagine what might happen if I told him I wanted him. If I gave in to the need that's been building inside me all day.

I imagine how it might feel to have him push me down on the bed. How his hands would feel against my curves. Would he take his time, kissing me slowly, dragging out each moment? Or would he hurry, ripping my clothes off with brazen excitement?

The thought chases shivers down my spine until reality takes over, and I'm promptly reminded that there are two very good reasons I'm not supposed to want that.

For one thing, I know myself well enough to understand that *casual* and *intimacy*, like rum and tequila, are two things that don't mix for me. I need commitment. Consistency. Certainty. Things Jack certainly isn't offering.

And second, unlike everyone else, I haven't yet given up on Carter and me—the mere thought of which is enough to jolt me out of my head and back into the room, where Jack's watching me.

"Right," I tell him with a stiff nod.

We make brief eye contact, the kind that feels like a silent wager—though what the terms are, I'm not sure—then I flop back against the mattress and shut my eyes, determined to ignore the guilty pound of my racing heart.

ONCE WE'RE PRETTY SURE THE INNKEEPER WON'T BE COMING BACK, JACK and I drift into silence. The only sound is that of the old house creaking around us.

I wonder if this place is haunted. I bet it is. Someone *definitely* died of bubonic plague here.

I'm about to ask Jack if he thinks our next unwanted visitor will be a ghost, but he speaks first.

"Can I ask you something?"

"Yes, I do think this place is haunted," I say, eyes still closed. "And no, I'm not telling you if Carter and I used butt plugs."

"Actually," he says, laughter cutting through his voice. "I was going to ask why you want to get back with your boyfriend so badly?"

My eyes flick open and I sit up on the bed. "What do you mean?"

"It's not really my business, but it seems like he was sort of an asshole to you. Why would you want to go back to him after that?"

My internal defenses instantly shoot up. Things might be complicated with Carter and me right now, but I'll be damned if I'm going to be lectured on what a healthy relationship looks like by Mr. Expiration Dating.

"First off, you're right, it's not your business. And second"—I shoot him an evil eye—"he's not an asshole. He's a nice guy."

"*Nice*?" Jack's eyebrows inch toward his hairline. "That's why you're so hot and bothered over him? Because he's *nice*?"

"I'm not hot and both—" I pause, catching myself. "I mean, there's more to a relationship than getting *hot and bothered*," I say instead.

He leans closer, examining. "Like what?"

My stomach pendulates and I can't help feeling as though I've walked into some kind of trap.

"What do you want?" I ask. "An essay?"

"I'm just asking why you want to get back together with the guy. Should be easy to answer since he's *perfect*, right?"

Okay, now I know it's a trap. But I hate the way he's looking at me. Like he thinks he knows everything. Like he's got me all figured out.

"Carter and I have been together for a long time," I say stiffly. "We have a life together." But Jack doesn't look convinced.

"That's why you want to get back together with him?" he asks. "Because you've been together a long time already?"

"Well, no," I say, choosing my words carefully. "That's not the only reason."

"Then what else?"

I take a breath, steeling myself. "What is this? An interrogation?"

He shrugs like the answer doesn't really interest him, but I can see the defiant look behind his eyes, like he's a bloodhound ready to sniff out any misgivings.

Annoyance pricks my skin. Just because I know Carter and I have issues doesn't mean I want to become ammunition for Jack's crusade against commitment. A commitment he doesn't know anything about.

He even said so himself. He doesn't do relationships. He doesn't get that Carter and I have been through a lot. That we have inside jokes and secrets and stories only the two of us know. Jack doesn't get all the ways my life feels like a tapestry of the experiences I've shared with him. Or that without him, I'm afraid everything will unravel.

"You're right," I say after a beat. "Carter isn't perfect and neither is our relationship. But we've been through a lot together and after the year I've had, I don't want to lose him too."

It's perhaps the most honest I've been with anyone, including myself, but Jack frowns, eyes narrowing in question. "I know I'm not exactly a relationship guru over here, but shouldn't wanting to be with someone be about passion? Love? Longing? Not fear."

It's that last word, *fear*, that makes my stomach lurch, acid rising in my throat. Of course I'm afraid. But it's also more complicated than that. Complicated in ways Jack doesn't understand.

"I thought love was the opiate of the masses or whatever it was you were saying on the train," I shoot back. "Now you're going to lecture me on what passion looks like?"

He puts his hands up in surrender. "I'm just saying, do you want to get back together because you *love* him? Or because you're scared of the alternative?"

"Of course I love him." I cross my arms over my chest, limbs suddenly heavy with indignation. "But that's not all a relationship is. There's also trust and history and shared intimacy. Things you can't get with expiration dating or a one-night stand," I add pointedly. "Things *you* probably wouldn't understand."

As soon as I say it a shadow ripples through his face, expanding from his eyes outward as though consumed by a ghost only he can see.

"You're right," Jack says stiffly. "I probably wouldn't."

He looks away, and I can't help but feel like I've stepped on some kind of emotional land mine.

Part of me wants to pause and dissect it, to explore the tiny layer of Jack that's just been pulled back. But another part of me suddenly feels claustrophobic. Like my skin doesn't fit right. Like this room is too small. Like I need to leave.

My eyes dart toward the door. "I think I'm gonna go outside. Get some fresh air."

"Alone?" he asks.

"Yes," I tell him. "Alone."

"But it's dark and you've never been here before." He sits up, pushing his hair out of his eyes, like he might try to stop me. "I don't think that's a good idea."

I reach for my jacket and sling it around my shoulders. "I'll be fine." Then, before he can protest further, I open the door and slip back out into the hall. Thankfully, the innkeeper is nowhere to be found and I'm able to disappear into the night air unseen.

Outside, a chilly wind licks at my neck, brisk enough to heighten my senses. I inhale deeply, hoping the crisp air will help clear my head, but I can't ignore the ball of emotion tunneling inside me, weighing down each step I take.

Jack is being presumptuous, not to mention judgmental. He doesn't know anything about Carter and me. He doesn't know about when I had food poisoning and Carter stayed up all night, holding my hair while I puked, or that Carter knows all my restaurant orders by heart.

Jack doesn't know what it's like to be with someone for eight years. To have your life be so inextricably entangled with someone else's that losing them feels like losing a vital organ. To fear the possibility of losing *everything.*

Jack doesn't understand any of it. And yet, despite my every instinct to write off his half-assed assessments of our eight-year relationship, there's a kernel of truth embedded in what Jack had said. An infuriating, inconvenient kernel.

I try to brush it off, but it only digs deeper.

I think about the night Carter and I hooked up after the break. I hadn't planned for it to happen, but I'd been sad and horny and lonely, so I'd sent him an ill-advised text that I was thinking about him . . . and that I wasn't wearing any underwear.

He'd texted back instantly, asking me to come over. I remember the jolt of excitement, the feeling that everything was going to be okay. But it hadn't been.

After we had sex, I assumed I'd stay the night at Carter's place—*our* place—but Carter got weird and told me it was probably better if I left. *So things don't get messy,* he'd said.

Part of me had wanted to fight with him about it, but another part of me didn't want to appear even more pathetic than I felt, so I left, fighting back tears until I made it to my car, where I cried the whole way home.

I really thought we'd get back together. That our night together was proof of the inevitability of our relationship. That sleeping together would somehow fix things and Carter would realize he couldn't live without me.

But now, in retrospect, I consider why I'd gone over there in the first place. It hadn't been because of some inextinguishable flame of passion in our relationship. Or even because I wanted to get laid. No, I'd gone over there because I was looking for proof that I still had some semblance of control over my life. Because it was easier to go back to him and his bed than it was to try to cope with the rising tide of instability and loneliness in my life. Because Jack's right. I am afraid.

Chapter 12

58 HOURS UNTIL THE WEDDING

When I return from my walk, Jack is sitting on the bed, eyes glued to his phone. But as soon as he sees me, he perks up. "Finally. I thought I was going to have to break down another door."

"Very funny."

I shift toward the bed and remove my shoes and jacket. I'm just hanging my jacket on the hook behind the door next to the garment bag with the veil when I see it: a tear in the bag. And not just a tiny little tear but a gaping hole, big enough that the lace is visible through the opening.

My stomach drops and all thoughts of Jack and Carter dissipate, instantly replaced with a more pressing need as I thrust open the bag.

Please, please, please don't let anything have happened to the veil. My eyes zip from the tulle to the custom lace flowers, searching for blemishes. Then I see it. The tiniest tear near the seam.

My mouth falls into an oval, hands flying to my face in what I imagine is a perfect re-creation of Edvard Munch's *The Scream.*

What am I going to do? Allison can't see this. She'll have a heart attack. Then she'll kill me, and we'll never repair our relationship because, one, I'll be dead, and two, she'll never be able to forgive me after this!

Panic strums my internal nervous system as I rack my brain, trying to figure out how this could have happened—how I could have been so careless—then it hits me. The restaurant. Something had caught on the door, but in our haste to flee, I'd ignored it. Now I wish I'd stayed locked in the bathroom. At least rotting in a public restroom would be better than whatever fate I'm now facing.

Jack must sense that something is wrong because he sits up straighter, eyes wavering across my face, and asks, "Ada? Are you okay?"

"There's a tear. In the veil," I say, voice shaking.

"What? Let me see."

Jack appears by my side, and I cringe as I point out the tiny tear that might as well be a formal execution notice. "See? She's gonna kill me."

"This?" Jack takes the velvety lace in his hands. "She'll never notice. It's barely bigger than the tip of a pen."

I cough out a laugh. "Oh, Jack, you sweet summer child. I don't know if you're aware, but this is a very expensive, one-of-a-kind Demi Karina veil. Not only will my sister notice it, she'll have a full-fledged meltdown and it'll be my fault!"

"No, she won't."

I turn to face him, brows scrunching. "What do you mean *no, she won't?* I just said—"

"I mean," he says, cutting me off, "that we can fix it."

"We?" My eyebrows shoot up. "How are *we* going to fix it? I don't know how to sew, and even if I did, I don't have a sewing kit on me."

"Well, lucky for you, I do."

I gawk at him. "You know how to sew?"

"And I have a travel-sized sewing kit that I always bring for emergencies."

For a minute I just stare at him, mouth dangerously close to hitting the floor. "Are you serious right now?"

"I always come prepared," he says with a casual shrug, like it's no big deal that he's just saved my ass from certain death. Again.

At first, I'm speechless. Because what even are words? And how could I possibly arrange them in a configuration that adequately conveys just how impressed, relieved, and downright astonished I feel right now?

"Okay, it's official," I finally say. "You are absolutely the hero in a rom-com."

A low, throaty laugh breaks in his chest. "Does this mean you're not mad at me anymore?"

"Mad at you? I think I love you," I say, clutching my heart like it might beat right out of my chest. "I'm trying to think of how best to demonstrate my thanks. Is naming my firstborn after you too much?"

Again, Jack laughs, and maybe I imagine it, but a blush colors his neck. "Don't thank me just yet."

He takes a tiny, travel-sized sewing kit from his luggage and meets me on the bed. As I stand beside him, our hips meet in a casual brush, subtle enough that I probably wouldn't notice—*if* every place his body touches mine wasn't humming with awareness.

I've never been a terribly observant person. Not the type to notice every subtle shift in expression or body language. But when it comes to Jack, I can't help how aware I am of him. How every movement, every pull of the face and brush of the knee draws my focus.

We spread the veil out across the bed, assessing the tear.

"What do you think? Can you fix it?" I ask.

"Shouldn't be a problem. We're lucky it's on the seam," he explains, pointing to the delicate lace flower on the seam. "If it was the tulle, we'd be in trouble. But if I do a slip stitch on the hole with invisible thread, it'll be good as new."

"Okay, I don't know what any of that means, but I'm *very* turned on right now," I say.

"Looks like I found out your kink after all. Who knew it was domestic skills?"

"Trust me. I'm just as surprised as you."

His lips pull up and I like the way his eyes catch mine. The little secret smile that lands in the corner of his mouth like he's trying and failing not to grin.

Jack threads a needle and gets to work. All the while I watch with rapt attention, oscillating between fear that he'll mess up and arousal at the competency porn playing out before me.

So much for packing away my dirty thoughts about Jack.

"So," I say, spreading myself out on the bed and propping my chin up on my elbows. "Do you also know how to churn your own butter?"

"Hilarious," he says, eyes remaining pinned to the lace.

"Hey, I'm just asking. You seem to be full of surprises. Banging down doors. Sewing. Improv acting skills," I say, ticking them off on my fingers. "What else can you do?"

"Some might say I'm a Jack-of-all-trades."

I slap my knee, barking out a laugh. "And he does puns too!"

His mouth quirks like he's trying to hold back his amusement, and I can't help the tiny whoosh of heat that rushes into my stomach.

We drift into silence, and I watch him work, enjoying the flex of his forearms a little too much as he draws the needle in and out of the fabric.

"So, where'd you learn to sew?" I ask. "I feel like it's sort of a lost art for our generation."

"*Our* generation?" he asks, one eyebrow flicking upward. "I thought I was *old*."

"Good point," I say, nodding sagely. "I'm sure it's not that impressive for someone who was alive during the Oregon Trail."

Jack shakes his head, grinning, and a piece of hair falls into his eyes. He brushes it away, but it falls back, determined to remain seductively strewn across his brow.

It shouldn't be a big deal. It's just skin—warm, supple skin—but right now the sheen of sweat gathering at his hairline, the dimple emerging on the side of his mouth, the swoop of dark hair threatening to fall into his eyes are more erotic than I can explain.

"My mom taught me, actually," he says, pausing to rethread the needle. "When I was in high school, I did a lot of sports, and my clothes were always getting tears in them. My mom got sick of repairing them all the time, so she taught me how to do it."

"Smart lady," I say. "Teach a man to fish and all that."

He smiles, but I can see the lines pulled taut around his eyes. It feels like a tiny mark in a scratch-off ticket, the barest hint of a reveal. But of what, I'm not sure. I only know that I'm greedy for more.

"So is that a yes or a no on the butter churning?" I ask.

His eyes rise to meet mine. "You're distracting me."

"Sorry," I whisper, inching back onto my heels. "I'll shut up."

"It's okay," he says, eyes hitching to mine. "You're a good distraction."

My heartbeat stumbles, heat inexplicably blooming in my

chest. Though I can't determine if that's from the way he's looking at me, with upturned lips and teasing eyes, or the way his mouth wraps around the word *distraction*, like he means to say *temptation*.

It doesn't take Jack long to finish, and when he's done, he holds the veil up for my approval. "What do you think?" he asks. "Will she notice?"

I examine the lace flowers, searching for imperfections Allison might notice, but it's perfect. Almost like it never happened. And before I can stop myself, I'm flinging myself into his arms.

At first he freezes, limbs stiffening against mine, but once the initial shock wears off, he hugs me back, pulling me into the firm wall of his chest.

I'm not sure if it's the fact that he just saved my ass. *Again*. Or that I can't remember the last time someone hugged me like this—like they really meant it—but I lean into him, relishing the heat of his body and the now-familiar scent of tangy cologne with a hint of something sweet.

"Thank you," I whisper into his chest.

"You're welcome," he says back, voice low, barely above a whisper. The sound of it vibrates inside me, making my skin run hot like I've just come down with the flu.

I expect one of us to break away, to end the hug, to return to whatever we were just doing, but neither of us does, and with each passing moment that we don't break away, I become more and more aware of how close we are. Of all the places we're touching. And all the places we're *not*. I'm even more hyperaware of my own rapidly increasing pace of breath and inconvenient heat simmering in my belly.

It's just a hug, I tell myself. A simple, friendly, uncomplicated thanks-for-saving-my-ass-again hug. But by the way my body is responding, we might as well be on top of each other. Naked.

I hook my gaze up, and for a brief second our eyes catch, twin electric currents pinging between our bodies. I wonder if maybe he can feel it too. But just as quickly as the pressure builds, the valve opens, and cold, sobering awareness washes over me. Awareness of what this must look like—what *I* must look like—and I jolt backward, untangling myself from him like his body is made of hot coals.

Jack's eyes narrow, lips parting into a confused frown, and I'm suddenly overcome with a powerful need to be anywhere that's not in Jack's direct line of sight.

"I'm gonna take a shower," I blurt out.

His jaw tightens, muscles pulsing at his temples. "Ada—" But I'm already across the room, hands flying to open the bathroom door.

"Try not to lock yourself in this time," he calls after me, but I don't turn back.

As soon as the bathroom door slams shut, I grip the sink, eyes lifting to meet my own reflection in the mirror. My face is flushed, skin glowing red in all the places I can still feel the ghost of his touch.

I splash some water on my face. Then I close the lid on the toilet seat and sit down, placing my head in my hands, waiting for my breathing to steady.

What. Was. That?

I mean, it was a hug. But not a regular hug. A really fucking hot hug. The kind that felt more like foreplay.

But maybe I'd imagined it. Maybe it hadn't been hot at all. Maybe I'm so starved for intimacy that I mistook a simple hug for something more *erotic*.

I replay the moment, searching for logic, something to explain away the dizzying tangle of feelings currently tying knots inside me.

I'd just been through a harrowing experience with the veil. And he'd saved the day. So it's only natural for me to feel a rush of affection for him. Right?

I let the thought take hold, allowing myself a brief respite from the flurries of panic and guilt swimming inside me. But deep down I know that the situation with the veil isn't enough to explain the surge of need I'd felt. Or the momentary wildness that had raged inside me. No, what I'd felt—am still feeling—was loud. Insistent. Demanding. Like a note played low, suddenly cranked to full volume.

I try to pack it away, to shove it into the depths of my mind where I don't have to think about it—*about him*—but it only grows more incessant, an incurably catchy tune I can't seem to shake.

WHEN I EMERGE FROM THE BATHROOM, I FIND JACK ASLEEP—ZEBRA EYE mask on—sprawled out across the bed like he owns the place. The blanket has slipped, exposing the hard ridges of his chest and abs.

Ugh. It's like he's taunting me.

I think about sleeping on the floor, but then I'd have to sleep with *the special blanket*, so I tiptoe to the bed and slide under the covers beside him, careful to shove the extra blanket all the way to the foot of the bed where it can't touch either of us.

I shut my eyes and try to concentrate on falling asleep. But my body doesn't seem to want to drift off. I toss and turn, trying to get comfortable until I remember that at home it's three p.m. Fucking jet lag.

I stare at the ceiling, willing sleep to come, but it's no use. I'm wide awake.

"Hey." Jack's voice breaks through the silence.

I thought he was asleep. Was he pretending?

"What?" I whisper back.

"Are you awake?"

"Clearly."

He rustles beside me. "I can't sleep. You?"

"No."

"What should we do?"

It's eleven p.m. here. And we're in what is likely one of the least interesting towns in the UK. There's nothing *to do.*

"How about we watch TV?" he suggests. "Or *the telly* as they say?"

I cast a glance toward the shadowy outline of the ancient TV box. "Something tells me that thing doesn't get cable."

"C'mon, we've got nothing better to do." He climbs out of bed, and I watch the dark outline of his broad shoulders as he makes his way over to the TV.

He spends a moment fiddling with the buttons until the screen flashes and TV voices and canned laughter break through the silence.

"Aha!" Jack pumps a triumphant fist in the air. "Looks like we only have one channel though."

Jack crawls back into bed and I scoot over to make room for him. His thigh brushes mine and my skin burns, every atom humming with awareness like I've been plugged in and jacked up with electricity.

I'm so absorbed in the closeness of him that it takes me a moment to realize what we are watching. It's some kind of British reality dating show. Or at least that's what I think it is until the shot widens, granting us a view of six naked men all standing in front of a clothed woman. And yup. That's a penis. On TV.

"What the hell is this?" I demand.

"Beats me," he says with a laugh. "I guess the Brits aren't quite so prudish about nudity on TV."

"Are you sure this isn't porn?"

"It's Channel Four."

A blush works its way up my neck as the camera pans to do a close-up of a particularly hairy man. Nudity isn't something that's ever embarrassed me—especially after years of fine arts class—but right now, staring at a penis with Jack right beside me sends strange feelings of heat and curiosity through my brain. None of which are G-rated.

I clear my throat. "So, uh, what exactly is the objective? She's supposed to pick one of them based on how they look naked?" I ask. "Isn't that sort of shallow?"

"Sorry, I didn't realize this wasn't sophisticated enough for you. Should I see if the news is on? Maybe a World War Two docuseries? I heard there was a good one about the Battle of the Bulge."

"I'm pretty sure we're already watching that."

A cackle rips out of him.

"I'm just wondering what the criteria is," I say, pointing to the screen. "Length? Size?"

"If that's what she's judging on, she's going to be disappointed. Everyone knows it's not about length or size, but what you can do with it," Jack says, giving me a knowing look as though he's just imparted some great wisdom.

I try to laugh, but the sound doesn't quite make it out because now I'm wondering whether Jack is speaking generally or . . . ? *Stop it! Don't think about Jack's penis. Or what he might do with it. Focus.* But focus on *what*, exactly? The naked men on TV? That doesn't exactly feel like a safe choice either.

I stare straight ahead, hoping he's too busy watching the TV to notice the heat creeping into my cheeks. We stay like that, both of us looking ahead, pretending to watch the woman choose between the final two contestants. But I can feel the tension radiating from his body. I feel it every time he shifts his weight and we touch for a beat too long before he pulls away and starts the cycle all over again.

"You know what this needs?" he asks after a moment.

"A trigger warning?"

"Food. I'm starving."

The last time he was starving it didn't really end in our favor. But he has a point. We haven't eaten in hours.

"It's the middle of the night. How are we going to find food?" I ask.

"We could order pizza?"

"At twelve a.m.?"

"Twelve a.m. is the best time to order pizza," he says. "It's a universally agreed upon concept."

My mouth salivates at the mere thought of warm, yeasty crust and melty cheese.

"Fine. I'm in."

Jack scrolls on his phone for a minute before putting it to his ear. I hear someone answer on the other line.

"Hi. Can we order a . . . ?" He looks to me and I mouth the words *large pepperoni with pineapple.*

He makes a face of disgust and vigorously shakes his head. "One large pepperoni, please," he says.

"And chips . . . Great. Okay, thanks," he says before ending the call. "Pepperoni *and* pineapple?" he asks. "I don't think I can trust you."

I laugh. "Why not? It's good."

"Fortunately for me, and all of humankind, they don't do pineapple on pizza here. Also, they don't do delivery. Takeaway only. You up for a little nighttime stroll?"

"Do I have to put pants on?" I ask, scrunching up my face.

"Pants are optional," he says. "But highly recommended."

"Fine," I say crawling out of our little cocoon of blankets and pillows. "I'll put on pants, but only for pizza."

I wriggle back into jeans and toss on a sweatshirt over my T-shirt.

As we make our way back downstairs the floorboards creak under our weight. Jack and I lock eyes and I can tell we've had the same thought.

"If she catches us, what are we going to say?" I whisper.

"That we're running out for sustenance after our marathon lovemaking session?" Jack tries, and I'm thankful the hall is dark enough to conceal the blush I know is crawling up my neck.

Outside, cold night air envelops us and my eyes quickly adjust to the shadowy street, blinking back the darkness.

"Do you know where we're going?" I ask, shivering in the chilly air.

He holds up his phone, frowning at the screen. "Says it's just three blocks this way."

Jack's tall frame towers beside me, casting long shadows on the concrete. Overhead, a swollen moon paints the street in swaths of yellow light.

We turn the corner onto a main street, when my phone vibrates in my pocket.

ALLISON

Is the veil okay? Make sure it gets here in one piece.

Seriously? How does she know? Does she have some kind of ESP telling her when the veil might be in danger? If only she had ESP to tell her it's maybe not a great idea to marry a guy you barely know.

I type out a quick, yes, it's fine, then shove my phone back into my pocket.

"Allison?" Jack asks.

"She won't leave me alone."

"Can't you just tell her to piss off?"

"I'm the maid of honor," I explain. "It's sort of in my job description."

After a beat, he asks, "Is it always like this with you guys? Fighting, I mean?"

"We used to be really close," I say, kicking at a pebble. "But things have been weird with us since she got engaged to Collin. Turns out telling your sister you think she's making a huge mistake that will ruin her life doesn't exactly go over well."

My throat squeezes, reliving how much it had hurt to find out that she was engaged to a man I'd never even met. The memory still stings, dragging me back into that moment. The confusion. The pain. The hollow clench in my chest when I'd seen the ring and known Allison was rushing into things and there was nothing I could do to stop her.

"I can't imagine Allison taking that well," Jack says.

"She didn't. She was pissed. She accused me of trying to control her, of not trusting her decisions with men. Which is true, I don't," I say, eyes cutting to his. "The last guy had a literal restraining order against him. And the guy before that tried to convince her he was allergic to condoms, so excuse me if I'm dubious of this whirlwind marriage."

I expect Jack to once again defend Collin, or perhaps turn the conversation into another example of why marriage is a bad idea. Instead, he takes a long breath, eyes snagging mine. "I'm really sorry, Ada," he says. "That's shitty."

I'm not sure if it's the weightiness under his voice or the warm, melting glow behind his eyes, but I feel like he means it. Like it's not just a throwaway comment or an empty statement, but a real moment of solidarity. And I can't help but feel the ache of loneliness that I've come to accept over the past few months start to recede just a little bit.

"We've fought before," I say after a beat. "But it's never been like this with her. Usually we fight, then make up twenty minutes later when she wants to borrow a shirt or something. But this time we haven't made up and . . ." An unexpected crack worms its way into my voice. "This wedding, this fight, it's all been really hard on me, especially after losing the business and Carter."

I think about how it felt to lose my business, to watch my sister grow distant, to feel like everything around me was unraveling piece by piece. I thought Carter would stick by my side, that he'd always be there for me the same way I'd been for him, but he slipped away, too, leaving me even more lost and confused and alone. And yes, afraid.

But it's not just a fear of being alone, of not getting my old life back, it's the feeling of helplessness, the confusion, the lack of control. It's seeing a future I'd thought was certain begin to fade away, replaced with bleak, untethered nothingness. A nothingness my brain can't fill in for me.

We walk a little farther until I say, "I guess it's why I've clung to Carter so hard. I've already lost so much, and I don't want our relationship to be one more thing I lose." As soon as I say it, I look away, embarrassed. "Sorry," I say to the concrete. "You probably don't want to hear about Carter again. I know you think I'm naive for wanting to get back together."

Jack shakes his head, eyes catching mine. "I don't think that, Ada." He pauses. "And I'm sorry about earlier. I shouldn't have overstepped like that. I was an ass. Again," he adds, wincing.

I take a deep breath, lungs expanding with cold night air. "It's okay," I say. "Maybe you were right."

His eyes flash with something unreadable. "About what?"

That I am afraid.

"Just that maybe being with someone for a long time *isn't* enough," I say instead.

As soon as I say it, I brace myself, expecting Jack to gloat and say *I told you so.* Instead, he asks in a tone that's surprisingly soft, "Are you saying you might be having second thoughts?"

The question tugs at my insides, tying them in knots I can't seem to untangle.

"I don't know," I say. "I'm just . . ." But I don't know how to finish that sentence, at least not in a way that won't make me feel sick. "I don't know," I repeat.

Jack nods, dark eyes warming in the yellow glow of a streetlamp. For a long moment neither of us speaks, but I'm newly aware of how close we are, how his hand keeps grazing mine as he walks beside me. I wonder if he's aware of me the same way I'm aware of him.

"I know we don't exactly see eye to eye on matters of the heart," he says after a minute. "But I feel like if you're going to do the commitment thing, then you should at least be with someone who is all in. Someone who appreciates you and wants to grow together, not someone with one foot out the door, looking for the next exit." He watches me tentatively as though waiting for me to push back. When I don't, he continues. "If you've got something good, something worth having, you do everything you can to keep it, right?"

The words ping around inside my brain like metal balls in a pinball machine, springing from one thought to the next.

He's right. I *do* deserve someone who doesn't get squeamish every time marriage gets mentioned, someone who doesn't need to take a break to see how he *feels about things.* Someone who is *all in.*

And yet, it's not that simple.

Maybe if every area of my life wasn't in varying degrees of upheaval. If the last year hadn't stolen my confidence brick by brick. If Carter didn't feel like my source of stability . . . But I can't take another risk, romantic or otherwise. Not when the only risk I've ever taken, the one thing that was just for me and no one else, was an abject failure. A failure that landed me in the exact position I'm in right now.

When I look back at Jack, his brow is furrowed, the corners of his eyes scrunched in thought, and I can't help but wonder where his mind is. If maybe it has to do with the *personal stuff* he mentioned earlier.

Part of me wants to ask him. To whittle down this unspoken barrier between us. But another part of me senses that whatever it is, like me, he's not ready to talk about it yet.

We don't say anything else the rest of the way to the pizza shop, but a strange kind of solidarity hangs between us. Like we're both fighting to stay above different waves. He doesn't tell me what's on his mind, and I don't say anything more about Carter, but I can feel the invisible threads between us tighten, keeping each other afloat.

THE PIZZA SHOP IS A GREASY TAKEAWAY SPOT WITH HARSH NEON LIGHT AND cold red plastic booths. Despite the lateness of the hour, the place isn't empty. A few drunk kids stumble in behind us followed by a group wearing soccer (football?) jerseys, talking loudly about the score of a match.

By the time we make it back to the inn I'm delirious with hunger and the scent of garlic and cheese wafting from the cardboard box is torture.

I shimmy out of my jeans and back into my cat pajamas before flopping back down on the bed.

Jack opens the pizza box and I moan with pleasure.

"Oh, I see," Jack says, sliding in beside me.

"What?"

"That noise you just made, that was a sex noise. A *real* sex noise," he says, mouth twitching. "Good to know."

I snort and reach past him for a slice, stuffing as much as I can into my mouth.

For a moment we chew in silence, savoring the tangy tomato sauce and greasy, melted cheese.

"Just like Italy," he says between bites.

I'm sure this crapfest of a pizza would mortify the Italians. But right now, this is the best damn pizza I've ever had.

"Just like Italy," I repeat, holding out my slice to his like we are cheersing.

He smiles and I smile back.

There's a kind of unexpected intimacy to the moment. Like a hug that lasts a beat too long. Or catching someone's eye in a crowded room.

"We should go," he says after a moment.

I frown, tugging at a particularly gooey strand of cheese. "Go where?"

"Italy."

"*We*?"

"Why not? It'll be a pizza field trip. I'll take you to that place I told you about, Pizzeria Vergini in Naples."

"You would want to go to Italy? With me?" I shoot him a conspiratorial look. "I don't know if you've noticed, but we're not exactly the best travel companions."

"Come on, you're not *that* bad as long as you clean your hair out of the drain and don't get locked in any bathrooms," he teases.

I give him a playful shove. "Excuse me, but you're the one who woke up cuddling me this morning, so it's not like you're perfect."

"First off, that wasn't intentional." He dabs at the corners of his mouth with a napkin. "And second, how about this: if one year from now you're still single, we go to Italy together."

He holds out a greasy hand and I look down at it, skeptical. "Is this one of those pity pacts where we promise to marry each other if we're both sufficiently desperate enough?" I ask.

He laughs. "I can assure you there will be no marriage pact. Just pizza. In fact . . ." His brow scrunches. "It's a pizza pact."

Part of me wants to tell him I'll probably be back with Carter next year, like I've been telling myself. But there's another part of me that likes the idea of making a silly promise with Jack. Even if we'll never have a reason to keep it.

"Okay," I say after a moment. "I'm in."

We shake on it, and for a second the moment fills with possibility. I imagine us together in Italy, drinking prosecco under the shadow of the Colosseum, or wandering the narrow passages of Venice as we stuff our faces with pizza and gelato.

It's a nice image. But while it's nice to dream about some kind of vague future trip we might take, like we're more than just two people headed to the same wedding, like we're real friends, I know it'll never happen.

We won't go to Italy. Just like I won't go to Paris. But it's nice to pretend.

We watch the rest of the episode and another and another until my eyes sag with tiredness. Jack says he's not tired yet, but he falls asleep first, chin dipping steadily toward his chest until he finally slumps against my shoulder. A piece of hair falls into his enviably long eyelashes, and I reach out to push it away.

Perhaps it's silly considering I'm in a janky old bed-and-breakfast watching a shitty reality TV show, but this is the best night I've had in a long time. And it occurs to me that if Carter were here—like he was supposed to be—then *this* wouldn't have happened. I wouldn't be here with Jack, eating pizza in bed, making future travel plans we'll never act on. I'd have been with Carter, somewhere else, doing something else. And somehow that thought disappoints me.

Chapter 13

50 HOURS UNTIL THE WEDDING

When I awake the next morning, I'm warm and snug like I've slept in a cozy little cocoon all night, and I burrow deeper into the nest of blankets, relishing their weighted comfort.

Who knew I'd sleep so well here? Must be all that fresh air. Or the pizza. Probably the pizza.

I yawn and stretch before looking down in horror to see that I'm wrapped up in none other than *the special blanket.*

"Ahhh!" I shriek, shoving the blanket off and scrambling to the other side of the bed as fast as I can. "How did this get on me?"

"You looked cold last night," comes the familiar timbre of Jack's voice.

I jump and turn around to where Jack is leaning against the doorway to the bathroom, watching me with amusement.

"And you couldn't find another blanket?" I demand. "Preferably one that won't get me pregnant?"

He laughs. "If you get pregnant, it won't be my fault. Not even my incredibly potent sperm are that good."

It's on the very unsexy word *sperm* that I realize Jack's wearing a pair of running shorts—*just* running shorts—and holding two paper cups. His face and chest shimmer with sweat.

"What's that?" I ask, pointing to the cups.

"Coffee. Here." He hands me a paper cup and my nostrils rejoice at the earthy scent.

"How long have you been up? And why are you half naked and sweaty?" I ask.

"I went for a run this morning."

I balk. Seriously? How is it that I'm a jet-lagged mess and he's all bright-eyed and bushy-tailed?

"I've also been arranging our travel plans with Mrs. Poyevich," he says.

"Mrs. Poyevich?"

"You know, our friend from last night?" He wiggles his eyebrows. "She asked me all about our wedding."

I take a long sip of coffee, feeling my senses come back to life. "And what did you say?"

"I told her we eloped because we're not really into big weddings."

"You choose now to go for accuracy?"

He laughs but doesn't contest my point.

"You should get up," he says, patting the edge of the bed. "We need to hit the road."

"You got train tickets already?" I ask, wondering what else he's been up to while I've been asleep. Saving the whales? Finding the cure for cancer?

Jack steps away from the bed, running his palm down the side of his neck. "Not exactly."

My eyebrows narrow into a *v*. "What do you mean *not exactly*?"

"So, hear me out . . ."

Great. What did he do?

"I got up early to get train tickets, but unfortunately there are no trains running directly from here to Glasgow today," he explains. "Apparently National Rail is still on strike."

I groan. And just when I thought my luck might be turning.

"*But.*" He gives me a persistent look. "I told Mrs. Poyevich about our predicament, and lo and behold, her brother loaned her a car a few weeks ago. A car she needs to return. He lives in Edinburgh, so I volunteered to drive the car back for her."

"Edinburgh?" I ask. "But we aren't going to Edinburgh."

"I know, but it's close enough, and we can take the bus from there."

I chew on my bottom lip, mulling over this blip in the plan. "Isn't this going to set us back time-wise?"

"Not necessarily. I've checked it all out. We can take the bus from Edinburgh tonight and still make the ferry tomorrow. It'll be fine," he adds, noticing my wary expression.

"And this is our only option?" I ask.

"Unless you want to stay here another night," he says, gesturing to *the special blanket*.

I grimace. *No thank you.*

"Fine," I tell him. It's not like we have another choice.

TWENTY MINUTES LATER, I EMERGE FROM THE BATHROOM IN A CLOUD OF steam and complimentary mint-scented shampoo, to find Jack pacing the room, phone glued to his ear, looking miserable.

"Fine," he says, waving his hand with an air of annoyance. "Sure. I'll send it over. Just tell her I'm not settling . . ." A deep sigh rattles in his throat. "If she wants to talk, she can talk to me herself . . . Yeah . . . okay . . . Fine. That's great." The muscles in his jaw twitch. "Thanks for calling, Doug." Jack doesn't say goodbye, he just slams his thumb into the screen and glares up at the ceiling mid–eye roll like it's personally offended him.

"Everything good?" I ask, pausing in the bathroom doorway.

"Fine." But based on the trio of creases forming in his forehead, he, in fact, doesn't look fine.

"You sure?"

"Don't worry about it," he says tersely.

I pretend the brush-off doesn't bother me, but as I'm shoveling clothes back into my suitcase, I can't help but notice that in the last thirty-six-ish hours we've spent together, all he's told me about himself is how he lost his virginity, that he prefers boxers to briefs, he's a lawyer, and apparently, he's never been in love.

I think back to our conversation on the curb. *Personal stuff,* he'd said. Of course, *personal stuff* is code for *we aren't close enough for me to tell you that.* Which is fair. We've only known each other two days. It's not like I'm entitled to know all about his life. But last night it felt like our relationship had moved into something possibly resembling friendship. But maybe we hadn't. Maybe I'd been the one to misread things this time.

We pack up our things in silence until Jack asks, "Want to get a drink?"

I look up from my suitcase. "A drink? It's like nine a.m."

"Yeah, but back home it's one a.m., which is a perfectly acceptable time to drink."

I open my mouth to tell him we should probably get going, that we don't have time for a drink, but just as quickly as I do, I realize it doesn't sound so bad. Besides, we're technically on vacation and everyone knows the rules don't apply when you're on vacation. Right?

"Fine," I agree. "One drink, but then we're getting on the road, right?"

"Then we're getting on the road," he agrees.

After we check out, we grab the car keys from Mrs. Poyevich, who yells, "Goodbye, Mr. and Mrs. Houghton," while waving exuberantly on our way out the door. We wave back, promising to send pictures of our firstborn.

Outside, the pale morning sun dips below the clouds, casting spouts of light along the narrow rows of cobblestone.

"Is this where you ran?" I ask.

He nods, eyes not meeting mine. "It was good to get out and clear my head."

He offers no further explanation as to what exactly in his head needed clearing, and we drift into silence as we walk along the high street, admiring the colorful storefronts.

Eventually, Jack guides us into a dimly lit pub named the George and Dragon with dark walls and an ancient wooden floor that creaks under our weight. Somewhere in the back, a staticky radio croons, announcing that Manchester just scored against Madrid.

The pub is already serving lunch even though it's ten a.m., and I decide to go for fish and chips while Jack orders a pint and a burger. After we order at the bar, we shuffle into a booth in the back. We've barely sat down when Jack reaches over and snatches a fry off my plate. I try to smack his wrist, but he's too fast.

"Hey! Get your own fries!"

"I'm starving after my run." He grabs another fry and pops it into his mouth. "Shocked you didn't ask for pineapple on them though."

"Ha ha. You're just lucky they don't have ranch here."

"When we go to Italy, I doubt you'll be able to get pineapple on your pizza. What does that tell you?"

When we go to Italy. The words send volts of electricity parading down my spine, even though I know he doesn't mean it.

We've only known each other for two days. This time next

year I doubt he'll even remember my name. Besides, he has no idea if Carter and I will get back together. And frankly, neither do I.

I cut into my food, taking a few bites of a flaky, crispy fish before I ask, "How about another round of questions?"

"Don't we know each other well enough now?" he asks, popping another fry into his mouth. "After all, I know that you're a screamer."

Unwanted heat blooms behind my navel and I take my time chewing before I answer.

"I know that your mom taught you how to sew, how you lost your virginity, and that your love of pizza runs deep," I say. "But what about your family? Any brothers or sisters? Are you close with your parents?"

"No brothers or sisters. Just me." His eyes dim. "And my dad and I don't talk."

"What about your mom?" I try, scooping a helping of fried fish onto my fork. "I bet she'll love hearing how you saved my ass with those sewing skills."

Jack picks up his glass, considers it, then sets it down again before finally saying, "My mom died."

I freeze, fork hovering a few inches from my mouth. For a moment I think I must have misheard, but the torque in his jaw and emerging shadow behind his eyes confirm that my hearing is just fine.

"What about you?" he asks, cutting through the protracted silence. "Are you close with your parents?"

I jerk back, frowning. "Whoa, you can't just drop a bomb like that."

"About your parents?" He gives a half laugh.

"No . . . about . . ." I lower my voice to a whisper even though we're the only ones here. "About your mom." Seriously? How can he joke about this? Then it occurs to me that the joking might be intentional, a deflection.

"It was a long time ago now." He waves his hand like he's flicking away a bothersome fly, but I can hear the ragged edge to his voice. The heaviness. And I can't help but feel like the curtain is being lifted, and instead of the Great and Powerful Oz, I'm face-to-face with someone entirely different from who I'd expected.

"Sorry, I didn't mean to make things awkward," he says after a beat.

"No, you didn't," I say quickly. "I was just surprised. That's all."

"It's okay, you can say it's awkward. Some people get weird about it."

I feel the canned clichés rise inside me.

Sorry for your loss.

She's in a better place.

Time will heal all wounds.

But none of them make it out. They feel too hollow, too derivative, too much like a Hallmark sympathy card.

"I'm sorry," I say at last, knowing it's inadequate.

He flicks a strand of hair from his eyes. "It's fine." I can tell it's a response he's grown accustomed to saying, almost like he's on autopilot.

"What happened? I mean, you don't have to tell me if you don't want to," I add.

"It's fine," he says again, rubbing the back of his neck. "She was in a scuba accident, actually."

He says the word *actually* like it's a modifier, something to soften the blow.

"It was about a year after my dad left us for someone at work." His mouth tenses, like whatever memory is buried in those words is still very real and painful. "I was fifteen and my mom started seeing a new guy. The first guy since my dad. They were on vacation in the Bahamas when it happened." His voice comes out stiff, robotic, like it's a story he's told innumerable times, and I instantly hate myself for making him tell it one more time.

"Where were you?" I ask, trying to imagine a fifteen-year-old Jack.

He picks up his fork, then sets it back down, adjusting it so that it's perfectly straight. "I was staying at Collin's house. His family sort of took me in after. Really made me feel like I was part of their family when I didn't have anyone else. I was lucky to have them."

My heart squeezes like there's an invisible fist tightening around it. I'm no fan of Collin, but I feel an instant wave of tenderness toward him.

"I'm glad you had them," I say.

A noiseless breath snakes between his parted lips, eyes capturing mine. "Me too."

Something hot flares in my chest, but I don't know if it's guilt or sympathy or something else entirely.

I wish I had something to say. Something helpful. But I understand there's nothing I can say. He's lived with this pain for almost twenty years and there's nothing that will make it any easier.

I consider reaching over and giving him a pat on the hand, some small sign to show him I care, but that feels too forward, so I shift my weight under the table so our knees rest against one another. Jack doesn't move and neither do I.

"Are you close with your parents?" he asks again.

I can tell he's trying to redirect the conversation away from himself. But I can't exactly blame him.

"Before my mom married my stepdad, it was just us girls and we were really close."

I smile, remembering Friday movie nights when Allison and I

would pull our mattresses off our beds and build a fort in front of the TV, waiting until we heard Mom's keys in the door so we could pop the VHS in. Despite Mom letting us watch any movie, we always wanted to watch *The Parent Trap*. It didn't matter that we'd seen it a million times, it was the comfort, the familiarity of knowing exactly how it was going to end. Like returning to a favorite pair of jeans that fit just right. To this day, it is still my sister's go-to comfort movie.

"I'm glad my mom found my stepdad," I tell him. "But those years when it was just the three of us will always be bittersweet to me."

"What happened to your dad?" Jack asks. "If you don't mind my asking."

"My biological dad was never married to my mom," I tell him. "He was in and out of our lives until I was six and Allison was a toddler, then he just dipped. We haven't seen or heard from him since."

"I'm sorry," Jack says, eyes softening.

"Don't be. He wasn't exactly a great dad. Which I suppose we have in common," I add, letting my eyes linger on his. He gives the barest hint of a nod and a loose strand of solidarity weaves between us.

"Allison and I never had a real relationship with him," I go on. "He was just this guy that came over once in a while to play with us or take us for ice cream. Then one day he stopped coming."

My spine pulls at the memory of all the nights I heard my mom crying when she thought Allison and I had gone to sleep, hating how that made me feel, even though I was too young to understand.

"How did you feel about your mom getting married?" Jack asks.

"I was twelve, so I was just happy to see my mom find someone who treated her well and made her happy," I tell him. "But when mom and Bill sat us down to tell us the news, Allison burst into tears. I had to take her into the other room and explain there was going to be a big party and cake and Mom would be so happy. I think she was used to it just being the three of us and she didn't like change. I remember when we moved into Bill's house, Allison and I got our own rooms for the first time, and Allison wasn't used to sleeping by herself, so for the first few months she slept in my room with me." I pause, smiling at the long-buried memory. "But eventually she warmed up to Bill and the new house."

"Do you like him?" Jack asks.

"I do. He's a great guy and he loves my mom, which is probably why I've always idolized their relationship. When they got together, he'd just gotten divorced, and my mom was a single parent. They both had emotional baggage, and every reason in the world to be afraid, but they chose each other anyways, and I think that's kind of beautiful."

As I say it, warmth pools in my stomach, spreading outward like I'm draped in a fuzzy blanket. I expect Jack to tease me, to tell me I'm buying into social programming or whatever. Instead, he smiles and asks, "Is that why you're such a hopeless romantic?"

"I wouldn't say *hopeless*. But it's certainly easier to believe in things like everlasting love and commitment when you see the way my stepdad looks at my mom."

I think about the times I've caught them slow dancing in the kitchen. All the interrupted moments my sister and I ran away screaming from because we thought it was gross to see them kissing. Now I can't help the tug of longing in the pit of my stomach. The desire for that kind of love. The kind that's hard-fought and won.

I used to think that's what Carter and I had. That the length of our relationship corresponded with durability—something worth preserving. But maybe that's not what love is. Maybe it's not hours clocked or years passed. It's a quiet certainty that you're not alone, that whatever comes—may it be joy or tragedy, success or loss—you'll have someone by your side through it all. That you won't have to face it on your own. Maybe it's finding someone who makes you feel a little less alone in the world.

The thought brings an ache to my throat and a pang to my chest.

Jack doesn't say anything, but under the table his knee bumps mine. Maybe it's an accident, or maybe it's not, but it feels nice, and I get that same sense of camaraderie I'd felt last night, like the tension between us has shifted, giving way to something like solidarity.

"You know," I say after a minute, "I had fun last night."

His eyes meet mine, gaze laced with a warmth I'm relieved to see. "I did too. Even if it's your fault we had to sleep in that crusty inn."

"For the last time, it wasn't my fault that I got locked in the bathroom."

He laughs and the sound loosens something inside me. "I'll let you off the hook, but only because if we'd made our train, we wouldn't have seen our new favorite TV show."

"Or eaten the world's most amazing pizza," I add.

He grins and a tingle runs the length of my spine, gathering in the hollow space behind my belly button.

"I'm glad you decided not to ditch me when you had the chance last night," I tell him.

"I wouldn't have ditched you, Ada."

"Because you're afraid of my sister?" I tease.

His bottom lip disappears between his teeth, and he shakes

his head. "I mean, yes, she's terrifying, but also . . ." His voice trails off, gaze dipping from my eyes, then lower, before settling on my lips.

A rush of awareness floods my body and suddenly I'm desperate for him to finish that sentence. To scrape back the layer of unspoken thoughts between us. Instead, he reaches under the table and puts his hand on the top of my knee. I expect it to be a transient gesture, there one moment, gone the next, but he leaves his hand long enough that it feels like his skin is sizzling straight through the fabric of my jeans. A bolt of unrestrained desire shoots down my center and I cast my gaze downward, hoping he doesn't notice the hues of pink streaking my cheeks.

We *definitely* shouldn't be touching like this—especially after hug-gate—but I can't bring myself to move away. Not until two men enter the pub, making the bell jangle over the door. The sound snaps us back to reality and we both jump apart like we've been caught doing something we shouldn't.

I look away, embarrassed. He clears his throat. Silence ensues.

"We should get going," he says after a moment.

"You good to drive?" I ask, eyeing his half-finished glass of beer.

Jack nods and grabs the keys, looking everywhere but at me.

As we exit the pub, returning to the crisp morning air, I try to stay cool, to pretend like whatever the hell just happened didn't set every nerve ending in my body on fire.

He's just being nice, I tell myself. But Jack's words from last night echo in my mind. *That's why you're so hot and bothered over him? Because he's nice?*

Of course he'd meant Carter, but now the words feel strangely pointed, like tiny, highly accurate arrows directed right at the most vulnerable parts of my mind. Parts of my mind that can't seem to stop thinking about the weight of Jack's hand. Or the way his eyes dipped to my lips, lingering just a beat too long.

I try to shake the thought free, but as we walk to the car in silence I can't help but feel like a door's opened inside me. A door I'm not sure I can close again.

Chapter 14

48 HOURS UNTIL THE WEDDING

"Are you sure this is safe?" I ask, examining the rusty hood of the 1974 Peugeot.

I'm no car expert. Scratch that. I'm barely able to operate a motor vehicle. I've had four speeding tickets and three driving infractions in two years—something Carter would incessantly tease me about. But this car doesn't look like it will make it forty feet out of the driveway, much less all the way to Edinburgh. The taillight is hanging out, the hood is rusted through, and when Jack started the engine it made a few popping noises that sounded like gunshots.

"It's fine," Jack says with a wave of his hand.

"Are you sure?" I ask again. "Because it looks like a metal death trap, and that's putting it lightly."

"It's only a hundred and seventy miles, we'll be fine. Don't you trust me?" he asks.

"It's not *you* I'm worried about, it's the car," I say, casting the steering wheel a dubious glance. "Are you going to be okay driving on the other side of the road?"

He shrugs. "How hard can it be?"

The answer: harder than expected.

First off, there are no traffic lights. Only roundabouts, which are extra confusing when you're driving on the other side of the road. I screamed the first time Jack tried to turn into the oncoming traffic out of a roundabout.

I figured things would get easier once we got onto the motorway, but Jack's depth perception is off because he isn't used to driving on the left side and we keep accidentally veering out of our lane.

We've already been flipped off six times. At first, I thought people were throwing up the peace sign until I figured out that holding up your middle and index finger is the British equivalent of the bird. Jack tries to explain that this has something to do with the Hundred Years' War between France and England, but I'm too busy trying not to die to listen.

Fortunately, several brushes with death and one tearful plea to drop me off at the next petrol station later, Jack seems to get the hang of it. Now we're on something called the M6 headed north toward Scotland. According to Google Maps we should arrive in Edinburgh in three and a half hours.

Jack fiddles with the radio and I secretly hope he picks something terrible to listen to—something like talk radio or Nickelback—so as to ease the burden of my little crush on him. Instead, he lands on an eighties station playing "Edge of Seventeen" and starts humming along. Dammit. He even has good taste in music.

"So . . ." he says, keeping his eyes focused on the road as Stevie Nicks's voice croons in the background.

"So . . . ?" I parrot.

Jack clears his throat. "I was thinking about what you said last night, about how you told Allison it was a mistake to marry Collin."

My insides pull tight, a dozen tiny, internal alarms all tripped at once. "I thought we agreed to forget everything I said about Collin?"

"But I thought things were different now," he says, tipping his chin toward me. "I mean, for starters, we're married."

My mouth twitches. "We're still married?"

He looks at me with mock horror. "Of course we are. Marriage is a lifelong commitment. Or at least that's what some girl on a train told me."

I know he's teasing, but based on the traitorous flop of my stomach, I don't think my body gets the memo.

"I know you said you don't trust Collin, or any of the men Allison's dated. But did Collin do something? Or is there a specific reason you don't like him? Besides the fact that he's the human equivalent of an unwrapped, under-the-seat Hershey's Kiss?"

"My sister's dated a lot of questionable men," I say, fidgeting with the hem of my shirt. "Everyone she's ever dated has turned out to be a creep or a criminal or a cheater . . ." My mind stalls on Bradley. "Or just a downright bad guy."

"So? Collin's not questionable."

I sigh, exasperated. "Of course he's questionable. He's ten years older than her. And they barely know each other."

"Age doesn't make someone questionable," Jack points out. "It's not like she's a minor. She's twenty-four."

I huff in frustration, letting my eyes zip to the window, where we pass a flock of sheep. "You don't understand."

"Okay, so explain it to me. We still have three hours until we make it to Edinburgh."

My lips firm. I hadn't wanted to talk about Bradley, but something in me needs Jack to understand. To get where my protectiveness is coming from.

"Before Collin, Allison dated this other guy. *Bradley*," I say. "And let's just say he wasn't a great guy."

"What do you mean?"

"Like he would tell her what to wear, and how to act, and got really jealous. He was sort of . . ." The word dangles on the tip of my tongue. *Abusive.* "He was kind of a jerk," I say instead. "I told her she needed to end things with him, but she was scared to."

Jack's brows dip into thoughtful ridges. "For some reason I'm having a hard time picturing Allison being scared to break up with someone."

"I know Allison acts tough and all, but it's not easy to walk out of a situation like that. Especially when every time he did something like scream at her or cause a scene, he'd be back a week later begging for forgiveness, telling her he was sorry, but also that it was somehow her fault in the first place and really *she'd* brought it on herself."

"That's fucked up. I had no idea."

Out of the corner of my eye I see Jack swallow hard, and I can't help the tiny ping of vindication inside my chest.

"Allison was afraid he wouldn't take it well if she broke things off," I go on. "So I helped her pack up all her stuff while Bradley was out. We changed her cell phone number and deleted all her social media profiles so he couldn't find her. But somehow Bradley got her new number and he started texting her scary stuff every day, getting mad at her for leaving him and saying she was going to regret it."

I bite back the bitter memories rising inside me. All the nights Allison called me in tears, crying so hard she could barely talk. Nights I'd fall asleep with my ringer at full volume just in case she needed me.

Jack shakes his head, shock and something darker swallowing his expression. "What happened? Did she get rid of him?"

"Eventually I helped Allison get a restraining order against him and he stopped bothering her," I say. "But for a while she was afraid to leave the house and I moved her in with Carter and me until she could find somewhere new to live."

Jack's eyes stay trained on the road, but his gaze narrows, brows pushing into a furrow. After a pause, he says, "I'm sorry that happened. But is this about Bradley or about Collin?"

"Neither. It's about Allison," I say sharply. "Everything with Collin happened so fast. And I'm worried they're rushing into things, that she's not really thinking about this, and I'll have to come and clean up the mess. Like I always do."

Jack's mouth tightens, expression sharpening on the road ahead. "I get that what happened with this Bradley guy was bad, but aren't you being sort of unfair? Collin isn't Bradley."

Frustration tugs at my chest. Jack doesn't understand. He doesn't understand what it was like when Bradley would leave Allison voicemails every day telling her she was worthless without him. Or when she'd call me crying and hysterical over his latest outburst.

Jack also doesn't understand that the only reason she was able to get out of that relationship was because of me. Because *I* cut the cord. Because *I* helped her move out. Because *I* changed her phone number and filed the police report. Now I'm afraid something like that could happen again. Maybe not the same exact thing, but I've been through this enough times to know that my sister's relationships always end the same way. With Allison crying and heartbroken, and me picking up the pieces. And I don't see why this will be any different.

"I thought you'd understand my reservations," I say, voice thickening. "Given that you're against marriage and all."

A muscle in Jack's jaw jumps, tension straddling the bridge of his mouth. "This isn't about marriage, this is about me trying to understand why you hate my best friend."

"I don't *hate* him," I say. "I just don't want my sister to make another mistake, especially one that *I* could have prevented her from making."

"But you have to let her make her own mistakes. Even if you think you know best. So what if things don't work out with her and Collin? Then you'll be there for her when she needs you. You're her sister, not her keeper."

"You don't get it," I tell him. "Allison's not a cynic like you. She wears her heart on her sleeve. She falls in love hard and fast—which is great if you're Meg Ryan in a Nora Ephron film, but not so great in the real world where there are predatory jerks who take advantage of people like my sister."

Jack's mouth sets into a hard line, visible threads of annoyance weaving across his features. "I understand that you're protective of her, but she's a grown-ass woman. She doesn't need you to save her. Especially not from Collin," he says, giving me a heavy side-eye. "He's a good guy, Ada. He'll treat her right."

I squeeze my lips tight, trying to mask the emotion rising in my throat. "I get that Collin is your bestie and you have to defend him, but the way I see it, he's a glorified frat star who touches boobs for a living. So excuse me if I don't trust the guy."

Jack takes one hand off the steering wheel and runs it through his hair. "*Yes,* Collin does breast implants, which is a very real and valid profession, by the way." He pauses to shoot me a cutting glance. "But I'm gonna assume you don't know that he also does reconstructive surgery for domestic abuse and burn victims, or that he's one of the best people I know. So *no,*" Jack says, voice tightening, "he's not exactly the douchey *frat star* you have him pegged as."

"But—"

"And I'm sure you don't know about the time Collin drove all the way to Canada to get some special tea for her when she was sick, or when she had food poisoning and Collin stayed up all night with her. Or the time her dog got something stuck in its throat so Collin drove them to the vet at three a.m. Or the—"

"Okay, we get it," I interrupt. "Thanks for the reminder that my sister basically wants nothing to do with me."

"I'm just saying, if you want to judge Collin based on the actions of some loser Allison *used* to date, okay, fine, but you're wrong about him," Jack says, eyes briefly cutting to mine. "Support this marriage or don't, but don't blame Collin for your own prejudices."

My stomach constricts and I sink lower in my seat, bottom lip disappearing between my teeth.

Part of me wants to double down, to tell him he doesn't get it. That he wasn't there when Allison went through the aftermath of Bradley when she cried herself to sleep for months. That it wasn't just Allison who was hurt. It hurt me too. It hurt me to see her like that and I'm terrified of it happening again. But another part of me feels caught, like Jack's uncovered an ugly side of me. A side I didn't want anyone to see.

"I thought you don't believe in relationships," I say after a beat.

His eyes darken. "I don't."

I sit up straighter. "So aren't you being hypocritical? I can't be concerned about my sister's well-being when she decides to marry some guy I don't even know? But you can tell Collin not to get married?"

His jaw sharpens. "That's between Collin and me."

"*What's* between Collin and you?"

He inhales sharply followed by a noisy exhale. "It's personal," he says.

There's that word again. *Personal.* Aka off-limits.

"So you're not gonna tell me? I thought you were my husband."

Jack shifts uncomfortably but doesn't say anything. Okay. Ouch. He can make jokes, but I can't?

"Did something happen between you two?" I try. "Is that the reason you aren't looking forward to the wedding?"

"We're fine." But there's an edge to his voice that sounds decidedly *not* fine.

"But you didn't answer my question."

I try to catch his eye, waiting for an explanation, but he keeps his focus pinned to the road ahead.

Irritation rises in my throat like bile. Apparently we can mindlessly flirt and eat pizza in bed and muse about my relationships with Carter and my sister, but that's it. My personal life is up for consumption. His is not.

WITH THE EXCEPTIONS OF ONE OF US COMMENTING ON DIRECTIONS OR ASK-ing to change the radio station, the next hour passes in silence.

I force my attention out the window, hoping the velvety farmland and winding country lanes will somehow unwind the knot of tension clenched inside me.

We're just passing signs for Northumberland National Park when the car gives a little thump followed by metal crushing against asphalt.

"What was that?" I ask, jerking my head up.

The muscles in Jack's jaw stiffen, but he doesn't say anything as he pulls us over to the side of the road.

"I don't know. Let me check it out," he says, killing the engine and hopping out of the car.

I hope Jack knows something about cars, because if we have to count on me, we will be stuck here forever.

I wait a full thirty seconds before I get out of the car.

"Everything okay down there?" I ask, craning my neck as he bends down to examine the car's underbelly.

"Tire's shredded," he says, shaking his head.

I take a peek and sure enough the entire tire on the back right-hand side is blown out, and all that's left are the shredded remains of rubber wrapped lazily around the rim.

Great. Just great. I knew this car was a bad idea.

"What are we going to do?" I ask.

"As long as this car has a spare, we'll be fine." Jack pops open the trunk and sticks his head inside.

"And if it doesn't?"

He stares blankly at me. "We die."

I purse my lips. Okay, not helping.

"Do you even know how to change a tire?"

"Yes, Ada," he says with a hint of annoyance like I've just suggested he doesn't know how to brush his teeth. "I can change a tire."

He pulls up the plastic bottom of the trunk to reveal a skinny spare tire.

"This will work." He removes his jacket and tosses it onto the passenger seat. Then he crouches down beside the blown-out tire to examine the damage. "Is there a wrench in the back?" he asks after a minute.

I scurry to the back of the car and peer inside the trunk. I don't even know what I'm looking for. What kind of wrench? Aren't there different types?

My eyes land on a metal cross. That must be it. I hastily grab it and hand it to Jack.

"Here," I say, pretending I'm totally confident I knew exactly what to look for.

He presses the wrench into the hubcap and begins to screw it (or maybe unscrew?) counterclockwise.

I find myself momentarily mesmerized by corded bands of muscle flexing under his forearms until he says, "Now I need the jack."

"The what?"

"The jack," he repeats, this time louder.

"Like your name?"

"Yes, the jack as in *me*," he says flatly.

"Jeez. You don't have to be so bossy," I mutter over my shoulder as I open the trunk.

The jack. I need to find the jack. What's a jack? I push aside an empty gas can and a box of jumper cables. What if there is no jack? What then? Are we stuck here forever? I have AAA, but I doubt that works in the UK.

Jack appears beside me, craning over my shoulder. "This," he says, picking up a diamond-shaped tool with springs. "This is a jack."

Not fair. I totally didn't even see that.

"Have you ever changed a tire before?" he asks.

I shake my head and Jack's eyes widen with surprise.

"No one ever showed you how? Not even your *perfect* boyfriend?"

Again, I shake my head. Carter was good at a lot of things, but he wasn't exactly Mr. Fix It.

"Come here," Jack says, ushering me toward him. "I'll show you."

I kneel beside him, pretending his firm but kind tone doesn't awaken little thrills across my body.

He begins to jack the car up. Oh. *The jack.* That makes sense now.

"We have to crank it up so that it takes the weight off," he explains, pointing to the crank. "Do you want to try?"

I take the crank and give it a push just like he did, but it doesn't move. "I don't think I'm strong enough."

"Here." He puts his hand on top of mine, guiding me.

We continue like that, muscles moving in tandem, using our combined strength (okay, fine, mostly his) until a water droplet lands on my face. For a moment I think I might have broken a sweat, until I look up and a few more land in my eyes.

"It's raining," I say, like that's not abundantly obvious.

"You can sit in the car," he says, eyes focused intently on the jack. "I'll get this done."

"No way. I'm not going to sit in the car while you get rained on." I reach inside the car and grab his jacket. "Here," I say, holding it up, outstretched, over his head. But my makeshift covering only works for a little bit until the rain starts coming down diagonally.

"You should get back in the car," he yells over the sound of the rain pummeling the concrete. "You're going to get soaked."

"It's fine! I'm from Seattle," I yell back.

Not gonna lie. It's sort of hot. Him, crouched on the side of the road, wet T-shirt sticking to the contours of his chest like a second skin, muscles flexing.

My mind flutters back to last night and a burning sensation floods my chest. As much as I enjoyed watching Jack sew delicate lace, watching him change a tire in a wet T-shirt is infinitely better.

But the warmth in my chest tells me it isn't just Jack's varied repertoire of skills that I'm finding compelling. It's the feeling of being cared for, of being looked after.

With Carter, it often felt like I was the one taking care of him, the one constantly managing his emotions, whether that be supporting his latest career endeavor or tiptoeing around the topic of marriage. But my feelings were my own to manage.

The same is true with Allison. I've always been the one looking after her and cleaning up her messes, and never the reverse. Which is fine. I like fixing things and taking care of those I love. But as I try not to stare at the stubborn piece of hair in Jack's eyes, or the single drop of rainwater taking a seductive stroll down his neck, I realize there's something nice about being the one told to sit in the car while someone else fixes it.

A few minutes later Jack announces he's done, and we climb back into the car.

It's not until I'm seated that I notice my bra is now visible through the thin fabric of my own wet T-shirt. My nipples are also hard as rocks, but I'm not entirely sure I can chalk that up to the cold.

"If you can see my bra, please don't say anything," I say, reaching for the heat control, which is of course broken.

"Don't worry," he says, eyes flashing to mine. "I won't say anything about your pink bra."

I roll my eyes and look away, pretending his words—and his gaze—don't awaken little thrills across my skin.

This morning I'd wondered if we were still strangers or if we'd made the jump to friends. But maybe we're neither. Maybe we're something else. Some blurry third option that I can't—or won't—name.

Chapter 15

46 HOURS UNTIL THE WEDDING

"Can we stop? I have to pee."

Jack groans. "You literally just peed fifteen minutes ago."

"But now I have to pee again," I tell him, knee bobbing up and down against the seat.

"Well, maybe you should have thought about that before buying a giant energy drink at the petrol station."

"I'm jet-lagged!"

"You're not the one who has to drive. Why don't you get some sleep?" he suggests.

"I can't sleep! What if you run us off the road and kill us both? I have to stay vigilant."

Jack snorts, but the barest hint of a grin worms around the corners of his mouth and I like it just a little too much.

I return my attention to the window, where I attempt to concentrate on the expanses of lush greenery and the crumbling exteriors of stone structures forgotten by time. But I'm finding it hard to focus. And not just because my bladder is full.

Jack's driving with one hand on the steering wheel and the other hand on the back of my seat. I can't explain why, but this position is disarmingly attractive, as is the still-damp T-shirt clinging to his chest, and I have to physically tear my gaze away when he asks me to check the directions on my phone.

As I reach for my phone, I realize that I haven't looked at it since yesterday. Usually I'm glued to it, checking to see if Carter's messaged me or if Allison needs something. But what with missing the train and the veil and, well . . . *Jack,* I guess I've been distracted.

I expect half a dozen to-do list items from Allison, but there's only one text. From Carter. Sent eleven hours ago.

My stomach plummets like I'm on that haunted elevator ride at Disneyland and my fingers fly across the screen to open the message.

CARTER
I hope you're having a good time in Ireland. I know we said we wouldn't discuss our relationship for another two weeks, but can we talk?

I read the message again, combing through each word like it's an ancient language only I can translate. But the more I read it, the less I understand.

Does this mean he wants to get back together? *Or* . . . My throat tightens. Does this mean he wants to break up for good?

My chest swells. My breath comes in small, shallow bursts.

I thought I'd have time to prepare. That we'd meet up in person. Or at least, I'd be given some kind of warning. I didn't think he'd text me out of the blue and just ask *to talk.*

"Ada?" Jack's voice is muffled and distant, like he's speaking through a homemade tin can phone. "What's wrong? Are you okay?"

It should be a simple question, but it's not.

"I'm fine," I lie, lips forming a thin line.

But Jack doesn't believe me because a moment later he's taking a hard left, pulling the car onto the shoulder.

"What is it?" he asks, voice thick with worry. "Are you feeling okay?"

I shake my head. "It's nothing."

"You look like you're going to be sick." He leans over the seat and pulls out a bottle of water he bought at the petrol station. "Here. Drink this."

I take the bottle and chug, grateful for something to do with my face and hands.

When I finish, I wipe my mouth with the back of my hand. "Now I'm definitely going to have to pee again," I tell him.

His eyes waver across my face. "What just happened?"

I chew on my bottom lip, debating the wisdom of telling him the truth. After all, he's made it clear he's no fan of Carter. But Jack's all I have right now. Besides, he's a guy. Maybe he can help me decipher Carter's message.

I hold up my phone, showing him the message. Jack takes it, and I watch out of the corner of my eye as his expression stiffens.

"What do you think this means?" he asks after a minute.

"I don't know," I admit. "What do you think?"

Jack looks past me out the window, where a flock of sheep is milling in a pasture adjacent to the highway. After a minute, he says, "I don't know Carter. I can't guess what he's thinking. But whatever it is, it sounds like it can't wait."

Something sharp pulses under my ribs.

"Does this mean he wants to get back together, and he can't

wait until I get home to tell me? Or maybe he's met someone else?" My throat shrinks, breath stuttering to a standstill. Just because my feelings toward Carter are complicated doesn't mean I'm ready to find out Carter's with someone else. Not now. Not like this.

After a handful of seconds, Jack's eyes lift to mine, studying. "Ada, forget about what he wants for a minute. What do *you* want?"

The question runs a few laps around my mind before finally taking hold. *What do I want?*

All this time I've been focused on Carter. On what Carter wants. On whether Carter will want to get back together with *me.* But I haven't stopped to consider what *I* might want. Or that I, too, have a say in the matter.

Do I want to go back to Carter because I'm afraid of losing the one constant in my life? Because I'm afraid, full stop? Or do I want something else? Something I haven't allowed myself to consider until now?

As if on instinct, my brain flicks back to last night, to Jack and me eating pizza in bed, laughing until our stomachs hurt, planning trips to Italy we'll never actually take.

It's not that I think that—whatever *that* is—is a realistic depiction of what I could have without Carter. But for so long I've convinced myself that life without the architecture of Carter would be terrible. That I'd be lost and rudderless. But if last night had been a tiny glimpse into what life on the other side could be like, then maybe the future might not be so scary.

When I look back at Jack, he's watching me with a kind of careful consideration, like he can see the heavy whir of thoughts pressing up against the inner walls of my mind.

I try to summon an answer to his question, but I don't know how to explain everything I'm feeling, all the words I'm still too afraid to admit, even to myself.

That I miss Carter, but that I also feel guilty for not missing Carter *enough*.

That I don't know who I am without Carter. But I'm starting to suspect there's a part of me that wants to find out.

Most of all I don't know how to explain the other thing, the thing that twists and flails inside me like I've swallowed something alive. I don't know how to explain what it feels like when Jack's eyes meet mine, or what happens to my stomach when he laughs. I don't know how to explain the jolt of electricity under my skin when we touch. Or how confusing this all is.

I don't know how to explain any of it, so I don't.

"How should I respond?" I ask.

Jack coughs out a strangled laugh. "I can't tell you what to say, Ada. That's up to you."

"I know, but should I text him back? Or should I wait? I wouldn't want to come off *desperate*," I add, giving Jack a knowing look.

He tilts his head, gaze narrowing in thought. "We're about an hour outside of Edinburgh. Maybe you should take the rest of the day to think about it. Decide what you want. Besides"—Jack checks the car's analog clock—"it's four a.m. back home. I doubt Carter's in a position to talk right now."

He's right. I have no choice but to wait and think.

Chapter 16

44 HOURS UNTIL THE WEDDING

When we finally reach Edinburgh, the sun is breaking through the wall of steely gray clouds overhead, sending beams of light like spotlights on a stage.

After we drop off the car at Mrs. Poyevich's brother's place and store our luggage in pay-by-the-hour lockers for backpackers, Jack and I waste no time exploring Edinburgh.

We start with high tea at the Balmoral Hotel on Princess Street, where we eat overpriced scones and tiny sandwiches while dodging disapproving looks from hotel staff for being painfully out of dress code. After we're stuffed with enough clotted cream and cake to make Marie Antoinette proud, we wander the narrow passages and cobblestone alleyways of Old Town leading up to Edinburgh Castle under the watchful eye of stone turrets and stained-glass windows and centuries of history.

As we climb the steep passages, I push all thoughts of Carter and the conversation we still need to have to the back of my mind, instead determined to focus on what's right in front of me: the sprawling view of Edinburgh. The stitch in my side. The damp air, threatening to turn to rain. The crooning voices of buskers on the Royal Mile. The thousand years of history all crammed into a narrow maze of cobblestone and brick, worn and weathered by time.

All around us the city hums with a kind of magnetic energy. A reminder that we are but transitory visitors in a long, rich history that started long before we arrived and will continue long after we leave.

It makes me feel alive in a way I haven't felt before. Like all my life I've just been wandering around in a zombielike haze until this moment when everything shifted from dull and faded to sharp and brilliant. Sounds feel louder, colors more vibrant. Even my body feels lighter, looser, like I've managed to shed twenty pounds in a matter of minutes.

I wonder if it's the magic of Edinburgh. Or if traveling always feels this way. But deep down, past all my excuses, I know that the quiet purr of contentment vibrating inside me isn't so much about where I am or what I'm doing, it's about who I'm with.

As we stroll in and out of kitschy souvenir shops and stores selling hundred-year-old whiskey, Jack tells me about playing Little League with Collin, and how his favorite birthday memory was going to the zoo when he turned ten. He tells me about staying at Collin's family's lake house every summer, and how when it was time to go home, he'd cry because he didn't want to leave. We trade stories about school dances and first crushes and bad teenage fashion choices (apparently Jack had an eyeliner phase in high school), and I absorb each detail like a sponge eager to soak up every last drop of him. But even still, I find myself greedy for more Jack.

Jack, who is funny and smart and does a terrible impression of a Scottish accent. Jack, whose body my subconscious can't stop tracking. I'm continuously aware of his proximity, his heat, the way his frame vibrates when he laughs, and all the accidental hand grazes I'm having a harder and harder time convincing myself are actually accidents.

AROUND MIDAFTERNOON, THE DARK CLOUDS CONGEAL AND THE SKY MORPHS from gray to a deep charcoal. And with cinematic timing, it begins to rain. Again.

I attempt to cover my head with my arms, but it's no use. Unrelenting streaks of cold rain pummel the cobblestone, soaking us for the second time that day.

"Come on," Jack says, taking my hand in his. "Let's get inside somewhere." This time the weight of his hand in mine feels natural, like a choreographed dance we've practiced before.

As he pulls along, it starts to rain harder, coming down in thick, heavy sheets, entirely different from the Seattle rain that rains *around* you rather than *on* you. It's raining so hard that it isn't until the door shuts behind us and we are safely out of the rain that I notice we've found our way into a bookshop. On either side of us, tall wood shelves form narrow rows, each section feeding into the next like a giant maze.

I'm so absorbed in the over-stacked rows of worn paperbacks and bright new releases that it takes me a moment to realize that Jack's still holding my hand. I wonder if it's unconscious, if maybe he's also too absorbed in the shop to notice. But after a few beats of continued hand-holding, it becomes apparent that that can't possibly be the case.

I decide to count to five, then I'll let go. But five comes and goes and I still don't let go. And neither does he.

My pulse ratchets up, loud enough that I wonder if he can hear it over the lo-fi beats playing in the background.

I should let go. *We* should let go. There is no reason for a pair of non-romantically involved adults to hold hands in a bookstore. But it's like the weight of his hand, the heat of his skin, is causing every last functioning brain cell to revolt.

I'm wondering how long we're going to do this, or if we'll be stuck in hand-holding purgatory forever, until a man bumps my shoulder from behind and I stumble forward. The man murmurs a quick apology, but the brief contact is enough to break the spell. Jack drops my hand like it's scalding hot.

"Sorry," he mutters. But he doesn't say it like an apology, more like the kind of offhanded *sorry* you mutter while sidestepping a stranger in the supermarket.

My cheeks grow warm, and in an effort to look preoccupied, I reach for the first book I see.

Men Are from Mars, Women Are from Venus.

Ah, yes. How appropriate.

I pretend to riffle through a few pages. But I can't focus. My brain is too aflutter, too scrambled, not with thoughts, but with flashes of sensory detail. The weight of his hand. The brush of his knee. The slow, easy curl of his mouth when he smiles and the cloud of sexual chaos that promptly rages inside me.

I try to tell myself I shouldn't feel this way, that it's not a good idea to continue harboring this crush on Jack when I know he and I don't want the same things, but the thought that was once loud and insistent dulls to a quiet murmur, waning under the pressure of too many feelings and not enough options to categorize them all.

"COME ON!" JACK URGES, HIS VOICE CARRYING DOWN THE HILLSIDE. ABOVE us the gray sky morphs into a light blue as the clouds shift and sunlight filters in through the gaps. I cast a quick look over my shoulder and I'm almost dizzy knowing how high up we are.

After the rain broke, Jack insisted we get a panoramic view of the city. I assumed he meant from the top of a tall building—*not* hiking to the top of an active volcano! But alas, here I am, halfway to the summit of Arthur's Seat, the main peak in Edinburgh's surrounding group of hills.

My thighs burn and sweat gathers at the back of my neck, but I push forward, knowing the view at the top will be worth it. That, and after days cramped in trains, cars, and airplanes it feels amazing to work my leg muscles and feel the fresh air on my face.

"How did you know about this hike?" I call ahead to Jack, who is a few feet in front of me on the path.

He turns around just as a gust of wind feathers across his hair, sending dark tresses into his eyes. "From this little-known travel guide," he says. "Maybe you've heard of it? It's called Google."

I laugh but my voice is lost to the wind.

As we climb, there's this steady beat inside me, the feeling of knowing this is exactly where I'm supposed to be right now. It's one of those rare moments, almost like an out-of-body experience, where you step outside yourself and think, *This moment, right here, this is what it's all about. This is what I've been waiting for.*

Not much farther ahead there's a bend in the path, and suddenly we are at the top of a ledge jutting over a cliff where we can see everything: Edinburgh Castle perched atop the rugged remains of an ancient volcano. Spires and steeples pressing skyward. A thick coat of mist from the earlier rain hovering just above the surface. It's eerie and powerful and just a little magical. The kind of scene I'd love to capture on canvas.

I imagine the broad strokes of green I'd use. The texture to show the grass rustling in the breeze. The way I'd mix the blue and black to get the gray color of the sky just right. I visualize the brush in my hand, hovering just over my blank canvas, anticipation coursing through me as nothing becomes *something*.

"I read that some people think this is supposed to be Camelot," Jack says, coming up beside me. "That's why they call it Arthur's Seat."

"I believe it," I tell him, finding it easy to imagine the sprawling expanse of green below as a magical kingdom.

Ahead of us, a group is taking photos and I find myself drawn to a woman with a sleeve, pausing on one design in particular, an intricate tree with roots stretching across her bicep. The line work is exquisite, and I can't help but feel like I've seen it before somewhere.

Then it hits me. *I have.*

My heart starts to race and, as if by impulse alone, I walk toward her, excitement building with each step.

"Excuse me?"

The woman turns to face me.

"Hi," I say. "I'm Ada. I don't know if you recognize me, but I did your tree tattoo." I point to her arm and she follows my gaze.

Awareness flows through her features. "Oh my gosh, of course I remember you! I spent six hours in your chair howling with pain. How could I forget?"

I laugh. "I'd know that arm anywhere."

She beams at me, clearly just as thrilled as I feel. "Wow. What a wild coincidence, running into each other all the way in Scotland!"

"Yeah, wild," I repeat. But it's not wild. *It's fate.*

"I heard you closed shop," she says. "Which is too bad. Your line work was phenomenal."

A blush crawls up my neck. "Thank you."

"I was hoping I could commission you for another piece," she says. "I don't suppose you take on freelance, do you?"

"Well—" I start to say, ready to give my usual diplomatic answer about how I'm not taking commissions right now, but just as the words start to take shape, so does an idea.

It starts as nothing more than an ember. A cautious little spark. But then it catches fire, rapidly expanding inside my brain until I'm consumed by the possibility of it.

Yes, I'm scared to try again. I'm scared to fail. I'm scared to be vulnerable with something as tender and delicate as my dreams. But I want this. Perhaps more than I've wanted anything in a long time. And before I can consider it further, I hear myself say, "I'm actually opening another shop."

Her eyes double in size. "Really?"

A million questions lurk under the surface. Questions I don't know the answers to. But what I do know is that right now, in this moment, I want nothing more than to do exactly as I've told this woman. I want to reopen the shop.

"Really," I confirm, this time with more confidence.

We talk for a few minutes more and she shows me some ideas she has for a sailing ship she wants on her left shoulder. Then we swap contacts and I promise to let her know as soon as the business is back up and running.

By the time the conversation ends, I'm a teakettle practically frothing over with excitement. And nerves. But mostly excitement.

It won't be easy, it will be really fucking hard, but this is something I want to work hard at.

"Who was that?" Jack asks after I say goodbye to the woman.

"*That* was a sign," I tell him, practically vibrating out my skin.

"What kind of sign?"

"Remember how I told you I always wanted to see one of my pieces in the wild?"

Jack looks over at the woman, now snapping a photo with her girlfriend, then back to me, understanding washing over his expression. "Wait. You did a tattoo for her?"

My head bobs up and down, eyes shining. "And what's even

better is that I think I just found my first client for the new shop! She asked me if I'm still doing custom work."

"And what did you say?"

"I told her I was."

Jack's gaze warms, the skin around his eyes crinkling. "That's great, Ada. What changed your mind? Besides fate," he adds.

I look around us, taking in the windswept plateau and the jagged cliffs falling off into an endless horizon. Maybe it's this beautiful place. Or the magic of traveling. Or maybe it's the fact that over the course of the last few days everything that could go wrong has, and yet somehow I feel a little braver, a little bolder, like maybe things not working out isn't always a bad thing. Maybe with rejection and failure also come silver linings and new beginnings.

"I don't know," I tell him. "I just feel confident, I guess."

His mouth stretches into a smile. "We'll have to celebrate later," he says, and I can't help the way my limbs feel almost jittery with excitement, like I'm overcaffeinated. It's not just at the idea of celebrating, but that there will *be* a "later." With Jack. The possibility of which balloons inside me until I'm practically levitating.

"That sounds great," I tell him. "But I kind of want to do something now. Something fun."

"Like what?"

My eyes dart across the expanse of grass then back to Jack. "How about cartwheels?"

Uncertainty flashes in Jack's eyes. "Cartwheels?"

"I haven't done one in years, and this"—I gesture to the grassy plateau—"is the perfect spot."

He shakes his head. "No way."

I put my hands on my hips. "And why not?"

"Because," he says, voice crackling with laughter, "I have a JD, Ada. I'm a serious person. I don't do cartwheels."

"Oh, you're a *serious* person? Were you a serious person when you were making fake sex noises last night?"

"I think you and I both know that was *very* serious business."

"Well, so is this. How about I do one first?"

I raise my arms overhead, look down at the ground, and aim. My hands squelch in the mud, and I kick one leg over my head and then the other. My shirt rides up and cold air hits my exposed stomach. I land with a flourish.

"Ta-da!"

Jack applauds and I do a little curtsy.

"Your turn," I say.

Jack steps back, as though afraid cartwheels might be contagious.

"Come on, just one. For me?" I give his wrist a tug. "Pleeeeeeeeease."

His mouth scrunches in the corner of his jaw like he's going to argue. Instead, he rolls his sleeves up past his forearms and I find my eyes homing in on the defined muscles popping under his skin.

"Fine," he says. "*One* cartwheel."

Jack screws up his face in concentration, shifting his weight back and forth like he's mentally preparing himself.

I watch him, waiting. But he doesn't move.

"Here," I say, stepping forward. "It's hand, hand, foot, foot." I mime the pattern for him.

"I don't need a lesson," he says with a *hmph*. Then he takes a deep breath and hurls his body toward the ground. Jack sticks out his arms just in time to not faceplant, but his legs aren't in the air fast enough and he tumbles into the grass, landing right on his ass.

For a moment I'm worried he's hurt, but a second later, Jack's face splits into a grin and he flops backward, laughing. "Am I dead?"

"Solid 9.76 except for the dismount." I sit down beside him, not even caring that my jeans instantly soak through in the wet grass. "Does anything hurt?"

Jack presses his palm to his forehead as though assessing for damage. "Just my ego. I think it's bruised."

"The Lord has to keep you humble somehow."

I lie on the grass beside him, heads pressed together. We're close enough that I can smell his cologne. Tangy with something sweet.

"See, wasn't that fun?" I tease.

"No."

"Come on, Simone Biles, don't lie. You know it was fun."

He rolls over onto his side, facing me. "I think I liked watching you do it better."

I give him a jab in the ribs, and he cocks his head, mouth sliding into that easy smile when he knows he's being cute.

It's funny how after only a few days together I already know some of his mannerisms. The glint in his eyes when he's trying to get a rise out of me. The crease in his forehead when he's thinking. The curl of his lips when he's trying not to laugh. Each expression is like a puzzle piece, although what it all adds up to, I'm not sure yet.

"We should take a picture," he says after a minute.

"So you can remember your failed Olympic dreams?"

"I never take photos anymore," he says with a shrug. "It's like the last year of my life never existed." His tone is easy, but I can tell there's something he's not saying.

I shift closer, letting my hip nestle against his. "Why not?" I ask.

"I guess it wasn't worth remembering."

Again, he shrugs, like it doesn't matter, but a shadow passes over his eyes, and I can't help but wonder if it really wasn't worth remembering, or if he doesn't *want* to remember it.

The thought makes me sad, not just because it's depressing, but because it's a clear reminder that despite the last few hours together, he's still keeping me at arm's length. Close enough to tell me about Collin's lake house and hold my hand in a bookstore, but not close enough to tell me about the hurt draped across his face like a heavy curtain.

Jack holds up his phone and we put our heads together, beaming into the front-facing camera. Our cheeks are rosy from the cold and our hair sticks out as a breeze ripples past.

As we freeze on his screen, caught in place, I wonder how I'll remember this moment a year from now, two years from now. Will Jack and I be friends? Will we still talk? Or will he be a stranger from my past? Someone who drifted into my life for three days and then drifted back out. The thought forms a wedge in my throat that I can't seem to swallow past.

After he snaps the photo, he stands up, wipes his palms on his now-wet jeans, sticks out his hand to me, and helps me to my feet.

"Here. You've got . . ." He reaches to wipe blades of grass from my hair and goose bumps spread down my arms like wildfire.

"Thanks," I say, voice snagging.

He blinks at me, and I can feel him trying and hesitating to speak before he says, "I found something you might like."

My insides give a little skip. "You did?"

His mouth moves into an uncharacteristically shy smile as he holds out his hand, showing me a perfect four-leaf clover sitting in the middle of his outstretched palm. The ultimate symbol of luck.

A gasp breaks in the back of my throat. "How did you find this?"

"I might have been keeping my eyes open for one."

My limbs suddenly feel unsteady, one strong gust away from toppling over.

"I thought you don't believe in luck?" I ask.

"I don't. But you do." He holds up the clover, eyes landing on the spot behind my ear. "May I?"

I nod and he gently moves my hair away from my face, tucking the clover behind my ear. His fingers brush along my scalp and everything in me squeezes tight.

When he pulls back, I strike a little pose, one hand on my hip. "What do you think?" I ask. "Do I look lucky?"

He studies me a minute before answering, and I feel his eyes everywhere, like he's taking me in, particle by particle. "You look happy," he says at last.

"I am happy," I tell him. And I mean it. For the first time in a long time, I feel hopeful. And not just about Sleeve It to Me. But about everything.

I don't know what's going to happen, or what Carter's going to say when we finally talk, but maybe that's okay.

I think about the past few days, how seemingly nothing's gone to plan, how pretty much everything that could go wrong has, and yet I'm okay. A little jet-lagged. A little sweaty. A little broke. But *okay,* nonetheless. Maybe that is yet another sign. A sign that no matter what's next, I'll survive.

As we make our way back down the hill with muddy clothes and sore cheeks, Jack's earlier question surfaces inside me like a clump of ice lodged in the back of my head that little by little has begun to thaw its way free.

What do you want?

This, I think. *I want this.*

This high of being here, on a windswept plateau overlooking a beautiful city, exploring new places, trying new things, doing cartwheels and making plans with men who smell tangy and musky with a hint of something sweet. Whatever this feeling is, I want more.

Yes, I'm scared to let go. To be alone. To fail. To divest myself of the future I've pinned the last eight years on.

But past the fear is a flicker of possibility. It's tiny, nothing more than a glint in the dark. But it's enough. Enough to push me over the edge, headfirst into the unknown.

Chapter 17

40 HOURS UNTIL THE WEDDING

After the hike, we both collapse onto the bus to Cairnryan, sweaty, a little out of breath, and very, very happy.

We sit in comfortable, tired silence until Jack says, "I got you something else," before reaching into his luggage, wedged between his knees.

"Another four-leaf clover?" I ask excitedly.

He shakes his head, grinning. "Better." Then he hands me a pocket-sized guide to Paris.

I suppose the right thing to say would be, *Wow, thanks so much*, or *You shouldn't have!* But instead, what comes out is, "When did you get this? We've been together every second of the day."

Jack laughs. "Well, not *every* second of the day. I saw it in that bookshop in Edinburgh and thought of you."

His words have a ripple effect that starts in my throat then slowly sinks lower into my chest and then my stomach, spreading outward as though putting down roots.

"What's it for?" I ask, brushing my thumb over the spine.

"Well, most people read books, but I guess it might make a nice coaster too."

I give his arm a whack. "Okay, smartass. I mean why'd you get me this?"

"I thought you'd like it. That maybe you could use it when you go to Paris."

My heartbeat stumbles, then fully trips over itself. *He not only remembered that I want to go to Paris but bought me a book about it? In the hopes that I'd go?*

I don't know what to think, or say, only that there's a slow and steady pulse pressing against my sternum, the kind that feels like wishing on a star or a birthday candle. Like wanting something so bad that you can feel it thumping inside you, magnified and electric.

"Thank you," I say after a beat. "That was really thoughtful."

"You're welcome."

I study Jack, eyes narrowing in consideration.

"What?" he asks, voice laced with a half laugh.

"You're secretly a softy, aren't you?"

Jack presses a hand to his chest, clutching metaphorical pearls. "I am *not* a softy."

"You totally are," I say, poking him in the ribs. "But don't worry." I lower my voice to a whisper. "I won't tell anyone. Your secret softy persona is safe with me."

Jack snorts, but not before I catch sight of the trail of pink climbing his throat.

"I hope you make it to Paris someday," he says with resolute stiffness. "It's a great city."

"I hope I do too," I tell him.

And this time I mean it.

Jack casts me a half smile before returning his gaze to his

phone. I try to focus on the passing Scottish countryside, but the same heat I'd felt when we held hands in the bookstore returns, this time deeper, like it's managed to burrow under my skin, running through my veins like jet fuel.

AFTER AN HOUR, JACK DOZES OFF.

When I look over, the first thing I notice is how cute he looks when he's asleep, all soft-jawed and peaceful. The second is that he's still got his phone in his hand. A new message flashes on the screen and the phone buzzes, but he doesn't wake up. Curiosity prickles inside me.

I can't say I'm not tempted to take a peek. He's so private. Meanwhile, I've told him so much about me.

I really shouldn't . . . but I'm already leaning over far enough to catch a quick glance at his screen where the message appears in a flash before the screen goes black.

LEXI

Can we grab dinner when you get back?

I want to see you

My entire body jolts as though zapped by electricity.

Lexi? Who's Lexi? A hookup? Someone he's casually seeing? A figure skater?

Jack shuffles in his sleep and I quickly turn toward the window, pretending to be engrossed in the passing scenery.

It shouldn't matter who he's talking to—or sleeping with. It's absolutely not my business. But I can't help the stab of jealousy, followed in quick succession by a hot whoosh of embarrassment. I've known the guy less than three days. We're road trip buddies who sometimes hold hands in bookstores and buy one another thoughtful gifts. But that's it. I have no right to feel jealous. And this inconvenient crush on Jack is just that. *A crush.*

But unlike the long, painfully drawn-out crushes I used to harbor in high school—the kind that I'd nurse and tend to for years—this one comes with a hard expiration date.

Tomorrow we'll arrive at the wedding and *this*, this confusing, tightly wound thing between us, will unspool. I'll go back to my life, and he'll go back to his—a life of *Lexi*s and mysterious phone calls he doesn't want to talk about.

I, TOO, MUST DOZE OFF BECAUSE I'M JOLTED AWAKE BY THE BUS COMING TO a stop.

"Ada." My eyes flicker open and Jack's blurry face comes into view.

"Huh?" I blink a few times before realizing my head is nestled into the crook of Jack's shoulder. I sit up straight, now instantly awake. "Shit. I'm sorry. I didn't mean to fall asleep on you."

His gaze bounces over me, jaw ticking as he swallows. "No worries."

After grabbing our things, we disembark with the other passengers whose final stop is Cairnryan, a sleepy seaside village comprised of a single high street and a port where we'll catch the ferry to Belfast in the morning. It's totally different from the electric thrill of Edinburgh, but charming in its own cozy sort of way.

By the time we arrive at the small guesthouse next to the ferry terminal, dusk is settling on the horizon, painting the sky in stripes of candy-colored pinks and purples.

Fortunately, this establishment doesn't ask if we are married, and we check into our room, a dated second-floor walk-up with a lingering odor of cigar smoke and dark green, seventies-esque bedspreads, without issue. This time there are two single beds.

Good, I tell myself. Physical distance is probably for the best. Not just because in a matter of hours we'll arrive at the wedding and our time together will end, but because Jack and I don't want the same things. He's been very clear about that, and so have I.

The last few days have existed in a bubble. A bubble that will soon pop without guarantee that our friendship—or whatever this is—will continue past it. It's best not to get too attached.

AFTER WE PUT OUR STUFF IN THE ROOM, JACK AND I DECIDE TO CHECK OUT the pub because, as he puts it, *What else are we going to do?*

I expect the place to be quiet—after all, the village is a single street—but to my surprise, the pub is packed.

"This must be the spot," I yell, trying to be heard over the din of conversation and drunken laughter.

"Must be," Jack yells back.

The crowd pushes against us like a heavy tide and Jack takes my hand, guiding me past the throngs of inebriated patrons crowded around worn wooden tables and a long, polished bar.

We manage to snag a booth near the back, then Jack disappears to order us drinks. A handful of moments after he's gone, his phone vibrates from where it sits face up on the table. I can't help but wonder if it's more texts from Lexi.

But before I can indulge yet another masochistic urge to snoop, Jack returns, holding a bottle of Scotch and two glasses.

"Hey," I say in my best *I totally wasn't looking at your phone* voice.

"Hey." He casts his phone a glance where it continues to vibrate in the center of the table.

"Looks like you're pretty popular," I say.

Jack takes one look at the screen, frowns, then shoves the phone into his pocket. "It's just Collin."

"Everything okay?"

He gives me a sidelong glance, two ridges forming between his brows. "Just wedding stuff."

"Not a strip club catastrophe, I hope," I tease, but either Jack doesn't hear me or it's more *personal stuff* he doesn't want to share, because he reaches for the bottle of Scotch and pours two glasses.

"You got a whole bottle?" I ask, casting the fancy label a dubious glance.

"It's our only night in Scotland. Go big or go home, right?" He sees the look on my face and adds, "My treat."

"You've already been so nice to me. Let me buy."

I'm almost positive I can't afford it. But I hate the thought of owing Jack. At least more than I already do.

Jack shakes his head. "No way. You've got a business to save up for."

My cheeks warm, flattered. "Are you sure?"

"Consider this an investment in your new venture." He nudges a glass toward me. "Now, drink up."

I eye the contents of my glass. "You're not trying to get me drunk, are you?"

"Why would I? You've already told me all of your secrets."

"Not true. I didn't tell you where my tattoo is," I counter.

"You mean the one on your ass?"

"It's not on my ass."

Jack laughs, a low, throaty sound that nestles in the hollows of my stomach. "How many drinks is it going to take to get you to tell me?" he asks, eyes steadily holding mine. "Because I'm prepared to stay here as long as it takes."

"As generous as that offer is, maybe it's time for you to tell me some of your secrets."

"I don't have any secrets," he says a little too quickly.

"Liar. Everyone has secrets."

He leans back in his seat, a flicker of intrigue in his eyes. "Fine. Let's have a drink, and maybe you'll find out."

Jack lifts his glass, eyes finding mine. I do the same.

"What are we toasting to this time?" I ask.

His expression turns pensive. "How about to Sleeve It to Me 2.0?"

I can't help but smile. "Do we still need to make eye contact?" I ask. "Or are we good on the whole seven years of bad sex thing?"

"One can never be too careful," he says, giving me a look that scorches right down my center.

"To Sleeve It to Me 2.0," I say, glass hovering midair.

"May she rise again," Jack agrees.

He clinks his glass against mine and we drink. The Scotch tastes hot and smoky, like bottled flames. When we finish, we both slam our glasses on the wooden tabletop.

"So, have you thought more about what you're going to do?" he asks. "About, you know . . ." His voice trails off, but I know what he means.

My eyes shoot down, suddenly afraid to verbalize the thoughts that have been swimming in the periphery of my brain all day.

It's one thing to *think* about not going back to Carter, and another thing entirely to say it out loud. Like saying it will make it real.

"I have," I say at last.

"And?"

I take a deep breath. "After I lost the business and things fell apart with my sister, I think I clung to Carter because he felt like the last thing in my life I could count on. But then that fell apart, too, and suddenly it felt like my whole world was crumbling around me and there was nothing I could do but hope Carter would want me back. I felt lost and helpless, like my life wasn't really mine and I was just in a holding pattern waiting for Carter to come back and rescue me from the uncertainty. But I don't want to live like that anymore."

As soon as I say it, I expect the swift ache of fear to take hold. The sinking feeling that I've made a mistake. Instead, I feel lighter, like the laws of gravity have been lifted and now I'm free-floating, a bodiless version of myself.

"And it's not just about Carter," I continue. "For so long, I've let my relationships with others define my identity. I'm Allison's big sister. My mom's eldest daughter." I wave my hand as though gesturing to invisible versions of them.

"I'm not even totally sure who I am without those relationships reflecting my identity back to me, telling me who I'm supposed to be and what I'm supposed to do." I pause, searching for the words that have haunted me all day. "But maybe this is a new beginning for me. A chance to figure out who I am apart from the people in my life who expect things from me. To figure out what I want."

Jack nods, dark eyes focused on mine with a gaze so intense I imagine my words are electric currents transmitting directly to his brain. "And what do you want?" he asks.

I chew on his words, savoring the question. It's the same one he asked me hours ago, but now I think I have a better idea how to answer.

"I know it's risky, but I want to reopen Sleeve It to Me."

A grin tugs at the corners of his mouth and I mirror his expression. "You should do it," he says with the same levity as when he told me I should go to Paris. Like it's easy. Like all I have to do is reach out and take it.

"And I want to move out of my parents' house, and I want to paint again," I tell him, voice speeding up with excitement. "And I want to fall in love. Not yet, not right now, but when I'm ready, I want to find the kind of love my mom and stepdad have. The kind where the future is full of unknowns and uncertainty, but we choose it anyway, because no matter what happens, we'll be in it together."

Maybe it's the alcohol coursing through me, or the speed with which I'm talking, but when I finish, I'm breathless, cheeks stained in swatches of heat.

Jack's eyes glow, turning from inky black to a warm brown. "You should get all those things," he says. "You should get everything you want, Ada."

I shoot his glass a suspicious look. "*You* should stop drinking whatever is in there immediately because I'm pretty sure they've laced it with something."

A smile plays on his lips, but it's worn down, hidden behind a sharp range of shadows and the same haunted look I saw last night.

Under the table his knee bumps mine. I bump him back.

Chapter 18

38 HOURS UNTIL THE WEDDING

There's a small stage behind our table where a band picks up their instruments.

The first song is morose and thick with emotion—something about a woman whose lover has left for battle—but since I'm not exactly fluent in the Scottish brogue, I only catch about twenty-five percent of the lyrics.

The next song is lively and the crowd claps along as the fiddler plucks the strings with a surgeon's precision. I'm a little (okay, a lot) tipsy from the Scotch and I sway back and forth to music in a happy, drunken stupor.

As the song ramps up, people pair off and begin to dance, bodies bouncing through the jaunty notes.

"Want to dance?" Jack asks, holding out his hand to me.

I look down at his outstretched palm, and I'm briefly reminded of my earlier resolution to create more space between us. But now, several drinks in, with my resolve weaker and my inhibitions lower, I take his hand.

As he leads me away from the table, cutting a path toward the band, the churning crowd presses against us, sending me right into Jack's chest. He grips my waist, steadying me.

"You okay?" he asks, dropping his mouth to my ear, where hot breath tickles my skin. I nod as my stomach fights a series of roller-coaster-style dips that don't have anything to do with the Scotch.

The beat picks up and his fingers fold around me, pulling my body flush against his. My chest flutters from the closeness.

We rock back and forth, swaying outside the beat until he catches my eye and we both laugh, aware that neither of us has any idea what we're doing.

"I don't know the steps," I admit.

"Me either. We'll have to make them up."

We turn and spin until I'm dizzy and laughing and not entirely sure which way is up. But what I am sure of is that I like Jack's hands on my waist. I like our bodies pressed together. I like it *a lot*.

I wait for thoughts of caution reminding me that this isn't a good idea, that we shouldn't be so close, but they don't come. Instead, alcohol pumps through me, clouding over the rational part of my brain, blurring out any earlier resolutions I might have made.

I'm no longer thinking, just feeling. Feeling his fingers skating along the band of my jeans and the tantalizing way his knee parts my thighs, gently coaxing them apart.

We're close enough that I can count every freckle on his chin, every crease in his forehead, and I find myself wondering how many hours I'd spend in front of a canvas trying to get the shade of his mouth just right. How it would feel to press my lips to his. To taste him. To have his scent draped over me like a blanket.

He's saying something, and by the way his eyes flash, I know it's supposed to make me laugh, but I can't focus. I can't hear anything except the crescendo of my racing pulse.

I fake a laugh, pretending to have heard what he just said, but Jack knows me too well.

"Ada?"

"Hmm?"

"You okay?"

No. No I'm not okay.

"Just dizzy," I lie.

Searching eyes fall heavily on mine, then lower, dropping to my mouth. I'm not sure who leans in first. Maybe it's him. Or maybe it's me. But his day-old scruff brushes against my jawline, and everything slows to an exaggerated pace, distorted and warped like it's happening inside a fishbowl. Even the music has dulled to a low thump in the background.

I wait for one of us to pull back, to acknowledge that we're way too close, touching in too many places, but I don't move. And neither does he. Instead, we linger, lips hovering centimeters apart, close enough that it's hard to tell which shaky exhale is mine and which is his.

He shifts nearer, lips grazing my cheek, and I wonder with almost feverish desperation if we're going to kiss. Or if we'll float in this decadent purgatory forever. But just as my heart crawls into my throat with anticipation, the music stops, and the moment expires with it.

A round of applause breaks out around us, but neither of us pull away. We stand there blinking and immobile like the lights have just come back on in the movie theater and we're unsure how to reenter reality.

But even though we've stopped moving, it feels like we're still spinning. Or maybe like the room itself is spinning.

My first thought is that I'm dizzy from dancing, but then my stomach rolls and all thoughts of Jack and his mouth instantly disappear as I bend at the knees, overcome by a wave of nausea.

Jack places a protective hand on my lower back. "Ada? What's wrong?"

"I don't feel good," I tell him.

"Let me get you some water."

But I don't have time to wait for water, because I feel the Scotch about to make a reappearance. I turn on my heels and elbow my way through the crowd. My feet scrape against the sticky wood floor, followed by desperate hands pushing open the door. As soon as I'm outside, my mouth stretches wide, accepting deep gulps of cool air.

I must have drunk more than I thought. Probably because I was distracted. Jack Houghton is officially a health hazard.

"Ada?" I open my eyes. Jack is standing in front of me, face clouded with worry. "Your face is green."

Great. Green isn't my color.

My insides lurch, and I put my hands on my knees, waiting for the inevitable. One shaky breath later, the contents of my stomach empty out all over the concrete.

Jack pulls my hair from my face, while his other hand rests on my lower back, rubbing in slow circles. "You're okay," he whispers.

My eyes burn and my legs wobble and I stumble, falling clumsily into his chest. "I'm sorry," I whisper. "I drank too much."

"There's nothing to apologize for." His arms wrap around me, pulling me into his warm chest.

I nod helplessly, eyes welling with tears. I don't really know what I'm crying for—if it's shame or disappointment or the overwhelming surge of every repressed feeling I've tried to pack away over the last few days—but suddenly it's all frothing toward the surface, spilling down my cheeks in thick, wet streaks.

The rhythmic tempo of Jack's hand stroking my back stops,

and I worry I've officially scared him off. But then he leans in, close enough that his stubble scrapes my cheek, and says in a voice so soft and gentle it comes out more like a whisper, "Come on, let's get you to bed."

"Jack—" I start to say, but before I can protest, he scoops me up in his arms, cradling me against his chest, and carries me away.

Chapter 19

37 HOURS UNTIL THE WEDDING

Jack's hands sink to my hips, contouring to fit the shape of me as he sets me down on the single bed closest to the bathroom. I assume I'll feel some level of simmering humiliation in the morning when I'm hit with the reality that Jack literally carried me to bed, but right now I'm too drunk and too dizzy to care.

"Carrie Underwood was right," I say with a groan. "I should stick to fruity little drinks because I *cannot* shoot whiskey."

Jack's laugh echoes all the way from the bathroom, where he's filling up a cup in the sink. When he returns, he sits beside me at the foot of the bed. "Here. Drink this," he says, nudging a cup of water in my direction.

I take one look at the cup, wonder if I might puke again, then swat his hand away.

Jack's mouth twitches with amusement. "Oh, so you're this kind of drunk?"

"I'm *not* drunk," I protest.

False. I'm *definitely* still drunk. And the room is spinning. Or maybe I'm spinning. It's hard to tell.

"Come on, please just drink your water," he says, giving me an insistent look.

"Fine. You're so bossy."

I take a few dainty sips until he gives me a look, and I begrudgingly finish the glass, wincing as I taste the acid on my tongue.

"You feel better now?"

Jack's face zooms in and out of focus, eyes too big for his face, body all out of proportion. I feel like I'm inside a Matisse painting.

"The room won't stop spinning. And you have two heads," I tell him. "You should probably get that checked out."

He laughs. "I might have two heads, but you have vomit on your shirt."

I look down. Dammit. He's right.

"I'm gonna grab you a clean shirt, okay?" He moves toward my suitcase, but I shake my head. Confusion threads through his expression. "You'd rather wear a shirt covered in puke?"

"I don't want you looking in my suitcase," I say, words all slurring together in one long breath.

He frowns. "Don't tell me you're the one with cocaine after all. Because that would be quite the plot twist."

"I don't want you to see my vibrator."

As I say it, I'm only vaguely aware that I shouldn't.

Jack cocks an eyebrow. "You think I haven't seen a vibrator before?" he asks.

"It's embarrassinggggg," I whine, covering my face with my hands.

There's a flicker of surprise behind his eyes, but just as quickly as it appears it fades into something unreadable. "Fine. I'll get you one of my mine."

Jack rummages in his suitcase before returning a moment later with a T-shirt.

"Arms up," he instructs, and I raise my hands like a toddler, letting him guide me out of my shirt and into his. It's big and soft and smells just like him. Tangy with a hint of something sweet.

I reach for the button on my jeans, but I'm too drunk and my fingers can't get a hold of the metal.

"Jack? Can you help me?"

Jack's jaw tightens, the lines between his eyebrows sinking into deep ridges. "I'm not sure that's a good idea," he says at last.

"Please? I don't want to sleep in jeans."

His mouth flatlines, but he steps toward me and brushes my hands away so he can finish undoing the buttons.

"Lift your hips," he commands.

You're going to regret this tomorrow, a panicky part of my brain whispers, but I do as I'm told anyway, too drunk to care that Jack's undressing me, or that I'm wearing underwear that looks like it should say *Tuesday* on the back.

He shimmies my jeans down my legs and tosses them onto my suitcase, where they land in a crumpled heap.

"I'm gonna take a shower," he says, turning toward the door like he can't get away from my pants-less body fast enough. "Yell if you need anything."

"Jack?"

He pauses, turning back to face me. "Hmm?"

"Can I ask you something?"

His eyes stall on me and I love the way they look right now, brimming with light and warmth and heat.

"What would have happened if we'd hooked up that first night?"

There's a part of me that knows I shouldn't ask, but I'm too drunk to remember why. All I can think is that I want to know. I *really* want to know.

Jack's eyes go wide like a deer in the headlights. "What?"

"What would—"

"No, I heard you, I just . . ." Jack rubs the side of his face with the heel of his palm, eyes snapping toward the bathroom door like he's looking for an escape route. "I don't know. I probably would have kissed you," he says at last.

Heat pours over my skin, slipping into all my nooks and crannies.

"Then what?" I ask, heart skipping a feverish beat.

Jack swallows hard, eyes sliding into the carpet, and my pulse jumps in anticipation. But when he looks back at me, his gaze is hard, resolute. "You should get some sleep, Ada."

He lets his attention linger on me a beat longer before disappearing into the bathroom. A moment later, I hear the shower turn on.

The room is still spinning, and dizziness presses against the back of my throat. I shut my eyes and rest my head against the mattress before tumbling into a fevered, drunken sleep.

***

A DISTANT TRILL PULLS ME FROM UNCONSCIOUSNESS, AND I SLOWLY BLINK back the haze of sleep. The room is dark except for slices of moonlight sneaking past the curtains, painting stripes of pale light across the carpet. Through the darkness I can see Jack's shadowy form asleep in the other bed.

The trilling sound continues, and it takes me a moment to realize that it's my phone.

I'm about to silence my phone when I see the name on the screen.

It's Carter.

His name acts as an instant shot of espresso, peeling back the blurry film of sleep as I reach for the phone. But I'm too late and the call goes to voicemail. A second later, a text pops up on the screen.

CARTER
Can we talk?

I look at the time. It's two a.m. here, which means it's six p.m. back home. Part of me wonders if I'm still too drunk, too sleepy for this. I could go back to bed and sleep off the remaining dregs of drunkenness and talk to him when I'm fully sober. But another part of me wants to just get this over with.

Fingers racing, chest thumping, I type a response. Gimme a second

Three dots appear, telling me he's typing.

CARTER
Okay

I pull on a sweatshirt and slip outside, where pale moonlight casts shadows along the hotel walls. Overhead, a sugary smattering of stars flecks the inky sky. My bare feet sting against the cold concrete and I shiver, pulling my sweatshirt closer to my body. In the distance I can hear the shouts and laughter of merrymakers outside the pub.

I take a deep breath and press the receiver to my ear. He picks up on the third ring.

"Hey, Ada." His voice comes through smooth and achingly familiar. My heart squeezes. "How are you?" he asks.

"I'm good. Or as good as I can be at two a.m."

"Shit, I'm sorry. I forgot about the time difference. Is now a bad time?"

"It's fine," I tell him, sneaking a glance back at the hotel room door, hoping Jack really is sound asleep.

"I'm glad you answered my text," he says. "I got worried when I didn't hear from you."

"Sorry, I just, uh . . ." I look out into the blackness stretching in front of me. "It was a long day."

"Wedding stuff?"

I don't really want to explain the whole flight cancellation and road trip with Jack situation, so I say, "Yeah. Sort of."

"So . . ." There's rustling on his end and I wonder if he's pacing like he usually does when he's nervous. "I wanted to see if we could talk when you get back from Ireland."

"Talk about what?" I ask, trying to keep my voice even and not like my heart is hammering wildly inside my chest.

There's a pause before he says, "About us. About getting back together."

Suddenly, I'm queasy all over again. But this time it has nothing to do with Scotch.

"I know we have two more weeks before we said we'd talk," he goes on, voice speeding up like he's in a hurry to get it out. "But I miss you, Ada. I've been thinking about you going to Allison's wedding alone, and I realized how much I wished I was there. With you."

My stomach jolts, a million warning bells clamoring in my head.

Carter misses me. Carter's been thinking about me. Carter wants to get back together.

In every imagined version of this scenario, I thought I'd be thrilled. That my insides would turn warm and gooey. After all, this was what I wanted. What I've been waiting for. It's the exact scene I dreamed of all those nights I slept with my phone on the highest volume just in case he called. Instead, it feels like there's a heel on my windpipe, blocking my airflow.

"Ada?"

It takes me a minute to realize he's saying my name.

"Ada? Are you still there?"

Somehow, I find my voice and creak out an unsteady "Yes. I'm here."

"I'm going to Moab next week to do some freelance photography," he continues. "And I was thinking you could come with me." There's a thread of earnestness in his voice that makes my heartbeat stumble over itself. But there's no apology. No, *I'm sorry for walking away when you needed me most.* He just expects me to go to Moab with him, like this break was just a little blip in the road. Like I'm a career he can just bounce back to at his leisure. Like I didn't cry myself to sleep for weeks over him.

I press my palm to my forehead. "Carter, this is a lot to think about."

"I know, it *is* a lot, but it would be good for us to talk and spend time together."

"Carter, I—" But my breath stalls and I lean against the cold concrete, legs suddenly wobbling like jelly. "I don't know," I finish.

"You don't know if you want to go to Moab?"

"No, not Moab . . ."

For a moment I consider how easy it would be to tell Carter, *No, of course I want to get back together.* How easy it would be to slide back into our old life. To pick up where we left off and pretend like the last few days hadn't happened—hell, like the last three months hadn't happened.

I imagine him picking me up from the airport. Me moving

back into his place and us resuming our life. The clockwork regularity of date night on Saturdays and takeaway pastries from our favorite coffee shop on Sunday mornings. I'd be lying if I said there wasn't at least a small temptation to return to normalcy. But the truth hammering inside me, the truth that's now impossible to ignore, is that I don't want that anymore.

It happened quickly, like a trail of dominos tipping over in rapid succession. But now that I've removed the blinders and started to see my life—*our life*—for what it was, I'm not sure I can put them back on. I'm not sure I can go back to the way things were.

I think about what Jack said when we walked to the pizza shop, about being with someone who is all in. Maybe there was a time when Carter was *all in*, when I was his person and he was mine. But he hasn't been for a while, and I can't go back to waiting on a proposal that may never come, just like I can't go back to managing his emotions and walking on eggshells, all while negating my own needs. Most of all, I can't return to him because I'm afraid of change. Because I'm afraid to let go.

It's not fair to me. And it's not fair to him either.

I take a deep breath. "I don't think it's a good idea to get back together, Carter."

For a long moment he doesn't say anything, and everything in me pulls tight, bracing myself against whatever's coming next.

"I thought you'd be happy," he says at last. "I thought you'd want to get back together."

Me too.

"I did," I tell him. "But I realized some things over the last few days."

"Like what?" I can hear the tug of irritation in his voice, like he's annoyed I'm not leaping at the chance to get back together.

"Like I don't think we want the same things anymore," I tell him. "I don't think we've wanted the same things for a long time." I pause, collecting my breath. "And I think it's time to end things. For good."

There's some shuffling on his end before he finally asks, "Is there someone else?"

A hot whoosh of awareness rips through me.

I can still feel Jack's hands on me. The weight of him pressed against my chest. I can still smell the Scotch on his mouth as he'd leaned in, lips hovering above mine. I can still feel the excitement in my belly as I wondered if Jack would kiss me. Jack, who is sexy and thoughtful and makes me feel cared for. Jack, who *doesn't* do relationships.

"No," I tell him. "There's no one else."

"Oh." But I can't tell if there's relief or frustration behind that *oh*. "So this is about me?" he asks.

"No, Carter," I say, voice tightening. "It's about me. It's about the fact that I'm not sure who I am outside this relationship, but I want to find out. On my own." I'm surprised by the evenness of my tone and the clarity of my words, and all the while my heart is pounding against my ribs. "I think it's for the best. For both of us."

Silence stretches between us, and I don't realize I'm holding my breath until finally I release a shaky exhale, watching the hot air rise like plumes of smoke.

"Maybe you're right," Carter finally says. "Maybe this is for the best."

I wait for the precipitous lurch of my stomach. The feeling of being knocked off my feet as my world crumbles around me. Instead, his words wash over me with an unexpected calmness. Like we're both taking one big, collective exhale and releasing the coils of tension that have been wrapped around us for too long.

The seconds mesh into a silent minute, filling with all the

other things I think about saying but decide not to. We make lofty promises to talk again when I get back, with the full knowledge that we probably won't. Then the phone call ends, and so does our eight-year relationship.

For good this time.

Chapter 20

35 HOURS UNTIL THE WEDDING

As soon as the call ends, I wait for the surge of absolution. The calm acceptance that I've done something empowering. After all, I know ending things with Carter was the right thing to do—the necessary thing—but my heart hasn't quite caught up with my brain just yet. It's still sore and bruised and tender, and I sink to my knees, crushed by the weight of it.

Once I start crying, I can't stop. I cry until I'm choking on my own breath, eyes blurring, throat raw.

But I know, in between inelegant sobs, that the sheer volume of tears can't be explained by Carter alone. It's not just the end of our eight-year relationship that I'm crying over. It's *everything*. It's the sharp, painful release of hope. The unknown of what comes next. The ache in the hollow pit of my stomach, reminding me that the fantasy I'd clung so tightly to was nothing more than a mirage.

I think back to what Jack said the night we met, about everyone being the villain in someone else's story. All this time I thought Carter was the hero in mine. The knight in shining armor. The handsome prince. But he wasn't. He wasn't the villain either. He just *wasn't right*. And somehow that quiet truth is almost harder, more painful to accept.

I'm crying so hard I don't hear the door open or the footsteps on the concrete until he's standing over me.

"Ada?"

I jerk my head upward to see Jack, barefoot, wearing boxer briefs and a wrinkled T-shirt that clings to his chest like a second skin. His hair is a mess, and his eyes are still bleary with sleep. But as soon as his gaze meets mine, his eyes widen with concern.

"What's wrong?" he asks, squatting down beside me. "What are you doing out here?"

"Nothing." I look away, trying to hide my tearstained face.

"Ada." His voice softens. "What's going on? What happened?"

Maybe it's the slice of moonlight painted across his face, or the tenderness of his voice, but something about it coaxes the words to the surface.

"I . . . I . . ." I choke on the words, my voice snagging as a tearful hiccup escapes me. "I ended things with Carter. For good."

Jack doesn't ask any questions. Not *when* or *why* or *how*. Instead, he pulls me into him, hard body melting against mine as he strokes my back.

There's a brief moment of hesitation, a quiet reminder that I shouldn't, but the thought is muted against the warmth of his body, and I burrow into him, letting him take my weight as I collapse into a fresh wave of tears.

I should probably be ashamed of the fact that I'm sobbing into the chest of a man I've only known a few days, that I've soaked his shirt with my tears, but it feels good to finally release the pent-up swell of emotions I've clung to for months.

Of course I've cried over Carter since the break. But always in private. Alone. Where no one could see me. Where no one could worry about me or ask questions I didn't want to answer. But as Jack's hands travel up and down my spine in comforting waves, I allow myself to relax into him, dissolving into the warm, solid weight of his arms.

"Well, aren't you going to say it?" I say after a minute.

"Say what?"

"*I told you so.* You were right. I was wrong. About all of it."

His hands halt their movement and I watch Jack's expression, aware of the slow path of his mouth as it moves from surprised to something else. Something sharper, more rigid. After a minute, he says, "I don't think you were wrong, Ada. I think you were *brave*."

I blanch, taken aback. "Brave?"

Slowly, he nods. "I think it takes a lot of courage to not only walk away from a relationship that's not serving you, but to still believe that real love is out there, and to be vulnerable enough to keep looking for it."

If I wasn't so shocked, I'd laugh. "But . . ." I frown, searching his face. "Aren't you going to tell me that love's a social construct? That I'm foolish for wanting to find it?"

He doesn't answer right away. Instead, his jaw tightens, brows clenched in thought. Finally, he says, "I think you deserve to find someone who is willing to do whatever it takes to be with you. Someone who is all in. Someone who understands how epically funny and sexy you are . . . I mean, *fuck*." He shakes his head. "If Carter didn't spend the last two and a half months wondering how the hell to get you back, then . . ." But I don't get to hear what Carter should have done because his voice trails off, cheeks turning pink.

Sexy?

Did Jack just say I'm sexy?

"What I'm trying to say is that I've been that guy, Ada. The guy who was willing to do anything to be with a girl. And you don't wait around. You don't ask for breaks. You don't lead her on for eight years. I know what it's like to be willing to crawl over broken glass to be with someone. And when you really love someone, that's what you're willing to do." His voice stretches, a beat of desperation coursing through his words, and I can't help but feel like the rug's been pulled out from under me. Since when does Jack Houghton know what it means to fall in love?

"What are you talking about?" I ask. "I thought you *expiration date* or whatever?"

His jaw muscles clench as silence swallows up the air between us. Finally, he says, "I'm getting divorced, Ada."

I blink once, twice.

Divorced?

But that can't be right. In order to get divorced, you have to first be married, and Jack doesn't do commitment. He thinks marriage is a scam.

I sit up, eyes latching to his. "What are you talking about?" I repeat. "You shit on marriage and relationships—" But I stop myself when I see his face visibly sink.

"Ada . . ." He draws a shaky breath. "It's all a fucking way to cope, okay?"

I try to untangle what he's just said, to fit it into what I know about Jack. But it's like I've started watching a movie from the end, and now I have no idea what's going on.

I study the downward tilt of his mouth, the sag of his features, the way the outdoor lighting casts hazy shadows across his face, and slowly the truth bobs to the surface, clear and unfoggy in a way it wasn't before.

Jack is getting divorced.

Because Jack is married.

His words shift inside me like sandstone, slowly rearranging the landscape of my memories over the past few days. The phone calls. The texts. Everything he said on the train. The fucking gift card he's getting Allison and Collin. All of it reshuffles in my brain until finally it forms a recognizable image. Something that makes sense.

There's so much I want to ask, so many things to unpack, but all I can manage is, "The phone call the other day with that guy, Doug, that was about your divorce, wasn't it?"

He lets out a long sigh and rubs the heel of his palm against his temple.

"That was my lawyer. Her and I been separated for almost a year, but we're finally making it official."

We. There's something so belabored about his use of *we,* like the mere utterance of the pronoun is exhausting to him.

"The whole thing's been a disaster," he continues, eyes going dark. "She wants the house. We've been fighting over it for months."

She wants the house.

The question appears on my tongue, even though I think I already know the answer. "What's her name?"

"Lexi."

"Lexi," I repeat, trying her name out. It tastes like salt when you expect sugar.

Lexi, who still texts him. Lexi, who wants to *grab dinner* when he gets back. The knot in my throat tightens like a noose.

"Why didn't you say something?"

He sighs, features withering. "Maybe I didn't tell you the truth for the same reason you kept telling yourself you wanted to get back with Carter—because it's easier that way."

His eyes flash to mine like he can see me all the way down to my splintered center.

"You were right the other day, when you said I was cliché," he goes on. "*The guy who engages in meaningless hookups with women whose names he won't remember, professing he doesn't fall in love.* Couldn't have said it better myself," he adds with a humorless laugh. "I'm the cliché, cynical divorced guy trying to fuck my way out of being depressed. And spoiler alert, it's not going very well."

It takes me a minute to realize he's quoting me, but when I do, pangs of unease twist and flail inside me.

"I shouldn't have—"

"Don't," he says quickly. "You were right. And I'm sorry I didn't tell you. I should have been honest."

"It's okay," I whisper, placing a hand on his shoulder. "It wasn't my business."

He shakes his head, frustrated. "No, I should have told you. It wasn't fair of me to keep that from you, not when you were so transparent with me."

Our eyes latch, an unspoken thread of thoughts siphoning between us.

"We don't have to talk about it if you don't want to," I tell him.

That's not necessarily true. I want to hear about it. Every word. I want to know all about the woman he had been in love with, maybe even is still in love with. But I also want to be sensitive.

For a long moment he doesn't say anything. He looks past me, out into the expanse of darkness around us. I watch him, uncertain if this is where the conversation ends.

After a beat, he says, "Lexi and I rushed into things. It was like everything was in fast-forward with us. We were reckless and in love, and a whirlwind wedding felt like the right thing at the time. In retrospect, I think we both felt like we had to rush, because if we stopped to contemplate what we were doing, we wouldn't have done it."

He pauses, expression wavering as a riptide of shadows washes over his face.

"Things were always rocky with us," he goes on. "But I thought that's just what passion looked like. I thought that was just what couples did. They fought. They yelled. They said things they didn't mean. They left for days without notice only to come back and make up.

"Then the fighting reached a boiling point that was unsustainable, so I insisted we start going to couples counseling. But things didn't get better. We kept fighting. The same fights over and over again. Like it was the hurdle we couldn't seem to clear. Everything always went from zero to sixty. It was like there was something about the other person that just set us both off." His shoulders slump as though the weight of trying to figure it out is a burden he's stilling carrying.

"A year ago we decided to separate. I didn't want the separation, but it seemed like the best idea at the time. I think in the back of my mind I figured we'd work it out and she'd come back." He pauses, deep lines bracketing either side of his mouth. "But she didn't. Instead, she told me she wasn't sure she ever loved me and that she wanted a divorce."

For a long moment neither of us says anything. We hover there, the space between us shrinking like someone's swallowed up all the oxygen.

I search his face, trying to find the right words. "Do you think there . . . ?"

"Do I think there was someone else?" he asks.

I dip my chin into a timid nod.

The creases around Jack's eyes deepen. "I don't think so. Or at least when I asked her, she said no. I think she was just unhappy, something that compounded over time until she realized she didn't want to be married anymore. That she didn't want *me* anymore."

He sounds defeated, resigned, like the cocky, self-assured man

I've slept beside the last two nights has burned off, leaving behind only the charred, broken bits. It makes me ache in ways I don't think I fully understand.

"I've thought about it a lot," he says. "I've replayed it over and over, trying to figure it out, like it was some kind of relationship Rubik's Cube, and if I could just crack it then I could fix things."

"It's not your fault," I tell him. "You can't blame yourself."

"I know. But maybe that's worse. Like there was nothing I could do. She just didn't love me anymore."

As he says it, his whole body sags, exhales coming out shallow, like he's just tumbled over the finish line, out of breath and out of steam.

He looks so raw right now, and for a minute I just stare at him, attempting to contend with the unfamiliar expressions of hurt and vulnerability I've only ever caught stray glimpses of.

A new ache emerges as the remaining pieces shift into place. Jack's guardedness. His comment about crawling over broken glass for someone he loved. Why Jack had had such strong thoughts about Carter.

It wasn't because he was a cynic. Or even judgmental. It was because he'd been hurt. *Badly.*

The ache builds to a deafening throb, pounding in my ears, indistinguishable from my own pulse.

When I finally speak, my voice comes out as raw as I feel. "I'm so sorry, Jack," I whisper. "I'm so sorry she hurt you." I reach for his hand, tentatively lacing my fingers through his. He squeezes my hand back, and for a long moment neither of us says anything. We just stay like that, hands clasped in the darkness, a new kind of wavelength vibrating between us.

Our pain might come in different shapes and sizes, born of different circumstances, but here, in the shadows, fingers intertwined like lifelines, it's hard to see where my hurt ends and his begins.

"She still reaches out sometimes," Jack says after a minute.

I think about the text I saw. My chest tightens.

"What does she want?" I ask.

"She says she wants to talk. Always framing it like I'm the one who won't give her a chance." He shakes his head, a ripple of frustration crossing his face. "Sometimes I think she's just trying to fuck with me. Like she wants to prove I still have feelings for her."

"Do you?" I ask. "Still have feelings for her?"

I feel like I'm poking a bruise to see if it's still sore, but I can't help it.

He lets out a belabored sigh, dark eyes trailing down to the ground. "She was my wife. We talked about having kids and growing old. We made vows to one another. We had a life together. I can't just pretend like none of that happened. Like the last five years hadn't been real. But sometimes I wish they hadn't. Sometimes I wish I'd never met her." He winces like the words taste bad.

I squeeze his hand. "Trust me. I get it. I . . ." But I let my voice trail off and instead wrap my arms around him, pressing my face into the crook of his shoulder. Jack's body stiffens with surprise, but slowly, he gathers me into the solid warmth of his chest.

I can't say for sure, but something about the way he's clinging to me makes me wonder if he's talked to anyone about this. Or if he's been carrying this burden alone. The thought makes my heart ache all over again, and I hug him tighter, willing my body to say all the words I can't form.

I'm sorry she hurt you.

I'm sorry you've been carrying this alone.

I'm here.

For a long moment, neither of us move. We stay there, both of us holding one another until Jack pulls back, limbs jerking upright.

"Fuck. I'm sorry," he says, brow scrunching against the moonlight. "You're upset about Carter and I just made this about me. Jesus, I feel like an asshole right now."

I shake my head. "No, it's okay. I'm glad you told me. I'm here if you want to talk about it . . . or not talk. That's cool too." I give him a reassuring smile.

He holds my gaze a moment longer before pulling me back into his chest. "I'm sorry about Carter," he murmurs into my hair. "I'm sorry it ended the way it did."

"I'm just glad you're here," I whisper back. "I know you didn't have a choice and we sort of just ended up on this trip together, but I'm glad it was you I got stuck with."

He holds me tighter. "Me too."

Jack draws his thumb up and down my spine, and I allow myself to sink into him, feeling the warmth of his body and the slow, methodical rise and fall of his breathing. *Thump. Thump. Thump.*

He's safe and warm and for the first time I allow myself to seriously wonder what could have happened that first night. If Jack had tried to kiss me and if I'd let him. If I'd said, *Fuck Carter,* and slept with Jack.

It probably would have been a mistake, but what if it hadn't . . . ?

I think back to the pub, what could have happened—what almost did—and I'm filled with an insatiable tug of *what if.*

Maybe it's not the most appropriate thought to be having right now when he's just told me about his divorce, but I feel greedy for him. Like now that he's let me in this much, it's not enough. I want more. I want to break open the tiny crack in his wall until I can see everything. Until I can have all of him.

I'm not sure who catches whose eyes. Maybe it's him, or

maybe it's me. But our eyes latch and I wonder if he's thinking the same thing. If he's tormented by the same *what if* I am.

My skin singes with the memory of his hands on my waist. Of his lips hovering over mine. The brief moment where I'd wondered, with almost feverish hope, if he'd kiss me.

The memory falls around me like a heavy curtain, blocking out everything else, and the confusing tugs of want that have coalesced around the edges of my mind all day bob to the surface, this time louder, more urgent.

There's a tiny voice in the back of my head that wonders if I'm moving on too fast. If I ought to slow down, grieve Carter a little more. But I don't want to slow down. I'm tired of waiting for someone else to make me happy. Maybe I'm finally ready to chase what *I* want.

What if. The words pound against my skull, egging me on.

What if.

What if?

Maybe it's the final remnants of Scotch still circulating in my bloodstream, or the warm, fuzzy feelings of shared intimacy, but before I can consider it a moment longer, I lean in, cupping his jaw in my hands, and press my lips to his.

A surprised groan vibrates in the back of his throat as our mouths meet, and I draw a sharp breath, inhaling his scent, feeling his body seize against mine. But as quickly as it starts, Jack places a hand on my shoulder and gently pushes me away.

I shrink back, cheeks burning. "Ohmygod. I'm so sorry!"

"Don't be." But his eyes are wide like he's caught under a spotlight.

I press a hand to my forehead like I might be feverish.

I don't know what came over me. I thought we were having a moment. I thought . . . But all the rationale that had made perfect sense seconds ago dulls under the heady pressure of his gaze.

"I'm sorry," I say again. "I don't know what I was thinking."

"It's fine," he says, looking anything but fine. "You're . . ." He falters, expression softening. But it's not the way someone would look at a lover, more like how a parent might look at a small child who has fallen and scraped their knee. Like he feels sorry for me.

"I'm *what*?" I ask, voice stretched thin.

"You're still drunk. And you're upset about Carter. You're emotionally . . ." He twirls his hand in the air, grasping for a word. "*Emotionally vulnerable.*"

Who is he trying to convince here? Me or him?

Frustration and shame twist together, forming one long braid inside me. Shame that I just did that. But also frustration that he didn't kiss me back. That he'd looked at me like that. That he'd let me believe he might want this too.

I'd seen the way he looked at me in the bookstore. The way he'd held my hand too long. The way he'd pulled me close on the dance floor.

"So what?" I ask, shifting back, away from him. "The other night you were ready to fuck after a couple of beers, and suddenly you've got a conscience?" As the words tumble out of me, hot and heavy, I know I'm being unfair, especially if the roles were reversed. But I'm mad. Mostly at myself. Mad that I allowed myself to get caught up in him and this ill-advised crush.

Jack shakes his head, exasperated. "No, Ada. That's not it."

"Then what is it? Tell me." I search his face, silently begging him to tell me he wanted me the way I wanted him. But he looks away.

"We should go to bed," he says.

"Jack—"

"You should get some rest. We both should." There's a finality to his voice that feels like a heavy door closing in my chest.

I open my mouth to protest, to accuse him of something, but nothing comes out.

He stands up and gives me his hand. I look down at it. He's offering me an alibi. And I ought to take it. I ought to play along. Agree that I'm still drunk as I stumble on my way to bed. Maybe even slur my words. Whatever I need to do to absolve myself of the mess I've just made.

But the truth is I'm not drunk.

I knew what I was doing. I wanted to kiss Jack. *I still do.*

Chapter 21

29 HOURS UNTIL THE WEDDING

When I wake up the next morning, everything hurts and my mouth tastes like the floor of a public restroom. Not that I know what that tastes like from experience. But based on the sour taste coating the back of my throat, I can guess.

"How do you feel?" The sound of Jack's voice rumbles in my eardrums like thunder in the distance, slowly pulling me out of the thick haze of sleep.

"Like I'm gonna die," I say, pressing my thumbs into my temples.

"Just wait until you get to your thirties," he says. "You won't be able to have one drink without getting a hangover."

"Great. So much to look forward to." I shut my eyes, willing the pain in my head to stop. "Will you please just toss my body into the sea? Tell my parents it's what I wanted."

"You mean after all this trouble to get to the wedding? No way. You're getting there dead or alive."

I try to laugh, but my throat is too sore.

"Our ferry leaves in thirty minutes. Are you gonna get up?" he asks. "Or should I plan to deliver you to this wedding in a body bag?"

"I'm getting up," I tell him. "No need to call the coroner yet."

I start to crawl out of bed when my eyes snag the unfamiliar logo emblazoned across my chest. *Portland State.* Wait a minute. This isn't my shirt. Why the hell am I wearing this?

Jack must notice the confusion on my face because he says, "You can keep it if you want. I have like three of those shirts."

My blood runs cold, unsure whether to focus on the fact that I'm wearing *his* shirt—which smells like him—or the question of *why* exactly I'm wearing it in the first place.

"We didn't . . . ?" I start to ask, but Jack shakes his head, features turning stony.

"No. Nothing happened," he says quickly. "You threw up on yours, so I loaned you mine."

Oh.

I freeze in place as, little by little, memories of last night thaw their way free. The pub. *Wayyyyy* too much Scotch. Dancing. Throwing up. Jack carrying me to bed. The phone call. Carter. Then . . . Oh God . . . *the kiss.*

No, correction, not *the kiss*. The *almost* kiss. The *rejected* kiss.

I wince. How is it possible that Carter and me officially breaking up wasn't the worst thing that happened last night?

I look down at the bed, wondering if there's any chance I can crawl under the covers and hide for, say . . . *eternity*? But considering we have to leave in thirty minutes, a world-ending meteor is probably the best I can hope for.

When it appears that's not likely, I climb out of bed—tugging at the hem of his shirt to make sure it covers my ass. At least I'm wearing underwear. So that's something.

"You want some coffee?" he asks.

I perk up. "You have coffee?"

"And a croissant."

My mouth instantly waters, embarrassment momentarily subsiding in favor of a much more pressing need. Carbs. I *need* carbs.

Jack hands me a waxy bakery bag and a coffee-to-go.

Is this some kind of peace offering? A symbolic gesture of *you tried to kiss me last night but it's okay, I forgive you*? But I'm too hungry to care.

I greedily bite into the flaky, still-warm croissant. "Oh my God," I groan as crumbs cascade down my chin. "Where did you get this?"

"There's a café just around the corner."

"Please tell me you didn't get up and go for a run?"

He winces. "No way. I'm too hungover."

Our eyes meet and the contact feels like friction, a subtle acknowledgment of what happened last night.

Part of me wants to talk about it. To get it all out in the open. If nothing else, then we can move on. But another part of me wants to pack the whole messy affair away and pretend it didn't happen. Anything to shield myself from the stomach-churning embarrassment that charges through me every time I look at Jack.

But what bothers me the most isn't that I kissed Jack. Or even that I embarrassed myself. It's that there's a part of me that thought Jack would *want* to kiss me back. That whatever carefully managed self-control had snapped in me might also snap in him.

I think about the way he held my hand in the bookstore. How I'd caught him looking at me. The way he'd opened up to me about his divorce. How close we'd danced last night.

At the time, those had felt like tiny stars in a bigger constellation proclaiming that perhaps my crush on Jack wasn't entirely unrequited. But maybe it had all been in my head. A byproduct of too much Scotch and close proximity. Or worse, maybe *I* had been the one to throw myself at him, acting off illusory clues and invented signs.

He called me sexy—that, I can be sure of—but maybe he'd meant it in a *you're objectively attractive* sort of way, and not in an *I really want to kiss you right now* sort of way.

But it's also possible that he hadn't wanted to kiss me given the circumstances. After all, I'd been crying over my ex. And there's a high probability that I was covered in snot and still smelled like vomit. Not exactly hot. Or romantic.

"Ada?"

I jerk my head up, facing Jack.

"You gonna get ready?" He taps his index finger against his Rolex. "The ferry leaves soon."

Right. The ferry that will take us to the wedding where we will go our separate ways. The beginning of a gradual distancing, a slow but painful fade into oblivion.

But maybe this is for the best. Not just because of what happened last night, but because no matter how I spin it, we're two ill-fated meteors destined for implosion. He's getting divorced and I just got out of an eight-year relationship.

The flimsy logic that had egged me on last night now feels utterly laughable. An obvious blip in judgment.

What did I think was going to happen? That we'd kiss and he'd declare his feelings for me? That he'd sweep me off my feet, take me to bed, and make love to me? Tell me I was some kind of exception to literally everything he'd told me about himself? Then we'd ride off into the sunset together?

Not likely.

But as much as I try to convince myself it's all for the best, it doesn't stop the pound of want aching inside me, the feeling of being homesick for somewhere I've never been.

I'm sure there's a long, eloquent German word with too many consonants to describe exactly what I'm feeling, but right now it just sucks.

ONCE ON BOARD THE FERRY, WE STAND ON THE OUTER DECK, WATCHING AS the Scottish coastline disappears into a misty haze.

I lean against the railing, letting the crisp sea breeze lick my face. Jack stands beside me, a careful distance between our hips. We haven't spoken since our brief exchange this morning, but I feel the tension drifting between us like smoke from an invisible fire.

I wonder if this is how it will be from now on. Awkward silences and careful avoidance.

I look down into the steely gray water, watching the whitecaps tumble and roll in the frothy sea, not entirely dissimilar from the waves in my own stomach. I sneak a peek at Jack, who doesn't seem to be faring any better than me. His head sags at the neck, face the color of ash. I wonder if he's going to puke.

Things might still be awkward, but our mutual hangovers have at least leveled the playing field.

After a moment, I say, "I'm sorry about last night. It wasn't fair of me to get mad at you."

Jack lifts his head, bloodshot eyes focusing on mine. "It's okay," he says. "You were upset. It was a mistake."

I search his face, trying to discern whether he means *I* thought it was a mistake. Or if he's calling it a mistake. But there's a guardedness to his expression, like whatever walls came down last night have been hastily reconstructed.

"You're right," I say after a beat. "I was upset. It shouldn't have happened."

He nods and I watch the column of his throat slide up and

down as he swallows. "It's better this way. It would have made things too complicated. No mess, no fuss. Right?" He catches my eye, giving me a knowing look, like he expects me to agree.

No mess, no fuss? I know what he means, but somehow hearing our would-be kiss described as a paper towel ad leaves me feeling queasy. Is that what he thinks of me? Messy? Fussy?

But it doesn't matter, because he's right. It would be *too complicated.* If anything happened between us, he'd be able to walk away unscathed—just another hookup with an expiration date. Meanwhile, I wouldn't be able to untangle myself so easily from the growing web of feelings I have for him.

Offer's expired, he'd said at the inn.

At the time I'd thought he'd been trying to save face after I rejected his proposition. But now I wonder if he'd known something I hadn't. If he could tell I was attracted to him and was merely trying to protect me. If he'd realized that I wasn't someone for whom casual entanglements would bode well.

Thick strands of embarrassment wind around me. God, I feel like a teenager all over again. Like I'm fourteen, nursing a painful crush on a hot senior.

But there's still time for me to fix this. To save face.

"I'm sorry," I say again.

"Don't be." Then he gives me a look that I interpret to mean, *You're forgiven, let's just drop it.*

"Can we still be friends?" I ask.

His eyes move back and forth across my face, expression draped in uncertainty. Finally, he says, "Of course we can still be friends." But he doesn't sound enthused as much as resigned, like the idea of being friends with me is a plea deal he's been forced to accept.

I wait for the swell of relief. The feeling of having cleared a major hurdle. Instead, I feel like a trapdoor has opened up beneath me and suddenly I'm in free fall, no solid ground to catch me. Because as much as I'd like to forget all about last night and move forward as *friends,* I'm not sure I can be just friends with Jack.

He's drawn a bold and totally obvious line in the sand, lining it with caution tape that reads, *Danger, do not come any closer, I am emotionally unavailable,* and suddenly I'm hopelessly illiterate.

Chapter 22

23 HOURS UNTIL THE WEDDING

Ashforth Castle, once the ancestral home of nobility, is now a luxury hotel and Condé Nast Top Ten destination where people with way too much cash can live out their wildest fairy-tale wedding dreams.

I press my nose to the glass as the cab takes us down a tree-lined drive framed by rolling green pastures and manicured gardens. At the end of the drive, spiraling turrets covered in tendrils of ivy peek above the treetops. I can't believe *this* is where Allison is getting married. In a *literal* castle. I turn to Jack, eyes wide, mouth agape.

"I don't think we're at Mrs. Poyevich's inn anymore," he whispers.

We share knowing smiles, the kind that make me think—if only briefly—that maybe we really can be friends.

After we've collected our luggage, we walk up the carpeted stone steps and into the gilded lobby, where crystal chandeliers hang from ornate wood-paneled walls and plush, velvet armchairs surround a crackling wood-burning fireplace.

A doorman in coattails and a top hat tips his brim to us and ushers us toward the front desk. "Checking in?" he asks in a thick Irish accent.

I'm about to respond when out of the corner of my eye I spot my mom tottering toward us in square heels and a too-tight skirt. From afar she looks perfectly made-up, but as we get closer, I see the web of stress lines stretched across her forehead, and the messy flyaway grays dotting her scalp tell me she's been running nervous fingers through her hair.

"Ada," she says, wrapping me in a tight hug as though I've just returned from war. "We'd almost given up on you."

"Hi, Mom." I hug her back, inhaling the familiar scent of cloves and lemon soap.

"We were so worried! Are you okay?" She pulls back as though trying to account for missing limbs.

"We're fine," I tell her, catching Jack's eye. "Everything's fine."

"Good. Good."

She forces a tight smile, which only accentuates the creases under her eyes. I doubt she's slept much since they arrived, and I feel an instant stab of guilt for not being here sooner.

"How's everything been?" I ask. "Anything I can help with?"

"Everything's fine. Well . . ." She pauses, lips squeezing like she's tasted something sour. "Not *fine*. I've had to go over the dinner menu three times since yesterday. And it looks like it might rain tomorrow, but I haven't heard anything about a contingency plan and—"

I place a tender hand on her shoulder. "Don't worry. I'm here now. I'll take care of it."

Her lips thin into a smile, relief sweeping across her features.

My mom and I have always had a good relationship, mostly because we know our roles. She's the worrier, and I'm the eldest daughter who knows how to come in and fix things.

"Hello, Mrs. Gallman," Jack says, stepping out from behind me. "I'm Jack Houghton, Collin's best man."

He sticks out his hand and her eyes instantly brighten in a look I know well.

Great. We haven't been here five minutes and she's already moved on from contingency plans to assessing Jack as a *potential suitor for my daughter.*

I should have warned him.

"Pleasure to meet you, Jack." She takes his hand and gives it a squeeze. "And what do you do?"

Cutting to the chase, I see . . .

"Mom—"

But she waves a hand, cutting me off.

"World's oldest profession, I'm afraid," he says with a self-deprecating grin.

"Prostitution?" I supply.

My mom shoots me a death glare.

"Close. Lawyer, actually," he says, an easy smile spreading over his features.

Her eyes widen like a lioness who's just caught sight of a zebra. "A lawyer? Really?"

"Okay, well, I think we should get checked in to our rooms so we can change for the rehearsal dinner, right, Jack?" I say, giving his arm a firm tug.

But my mom keeps her eyes trained on Jack, completely ignoring me. "So, Jack, do you have a date to the wedding?"

Oh God. Subtlety has never been her strong suit.

"Uh, no. I don't." He gives her a strained smile.

"So your girlfriend couldn't make it?"

I sincerely wish I could whack her over the head right now.

He coughs out what I can tell is a fake laugh. "No girlfriend."

"Oh. That's too bad." Her mouth twists into an unconvincing pout.

"Mom, we *really* need to get settled into our rooms . . ."

"I just wanted to say how thankful I am that you and Ada were able to travel together," she says, continuing to ignore me. "Thank you for looking out for her."

"That's kind of you to say, Mrs. Gallman, but I think we looked out for each other." His eyes snap to mine, holding my gaze with a kind of heated intensity that makes my skin prickle.

I wonder if he's thinking about last night. Because it's suddenly *all* I can think about.

"Please, call me Christine," my mom says. "Now, come on. Let's get you to your rooms. I've already got your room keys."

She ushers us through the lobby and past a decadent tearoom where a harpist serenades diners.

"Sorry about that," I whisper to Jack as we follow a few steps behind her. "You can just ignore her."

"She seems nice," he says, eyes sparkling in the low lobby light. "Very . . . *enthusiastic*."

"Careful," I warn. "If you get her to like you too much, she'll try to set us up."

His brow tenses, considering. "That depends. Are you guys one of those families that do fun runs on holidays?"

"We're not monsters, Jack."

A grin ripens across his mouth, but there's a hesitancy behind it like he's aware the teasing is a mask, one we're currently both employing.

My mom leads us past a grand staircase, toward a set of elevators, and I quicken my pace to keep up.

"Jack, you're in three ten." She hands him his room key. "And

Ada, you're in three-oh-four, just down the hall." She hands me my key, then leans in and whispers, "Is there something going on between you two?"

My face bursts into the heat of a thousand suns. "Mom!"

She looks at me like I'm an avocado that's about to go from ripe to rotten at any moment. "What? I'm just asking. He seems like a nice young man."

Clearly, Allison hasn't told her about the Slovakian figure skaters.

"No," I whisper back. "There's nothing going on."

"Are you sure?"

"*Pretty sure,*" I say through gritted teeth.

Her face falls, but just as quickly, it's swallowed back up with a determined smile. "In that case, there's someone I want you to meet later. You remember Tom, right? The neighbor's son?"

"Not really."

"I texted you about him earlier. The engineer."

"Oh. Right." My gaze flits to Jack, who is either very absorbed in the zipper on his suitcase or pretending not to listen.

"He just bought a house, you know." My mom continues. "He's looking for a wife. Very stable man."

"Mm. Nothing gets me hot and bothered like *stability.*"

She gives me an aggrieved look. "He's a nice young man, Ada."

Talking to Stable Tom is pretty much the last thing I want to do, but I know it will make her happy and when it comes to making it through this wedding weekend, it's optimal that I keep everyone happy.

"I'll talk to him," I tell her, corralling my mouth into something resembling a smile.

She beams. "Great! I just know you'll hit it off!"

Doubtful.

I wave my mom off, telling her we'll see her at the rehearsal dinner, then Jack and I step inside the elevator.

"So, Tom, huh?" he asks as the elevator lurches upward.

I shake my head, exasperated. "We haven't even been here five minutes and my mom's already trying to play matchmaker."

"But didn't you hear? He's *stable*."

Jack's eyes catch mine, flashing with a kind of awareness, but I don't know if he means it as an innocuous tease or a subtle hint that I might have better luck with Stable Tom than him. Either way, I look away, fighting back the tightness in my chest.

Not a moment too soon, the elevator dings and we step into a plush carpeted hallway.

"I'm going to change, then I'll meet you in the lobby so we can go into the rehearsal dinner together, okay?"

"You don't have to wait for me," I tell him, not wanting him to think he's still obligated to hang out with me. We're here. We made it. The terms of the deal have been fulfilled.

"I want to."

"Oh . . ." I search for a loophole, something to mark this as the moment our journey ends, but I come up short. "Okay," I say at last. "I'll see you in twenty minutes?"

He nods and silence stretches between us, waiting to be filled, but neither of us does. I turn toward 304.

"Ada?"

I hate the way my heart beats hopefully against my ribs as I turn back to face him. "Yeah?"

He opens his mouth then closes it right away. A beat of stillness follows.

"See ya," he says at last.

"See ya," I repeat. Then I turn and walk toward my room, feeling his gaze on me the entire way.

Chapter 23

22 HOURS UNTIL THE WEDDING

As soon as I enter my hotel room, I understand exactly how Mia Thermopolis must have felt when she was first shown her royal bedroom in Genovia because *holy cow* is this room amazing.

My eyes zip from the floor-length windows draped in plush velvet curtains to the massive four-poster bed in the center of the room.

I can't believe I complained about coming to this wedding. I take it all back. Especially the part about the *overpriced castle.*

I sink into the zillion-thread-count bedding, already plotting how I can stay wrapped in this glorious duvet instead of going to the rehearsal, but alas, I think someone might notice if the maid of honor doesn't turn up.

I open my luggage, searching for the black midi skirt I packed for the rehearsal dinner. I used to call it my *date night skirt* because I would wear it out with Carter. He said he liked it because it made my ass look good. And he was right.

After I add a black halter top, a pair of dangly earrings, and a pop of red lipstick, I head back down to the lobby in search of Jack. I'm turning the corner past the elevators when I spot familiar broad shoulders straining under a charcoal suit jacket, that even with his back turned to me, I can tell fits Jack in all the right places. Standing opposite him is Collin, dressed in a dark navy suit, hair combed back like a nineties Wall Street tycoon.

I wait for Collin to notice me, but his eyes stay grounded on Jack, expression darkening. "I'm freaking out," he says, voice a low rasp. "What if this whole thing is a mistake?"

"It's not," Jack says, shoving his hands into his pockets. "I told you last night, it's just cold feet. Everything is going to be fine."

My body stiffens, pulse throbbing against my neck.

I should probably turn around, pretend I didn't hear anything, but my feet stay rooted to the floor.

"You were the one who told me not to get married. So, what? Now you think I should?" Collin asks.

Jack shifts his weight, adjusting his stance. "You love her, right?"

Collin runs a hand through his sandy hair, jaw tightening. "Of course I love her, but what if it's not enough? What if we can't make it work? We've known each other less than a year."

"Come on, Collin," Jack says, voice firm. "The wedding is tomorrow. You need to get a grip."

The muscles in Collin's throat flex as he swallows. "Is this how you felt before you married Lexi?"

Jack's shoulders grow rigid. "Things with her were different. You know that."

Collin opens his mouth to respond, but just as he does, his eyes sidestep to me. I instantly pull my gaze away, pretending to be engrossed in a painting and *not* like I was eavesdropping.

Collin clears his throat. "Hey, Ada."

At the mention of my name, Jack turns around, eyes dragging

up and down my body with unfettered interest, something that would have normally built a fire in my stomach. Instead, blood pumps loudly in my ears, palms growing sticky with panic.

"Ada," Jack says, voice a little breathless, like he's taken the stairs too fast.

I force my eyes up, pretending to have just noticed them. "Hey, I didn't even recognize you guys. You look so . . . fancy," I say with a nervous laugh.

Collin forces a tight smile as he slides a hand around my shoulder and pulls me into a very youth group-y side hug. "How was the trip here?" he asks.

"Fine. Good," I say, hoping to mask the chaos breaking loose inside me, but I can't seem to catch a breath. Or swallow properly. It's like my throat's been coated in tar.

I think back to last night, to Jack's phone buzzing on the pub table. To his terse "just wedding stuff" as he'd taken one glance at the screen and stuffed it back in his pocket.

Is that why Collin had been blowing up Jack's phone? Because he was *freaking out* about getting married?

The thought makes my stomach pendulate, acid rising in my throat.

Though I'm not sure which is worse: That Collin's having second thoughts about marrying Allison? Or that Jack knew—at least since last night—and didn't tell me?

Jack tilts his head, examining my face. "Ada? Everything okay?"

I think about confronting them, demanding that they explain what the hell is going on, but a voice of reason intervenes to remind me that on the other side of those doors are a hundred guests, none of whom have traveled six thousand miles to hear the maid of honor lay into the groom and best man. Or maybe they have, but that's not a show they'll be getting tonight.

No, I'll have to handle this more discreetly.

"I'm fine," I say again. "Totally fine."

Jack frowns, clearly dubious, but doesn't say anything.

"We should go in there," Collin says, pointing to a wide set of double doors. "You know how Allison doesn't like to wait." He flashes us a faulty grin that doesn't quite reach his eyes, before gesturing for us to follow him.

As we step into the party, my brain whirs to action, attempting to formulate a plan.

Should I tell Allison that Collin's having second thoughts?

No, of course not. She'll panic. I'll have to figure this out on my own.

But how? Convince Collin to go through with a marriage he isn't sure about? That's not exactly a stellar plan either.

Ahead, I catch a glimpse of Collin's profile. He's smiling and laughing as he greets guests, but behind his eyes there's a rigidity that makes my gut twist.

This is exactly what I was worried about. That Collin and Allison were rushing into things. That Collin couldn't be trusted. And now I'm going to have to clean up the mess the way I always knew I would.

ALLISON AND COLLIN OPTED FOR A REHEARSAL DINNER SANS AN ACTUAL rehearsal since, as Allison put it, she didn't want to *steal the thunder of the real thing*, which means it's just an excuse for another expensive party.

Hors d'oeuvres and champagne flow freely from the silver trays of cocktail waiters. There's even a jazz band in the corner. But I'm not paying attention to any of it. All I can think about is knocking back a drink and figuring out what the hell I'm going to do about Collin.

I'm making a beeline to the open bar when I'm intercepted by Bill, who promptly wraps me in a big bear hug. "Kiddo, you made it," he says, squeezing me tight.

"Hey, Bill." I hug him back, inhaling the familiar scent of Old Spice.

In true Seattle fashion, Bill is wildly underdressed in khakis and a North Face puffer vest.

"How was the trip here?" he asks. "Allison said something about you traveling with the best man?"

As though of their own accord, my eyes find Jack on the other side of the room, engrossed in conversation with Collin's friends. My gaze pulls his and he looks up, eyes meeting mine, but I snap my attention back to Bill.

"We made it in one piece," I tell him.

"Well, it's lucky you two found each other," Bill says. "We were worried you weren't going to make it."

"Lucky is one way of putting it."

"Do you, uh . . ." His brow furrows. "Need money or anything? I'm sure it wasn't cheap traveling all that way."

I shift my weight, suddenly feeling like my clothes are too tight.

"I'm fine," I lie.

He nods, but lingering traces of worry still line his eyes. "Any leads on the job hunt?"

"A few."

His eyes warm. "That's great, kiddo. Glad to hear it."

I don't like lying to Bill, but it's not a good idea to tell my parents about my plans to reopen Sleeve It to Me. Not with Allison's wedding—and possible fallout—looming on the horizon.

"So, how's everything been here?" I ask. "How are Allison and Mom?"

"Oh, you know, a crisis a minute, but we're getting through

it," he says good-naturedly. "I think your mom is trying to distract herself from the stress of the wedding by trying to set you up with someone. The neighbor's kid, last I heard."

"Oh, I heard," I tell him. "I think she's hoping it will be a double wedding."

Bill laughs, then lowers his voice to a whisper. "Don't worry, I'll talk to her. She's just stressed, is all. You know how she is. Just wants the best for you girls."

I cast Bill a grateful smile.

"And Allison's been looking for you," he says. "She keeps asking if you're here yet." Bill's eyes drift across the room and I follow his gaze.

In the corner of the room, every bit the center of attention, is Allison, dressed in white, blond hair cascading down her back in perfect waves, the very image of the blushing bride.

When I look back at Bill, his eyes are already misting over.

"Oh, Bill," I say, patting his arm, a nervous laugh bubbling out of me. "It's not even the wedding yet."

"I know, I know . . ." He shakes his head. "I knew this day would come; I just didn't know it'd come so fast. I blinked and you girls grew up."

I'm about to tell him he doesn't have to worry about me getting married anytime soon, when I see Allison making a beeline in my direction.

"Duty calls," I tell Bill. He gives my shoulder a squeeze before sauntering off in the direction of the bar.

"Finally!" she cries. "I was about to promote Britney to maid of honor!"

I give her a pinched smile. "Not too late."

She rolls her eyes before wrapping me in a hug that's just a little too tight to be entirely friendly. "Where's the veil?"

"What veil?" I ask, bringing my hands to my face with cartoonish surprise.

She glares at me. "Not funny."

"It's up in my room," I tell her. "And don't worry. Your precious veil is in mint condition."

Apart from the minor surgery Jack had to perform, that is. But she doesn't need to know about that. That will be my and Jack's dirty little secret.

Speaking of Jack, my eyes scan the room until I find him talking with an older couple I assume are Collin's parents. They're both laughing at something he's just said.

"So," Allison says, following my gaze. "I see you and Houghton made it here in one piece."

"We got along, actually," I tell her. "He's a nice guy."

She scoffs. "Don't tell me you fell for it."

"Fell for what?"

"His whole *charming routine*," she says, using air quotes. "He's just trying to get in your pants, you know."

The air in my lungs thickens.

"Trust me, he's not," I tell her, just as a waiter passes us with a plate of small puff pastry–type things. Thankful for the excuse to do something with my hands and face, I stuff one into my mouth.

Holy crap. This is delicious.

"What are these?" I garble between bites of meat and pastry goodness.

"Mini sausage rolls," Allison says. "Apparently they are really popular here."

"These are amazing," I say, grabbing four more.

Allison takes one, too, and I wrinkle my nose. "I thought you weren't eating gluten anymore? Didn't you say it made you break out?"

"But I'm starving." She shoves two into her mouth, smudging her perfect cherry lip. "I've been so busy with wedding stuff I haven't eaten all day."

"I can go find you something else," I say, eyes darting around the room for another waiter. "Maybe I can see if they have rice crackers or—"

"It's fine."

"No, I'll just—"

"Ada. Seriously." She gives me a firm look. "I'm *fine*."

I put my hands up in a sign of surrender and finish chewing.

"So, how are you feeling about the wedding?" I ask, brushing the crumbs from my mouth.

"Good. There was a thing with the dinner menu, but—"

"No, I mean about getting married. To Collin," I clarify.

"Oh." She looks visibly uncomfortable. "Fine. I guess," she answers stiffly.

She guesses?

"How's Collin? Is he excited?" I ask, trying to keep my voice neutral and not at all like I'm keeping a nuclear secret.

Allison's perfectly made-up gaze shifts to the floor. "I think so."

"What do you mean *you think so*? Did he say something?" I study her expression, looking for clues that she might sense something's wrong.

"No, we've just both been so busy we haven't had a ton of time together."

Interesting. Is Collin avoiding her? Because he's having doubts?

"So you still want to do this?" I ask, eyes probing hers.

Her brows dip into a scowl. "*This*?"

"*This*." I gesture around the room. "*Get married*. Because if you don't, it's not too late, you know." I lean in, lowering my voice to a whisper. "We could call the whole thing off if you want. I'm pretty sure I can wrangle up a horse for you to escape on like Julia Roberts in *Runaway Bride*. Just say the word."

Allison pulls away from me, mouth tilting into a pinched frown. "I knew you were going to do this."

"Do what?"

"Come in here and . . . and . . ." Her voice sputters, eyes popping. "And try to convince me not to marry him!"

"I'm not," I say quickly. "I just want to make sure you feel totally comfortable with your decision to enter into a legally binding contract that expires only in death."

Allison glares at me. "I know you don't like Collin. But I'm going through with it, Ada. And if you don't like it, too bad." And with that, she storms off, white dress billowing behind her.

Great. Now Allison's mad at me. Or *madder*, I guess. But that's not my biggest problem right now. My biggest problem is that I need to figure out what the hell is going on with Collin so I can fix it before it's too late.

I spot Jack on the other side of the room and I make my way toward him. He's mid-conversation with Collin's parents when I grab his arm.

"I need to talk to you," I say, not bothering to apologize for interrupting.

He frowns. "Right now?"

"Yes, right now." And before he can protest, I'm dragging him out a set of glass doors and onto the darkened patio overlooking the lawn.

"What the hell, Ada? What's going on?" Jack demands, as the door shuts behind us, muffling the sounds of clinking glassware and laughter.

I turn to face him. "When were you going to tell me that Collin is having doubts about marrying my sister?"

His gaze widens as comprehension slogs through his features. "You heard us talking?"

"I did."

Jack runs a hand through his hair, currents of frustration weaving through his features. "You weren't supposed to hear that," he says after a pause.

"So, what? You were just going to hide the fact that Collin's freaking out about marrying Allison?"

Jack shakes his head, jaw muscles pulling taut. "It wasn't like that."

"Then what's it like? Because it sounds like you knew that Collin was having second thoughts and you didn't tell me!"

As the words fly out of my mouth, echoing in the darkness around us, I feel almost jittery, like my finely curated restraint has finally snapped, and I'm no longer in control.

Jack looks away, eyes not meeting mine. "He's just nervous, is all."

"Because *you* told him marriage is a trap?" I counter.

"I have it handled, okay?"

"How?"

His lips draw apart, close, then part again. "Just let me deal with it," he says.

I step closer. "Oh, because you've been dealing with it so well?"

His eyes darken, emulsifying into two black pools, and for a minute I think he's going to push back, tell me I'm wrong. Instead, he draws a long, jagged breath that rattles as though torn straight from his gut.

"I'm sorry," he says at last. "I know I should have told you how Collin was feeling, but I didn't want to worry you. You were already freaked out about Allison and this wedding, and I didn't want to make it worse. I figured it was my mess to clean up since I'm the one who told Collin not to get married." He pauses, shaking his head in frustration. "But this is just one more thing I've managed to fuck up."

My body stiffens like I'm preparing to be struck by lightning. I want to get mad, to accuse Jack of ruining everything. But somewhere past the haze of my own anger and fear, I can see that whatever's going on between him and Collin, it's weighing heavily on Jack, and piling on him won't solve anything.

I release a heavy breath, letting the tension float outward, away from my center.

"You should have told me," I say at last.

"I know. I'm sorry," he says again.

Our eyes latch, a flicker of understanding passing between us.

"How long has Collin been feeling this way?" I ask.

He kicks at a pebble, sending it into the blackness. "He told me about a week ago that he was nervous, but I honestly thought the whole thing would blow over. That he'd get to Ireland and forget all about his cold feet."

"Is that what you meant when you said it was between you and Collin?" I ask, thinking back to what Jack had said in the car.

Jack looks away, brow scrunching against the moonlight, and I think I'm about to get another brush-off, but his chin tips into a slow nod, dragging his gaze back to me. "Our relationship's been strained since Lexi asked for the divorce, but that's mostly my fault."

I step closer, eyeing him carefully. "What do you mean?"

"I mean that telling my best friend not to marry the love of his life is a pretty shitty thing to do," he says, eyes landing on mine with the kind of force that feels like friction. "Especially when Collin has always been there for me."

He looks down at the Rolex on his wrist, wincing like it contains bad memories.

"After my mom died, I stopped trying at pretty much everything. It was like the part of my brain that was supposed to care about stuff just stopped working, and slowly everyone in my life gave up on me. Teachers. Friends. Everyone except Collin. He's the one person who stood by my side through all of it." Jack pauses, moonlight-struck eyes lifting to meet mine before he says, "I know you're worried about Allison, but I promise Collin's a good guy. He's just nervous. That's all."

I want to jump in and explain why Collin can't be trusted, now perhaps more than ever, but something about the earnestness on Jack's face and the tenderness with which he speaks about Collin gives me pause, and slowly I retreat.

Maybe Jack was right and I've allowed past experiences to cloud my judgment of Collin.

Maybe this whole time I've been attempting to paint Collin in broad strokes of black and white, when really what I need are finer, more detail-oriented brushes, the kind that leave room for nuance.

"Sounds like Collin's a good friend," I say at last.

"He is." There's a guardedness to his expression, letting me know he hasn't yet forgotten my criticisms of Collin. "He's one of the best people I know."

"And you think he loves her?" I ask.

Jack blinks, then slowly he nods. "I remember Collin texted me the morning after his first official date with Allison. He told me he didn't want to jinx it, but he was pretty sure she was *the one*. I've never seen him fall so fast, or so hard."

Jack's words tunnel inside me, carving out new pathways in my brain.

All this time I've been concerned about Allison getting hurt. About minimizing damage. About protecting her. But I haven't stopped to ask if she and Collin are actually good together. If they make each other happy. If this wedding and subsequent marriage is something worth saving.

The realization fills me with guilt. The kind that's heavy in my gut.

When I look back at Jack, streaks of moonlight paint stripes across his face. His eyes hold mine, so delicately it's like I'm made of glass. Like I could shatter at any moment.

"But is that enough?" I ask.

It's the same question Collin had asked Jack. But it's a fair one. I'd loved Carter. Just like Jack had loved Lexi, and my mom had loved my dad. But it hadn't been enough. Because love isn't always enough for things to work out. To make people stay.

Jack's gaze softens, lips bowed in a tender crease before he says, "I can't tell you what's going to happen, but I can tell you that no matter what, Allison is going to be okay. If I have to make a PowerPoint presentation reminding Collin of all the reasons he loves Allison, then I will. And if I have to smuggle Allison out of the castle on horseback myself, then I'll do that too." He pauses, swallowing. "I'm just trying to tell you that we're in this together and I've got your back. I promise."

Maybe it's his words, or the determination with which he says them, but the tightly wound knot inside me loosens and suddenly I'm crying. Not cute, little tears, but full-on, bone-rattling sobs. The kind I can't control.

Jack only lets a beat pass before he puts his arm around me, tucking my head under the crook of his chin. "Hey, it's okay," he whispers into my hair. "You're okay."

The tears come harder and faster, but his grip only tightens as his arms gather me against his chest.

A sliver of my brain is embarrassed for sobbing into his chest like this again. But there's something about the way Jack's holding me—about the gentle hand on my back—that makes me feel like it's okay to cry. That I don't have to be strong or capable or in control. That Jack's arms are a safe place to fall apart. So I do. I cry and I cry until I'm not totally sure what I'm crying for anymore. Only that Jack feels too warm, too solid, too good, and I'm not ready to let go. Not yet.

Eventually I pull back, sniffing and wiping under my eyes. "I'm sorry," I say.

He runs his thumb under my chin, wiping away a stray tear. "For what?"

"For crying. For being a mess. Again." I gesture to myself.

Moonlight catches his eye, bringing lighter flecks of brown and caramel to the surface. "You don't have to apologize," he says. "You love your sister and it's scary to think she might get hurt. I get it."

I let his words wrap around me like a warm, weighted blanket as Jack tucks me back into his chest, where his skin is warm and his heart taps out comforting rhythms against mine.

"I think what scares me most is not being able to protect her," I say after a minute. "That things with her and me will never go back to the way they were. That she'll never be my best friend again."

"You're a good sister," he says, stroking my hair. "And I don't know how long it will take, but eventually you two will find your way back to one another."

My eyes drift up, finding his. "You think so?" My voice comes out raw, like my vocal cords have been stripped down to their core.

"I know so." Then he takes my hand, lacing his fingers with mine, and for a minute we stay like that, pressed together like we're each afraid the other might float away. It feels good. Not just the closeness, but knowing that I have someone who is looking out for me. Or maybe it's just as Jack told my mom. Maybe we're both looking out for one another.

A cool breeze catches my tearstained cheek and I shiver.

"Here." Jack shrugs his way out of his suit jacket and drapes it over my shoulders.

It smells like him, tangy with a hint of sweetness, and I shiver again, but this time it's not from the cold.

"My clothes look good on you," he says. "Maybe you should have stolen my suitcase after all."

"I wasn't trying to steal your suitcase, it was just—"

"Bad luck?" he tries.

My cheeks warm despite the cool night air. "I was going to say good luck, actually."

Jack's jaw softens, a hint of smile creeping into his features. "I agree. It was good luck."

Our gazes hold for a string of seconds, twin grins stretching across both of our faces until laughter and the low hum of voices drift through the door, reminding me that our presence is probably missed.

"You want to ditch the rest of the rehearsal dinner?" I ask.

His gaze skates toward the door then back to me. "I think they might notice if we're gone."

"Who cares," I say, giving his arm a tug. "We're in Ireland, let's go to a pub or something. I promise to not throw up this time," I add.

A husky laugh catches in the back of his throat. "You're just trying to get out of meeting Stable Tom, aren't you?"

My mouth quirks. "Maybe."

"As appealing as that offer is, we'd better get back in there. They're likely to notice if the best man and maid of honor are missing."

I want to protest, to make this moment stretch just a little longer, but he's giving me one of his dashing smiles that I find so hard to refuse. Damn him and his perfect dental hygiene.

"*Finnnneeee,*" I say. "But only because those mini sausage rolls were so good."

"Those were good," he agrees. "I had, like, twenty."

"Same. Do you think I could fit some in my purse for later?"

Jack smiles at me, his eyes crinkling. "Only if you get some for me too."

"Deal."

As we walk back inside, I find it harder and harder to ignore the tug in my chest, the ache of want, burning bright and electric inside me.

I ought to pack it away, shove it into the dark corner of my mind where I store song lyrics and random facts about celebrities. But my feelings for him feel too large, too overwhelming. Like a massive tsunami building in the distance, one whose force I can't outrun. All I can do is shelter in place and brace for impact.

Chapter 24

19 HOURS UNTIL THE WEDDING

As the maid of honor, the responsibility of planning Allison's last night as a single gal falls on me. Which is how Allison, the two other bridesmaids, and I end up at a sticky Belfast karaoke bar, chugging watered-down vodka sodas, singing along to a particularly heartfelt rendition of ABBA's "Gimme! Gimme! Gimme!" with a hundred of our closest Irish friends.

I don't know either of the other bridesmaids very well, except that Carmen speaks in fluent TV quotes and movie references, and that Britney was Allison's *big* in the Greek system at college—something I find profoundly annoying. Allison is always going on about her *big* and how *cool* and *awesome* she is, and I'm like, *Hello, your actual biological big sis is right here. What am I? Chopped liver?*

At the moment, my sister and her friends are entangled in one another's arms out on the dance floor, shrieking every time the song changes. Miraculously, it's been "our song," the last three songs in a row, none of which I recognize, which means I am officially too old for this.

I'm also too old for the sparkly pink cowgirl hats we're all wearing courtesy of Britney, who thought they fit the theme of "A Night of Lasts in Belfast." I'm not sure what the hat has to do with the theme, but the important thing is that Allison looks happy—and not like she suspects anything might be wrong with Collin, or otherwise. She's also too drunk to remember she's still mad at me, so that's something.

Three pop remixes later, it's our turn to take the karaoke stage.

Naturally, Allison goes first and performs Beyoncé's "Love on Top."

She's shimmying to the music, trying to hit a high note, when Collin appears at our table, followed by Jack and the two other groomsmen, Tony and Braden—who, in my mind, can be interchangeably referred to as Meathead One and Meathead Two.

"What are you guys doing here?" Britney yells over the music. "This is supposed to be girls only!"

"Sorry, ladies, we didn't know you'd be here too," Collin says, sharing a knowing smirk with Jack that makes me wonder if their presence really is a coincidence.

The boys all order drinks and take a seat at our table. Even though there are plenty of other open spots, Jack sits beside me. He's wearing the same outfit from earlier, except now he's lost the tie and jacket, and his shirtsleeves are rolled up to his elbows, showing off the veiny ridges of his forearms. If I didn't already wish I wasn't wearing a sparkly pink cowgirl hat, now I really do.

"Hey. Nice hat," he says, tipping the brim.

"I thought you were going to a strip club?" I ask.

"We were, but I thought this would be a better show." He pauses, looking me up and down. "Clearly I was right."

I'm thankful for the poor lighting, hiding the blush I'm sure is working its way up my neck. "How did you know we'd be here?"

His body bends toward me, knee brushing mine under the table. "Wild guess?"

"You sure you're not just following me?" I ask. "The last three days weren't enough for you?"

"Not nearly enough," he says, nudging my knee.

His eyes skip to mine, a scorching look behind his gaze, and a hot whoosh rips through me.

Eager to focus on literally anything else, I turn to Allison, watching as she returns from the stage and promptly drapes herself across Collin's lap. He wraps his arm around her shoulder, thumb skating back and forth across the same spot on her arm before leaning in and whispering something in her ear. Whatever it is has my sister blushing and giggling.

"Collin seems better," I whisper to Jack. "Have you talked to him?"

Jack cups my hand with his, giving it a quick squeeze. "Everything's going to be fine," he whispers back. "I promise."

It's not a real answer, but the comfort of his hand in mine is a fast-acting relief and I let myself relax. Or as much as I can with Jack's knee bouncing against mine.

Even now, after he's made it clear he doesn't want anything more, I can't help but continue to feel magnetized by him, endlessly aware of his body, his heat, the subtle shift of his weight. Every flex of the hand and tick of the jaw. He's an app I can't stop opening. A habit I can't break.

Every time his gaze latches on to mine, something in me catches fire, and those feelings I've tried to turn off turn right back on, magnified.

After Britney belts out "Jenny from the Block," Collin puts on a very lewd performance of "Clumsy" by Fergie that includes plenty of provocative hip movements and body rolls. I watch with one eye shut. Meanwhile, Allison shrieks and catcalls like she's at a Magic Mike Live performance. When Collin finishes, Allison pulls him in for a smoldering kiss that feels a little indecent in a club full of people, but hey, it's better than hearing the wedding's off, so I'll take it.

Next, Collin ropes Jack into performing some obscure nineties punk song I've never heard before. It must be some kind of inside joke because they can barely make it through a single lyric without cracking up.

Alcohol is clearly a factor, but I like seeing this side of Jack. A side that looks relaxed and at ease, wholly different from the man I saw last night, weighed down by hurt and broken promises.

When they finish, Collin reclaims his seat beside Allison, but Jack remains on stage, eyes locking on me as he wiggles his index finger in my direction.

I freeze, drink halfway to my lips.

"Come on, Ada," he says in a singsong voice. "You know you want to."

I shake my head like a dashboard bobblehead. "No, thanks. I don't sing."

He juts out his bottom lip. "One song?"

"Come on, Ada, do it!" Carmen cries, followed by a chorus of "Yeah, come on!"

I'm not a performer. I don't even like singing "Happy Birthday" out loud. But based on the way everyone is looking at me, chanting various versions of "Come on, Ada! Do it!" I have a feeling I'm not getting out of this one.

"Fine," I resign. "One song."

Jack's face breaks into a grin, the kind that feels like it's planting seeds and blossoming in my chest. Or maybe it's not the smile. Maybe that's just the way I feel when I look at him. When I do *anything* with him.

"I promise it will be worth it," he says. Then he gestures for me to join him on the stage where the lights are too bright and the temperature too hot.

We each take a microphone as the electric intro beats of Donna Summer's "Hot Stuff" flood the speaker system. Jack catches my eye, giving me the faintest hint of a nod, and even though we're on a stage in front of a crowd of people, it feels oddly intimate. Like it's just us.

The first lyrics pop up on the screen and my hands instantly turn clammy. Jack lifts his microphone and, with surprising bravado, belts out the first verse.

He's not bad. But what he lacks in technical singing abilities, he makes up for with Elvis-style hip gyrations and cartoonish body rolls.

I cover my face with my hands, laughing so hard I don't notice the next verse pops up on the screen until Jack gestures to me that it's my turn.

The first verse comes out shaky, but by the time the chorus comes I'm no longer thinking about Allison or Collin or the wedding. It's just Jack and me, laughing and dancing our way through the rest of the song in a wild display of bad vocals and even worse dance moves.

At one point, Tony throws a twenty-pound note on stage and I stuff it into my bra. Everyone cheers, but the sound is a distant roar in my ears, overshadowed by the heat of Jack's palm as he spins me in a lazy circle.

It's so cheesy, so over the top. And yet, I'm completely powerless to the swell of want that gathers in every hollow and nook of my body, and for one time-bending moment, nothing exists outside the heat of his gaze or the pressure of his hand.

When the song ends, the room blurs around us, swimming with a variety of colors and patterns entirely indistinguishable from one another. The only thing that remains sharply in focus is Jack. The sweat gathering on his brow. The piece of hair draped across his forehead. The warmth of his hand in mine as we take a bow.

As we walk off the stage, Jack leans into my ear and whispers, "Was that so bad?"

"That was payback for the cartwheels, wasn't it?"

He grins unevenly. "I'm sure I have no idea what you're talking about, Ada."

His hip scrapes mine and my heart thumps, blood pounds in my ears, every *check engine* light in my body blaring. I need to think. To breathe. To instill some level of sanity back into my thoughts.

"I'm going to the bathroom," I blurt.

I'm barely aware of where I'm going as my feet carry me down the long dark hall toward the neon sign that says TOILETS, only that I need space from Jack and all his pheromones.

Inside the bathroom, I grip the counter and stare at myself in the mirror. Flushed cheeks and deer-in-the-headlight eyes look back at me.

What just happened?

Sure, maybe it was just a fun song between friends at karaoke. Maybe I've misread things. *Again*. But I know that's not true. Not this time.

I take a deep breath and splash some water on my neck, willing my heart rate to slow down.

A second later, the door flies open and in comes Britney, carrying the sound of laughter and music through the door with her.

"Hey, nice job up there," she says, dipping her hands under the faucet beside me.

I force a smile. "Thanks."

"So," she says, dropping her voice to a conspiratorial whisper. "Is there something going on with you and Jack?"

I freeze. Oh God. Is it written all over my face?

"No. Of course not," I say, forcing the corners of my mouth upward.

She gives me a look like she doesn't believe me, then reaches for a paper towel. "You sure? I haven't seen that much chemistry on stage since Madonna and Britney kissed at the VMAs."

Sparks of heat flood my cheeks and I run my hands under the faucet, splashing cold water onto my face with renewed vigor.

She tips her chin. "Are you all right? Do you need water or something?"

"I'm fine. Totally fine. Just dizzy from singing." I wave my hand airily and mold my cheeks into a terse smile.

Britney's face pinches. "You sure? I have some Pepto in my purse . . . ?"

I shake my head again. She gives me one more careful look before disappearing back out the door.

As soon as she's gone, I lean back against the wall.

Is that what we looked like? Like we were all over each other? Like we had chemistry?

There's a part of me that knows I ought to be embarrassed. But somehow I'm not. Perhaps because it's validating to know I didn't make the whole thing up.

After I wash my hands, I exit the bathroom. The hall outside is dark and I bump into something hard. But it's not something. It's *someone*.

I stagger backward until firm hands grip my shoulders, steadying me.

"Sorry," comes a familiar voice.

I look up. It's Jack.

His hands slide down my bare arms, lingering on my waist. The touch is light, barely more than a graze, but it doesn't stop the electric ping of awareness under my skin or the dizzying array of Olympic-level backflips my stomach is currently performing.

He rejected you, I remind myself. *We're just friends.*

But the way he's looking at me—dark eyes tracing patterns across my face like there might be a quiz later—is saying otherwise.

"I was just in the bathroom," I say.

"Glad to see you didn't lock yourself in this time."

I blink. "Excuse me?"

"I'm joking."

Right. Joking. But my brain no longer has any grasp of the meaning. Only the fact that Jack's hands are still inexplicably on my waist, and suddenly I'm leaning into him, like his body is a Venus flytrap and I'm but a helpless spider being lured into its teeth. Except, unfortunately for me, I'd like to get eaten.

For a moment we just stand there, hovering alone in the dark, empty hall—the only light coming from the sign blinking overhead. Some rap song I vaguely recognize comes over the sound system and the bass thumps in time with my own racing heart.

I'm not sure what makes me do it, if it's the post-performance adrenaline still coursing through me or simply because I want an excuse to keep touching him, but I reach into my bra and pull out the twenty Tony threw on stage. Jack follows my hand, eyes widening.

"Here. To put toward my debt," I say, flattening the bill against his chest.

His hand brushes mine as he takes it. "I think you'll have to do a lot more performances to pay off the rest."

"How much do I owe you at this point?" I ask. "Or is it like the IRS where I have to guess and if I get it wrong I go to jail?"

Jack laughs, shifting close enough that I can smell the liquor on his lips. "I can get you an itemized list if you'd like," he says. "Though I'll warn you, my sewing fees aren't cheap."

"Damn. And what happens if I can't pay up?"

Jack licks his lips, eyes reflecting the light of the neon sign overhead. "Probably the stocks. Or debtor's prison."

I take another step toward him. "Joke's on you. I look super cute in orange."

His eyes travel down my face, lingering on my lips. "I bet you do."

The air between us feels charged and I can't help but feel like we're having two separate conversations. The one happening out loud, with words, and the silent one conducted through heated glances and rapidly shrinking personal space.

I don't want to get hurt again. And I certainly don't want to make yet another mistake. But I feel my defenses start to falter as the low buzz of sexual tension goes from crackling background noise to full-on ringing in my ears.

I think back to last night, to the excitement that had thrummed inside me. To the impulse I'd foolishly trusted and the burn of humiliation that had followed.

Part of me wants to memory-hole the whole thing and move on, but another part of me hums with curiosity. I want to know why he hadn't kissed me.

Was it because I'd truly read things wrong?

Or was it something else?

"Jack, can I ask you something?"

He blinks. "Sure. What's up?"

Maybe it's the hazy cover of darkness, or the alcohol still pumping in my bloodstream, but I feel brave enough to ask, "Did you not want to kiss me last night because I'd been throwing up and crying? Or . . ." I pause, letting my eyes trail across his face. "Did you just not want to kiss *me*?"

His gaze shifts from one of surprise to one that is visibly tense, and I worry I've stepped too far, that I've broken this delicate, glass-like thing between us.

He licks his bottom lip, forehead creasing before he says, "Of course I wanted to kiss you. But you were still drunk and upset about your ex. It wasn't a good idea. For either of us."

My breathing shallows, currents of energy zigzagging inside me. I try to think, to process the implications of what he's just said, but there are no thoughts, just the rapidly expanding heat in my belly and the surges of want gathering between my thighs.

For a second, nothing happens, we just float there, a flimsy distance separating us, before I hear myself ask, "Is this . . . ?"

His eyes narrow, searching through the darkness. "Is this *what*?"

"Is *this* a good idea?"

"Ada." His voice is low and gravelly, and my body warms from the sound alone.

His mouth opens slowly, as though moving at half speed, then he closes it again, a silent meditation happening behind his eyes. Then he says, in a voice so low I feel it rumble inside me, "Ada, if you want me to kiss you, I won't be able to stop myself this time."

I'm frozen, caught between his sticky breath on my cheek and the bass thumping in my chest. My brain screams for me to stop, to ask questions, to analyze and overthink every syllable of what he just said. But I don't. Instead, I look into his dark eyes and say the first thing I can think to say—the *only* thing I can think to say.

"I want you to kiss me, Jack."

Jack's gaze pores over me, seeping into my skin, and my blood thickens as everything slows around me. Even the music now sounds garbled and faint. Neither of us moves. We hover there, bodies suspended, an electric hum of anticipation coursing between us. Then Jack takes my head in his hands, fingers scraping the sides of my face as his mouth captures mine.

I expect the kiss to be urgent, demanding—like Jack—but instead, it's soft and reassuring, like each motion is asking for permission. *Is this okay?* his hand asks as it trails the curve of my chin. *And this?* His other hand brushes my sweaty hair from my forehead. I answer him with a kiss. *Yes. Touch me. Kiss me. Do it and do it now.*

The heat of his mouth draws me in, each breath pulling us a little closer, a little deeper. A slow, drugging kiss. Then another, this time hungrier, wilder, both of us testing the rapidly crumbling boundary between us.

"Fuck," he rasps into my mouth.

"I know," I breathe back. I'm not sure what it is exactly that I'm professing to *know*, only that whatever he's feeling, I'm feeling it too.

The cover of darkness eggs us on, teasing us with a façade of privacy, and he walks us back until my spine meets the wall. A tiny moan crawls up the back of my throat as his palm presses against my chest, keeping me in place with the lightest of pressure while his other hand slides down my body, molding around my hips. Everything in me liquefies. No bones. No internal organs. Nothing but formless swells of heat.

But I *need* more. The graze of a hand, the brush of a tongue is no longer enough. His hardness presses into me, telling me he feels the same way.

Jack tilts my chin, nudging the cowboy hat off my head.

"This fucking hat," he whispers, breath rough against my skin.

"I thought you liked it?" I mean for it to sound teasing, flirty. Instead, the words come out feverish and desperate, just like I feel.

"I did." His lips skim the side of my jaw, slipping higher until he's sucking on my bottom lip. "I liked it too much."

The taste of him decodes something inside me. Like he's reached into my most cavernous depths and opened a door to a room I didn't even know existed. And suddenly I forget where I am. Or that there are hundreds of people on the other side of this wall. All I can focus on are the pulse points of heat and pressure. All the places his hands are. And all the places I still need them to be.

I arch my hips toward him, begging him for more. He responds by inching his hand under my skirt, moving at a pace that's as torturous as it is delicious. He reaches the band of my underwear, and a needy, breathless whimper escapes me.

"You need to stay quiet," Jack whispers. "Can you do that for me, Ada?"

I'm about to tell him that I'm not sure what I'm capable of right now, when a voice comes out of the darkness. At first, I think it's Jack. But the voice is farther away, unfamiliar.

"There you are, we've been looking for you."

"Typical," another voice says. They both laugh.

The sound is muffled, warped, like I'm hearing it from under water.

Jack and I freeze, lips parted, still breathing heavily into one another's mouths. Our eyes meet, a silent bargain passing between us.

Maybe if we don't move, they'll go away.

But they speak again.

"Jack, we've been here five minutes and you're already groping some girl?" the one says.

They both snicker.

Okay, they are definitely talking to us. And if I'm not mistaken, I think our cockblockers are Meatheads One and Two. My eyes find Jack's through the darkness. He presses a single finger to his lips.

"Wait. Is that Allison's sister?" the other one asks.

Suddenly, my skin is too tight, pulse jamming against my ribs.

A beat passes before he says, "No, man, she's wearing a cowboy hat, remember?"

"Oh, yeah. Right."

My lungs deflate in a sigh of relief. Clearly they're too trashed to tell the difference between me and a coatrack right now.

"Jack, sorry to cockblock but we're heading out. Collin wants to go to another bar," the other says.

It takes Jack a moment to answer, but when he does, his voice is groggy and slow, like he's just woken up. "What?"

Tony and Braden both titter. "Dude, Collin's waiting for you. Tell your chick you'll booty call her later. Now come on."

There's a brief pause, one more uneven breath, then Jack and I yank apart. Even in the darkness I can see he's all flushed skin and swollen lips as he adjusts his pants, attempting to conceal his erection.

He gives me an apologetic smile, then he slips away, and I'm left standing alone, heart racing out of control as my brain struggles to play catch-up.

For a second, I'm too disoriented, too off-balance to think. No actual words form in my brain, only flashes of sensory memory. His hands pulling me to him, his lips, his mouth. God, *that mouth . . .*

I stumble backward until I find the wall, legs shaking like I've just stepped off a treadmill.

What the hell just happened?

One moment we were talking . . . *and the next* . . . Heat sinks into my center at the thought.

I wish I could say that whatever illusion I created for myself about Jack has now been shattered. That I got him out of my system. But far from it. Because now that I know what Jack tastes like, what his body feels like against mine, a type of Rubicon has been crossed. And it will no longer be enough to subsist off a meager ration of lingering stares and clumsy touches. It won't be enough at all.

Chapter 25

16 HOURS UNTIL THE WEDDING

The night ends with Carmen puking in the bathroom and Britney losing her shoes, but all in all the night is a success.

When we make it back to the castle, I make sure everyone drinks enough water before sending them to bed with two aspirin and a reminder to Venmo me eighty dollars in the morning.

I have a renewed appreciation for Jack as I wash Allison's face, perform her entire fifteen-step skincare routine, then help her under the covers—all while forcing her to chug glasses of water.

"Where's Collin?" she mumbles, water spilling down her chin. I wipe it away with a tissue from the bedside table.

"He's out with his friends," I remind her.

"Go get him," she whines. "I can't sleep without him."

"I don't know where he is," I tell her. *Not a strip club, I hope.* "Also, you're the one who wanted to sleep separately the night before because you said it was more romantic. Remember?"

She mutters something that sounds like *that's bullshit* before shutting her eyes and sinking back into the giant, fluffy hotel pillows.

I let three beats pass, waiting until her breathing changes to long, heavy breaths before deciding she's out. I'm just about to reach for the bedside lamp when she speaks again.

"I know you don't like Collin," Allison says, eyes still closed. "But I love him, Addy."

My heart squeezes. *Addy.* I know she's drunk and likely won't remember this conversation, but she hasn't called me that in a long time, and for a moment it feels like things are back to normal. Like everything is right with the world.

"I know you do," I tell her. Then I plant a gentle kiss on her forehead, turn out the lights, and return to my room.

Back in my room, I stare at my reflection in my bathroom mirror, watching the rise and fall of my chest. I'm still a little sweaty from dancing and my cheeks are still flushed with an alcohol-induced tinge, but I'm feeling focused and clearheaded now. And with each passing second, I'm feeling more confused.

I like Jack. A lot. And judging by the way his tongue was down my throat, he likes me too. But now what?

Was that a one-time thing, destined to never happen again? Or will he come to my room to pick up where we left off? I shoot a cursory glance at the door as though half expecting Jack to materialize.

But maybe the real question I should be asking is, What do *I* want?

Of course I want to sleep with Jack. But I also know myself. If I sleep with Jack, I'll want more than *just sex* and *no strings.* I already want as many strings as I can get when it comes to Jack Houghton.

But, my brain whispers, *if this is all I can have from him, maybe that can be enough. Maybe it has to be.*

I look at my suitcase, wondering if maybe I should change my underwear into something more presentable—you know, just in case—when I hear a soft *knock, knock, knock.*

"Ada?" Jack's deep voice calls from the other side of the door, and my entire body freezes as twin threads of anxiety and excitement weave together inside me.

It's two a.m. and Jack is outside my door.

Sure, he could want to talk. *Just* talk. Or maybe he's here to tell me what happened at the bar was a drunken mistake and redefine us as friends. Or maybe he just wants to check I made it back safely. Or not.

Hopefully not.

When I open the door, the top buttons on his shirt are undone, his hair is a mess, and is that . . . *glitter*? In his hand is a paper bag.

"Hey." He grins and the corners of my mouth pull upward, mirroring him.

"Hey," I say back.

Jack leans against the doorframe, his head tilted at an angle. "Can I come in?"

"Now? It's two a.m.?" I can hear my mother's voice. *Nothing good happens after midnight.* But my mom also thinks low-rise jeans are flattering, so what does she know?

Jack's mouth curves. "Are you hungry? I come bearing sausage."

Every cell in my body leaps to attention. "W-what?"

He shakes the paper bag in my face. "Mini sausage rolls. From the party."

Oh. Of course. Silly me. He means *literal* sausage, not whatever perverted euphemism my brain was imagining.

I open the door wider and gesture for him to come inside.

"I saw they were gonna throw out the leftovers," Jack says,

walking past me. "But I, like the good conservationist that I am, decided I knew a much better use for them."

"My mouth?" I try, but Jack apparently doesn't seem to notice the innuendo as he makes a beeline straight for my bed and falls back on the mattress.

"I'm exhausted," he says, sinking his head into the pillow.

"Me too," I tell him. But I'm not. I'm wide awake.

"Come here." He pats the spot next to him and I lie down, hips brushing his.

Not more than a few hours ago his tongue was in my mouth, but somehow lying here, side by side, feels much more intimate.

"This bed is amazing," he says to the ceiling. "It's like lying on a cloud."

"I know. These rooms are seriously nice."

He rolls his head to face me. "But I think I like Mrs. Poyevich's better."

The way his eyes land on mine feels like a balancing act. One where I'm trying to juggle too many plates and they're sure to all come crashing down around me.

A stray piece of glitter catches my eye and I flick it from his hair. "Did you guys end up at a strip club?" I ask.

"No, but some lady outside the bar flashed her tits at us. Does that count?"

I laugh and the bed shakes beneath us. "What changed your mind?"

His expression shifts, brows narrowing into a thoughtful *v* before he says, "I thought about what you said and I realized it might not be a good idea to take Collin to a strip club the night before his wedding. Especially with . . ." He gestures vaguely but doesn't finish the thought. But he doesn't need to. He's making good on his promise.

"So you stalked us instead?" I tease.

He grins. "I didn't have to. I heard Britney talking loudly in the elevator about where you were going."

"You just really wanted to see me make a fool of myself on stage, didn't you?"

"The first half of that is true." He pauses, eyes lifting to meet mine. "I just really wanted to see you."

The intensity of his gaze is suddenly too real, too palpable, too much like friction, and my eyes jump away, looking for something to focus on. They land on the bag of sausage rolls, and I reach for one. Not that the concept of a *sausage* is particularly helpful right now.

"Ohmygodthesearesogood," I groan between bites of buttery goodness.

He pops one into his mouth too. "These are better than *the pizza*."

"*The pizza*," I say, shutting my eyes. "I wanted to marry that pizza and have its babies."

"I can't wait for pizza in Naples."

"When do you leave?" I ask.

He shifts and the back of his hand grazes mine. "Day after the wedding."

Right. I'd almost forgotten his plans to go to Italy and how the window of time is closing in on us. Day after tomorrow he'll be gone. Then what?

We chew in silence until Jack reaches into the bag for another one. As he does, his shirtsleeves ride up, exposing the rigid veins crawling under his skin and something I didn't notice until now: a poppy on the inside of his wrist. Small and delicate, a jarring contrast to the rest of him.

Before I can even think about what I'm doing, I trace the smooth skin on his wrist. Goose bumps spread like wildfire up and down his forearms and I pull my hand back.

"I'm sorry," I blurt out.

His eyes hook up to mine. "It's okay. You can touch it if you want."

I smile unevenly, letting my fingers go back to tracing the pattern. I can tell it's a high-quality custom design. Highly saturated shading. Packed coloring. Consistent line work. It's the kind of piece that doesn't come cheap.

"It's really beautiful. Does it mean anything?"

"I got it after my mom died," he says. "It's a symbol of remembrance."

His gaze locks on mine, eyes so delicate it feels like one of us might crack.

"I love it," I tell him. "It suits you."

"Because I'm a secret softy?"

A half laugh judders out of me, and he shifts closer, knee riding up on mine, but I don't move away.

"It's surprising and unexpected," I say after a beat. "Like you."

He hums in response.

"Do you have any other tattoos?" I ask.

"I do."

I skim his body, taking in every inch of revealed skin. "Where?"

His mouth ripens into a grin. "None of your *beeswax*."

I give him a playful shove and Jack laughs. The tenor of it settles in the hollow of my stomach before sinking lower and finding a home in the space between my legs.

"So, now that you've seen mine, are you ever going to show me yours?" he asks, one eyebrow inching toward his scalp.

My bottom lip disappears between my teeth, poorly suppressing a grin. "Fine." I fold down the waistband of my skirt, showing him the mermaid on my hip.

The line work was hard to do myself from this angle, but I'm pleased with how it turned out. I especially like the way her tail disappears below my waistline with a seductive flourish. Something Jack also seems to be aware of.

He inhales sharply, eyes lifting to meet mine. "Can I?"

I'm not totally sure what he's asking, but I nod and Jack's fingers skate along my hip bone, tracing the shape of the mermaid's tail. It's a chaste gesture, hardly more intimate than a handshake, but the way he's doing it, slow and languorous, it might as well be his tongue.

"Does it have any significance?" he asks.

"When we were little, Allison and I used to play mermaid," I say. "We'd put our legs in pillowcases and pretend they were our tails, which usually involved us writhing on the floor pretending to 'swim.'"

Tender lines wrinkle around his mouth. "That's adorable."

"I don't think my mom thought it was very *adorable* when she'd get home from work and find us *swimming* when we were supposed to be in bed," I say with a half laugh, remembering all the nights my mom would work late and I'd be responsible for Allison and me. Usually, I was good about getting us to bed before Mom got home, but sometimes we stayed up too late and we'd have to sprint to our shared room and pretend to be asleep by the time her keys were in the lock.

Shhh, close your eyes, I'd whisper into the darkness.

The memory expands in my chest, making me feel unexpectedly hollow.

I know Allison's not a little girl anymore, that it's no longer up to me to make her dinner and put her to bed, but there's something sweet and tender about those fuzzy memories of childhood, memories of moments I'll never get back.

Jack tilts his chin, eyes wavering across my face. "Did you take care of Allison a lot growing up?" he asks.

"My mom tried her best, but being a single parent wasn't easy and she couldn't always be there," I tell him.

Jack nods, eyes tracing the outline of my features. "I guess that explains why you're so protective over Allison. Right?"

He says it like a question, but I can see the mental puzzle piece slide into place—the subtle shift behind his eyes—and I can't help but wonder if he's been building a picture of me the way I've been doing of him. If all this time he's been filing away snippets of information, hoarding them like trading cards he's hoping to collect the whole set of. The thought strikes across my core, igniting friction in my chest.

We slip into silence until Jack asks, "Can I ask you to design my next tattoo?"

"Depends. What are you thinking of getting?"

"Hmmm. Not sure yet." His body bows toward mine. "I was thinking about a compass rose, actually."

"Why that?"

"I like traveling. Seeing new places. Meeting new people." He pauses, eyes slicing to mine. "Especially strangers in hotels."

I'm newly aware of how soft and buttery the sheets feel against the backs of my thighs.

"We were never really strangers," I say. "We were always going to meet. It was sort of inevitable. Right?"

He nods, considering. "That's true. Maybe fate just sped up the process."

Fate.

The word scorches down my center like a match on granite and suddenly I know exactly what I want to do.

I reach for one of the complimentary hotel pens on the nightstand. "Can I?" I gesture to his forearm.

He sticks out his arm like he's giving blood.

I haven't so much as doodled since the break with Carter, and even before then, after losing the business, it was hard to summon the will to create. But now, I feel the surge of need rising inside me, powerful and all-consuming, like if I don't draw something right this minute, I might combust.

I can't say for certain where it comes from, only that I'm confident it has something to do with the man in front of me. The man whose presence feels like new air in my lungs.

As I sketch the outline of a compass on the inside of his forearm, using thick black strokes for the points and thinner lines for the sub-directions, I feel a kind of certainty coursing through my body. An awareness that this is what I'm supposed to be doing. This act of drawing—creating—even a silly sketch on Jack's arm, is when I am most perfectly myself. When all the chaos stills and suddenly everything feels okay. Everything feels right.

When I finish, I look up and see that Jack is watching me with a mix of awe and something else. Something heated.

"Like that?" I ask.

He smiles and I can't help the tiny tug of victory in my chest. "It's perfect. But now it's your turn."

"Mine?"

He holds out his hand for the pen and our fingers brush as I give it to him. He takes my arm and starts to sketch a triangle on the soft inside of my forearm.

"What is it?" I ask.

"Shh," he chides. "Don't disturb an artist while he's at work."

"Oh, so you're an artist now?" I tease.

I crane my neck to get a look, but he swats me away. When he pulls back a moment later, there is a triangle with squiggles in it.

I bark out a laugh. "What is this? A Rorschach test?"

"It's a slice of pizza. And not just any pizza. A pineapple pizza. See those chunks?" He points to deformed lumps.

I hug my arm to my chest. "I love it. I'm never washing this arm. Ever."

He laughs and his body vibrates against mine. We've inched closer now. Close enough that his breath warms my cheek, and memories of his hot, damp mouth pressed to mine race through me like a fast-acting drug.

The moment feels like foreplay.

And maybe it is.

We both swallow. Another breath. Another tempered exhale.

There's still a second for one of us to pull back, to stop things before they go any further. But neither of us does. Instead, he pulls me to him, cupping my jaw in his hands.

"I should tell you, I didn't come here to draw tattoos or eat sausage rolls," he says.

My breath hitches, pulse thumping against my rib cage.

"And what did you come here for?" I mean it to sound teasing, coy, but the tremble in my voice betrays me.

Jack's gaze lingers on my mouth before lifting to meet mine. There's captive hunger in his eyes—naked and obvious in a way that's palpable. "I came here to tell you I don't want to be just friends, Ada."

I open my mouth, hoping something funny or sexy comes out, but my throat is immobile. *Everything* is immobile as his fingers slide across my cheek and into my hair, drawing us closer. One more inch and our lips would be touching.

There's another beat of stillness, eyes holding in one last cursory gaze. Then Jack tips his chin to mine and whatever thinly veiled restraint we've been operating under snaps like a twig as our mouths collide in a desperate, frenzied rush of hot tongues and swollen lips and simmering need.

All I can think as he drags me to him is that *kissing Jack makes sense.* It makes sense the way the law of gravity makes sense. I can't explain the mechanics of it. It just does.

He kisses me fuller, deeper, hungrier. Each tip of the mouth and brush of teeth comes with a thrill that sends bolts of electricity racing down my spine. I want to swallow him. Or be swallowed. I can't decide. All I know is that I can't believe all the time we wasted not doing this.

"Come here," he rasps, pulling me on top of him. His hardness presses against me with aching urgency and a small, hungry sound escapes me.

"Do that again," he breathes, lips dragging against my neck.

"Do what?"

"That sound you just made."

I laugh. "I can't just make it again. I have to be prompted."

He pulls back, eyes falling over me in heavy waves. "Is that a challenge?"

That's all it takes for the floodgates to open inside me. Every hesitation, every thought of caution I've had over the course of the last few days disappears. I'm intoxicated by him. His body. His smell. His taste. All of it is both too much and not enough.

Before tonight, the idea of sex with Jack was just that, *an idea*. A hazy, improbable hypothetical. But now, as his hands wander between my thighs, awakening little flames across my skin, my mind races between the thrill of newness and the emerging realization that this is actually happening. This is real.

Our movements become more desperate, more hurried. My hands twist in his shirt, thumbs catching in the hem as I pull it up and over his head.

I'd known he was tall, that his shoulders were broad. But here, now, as my eyes take him in, getting lost in all the sharp corners and deep ridges of his chest, he's bigger, firmer, more solid than I realized.

Banded muscles wrap around me like tree trunks, somehow

both gentle and demanding, wanton and restrained. It's intoxicating knowing that he could rip my skirt, throw me down, easily take control, but instead he's careful, thoughtful.

Slowly, almost methodically, Jack slides the straps off my shoulder and undoes the clasp of my bra, letting the thin lace fall away from my chest. He moves with a well-maintained restraint that has my mind skipping ahead, wondering how he'll tease me. How long he'll keep me teetering on the edge before finally letting me have what I want. *What I need.*

"God, I've wanted this for so long," he whispers, breath hot on my sensitive skin as he dips his mouth to my nipple, circling me with his tongue.

"So long?" I tease. "You mean four days?"

"It was a hard four days. Emphasis on *hard*."

"You fooled me."

His lips curve. "I'm thirty-three years old, Ada. I know how to hide an inconvenient boner."

"Hmm." A contented laugh vibrates in my chest. "Tell me more about these inconvenient boners."

"Maybe later. I'm sort of in the middle of something." Then he pulls me onto his lap in a straddling position and kisses my neck, eager and determined.

Every vertebra liquefies. Nothing but molten heat fills every nook and cranny of my body as he cups my ass, jumbling every last residual thought in my head. A decadent groan echoes in the back of my throat, and he grips me harder, needier.

I reach for his belt. I can't wait any longer.

"Is this what you want?" he whispers, lips still grazing my throat.

Is this his way of warning me—a last-chance indemnity notice? That this will be a one-time thing? That we have an expiration date?

But I can't stop. We're in a car racing down the highway with no brakes.

"Yes," I breathe back. "I want this."

A determined hand splays across my thigh. Then higher, inching under the hem of my skirt. Close, but not enough. I wriggle in his grasp, desperate for more.

"Touch me," I plead, my skin singing with singular want.

Jack's lips curl into a stomach-twisting grin before kissing me again. His mouth never breaks contact as his hand travels under my skirt and between my legs, teasing the shape of me through my underwear, lingering over the spot I need his touch most.

"You're so wet," he murmurs against the hollow of my throat. "So *fucking* wet."

"Then stop fucking teasing me."

Keeping his mouth locked on mine, he pulls my underwear to the side and slides one long finger inside me. "Better?"

I can't answer, all I can do is make a pathetic little whimpering sound, which only encourages him.

His touch is light—vexingly so—and I grind against his hand, riding the rhythm of his strokes. He matches my intensity, making a come-hither motion, and I arch my back, eager for more friction. He slides another finger in and I gasp.

"Tell me what feels good." He sinks his fingers deeper. "There?"

"Yes," I pant.

"And here?" He turns circles with his thumb and forefinger.

"Yes. Fuck, *yes*." My lips part and an involuntary moan rises out of me. "I'm so close," I gasp, voice so breathless it's nearly unrecognizable.

He increases his tempo, fingers pumping in and out of me with perfect precision. "Do you want to come on my hand or my mouth?" he asks.

His words set off sparklers inside my chest, and it takes everything I have to utter back, "Mouth."

In one fluid motion, he picks me up, taut muscles hardening against me, and finally answers the question I asked the night we met: What would it be like to be thrown down on the bed by *those arms*? The answer: *fucking amazing*.

Together we tumble onto the mattress, a mess of arms and legs and ragged breath against skin.

He starts by kissing up the inside of my legs, moving at a pace so agonizingly slow, so restrained, I swear time starts moving backward.

I wiggle my hips, demanding more, but he ignores my request, instead leaving a trail of kisses all the way up to my hips until his tongue runs damp circles around my tattoo.

"So fucking sexy," he murmurs, voice hazy like he's lost in the moment. In me.

His tongue moves back and forth, up and down, drawing patterns on my skin. Then, just when I can't take it anymore, he hooks his thumbs in my underwear and tugs them down my thighs.

"Fuck," he mutters under his breath.

"What?" I ask, worried I'm about to find out, now, at age twenty-eight, that I have an abnormal vagina. "Is something wrong?"

He shakes his head. "You're perfect. Absolutely perfect." His eyes flash to mine, heated and heavy. Then his head is between my legs, gently coaxing my thighs apart and I lose all sense of time and space and thought.

I can't breathe. I can't think. All I can do is *want*.

His tongue circles my most sensitive spot, pausing and lingering, then losing track and starting all over again like my body is a maze he can't seem to find his way out of.

Need stretches inside me like a spiderweb as determined fingers sink into my thighs, and I lift my hips, eager to meet the pressure of his tongue.

"Yes. Don't stop. Jack . . . *Jack* . . ." I pant his name over and over until the syllables blur together and I'm just moaning.

How is it possible I've existed twenty-eight years on this planet and never known anything quite this good? This pleasurable? How is it possible that every flick of his tongue, every gentle sucking motion leaves me hungrier, more feral for him?

I realize, as he brings me to the edge for the third time, that every intimate moment before this pales in comparison, nothing more than a cheap imitation of what Jack can offer. That he can bend me to his will, playing my body like a finely tuned instrument and I'm nothing more than a gasping, panting heap of want, ready to beg for anything he'll give me.

"Jack, *please*," I finally ask.

"Please *what*?"

My body starts to shake with need, demanding he release me from this decadent punishment. "Please let me come."

He pulls back, eyes roving up to meet mine. "Are you begging me, Ada?"

I groan in frustration, pushing my hips into his face. "*Yes*, Jack. I'm begging."

With one hand gripping my ass, angling his mouth to my center, and his other slipping inside me, that's all it takes for me to tip over the edge into an onslaught of pleasure.

I cry out—not entirely dissimilar from my alleged porn star screams—and normally I'd be embarrassed about such a showy display of pleasure, but somehow Jack has managed to strip me of all shame. Like nothing else matters. Nothing except the slow, steady release of pressure between my thighs.

When I open my eyes, Jack's watching me, clearly pleased with himself.

"Wow . . . I . . ." But I can't even string together a sentence. "Wow," I say again, a lopsided grin stretching across my face.

He kisses me again and I taste myself on his tongue. "Good work, kid."

It's not until he pulls back, revealing the amused glimmer in his eyes that I realize he's alluding to the joke he'd made the first night in London. I don't know whether it's hot or funny or both, but the memory feels charged, like a million volts of energy all connecting at once inside me. All I know is that I need him. Now.

"I want you to fuck me now," I tell him. "*Please.*"

For a second, he just looks at me, blinking, until his mouth stretches into a wicked smile. "Say it again," he whispers.

A lurid laugh bubbles out of me. "You're so bossy."

"I think you like it."

I fight back a grin. "I want you to fuck me, Jack."

"You forgot the *please*."

I bite down on my lower lip. "Fine. I want you to *please* fuck me, Jack."

His hips roll over mine, and I haul him flush against me, desperate to close the gaps. A feral moan escapes barely parted lips, and my skin singes with the knowledge that I made him sound like that. That *I* had that effect on him.

Our movements are frantic now—rushed and brazen. We can't wait another second. He tugs my skirt down over my hips and I greedily reach for his belt, letting it fall to the floor with a thump. Then I coax his boxer briefs down his thighs and his erection springs free. My mouth goes dry, trying to calculate how exactly *that's* going to fit *there.* But Jack gently presses me into the mattress, and everything blurs.

We're skin to skin—nothing left between us—and I know right now, in between hazy thoughts of pleasure and need, that

I'll always remember this. That *this* is a moment that will be forever scorched into my memory—a catalog of skin and friction and sweat.

"Condom?" I gasp.

He reaches for his discarded pants, digging his wallet out of the pocket.

"Should I be worried that you brought condoms with you to deliver sausage rolls?" I tease.

He rips a foil packet with his teeth. "I told you, I always come prepared."

"This is the second time I'm thankful to hear you say that," I say.

A laugh breaks in his chest as he rolls the condom on and lowers himself between my hips.

I gasp at the sudden sensation. At the feeling of him wedged against me, long and hard.

"Is this good?" he asks, eyes pinned on me.

I bite down on my lower lip and nod. It's not just *good,* it's better than anything I've ever felt. So good that the word for it does not yet exist in the English language. Or perhaps any language at all.

He slides in a little deeper and everything shrinks to the space where our bodies connect. Where he's pulsing inside me.

"Ada, you're shaking."

"I'm just nervous," I tell him.

Jack pulls back, eyes dragging over me. "We don't have to do anything. We can stop."

In that moment I'd go anywhere with him, do anything with him. *Anything* but stop.

"No, it's a good kind of nervous," I tell him. "I want this. Promise," I add.

He eyes me carefully. "You sure?"

"Yes, Jack," I say, my voice a little breathless. "Please, just don't stop."

He slides the rest of the way inside me, body seizing as he fills me up.

As he goes deeper, his expression shifts, jaw clenching.

"What is it?" I ask. "Are you okay?"

He shuts his eyes. "I'm fine. I just . . . *fuck,* you feel *really* good. I might need to"—he winces—"go slowly," he says.

Jack's first few thrusts are slow and deliberate, an exercise in restraint. But as his pace increases, our movements become less rhythmic, losing all sense of tempo and structure until we're both crashing into one another, pupils blown out, lips parted, gasping.

I close my eyes, trying to hold on to the moment. The weight of Jack on top of me, inside me. The electric probe of his eyes locked on mine as we move together. But I can already feel it slipping away. Like there's not enough time. Not enough *him.*

He feels it too. I feel it in the hungry rhythm of our hips rocking together and the needy way his hands wind through my hair. I feel it in the determined heat of his eyes falling over me in heavy waves, like he's trying to commit me to memory.

Jack's thrusts slow down, tapering off into long, languid strokes before coming to a pause. Dark eyes sink into mine, deep enough to draw blood, and I realize it's the first time we've truly stopped moving since we started. It feels like stepping off a roller coaster. I'm standing still but the earth is still shifting and spinning underneath me.

"What?" I ask, frowning. "Why did you stop?"

His pupils are blown out, eyes wide and hungry. "I . . . I just want to look at you."

He's inside me for goodness' sake, but it's those words that bring a surge of heat to my cheeks.

"There hasn't been a whole lot I've wanted to remember in the last year." His thumb traces my jaw, holding my gaze captive like he's afraid if he looks away I might evaporate right out from under him. "But I want to remember this. I want to remember every single second of this night."

He holds my eyes, two, three beats longer, then he dips his chin to mine, pulling me into another kiss. But it's different from how he kissed me before. This one isn't rushed, in a hurry to escalate things. This is soft and slow as he takes his time, hugging the curves of each moment like I'm something to be savored in agonizing detail. It's tender and thoughtful and utterly unexpected from someone who claims to only *expiration date*.

And somewhere between the exploratory search of his damp mouth on mine and the breathy exhales I swallow as though they were my own, I fall a little harder, a little deeper. I fall far enough that I'm not sure I'll be able to find my way back.

Chapter 26

9 HOURS UNTIL THE WEDDING

We have sex twice more after that.

The second time we take our time exploring, touching, squeezing, grazing—hungry to have our fill of one another. To stretch this moment as long as we can.

The third time we come together in a sleepy, needy trance of fumbling grasps and bitten-off pleas, a little hungrier, a little more desperate, like we both know our time is running out.

There's a mutual awareness threaded behind every kiss, every touch, every hungry roll of the hips, that eventually the sun will come up and there will be veils to attend to, and catering to check on, and a bride and groom to worry about. But for a few hours, in the darkest part of the night when everyone else is asleep, it's just us. Nothing else exists. Nothing except his breath on my ear and my hands in his hair, our bodies tangled together in the sheets.

Afterward, we lie there, naked and sweaty in a cloud of oxytocin and bliss.

He kisses my forehead and tells me we're lucky we didn't break eye contact that first night at the hotel bar. I laugh and kiss him in agreement. Then he pulls me closer, and we fall asleep in a twisted knot of naked limbs and dried sweat.

When I wake up, I'm curled against the edge of the bed, arms and legs covered in prickly goose bumps. It's not until the cool air tickles my bare legs that I realize I'm naked. The sensation jolts me awake and I roll over to see Jack's bare chest rising and falling beside me. A single piece of hair hangs over his eyes, gently fluttering in the push and pull of his breath.

Little by little, memories trickle back. Jack's hands threading my hair. His dark eyes poring over me. The unbearable excitement of wanting him. Of being wanted.

But as much as I wish we could lie here, replaying last night over and over again, the pale morning light filtering through the windows reminds me that it will be time to get up soon.

A quick glance at my phone confirms this. It's just after six a.m., meaning I need to be in hair and makeup soon. Allison's orders.

"Hey."

I look up and see Jack's mouth pulling into a lazy grin. My heartbeat fumbles. Stalls. Then restarts like a faulty engine come back to life.

"Hey," I say back.

"How do you feel?"

A laugh bubbles in the back of my throat. "About the fact that we had sex? Pretty sore. But overall good."

"Sorry about that."

I jab his ribs. "You're not sorry."

His mouth cracks into an uneven smile. "You're right. I'm not. You want me to make it up to you by carrying you down the aisle?"

"That might look suspicious, don't you think?"

"Suspicious of what?"

"That we fucked."

He laughs and the sound is warm and throaty, and so deliciously sexy that it makes me want to mount him all over again.

"I think they might find out sooner or later," he says, giving me a look.

I'm not sure what he means by that, but the words stir inside me.

I'd gone into last night mentally prepared for the fallout. For whatever is supposed to happen after casual hookups. But lying here, heated eyes dancing back and forth, an obvious crackle of electricity sparking between us, it's hard to believe it was nothing more than a meaningless encounter.

I think back to the way he'd looked at me. The way he'd touched me. How careful we'd been with the time we had, like last night was something special neither of us wanted to waste. And I can't help but wonder, is it possible that this doesn't have to end? That maybe I—*we*—can have it all?

The questions hum inside me, an electric current tapping out hopeful rhythms against my chest.

I decide to test the waters. "So . . . it's already after six. We should probably get up. Right?" If he's looking for an excuse to leave, to end things now, I'll give him one.

"Five more minutes?" he asks.

Instant relief washes over me. "How about ten?"

His mouth stretches into a grin. "There's a lot we can do in ten minutes." Then he pulls me to him, mouth catching mine in a searing kiss that wakes me up better than a cup of coffee ever could.

In a flash, he's pushing me down onto the mattress, tongue slipping over mine, hands splaying across my ribs. A breathless moan breaks in his throat and I feel the sound everywhere all at once, a tiny, verbal confirmation that Jack wants me the way I want him.

Somewhere in between his hands on my breasts and the slow, sensual path of his mouth as it moves from my lips to my neck, I know we should talk about this. What it means or doesn't mean. What happens next. But my thoughts are too scrambled. Too lost in the promise of another orgasm.

Jack's thumb skates under my jaw, kissing me lightly before he says, "I want to use your vibrator on you."

I'm so caught up in the press of his thumb and the mounting pressure between my thighs that it takes me a second to process what he's just said.

I pull back, frowning. "Wait. How do you know I have a vibrator?"

"You told me about it when you were drunk," he says matter-of-factly.

"Was there anything I did that night that *wasn't* embarrassing?"

He laughs. "You didn't want me to see it. It was cute. In fact"—he pauses, dragging his eyes over me with unfettered hunger—"you should go get it. Unless you're still embarrassed, of course," he adds with a sly grin.

He doesn't need to convince me. A second later I return to bed, travel-sized vibrator in hand. Shivers chase down my spine as rough hands slide over my hips, dragging me closer, showing me where he's already hard.

"You have no idea what you do to me, do you?" he whispers.

"I think I may have some idea."

I take him in my hand, feeling every hard ridge and line of his erection. He groans, a primal sound ripped from somewhere deep inside, and I don't know what I love more, the sound itself or that I'm the reason for it.

His hands mold around my hips, holding me in place as his mouth slides across mine, teasing, hesitant, like he's not planning to kiss me at all. But then he does and the way his mouth catches mine in a decadent kiss feels almost serendipitous, like we've just happened to collide, and this kiss is the final domino in a chain of happy accidents.

My lips part in a wide, open-mouthed gasp as his hand trails down the side of my jawline, tipping my head back so he can capture the undercurve of my neck with his mouth. I'm so caught up in the wet heat of his tongue against my throat that I almost don't hear him whisper, "I want you on top."

I pull back, gaze tracing where there's a nonverbal *Is this okay?* primed behind his eyes. I dip my head into the tiniest nod. *Yes.*

He rolls on a condom and my breath staggers, pulse jumping in anticipation. There's one more sharp inhale, followed by a slow, shaky release. Then he's filling me up and I'm grinding against him, every muscle intent on bringing us closer, deeper. I'm already close when he turns on the vibrator and presses it against me.

It's the same vibrator I've used for years, nothing more than a means to an end, but in the hands of Jack, it transforms from mundane sex toy to something incomparably hot. Like he's managed to find a setting I had no idea even existed.

A string of curse words pours out of me as Jack's fingers dig into my hip, eyes locking on mine, telling me how beautiful I look on top. How good I feel. How wet. How tight. How he wants me to come for him.

I know I shouldn't want or need or hope for anything from him. But there's an ever-widening gap between the words in my head and the way he's looking at me. The heady pressure behind his eyes that feels like friction. Like he wants this—*needs this*—just as badly as I do. And my foolish heart keeps on hoping.

My orgasm comes so fast it takes me by surprise. Then he's coming, too, and we're unspooling together, breathy moans commingling in the air between us.

Afterward, we collapse against the mattress in a blissed-out haze, his fingers twisting mindlessly in my hair, both of us panting, covered in a sheen of sweat. I'm just catching my breath when I hear it.

Knock, knock, knock.

Was that—? Is there—? No, there couldn't possibly be someone at the door. But then the knock comes again.

"Ada? I need to talk to you," a voice calls from outside the door.

It takes me a minute to play catch-up as I blink back the orgasm-induced stupor still clouding my thoughts. But slowly the truth unwinds itself, breaking in past the Jack-shaped barrier crowding all rational parts of my brain.

"It's Allison," I whisper.

Jack's body seizes beside me. "What do we do?"

The primal part of me wants to throw caution to the wind and ignore her. After all, Jack and I still need to talk. But the rational part of me knows that's not going to fly. Not today anyway.

"You have to hide," I tell Jack.

His gaze widens, surprised. "Hide where?"

My eyes dart around the room, landing on the set of sliding doors opposite the bed. "The closet! Hurry!"

We untangle ourselves, tumbling out of bed, hands darting for discarded clothing.

"Ada? Are you awake?" Allison calls.

"Yes! One second!"

I throw Jack's boxer briefs at him and tug an oversized T-shirt over my head.

"Go! Go!" I whisper, practically shoving him into the closet with a pile of his own clothes.

I slam the closet shut, take a deep breath, and open the door. Outside stands Allison in a white bridal robe and curlers.

Call it sister's intuition, but as soon as my eyes meet hers, I can tell something's not right.

"What's wrong?" I ask.

She gnaws on her bottom lip, eyes welling with tears. "I'm sorry . . . I . . ." But the words don't make it out before she collapses into tears.

Worry strums my nerves as I wrap my arms around her, letting her bury her face in my chest. "Allison, what is it?"

"You're gonna be mad," she sobs.

"I promise I won't get mad," I say as I pat her hair.

Allison lifts her chin, glassy, tearstained eyes meeting mine. "Are you sure?"

"Allison, whatever it is, you can tell me," I say, trying to keep my voice soft and tempered, all the while my insides tangle themselves in worried knots, racing from one worst-cast scenario to the next. *She wants to call it off. She knows Collin was having second thoughts. Or worse, Collin's already called it off.* Last night, everything seemed fine, just like Jack said. But clearly that's not the case. Somewhere between me tucking Allison into bed and now, something changed.

She sniffs, withdrawing her body from mine. "I'm scared," she says at last.

I search her face. "Of what?"

Her bottom lip quivers. "What if you're right? What if we're rushing into things and I don't know Collin as well as I should?"

My heart bypasses my brain. I don't stop, I don't collect two hundred dollars, I go straight to panic.

"Did Collin say or do something?" I demand. "Because I swear—"

"No." She shakes her head, mouth forming a tight line. "Collin didn't do anything."

My chest loosens. "So what is it? What happened?"

Allison looks away, teeth sinking into her lips. "Nothing happened," she says, nearly exasperated. "It's just *forever* . . . that's such a long time."

I blink at her. "What do you mean?"

"We haven't even known each other a full year. I don't know if Collin prefers dogs or cats. Or if he thought the viral dress was blue and black or gold and white. Or what his favorite Taylor Swift album is." Allison's eyes widen as though just now realizing marriage isn't a FabFitFun subscription. "Oh my God, what if he doesn't like Taylor Swift? I *can't* marry a man who doesn't like Taylor Swift!"

Allison keeps talking, rattling off all the things she doesn't know about Collin. But I've stopped listening.

All I can think is, *I knew this would happen.*

I knew from the moment she showed me the big, sparkly rock on her finger that cost more than a year's rent that it was too good to be true. That it was only a matter of time before it all came crashing down.

But maybe I can still fix this.

My brain activates into damage control mode. First, I'll tell everyone Allison's sick. Then I'll start canceling vendors. I'm not sure if we can get any deposits back since it's the day of, but maybe if I grovel—

"Ada, stop."

I step back, frowning. "Stop *what*?"

"*This*." She gestures vaguely. "I can see what you're doing."

"I'm not doing anything," I tell her, simultaneously wondering if there is a back door she can sneak out of.

"Yes, you are," she huffs. "You're trying to figure out how you can fix it."

"Of course I'm trying to fix it," I snap. "What else do you expect me to do when you come to my room on the day of your wedding and tell me you're having doubts about marrying Collin?"

"I don't need you to fix it, Ada!"

Annoyance prickles inside me. "You *always* need me to fix it," I tell her, voice ratcheting up. "You needed me the night I drove twenty-seven hours to LA to come get you. You needed me when I flew home from New York after your ex dumped you! You needed me every time you went through yet another breakup!"

"I didn't ask you to do those things!"

"But you didn't exactly stop me from dropping everything to be there for you, did you?"

Her jaw clenches and she takes a step back. "I knew it was a mistake to tell you any of this. I'm just gonna go. Forget I said anything."

She turns to leave.

"Wait."

Allison pauses, hand hovering over the doorknob.

As much as I want to swoop in with a chorus of *I told you so*'s—to remind her that this is the exact thing I warned her about, the thing I've been afraid of this whole time—I'm reminded of what Jack said to me on the way to Scotland. *You're her sister, not her keeper.*

Allison doesn't need to hear *I told you so*—or even for me to try to fix it—she just needs me to be there for her. She just needs me to be her sister.

"Allison, come back," I say, corralling my voice into something softer.

"If you're just going to tell me you were right and *I told you so*, then—"

"I'm not," I say, cutting her off. "I just want to talk."

I sit on the bed and pat the spot beside me.

Tentative eyes skate to the spot, then the door, then back to me, before she finally sits down. "Fine. What?" she asks.

"Do you really not want to marry Collin?" I ask. "Or is something else bothering you?"

She shifts her weight, eyes dipping into her lap. After a heavy exhale, she says, "I do want to marry Collin . . . I just . . . What if this is one more thing I fuck up?"

"Why do you think you're going to fuck it up?" I ask her.

"Why wouldn't I?" she asks, voice wavering. "Every relationship I've ever been in has ended in disaster."

Her eyes meet mine, and I can see the vulnerability behind her gaze, the ache of worry I so badly want to scrub away. But I know that's not what she needs right now.

"You're right," I tell her. "You're probably going to make mistakes in this relationship. And so will Collin. But isn't that sort of the point of marriage?" I ask. "Two imperfect people trying to figure it out? Forever?"

Her gaze sweeps over me, probing. "You don't think that sounds intimidating or overwhelming?"

"I mean . . ."

I think about Jack and Lexi—and even my mom and Bill—and I get why marriage is scary. Especially when the odds of heartbreak are so high. But I don't think marriage is about finding someone who makes forever easy, because no one can do that. I think marriage is about choosing someone over and over again no matter how hard things get.

"I get why you're scared," I say at last. "Forever is a long time. And it's not going to be easy, not with Collin, not with anyone.

It's going to be hard work. But the question is whether Collin is the person you *want* to do the hard work with."

For a long minute Allison doesn't speak, and I worry this might be the moment she tells me she can't do this, that she's changed her mind. But slowly, Allison dips her chin into a nod. "I know I've made a lot of mistakes in the past, especially with guys. But this time it's real. I can feel it."

She swallows, eyes jumping down, then back up before she finally says, "Before Collin, I thought love was screaming matches and passionate make-ups and dramatic endings. That in order for something to be real, it had to be big and fiery and explosive. But it's not like that with Collin. He makes me feel safe and cared for. He's the first guy that's made me feel like I *deserve* to be treated well. That I'm worthy of love. Real love. The kind that doesn't need to play games or yell and scream to prove itself."

There's an unexpected intimacy behind her voice, like this is the first time she's told anyone how she really feels about Collin. The thought strikes me with unexpected tenderness.

"You really love him?" I ask after a beat.

She nods. "I do."

The admission manages to crawl past my final lines of defense, smothering me in a crushing mix of guilt and relief.

"I'm sorry for not trusting your relationship with Collin," I tell her. "But I was scared too. I was scared that you'd get hurt again. Especially after . . ." I know not to say Bradley's name in front of her. "I was scared that you were making this huge mistake that I wouldn't be able to protect you from."

"I'm sorry too. I'm sorry for shutting you out." Her bottom lip disappears between her teeth. "But, Ada, it's not your job to protect me."

I let her words wash over me, brash and unyielding. Jack had been right. Something I hadn't wanted to accept at the time. But now, hearing her tell me the truth decodes something inside me. Something I hadn't wanted to admit.

"You're right," I say, my voice filling with resolve. "It's just hard for me, especially when I feel like I've spent my entire life looking out for you. Sometimes I'm not sure how to do anything else, or what my role is if I'm not trying to protect you."

Her expression softens. "I know I've relied on you a lot in the past," she says. "But I don't want to rely on you anymore. Sometimes I just want to talk to you about stuff and not feel like you're gonna try to swoop in and save the day all the time." She pauses, struggling to keep her voice from splintering. "Sometimes I need my sister to just listen and be there for me."

My throat twists, a sharp throb emerging in my chest. The request seems so simple when spelled out like that.

"I can do that," I tell her.

The corners of her mouth tug upward and she gives my hand a squeeze. For the first time in a long time, I feel the gaps between us start to narrow. We haven't fixed everything between us, but it's a start.

"I'm glad you're here," she says.

My chest burns with hope and happiness. "Me too," I tell her.

We stay like that, hands clasped together, tender looks hovering behind our eyes, then Allison backs away, eyes flitting to the ground like she's just been caught doing something embarrassing.

"Well, I should get back to my room," she says. "The makeup artist is probably looking for me."

"I'll see you later then. Right?" I ask, just to be sure.

She laughs, and it feels good to hear. "Yes," she clarifies. "I'll be the one in white. Kinda hard to miss."

Relief swarms me. *Everything's going to be okay.*

Allison stands to go, and her eyes bounce around the room as though just now noticing the messy bed and last night's clothes littered across the floor as though haphazardly tossed there in a moment of passion––which of course they were. Her eyes snag on the other side of the bed, narrowing, and I follow her line of vision.

Oh shit.

Allison picks Jack's Rolex off the nightstand, pinching it between her thumb and forefinger like it's the primary clue in a murder investigation.

"Did you sleep with Jack?"

Damn. She's good. How did she do that?

"No! That's mine," I say, snatching it back.

Her forehead creases with a frown. "First off, this is a Rolex, which I know you can't afford. Second, this is a man's watch."

"So? You know I don't subscribe to gendered fashion norms."

She wrinkles her nose. "It smells like sex in here."

"No, it doesn't."

Does it?

Her hands find their way to her hips. "Don't lie to me, Ada. I can tell."

"Tell?"

How can she possibly tell? Is it the post-sex glow? Is my shirt on backward? I look down to be sure.

Allison waves her hand airily around the room. "Your vibrator's on the bed."

"So? I was using it alone—"

"*And* there's a hickey the size of Texas on your neck," she adds.

My hand flies to my neck, where sure enough I feel a swollen mark.

"You know," I say. "You should work for the CIA. I'd feel much better about our national security if you were in charge."

"Is that an admission?"

I purse my lips, trying to discern if this is really the conversation I want to have right now—especially with Jack hearing every word. But it appears my sister has no plans of letting this go.

"Okay, fine. Yes, I slept with Jack," I admit. "Happy?"

"How did this happen?"

I cough out a strangled laugh. "I never thought I'd be the one to have this conversation with you on your wedding day, but when two people—"

She gives me a frustrated look. "Ada, be serious. Have you been hooking up this whole time?"

"No," I say quickly. "Last night was the first time." *And maybe the last time.*

"So what happened?" she asks.

"Well . . ." But I don't know how to succinctly explain that forced proximity, vulnerable conversations, and mounting feelings of mutual attraction resulted in a feverish night of passion, so instead, I say, "Um, he brought me sausage rolls."

"*Sausage rolls?*" Her eyes widen. "Is that a sex position?"

"No! I just mean . . . Never mind." My heart races knowing Jack can hear all of this. "Are you mad?"

"You used protection, right?"

"Yes, of course."

"Then I'm not mad," she says. "You can sleep with whoever you want. After all the literal swamp creatures I've slept with, I have no room to judge." She pauses, eyes shifting to the floor. "But I thought you wanted to get back together with Carter."

"We broke up," I say, realizing as the words leave my mouth that she's the first person other than Jack that I've told.

Her gaze stretches wide. "When?"

"On the way here."

"So you decided to sleep with Jack? Like as a rebound?"

I shift my weight, bouncing from one foot to the other like I have to pee. "No, it wasn't like that."

"Then what was it like?"

"I . . ." My eyes skate to the closet, where I know Jack can hear all of this. "I don't know," I tell her. "It just happened."

Which is true. I didn't plan for it to happen. And yet, it feels wrong to tell Allison that last night was some kind of cosmic accident when it was nothing of the sort. At least not for me. But it's not like I can tell her I have real feelings for Jack and want us to live happily ever after, not when he's a few feet away, listening to every word.

For a long moment, Allison just looks at me, mouth slightly parted, eyes homing in on me like I'm a slide under a microscope. Finally, she says, "Listen, I'm happy for you to move on from Carter and get laid, but this is really out of character for you, and I guess I'm just surprised."

My chest constricts, heavy blood pounding in my eardrums as her words hit me in a nerve center I hadn't expected.

Part of me wants to tell her to mind her own business. That it's not her problem. But given the conversation we just had, that seems hypocritical.

Besides, she's right. This *is* unlike me. I'm dependable, reliable, consistent. The kind of girl who dates the same guy for eight years because she's afraid of change.

But then last night happened. And it had felt so good. So right. Like everything that happened over the past few days had been building toward that, a slow, steady wave that had finally crashed over both of us.

"There's nothing to be worried about," I tell her, lips pulling into a tight smile. "I'm fine. I can handle myself, Allison."

"I know, but . . ." She releases a heavy sigh, eyes cutting to the ground then back to me. "I don't know if he told you this, but Jack's getting divorced."

"I know," I tell her. "He told me."

Her eyes widen before narrowing again. "Okay, so you know that he's a mess?"

A seed of annoyance blooms inside me. "I don't see what the big deal is," I tell her, voice tightening. "It's a divorce, not herpes."

"He probably has that too." As soon as she says it, she winces. "Sorry, bad joke. I just don't want you to get your hopes up and think that Jack's gonna be your boyfriend. He does stuff like this all the time."

My mind travels back to last night. *Typical*, Tony and Braden had said. But last night had been different. *We* were different. Right?

"I know Jack has a *reputation*," I say, using air quotes. "But last night wasn't like that."

"Ada." She sighs my name like I'm a naive child who still thinks Santa Claus exists. "I know you're a big girl and you can handle yourself, but his divorce fucked him up and I don't want you to get caught in the cross fire and end up as collateral damage in his attempts to fuck his ex-wife off his mind. That's all."

I open my mouth to argue, to explain why she's wrong. Why she's the one being hypocritical right now. Why Jack isn't using me to fuck his ex-wife off his mind. But the words don't make it out. They stay jammed in my throat, trapped by the hornet's nest of insecurities she's just kicked.

My eyes flick to the closet door. I can't have this conversation, not here, not now, with Jack still in the room.

"Listen, I'm glad we talked, but I think you should go," I tell her.

Allison blinks back at me, clearly taken aback. "What?"

"I just mean you don't want to keep the hair and makeup people waiting," I say, taking her by the elbow and dragging her toward the door. "I'll catch up with you later, okay?"

Allison presses her lips into a zipped-up line, and I think she might argue, but then her chin dips into a tight nod. "Fine. I'll see you later."

She gives me one last look before disappearing out the door.

Chapter 27

7 HOURS UNTIL THE WEDDING

As soon as Allison's gone, the closet door opens and Jack emerges, tugging at the zipper on his pants. Last night's wrinkled shirt hangs open, unbuttoned.

"I'm sorry you had to hear that," I tell him.

There's a long pause. Too long. A slow pain spreads over my body, dull and grating like a headache.

Finally, he says, "I should go."

"You don't have to leave right now," I tell him. "You can stay."

I want you to stay.

But he doesn't answer, and I watch in silence as he slides his watch onto his wrist and buttons up his shirt.

"It's better if I leave," he says at last.

"Is it because of what Allison said?" I ask. "Because—"

He shakes his head, jaw tightening. "No, it's not that."

My limbs stiffen, blood turning heavy in my veins.

I want to believe nothing's changed. That he just needs to get ready for the wedding. But I know that's not true. I feel the shift in the air, like right before a storm.

He finishes buttoning his shirt then moves toward the door.

"So, I'll see you later?" I ask, desperately hoping he'll tell me what I want to hear. That he'll be back. That this isn't over.

He pauses, hand hovering over the doorknob. "I guess so." But he doesn't say it like, *I can't wait to make out with you later.* More like we'll have to see each other at the wedding.

It feels painfully final, and panic grabs my throat, stealing my breath as I grasp for something to say, something to make him stay. Something to change the course of this moment.

"Jack. Wait."

He hesitates before turning back to face me.

"I know you don't owe me anything, but can we at least talk?" My voice cracks against my will. "About us? About last night?"

He licks his lips, eyes trailing to the carpet. "I think I should just go."

I step back, feeling like I've been sucker punched.

This is worse than the worst-case scenario I had played out in my head. At least in that I'd imagined a gradual distancing, a slow but painful fade into oblivion. But this rapid withdrawal is *so* much worse.

"So this is how this ends?" I ask. "We meet our expiration date and you walk out of here like nothing happened between us?"

He shoves his hands in his pockets. "I don't think we have a choice."

I shake my head as though my body is physically rejecting what he's saying. "What do you mean we don't have a choice? Of course we have a choice. It doesn't have to be like this."

"Come on, Ada." There's a grating pull in his voice that I feel all the way in the pit of my stomach. "Last night was fun. Let's just leave it at that, okay?"

Heavy pangs of frustration churn inside me. Despite everything he's told me, I refuse to believe that last night, that the last few days, were simply *nothing*. Nothing more than sexual tension and meaningless flirtations. Maybe I believed that a few days ago. But not now. Not after last night. Or this morning. Not after he looked at me the way he did. Touched me the way he did. Not after everything.

"Jack, I get that you don't do commitment and that you had your heart broken, but was all this really nothing to you?" I search his face, looking for some kind of indicator that he doesn't mean what he said, that maybe I've misunderstood.

His entire face tightens. "Of course it wasn't nothing—"

"Then why—"

He holds his hand up. "Ada, *stop*." I freeze and Jack lets out a heavy exhale. "I can't be your fucking boyfriend."

His words hit me somewhere in my gut and I wince.

It's the same thing Allison said. But a million times worse coming out of Jack's mouth. Like finally confronting the monster under the bed that you've known was there the whole time, but you didn't want to admit it.

"Why are you so afraid of this thing between us?" I demand. "Would it really be so bad to at least explore it? To see where it goes?"

Veins pulse at his temples. "I *can't*, Ada. I told you that."

My heartbeat ratchets up, pulse slamming against my ribs.

"So last night was no different from the night we met? You were just trying to get in my pants? That was all?"

His mouth sets into a hard line. "That's not what I meant. That's not what this is."

"Then what is it?" I demand, hating the tug of desperation in my own voice. "Tell me. I can take it."

For a beat he just looks at me, like he expects it to be obvious, then in a low voice he says, "Your sister's right, Ada."

I frown, unsure where my sister fits into this. "What are you talking about?"

"What she said, about my divorce fucking me up."

I wince, remembering Allison's callous words. "She just meant that you were torn up over the divorce—"

"No, it's more than that."

For a moment he stares ahead, gaze fixed on the wall, before he finally says, "I thought it was clear that I'm in a bad place right now. I mean, come on, I told my best friend not to marry the woman he loves. That doesn't exactly scream *emotionally stable,* does it?"

"But—"

"As much as I wish I could forget about Lexi and my failed marriage and everything I did wrong, it's still on my mind *all the fucking time.*" He pauses, tension coiling around his features. "So, *no,* I'm not boyfriend material. Not for you, not for anyone."

My heart roars in my throat as I try to make sense of what he's saying, to catalog it and reorganize it in a way that doesn't make me feel like there's a weight on my chest, growing heavier and heavier. But the more I think about it, the more it makes sense. And the more it makes sense, the harder it is to breathe.

"I'm a mess, Ada," he continues, hurt bleeding through his voice. "I'm good for a one-night stand, but that's about it, okay?"

"But I'm a mess too." I gesture to myself. "When you met me, I was sobbing in a hotel lobby, for crying out loud. I'm the poster child for a mess."

The muscles in his jaw flex. "I just don't think I can give you what you want, Ada."

"And what do you think I want?"

"You want happily ever after and romance and certainty. You want what your mom and stepdad have. But I'm just getting out of a failed marriage. I'm not *Mr. Right,*" he says, voice cracking like a whip on the last syllable. "And you can't fix me, Ada."

"I know that, I—"

"Do you, Ada?"

I take a step back, the bitter edge in his voice knocking me off-balance.

"Because it sort of seems like you want me to take the place of Carter, and I can't do that. I can't be *the one* for you."

"I'm not asking you to!"

He shakes his head, tangled knots of frustration weaving across his expression. "What your sister said was true. Two days ago you wanted to get back with Carter, and now suddenly you want to be with me? Some guy you barely know whose life is a mess?" There's an ache of weariness in his voice that catches me off guard. "You ended things with Carter because he couldn't give you what you want, and good for you. But what makes you think that things with me would be any different? What makes you think I could give you what you want?"

"So is this about Carter or about me?"

"It's about the fact that *this*," he says, gesturing between us, "can't be anything. And that it's not fair to either of us to pretend like this thing between us wasn't doomed from the start."

"*Doomed?*" I repeat, voice shaking, caught somewhere between anger and hurt. "If this was so doomed, then why did you sleep with me? Why did you kiss me?"

"You asked me to."

"Seriously?" A humorless laugh escapes me. "You're going to blame last night on me? You're the one who came to *my* room, remember? I thought we both wanted it."

"I did. I just . . ." But he doesn't finish. Instead, he stands there, chest heaving, until finally he says, "It's not that I don't care about you, Ada. But I can't."

A heavy beat passes, dark eyes sweeping over me once more before he turns and moves toward the door.

I'd thought about this moment, anticipated it even, but now as it's happening, I can't help the hurt corroding the inside of my stomach. The painful realization that I've blown right past all my carefully constructed mental caution tape. That I've given my heart, my mind, my body to Jack without any assurances that I'd get anything in return. Just like I did with Carter.

The recognition of my own naiveté pours over me in heavy, suffocating streaks, snaking past the last shreds of hope guarding my heart.

Jack stops in front of the door. "Ada, I . . ." He swallows, and I hate the hopeful tug in my chest. "I'll see you at the wedding." Then he slips into the hall, letting the door shut with a tight thud behind him.

I stare at the door a full thirty seconds, waiting to see if he'll come back, if he'll tell me it was all a mistake, that he didn't mean it. But he doesn't, and I slowly sink to my knees, vision blurring behind a hot curtain of tears.

Chapter 28

7 HOURS UNTIL THE WEDDING

Through a blurry fog of tears, my eyes dance from the unmade bed to the bra peeking out from under it. Allison's right. It *does* smell like sex in here. And regret. And I'm suddenly filled with an unbearable need to be absolutely anywhere but this room.

I pull on the first clothes I can reach—a University of Washington hoodie, black leggings, and a pair of scuffed-up Chucks—and head for the door. My feet blindly carry me down to the lobby and outside into the crisp morning air.

Gravel crunches underfoot as I pass the horse stables, the scent of dirt and grass and horse manure filling my lungs.

It's quiet out here. Nothing but the gentle lap of the lake and the hum of the earth under my feet. A brisk morning breeze ripples past and I shiver, pulling my hoodie closer.

I scan the misty horizon, imagining the dark shades I'd use to paint the water's edge. The sharp contour of the hills looming in the distance. The varying shades of green, dripping with vibrancy like I'm seeing everything through a polarizing filter. The swift brushstrokes for rolling waves of green that seem to go on for miles, stretching and folding into a limitless distance.

Overhead, the sun shifts west across a pale sky, and I close my eyes like I did on Arthur's Seat, focusing on the thrum of my heart and the heavy rise and fall of my breath until all the sounds start to overlap and run together like a string of musical notes.

In the stillness, my mind wanders back to Jack. His touch. His mouth. His taste. The hum of his voice. The glimmer of *what if* I've allowed to dangle in front of me like a carrot on a string.

I should have known better. I should have prepared for this. After all, I'd told myself this was a possibility. But I'd given in anyway. Perhaps because there was some part of me that naively believed things with us were different. That *I* was different. That the last few days were enough to blow past everything I knew to be true about him. Everything he'd told me about himself. But I'd been wrong. Painfully, frustratingly wrong. And now I can't ignore the heavy dose of reality sliding down my back like an ice cube.

Doomed from the start, he'd said.

I wish I could tell myself that's not true, but he's right. Of course he is. Not just about himself, but about me as well.

I'm just getting out of an eight-year relationship. A relationship I haven't yet grieved or fully processed. And he's getting divorced—something that isn't even finalized. He's built towering walls around himself that won't come down anytime soon. Not for me. Maybe not for anyone.

I stand there a moment longer, feeling my lungs expand and contract against my chest, watching my breath rise like smoke in the crisp air until I notice white folding chairs being set up on the lawn, and I'm reminded that I should be getting back. I'm probably already late for hair and makeup.

I turn back toward the castle, mentally preparing myself for the amount of fake smiling I'm going to have to do today, when a distant noise catches me off guard. Something like scraping metal? Or gagging?

I scan the grounds until my eyes snag on a figure hunched over, bent at the knees, puking into one of the horse troughs by the stables. I freeze. Wait. Is that—? No. That can't be.

My feet squelch in the mud as I quicken my pace toward the figure. When I'm close enough to see who it is, I break into a full-on run.

"Collin?"

He lets out a belch before sinking to the ground, mud staining his pants.

I crouch beside him. "Collin? Can you hear me?" I shake his arm and his eyes flicker open.

"Allison?" he murmurers, voice groggy.

"It's Ada."

"Allison?" he asks again.

He's in worse shape than I thought.

"Collin, what happened?" A flash of scenarios ripples across my mind. The boys all getting wasted a few hours before the ceremony. Empty booze bottles everywhere. A trashed hotel room. Oh God. This is bad. How did he even get out here? And where are the other groomsmen? I look over my shoulder, half expecting Tony or Braden to stumble out from the stables.

"Allison, I'm sorry," he croaks.

"Collin, Allison's not here," I tell him. "It's me, Ada. I'm gonna try to help you." But as soon as I say it, I realize I'm not sure what I can do. He weighs twice as much as me. There's no way I can carry him.

"Collin? Can you hear me?" I try again. "Can you stand?"

His eyelids flicker for just a second before closing again.

Fuck.

I need a plan.

I'm just about to see if maybe the situation will grant me mom-lifting-a-minivan-off-her-child superpowers, when his eyes flutter half open. "Allison?"

God, not this again.

"No, it's Ada—" I grit my teeth, summoning all my strength as I try to lift him. But it's no use. He's too heavy.

I slump against the trough, eyes skipping from the drool on his chin to the suspicious stain on the front of his shirt. He looks terrible and I can't help but feel bad for the poor guy. Even if it is his own fault.

"Collin?" I try again, but he's out cold.

I sigh. This is probably the longest amount of time Collin and I have spent together, just the two of us.

A few days ago, I would have said it was because Collin and I don't get along. Because I don't trust him. But now I can't help but feel like it's my fault. Because I never gave him a chance or tried to get to know him. But maybe here, outside the stables, while he's covered in vomit on his wedding day, is just as good a time as any.

"Collin?" I try. "Can you hear me?"

His chin perks up.

"Do you want to marry Allison?" I ask.

Eyes still closed, he nods.

"And you really love her?"

For a long moment, he doesn't speak and I think he's passed out again. Then he holds up both hands spread apart. I frown. I don't understand . . . but then it dawns on me. He's showing me *how much.*

Warm relief pours over me.

Maybe I was wrong about Collin. Maybe he's a good guy just like Jack said. And maybe it's not too late to try to fix things.

"Collin," I say, taking a long breath. "I know I haven't been, uh . . ." I stall, looking for the right words. "As supportive of this wedding as I could have been, and that you and I haven't exactly gotten off on the right foot, but before you marry Allison there are a few things I want you to know about her. Like that her go-to comfort movie is *The Parent Trap*. And when she's hungover, she wants pancakes and hash browns. Her favorite Taylor Swift album is either *Lover* or *Reputation* depending on what kind of mood she's in. Her favorite flowers are roses, but only red or white ones. She hates salt and vinegar flavored anything. She'll tell you she won't get cold, but she always gets cold, so make sure she brings a sweater. And she'll act like she doesn't know what she's doing, but she will absolutely crush your ass at Scrabble." I pause, watching as a tiny dribble of drool makes its way down his chin. After a beat, I say, "I guess what I'm trying to say is that my sister means everything to me, and I just want her to be happy, so if marrying you is what makes her happy, then you have my blessing."

I search for some kind of acknowledgment that he got any of that. But still no movement.

"Okay, good talk," I say, giving his shoulder a firm pat.

I turn and look out at the lawn stretching all the way up to the castle, wondering if anyone is out looking for us. If maybe they'll send a search party when the groom doesn't show up for photos.

"Ada?"

When I look back at Collin his eyes are still closed.

"Yeah?"

"Allison misses you."

Emotion bottlenecks in my throat. "She does?"

But Collin doesn't answer. Instead, he slumps over and begins to snore.

I wait to see if he'll wake up again, but when he doesn't, I pull out my phone and call the one person who can help me right now.

He picks up on the third ring.

"Ada?"

"Hi . . . uh, listen . . . I know it's not a good time, but I need your help. It's Collin. He's a mess." I look down at where his chest rises and falls in time with his rhythmic snores. "Can you bring water?"

"Tell me where you are," he says. "I'll be right there."

■ ■ ———

AS SOON AS JACK SPOTS ME, I WAVE HIM OVER. WHEN HE GETS CLOSER, HIS dark eyes narrow and it's hard to tell if he's mad or just worried.

"I know you probably don't want to see me—"

"It's fine." He peers beyond me to where Collin sits, still slumped over, eyes shut, drool dripping from his chin. Jack winces. "He's in bad shape, huh?"

"How did this even happen?" I ask. "Were the guys pregaming this morning or something?"

"I have no idea, considering I was with you this morning." He shoots me a look I can't read. "He must have been drinking with Tony and Braden."

Hot bursts of memory pop behind my eyes. Jack's hands on my waist, guiding me on top of him. Lazy morning kisses and soft moans. I brush the thought aside.

"Did you bring the water?" I ask.

Jack hands me a bottle of water and I crouch beside Collin and tilt the bottle toward his lips.

"Collin, you need to drink this," I urge. Slowly his eyes flicker open, and he starts to drink.

"How do you feel?" Jack asks, kneeling beside me.

"Like shit," Collin mumbles.

"You look it."

Collin tries to grin. "Is Allison mad?"

"Lucky for you, she doesn't know yet. Right?" Jack looks to me to confirm and I nod.

"Please don't tell her," Collin pleads. "She's gonna kill me."

"Don't worry. I don't have a death wish," Jack says with a grimace. "Can you stand?"

"I don't think he can do much of anything right now," I say. "We'll have to carry him."

I scan the length of Collin's body, trying to figure out the mechanics of how Jack and I could carry him. But even if we can get Collin up and moving, he still looks like shit. His shirt is covered in mud and vomit. Not to mention he stinks to high heaven of booze. There's no way we can smuggle him back into the castle looking like this. Someone is sure to notice. Unless . . .

I turn to Jack. "I have an idea. Take off your shirt."

His mouth widens into a horrified *o*. "My what?"

"Your shirt." I gesture to his crisp button-down. "Take it off."

"And why exactly do I need to take my shirt off?"

"So you can switch shirts with Collin," I tell him.

"You want me to wear his wet, vomit-stained shirt?" he repeats, a groove appearing between his brows.

I wave my hand dismissively. "He's the groom, you're not. No one cares if you stink of booze and look like Charlie Sheen after a bad night."

Jack looks like he wants to argue but begins unbuttoning his shirt anyway. I bury my gaze, eager to look absolutely anywhere but Jack's naked torso, the same torso that a matter of hours ago had been pressed up against me in bed.

He clears his throat when he's done, signaling that the coast is clear, and I help Collin into Jack's clean shirt while Jack puts on Collin's dirty one.

"Good as new," Jack remarks as soon as Collin's dressed. "Just like *Weekend at Bernie's*." He catches my eye with a small smile, and my stomach gives a traitorous flutter.

"Do you think Allison will notice?" I ask.

Jack gives me a look. "It's Allison."

"You're right. But he looks a lot better. And he still has a few hours to sober up."

Jack reaches for one arm and I take the other. "On three. One . . . two . . . *three*." Together, we hoist him to his feet. Collin totters a bit, but Jack takes most of his weight, and the three of us hobble through the grass toward the castle like we're participating in a drunken version of a three-legged race. If anyone sees us, we're dead.

Jack must have the same thought because he asks, "What are we going to do if we run into someone? He still looks awful."

"Wait," I say, a little out of breath. We stop and I dig inside my purse, where I pull out a pair of sunglasses. "How about these?"

Jack makes a face. "Collin wouldn't be caught dead in cat-eye sunglasses."

"I don't think Collin is really in a position to be picky about fashion choices right now." I place the glasses on his face and step back, assessing. "Not bad, right?"

Flickers of amusement dance across Jack's features. "You're enjoying this, aren't you?"

"Maybe a little."

Jack's tight jaw loosens into a smile and something warm and liquid-like blooms inside my gut, but I shove it back down. *It's over,* I remind myself.

As we enter the lobby, the doorman tips his hat at us, and we give him our best *he is totally fine right now and absolutely nothing is wrong* smiles. I think he buys it. So far, so good.

We make it all the way to the elevators without passing anyone, when the elevator door dings and my mother walks out.

"Ada?" Her eyes travel from me, covered in mud with tangled hair and puffy eyes, to Jack, who looks like he's just tumbled out of a sewage heap, and finally over to Collin. She winces.

"Hey, Mom," I say, forcing a faux cheerful smile.

She wrinkles her nose as though she's just smelled something foul. Which she probably has. "What's going on?" she asks. "Is Collin okay?"

"Hi, Mrs. Gallman." Jack's eyes bounce to Collin as though just now noticing him for the first time. "Oh, Collin? He's fine."

The dent between her brows deepens. "Are you sure?"

I follow my mom's gaze to Collin, whose head has started to list forward. It looks like he's staring right at—*oh no*—my mom's chest.

This is bad. I try to adjust my hold on him, but his neck angles farther forward and the sunglasses slide to the bridge of his nose, like he's trying extra hard to get a peek. It's really *not* funny, except that, yeah . . . it's pretty funny, and I bite down on the inside of my cheeks to keep from laughing.

"Collin? Are you all right?" my mom asks, her face twisting with worry. When he doesn't answer, she looks to me. "Why are you holding him like that? Ada, what's going on?"

"He's fine," I lie. "Just a little horseback-riding injury. Nothing serious. Nothing to worry about."

Horseback-riding injury? Where do I get this stuff?

Jack gives me a look, but I discreetly shake my head, hoping he gets the memo to *just go with it!*

"Right. Horseback riding," Jack repeats. "Collin loves to ride. Helps clear his head," he adds with a knowing nod.

My mom frowns. "Horseback riding? But, Ada—"

Mercifully the elevator dings and the doors slide open.

"We have to go. See ya later, Mrs. Gallman," Jack says, and together, the three of us hobble into the elevator. As soon as the doors close, we both burst out into deranged laughter.

"Ohmygod," I gasp. "That was close."

"She was definitely suspicious."

"It looked like he was ogling my mom's boobs!"

"I mean, he does do that for a living," Jack says. "We could just say he was giving his professional opinion."

I snort. "Yeah, that'll go over well. He better be prepared to kiss some serious mother-in-law ass."

Jack presses the button for the third flood and the elevator whisks us upward.

After a beat, I say, "Thanks for your help. I don't know what I would have done without you."

"How many times have I saved your ass now? Four? Five? I'm losing count."

"One more and I get a free coffee, right?"

Jack laughs and it's friendly enough to feel like maybe we're back to being friends, but still strained enough to remind me we probably aren't.

"So does this mean you've forgiven Collin?" Jack asks.

I glance down at Collin. "We had a little heart-to-heart this morning."

The corners of Jack's mouth twitch like he's trying to smile, but the expression doesn't fully reach his eyes.

"Jack?"

Both of us look to Collin, whose eyes have flickered into half-moon slits.

"Yeah? What is it?" Jack gives Collin a frustrated glance as though he's not sure how many more antics he can take from his best friend.

Collin hiccups before drunkenly mumbling, "You guys are cute together."

I'm suddenly—and painfully—aware of how small this elevator is. How little air there is.

"He's smashed out of his mind," Jack mutters, not meeting my eye.

"Right," I agree, keeping my own eyes pinned straight ahead.

"No, seriously," Collin continues as though neither of us has said anything. "Jack, I haven't seen you as happy as you were last night in *years*."

Years?

Thankfully, the elevator dings and the doors open to our floor.

"I can take him from here," Jack says, hiking up Collin's weight as we step into the hall.

"You sure?"

"It's no problem. I'm gonna have to get him in the shower," he says, casting Collin a disgruntled look.

"Oh. Okay," I say, aware that this means our circumstantial comradery is now coming to an end. "Well, call me if you need anything, okay?"

"I will."

The seconds stretch out into a silent minute, both of us avoiding eye contact, before I finally say, "I'll see you both later."

I step toward my room.

"Ada?"

I hate the hopeful shudder that racks my body as I turn back to face him. "Yeah?"

Jack adjusts Collin's weight, eyes bouncing to the floor then up again. "I'm sorry," he says after a beat. "I'm sorry about everything."

I swallow past the thick knot in my throat. "I'm sorry too."

He nods, gaze lingering a moment longer before he disappears down the hall and into his room with Collin.

Chapter 29

4 HOURS UNTIL THE WEDDING

I don't know how long I stand in front of Jack's door. But the longer I stand there, the more overwhelmed I feel. Like all this time I've been treading water in the deep end, and it's finally caught up with me and I can't swim anymore.

I'm heartbroken that my relationship with Jack has been reduced to awkward pauses and stilted smiles. I'm disappointed that in a matter of hours, I'll probably never hear from him again. Most of all, I'm tired. Tired of trying to stay afloat. Of pretending I'm okay when I'm not.

My shoulders shake, insides cracking right down the center as I dissolve into a fresh wave of tears.

I'm crying so hard I don't hear the soft tread of feet on the carpet behind me.

"Ada, what's wrong?"

I look up through watery eyes to see Allison. Her hair and makeup are done, but she's still dressed in her bridal robe. Her gaze is pulled taut with worry.

I frantically wipe at my cheeks. "Nothing," I tell her. "I'm fine."

She makes a face. "You're clearly not fine, so either you can come to my room and tell me what's wrong, or you can identify Jack's body when it gets pulled out of the lake after *a mysterious accident*. It's up to you."

"How do you know it's about Jack?"

She sighs, exasperated. "Because I have two eyes and more than one functioning brain cell, Ada."

"But it's your wedding day," I say. "I don't want to burden you with my bullshit."

She puts her hands on her hips. "Ada, please. You've done nothing but put up with my bullshit for years, so for once, let me put up with yours."

"But—"

She shakes her head. "No buts, now come on. We're going to my room where you're gonna drink a mimosa and tell me everything. Got it?"

I nod helplessly and she takes me by the hand and drags me to her suite.

As soon as the door closes behind us, Allison is thrusting a mimosa (mostly champagne by the taste of it) into my hands and ushering me to sit beside her on the edge of the bed.

"Now spill," she commands.

"I don't know where to start," I tell her.

"How about the beginning?"

So I do. I tell her everything. Well, not *everything*. I leave out the part about the tear in the veil. But other than that, I tell her everything. About the night in London. About Carter. About dancing in the pub. About how I tried to kiss Jack. About karaoke and every ridiculous, terrible, wonderful thing that happened after that.

"You were right," I say, wiping under my eyes. "You were right about Jack. About all of it." My voice wavers on the last syllable, and Allison draws me into a hug, crushing my ribs to hers.

"Trust me," she says, petting my hair. "I've slept with a lot of guys I wish I hadn't. It'll be okay."

"But that's the thing," I tell her, voice cracking. "I don't regret it. I just feel foolish for thinking this thing between us might be real. That things with us were different."

Allison pulls backs, gaze wavering across my face before she asks, "Is that why you broke up with Carter? Because of your feelings for Jack?"

I consider her question for a moment before I answer. "No, I broke up with Carter for me. It's something I should have done a long time ago. But Jack . . ." I scrunch up my face, trying to summon the right words. "I know we didn't get much time together, but maybe that's why the last few days meant so much. Because we felt like a team. Like he really supported me. And not just to be nice or because he wanted something, but because he truly cared." As I say it, I feel the inevitable wave of emotion rise inside me once more, but I push it away, not wanting to go there.

Allison studies me, eyes tracing mine with the kind of practiced understanding that can only come from someone who truly knows you.

"You really like him, don't you?" she asks after a minute.

"Who?"

She playfully punches my arm. "You *like* Jack."

Yes, I think instantly without consideration.

"I do," I admit. "But I'm not ready to jump into another relationship and neither is he." I look into my lap, sighing before I say, "When I was with Carter, I made excuses for why he wasn't proposing, why the relationship wasn't moving forward. I spent years downplaying my own wants and needs all because I was afraid of being alone, and I don't want to do the same with Jack. Or anyone."

As I say it, the words gain traction inside me. Jack was right about me being afraid, but maybe what I was really afraid of wasn't change or uncertainty, it was a fear of being alone.

But I don't want to live that way anymore. I want to feel like I'm enough on my own. I want to feel comfortable as I am, with or without a partner by my side.

"I think I need to be single for a while," I say after a beat. "Maybe try out the whole Emma Watson self-partnering thing," I add with a half laugh.

Allison's mouth softens into a tender smile. "If you want to be single for a while, I totally support that. But the truth is there's no magic time when you're suddenly ready to be in love. Just like there isn't some switch in our hearts we can turn off when our feelings are inconvenient. I mean, look at Collin and me." She gestures to the sparkly ring on her left hand. "When I met Collin, I'd just gotten out of an abusive relationship, and I wasn't ready to date again. I was terrified of getting hurt, but everything with Collin just made sense whether I was ready or not."

I nod, thinking about how, five days ago, I'd never met Jack. All I knew was that I didn't like him. Then little by little the layers had peeled back and somewhere between London and here, I'd fallen for him. I didn't plan for it to happen. It just did.

"Besides," she continues, "just because now isn't the right time for you and Jack, it doesn't necessarily mean he's the wrong guy, right?"

I straighten up, brows furrowing. "But I thought you hated Jack?"

"I don't *hate* him," she says. "But I think two things can be true at once. Jack can be rough around the edges and messy and complicated. But I don't think he's actually a bad guy. I think he's just a guy who's going through some shit right now." She pauses, chewing on her bottom lip before she says, "Collin's worried about him, you know."

"What kind of worried?"

She sighs, shoulders lifting then falling. "I think he tries to act like he's tough, but he's hurting more than he lets on. Collin's been trying to get him to talk to a therapist about her."

Her. The ghost still haunting him.

"Did you ever know her?" I ask. "His wife?"

"I met her once when they got back together for like two seconds."

"What was she like?" I ask, unable to help myself.

Allison's eyes turn heavy and I can tell she's debating how much to say. "I don't know . . . she's a lawyer too. I think they met in law school. And really pretty. But like, not prettier than you," she says quickly. "She was one of those girls who always seemed out of reach. Like sort of aloof and cool, you know?"

"Yeah," I say, feeling my insides deflate.

I know the type. It's the opposite of me. While I'm open and wear my heart on my sleeve, girls like that are mysterious, closed off, unattainable. Effortlessly cool. I can see why Jack would be into her. *No,* I remind myself. *In love with her.*

"Were they good together?" I know I'm pushing things, but suddenly I need to know. I need to know what kind of person Jack had fallen for. What kind of person he'd *crawl over broken glass for.*

Allison shrugs. "I don't know, you'd have to ask him or Collin. But from what I heard, they had this very chaotic relationship. They'd fight and make up a lot. Things were always hot and cold."

I wince, knowing exactly what that means. They had lots of sex. Passionate, wild make-up sex. Visions of a faceless woman wound around Jack, bodies writhing together, infiltrate my brain and suddenly I feel a hot surge of jealousy. Jealousy that Jack loved her enough to marry her. That he'd wanted to be with her forever. No expiration date. But past the pangs of jealousy is a slow-churning anger. Anger she'd thrown it all away. That she'd thrown *him* away.

As soon as I think it, I feel silly. I have no right to be jealous or angry. He's not mine and he never was.

I turn my attention back to Allison, the person I should be focused on right now. "I'm sorry for dumping all this on you on your wedding day," I tell her. "Let's talk about something else. I spoke with the caterer yesterday and—"

She shakes her head. "Ada, it's okay to be upset. Your feelings are valid, even the inconvenient ones." Her mouth wavers, lips curling into an uneven smile before she says, "I know growing up you had a lot of responsibility on you, especially before Mom got married, but it's okay to need things from other people too."

"But it's your wedding day," I say. "Today is supposed to be about you."

Her smile softens. "I know, but you're my sister, and if you need me, then I'm here for you."

Her words unravel something inside me, and I realize as she gathers me against her chest that it's not just Allison who might need me. I also need her. That as much as I've tried—and failed—to fix things, to be there for everyone else, to always be the perfect daughter and sister and girlfriend, I can't do it. Sometimes I need someone there to catch *me*. To pick up *my* pieces.

After a minute, I pull away, collecting my breath before I say, "For years, I've told myself that you're the one who needs me. That I'm the big sister who is supposed to hold everything together. But . . ." An unexpected crack breaks through my words. "But I need you too," I tell her.

"It's okay to need me," she whispers. "I need you, too, sometimes. Like when I need you to tell me I shouldn't get bangs. Or to remind me where I keep my passport."

"Bottom left drawer of your nightstand," I say without hesitation.

She laughs. "God, I missed you."

I pull her back against my chest. "I missed you too."

We stay there, bodies pressed together like we're trying to make up for the last seven months, until Allison sits back, nose wrinkling.

"What?" I ask.

"I'm not sure I even want to know, but are you going to tell me why you're covered in mud?"

Chapter 30

THE WEDDING

Despite concerns that it might rain, sunshine breaks through the steel clouds, revealing blue skies in the distance. Rows of white chairs stand out amid the wide expanse of emerald lawn, and ivory rose petals lead the way to a crumbling stone wall draped in elegant bouts of ivy where, any moment now, Allison and Collin will say *I do.*

In the center of the wall stands Collin, a nervous smile on his lips, looking practically good as new in a black tux and white rose boutonniere.

"Collin cleaned up nice," I whisper to Jack, standing beside me as we await our cue to walk down the aisle.

"You'd hardly believe we found him in a trough a few hours ago," he whispers back.

I smile and he mirrors the expression, a brief flicker of solidarity passing between us, but I can feel the hesitation behind the upward turn of his mouth.

We haven't spoken since our moment in the hall—nothing

more than awkward *hello*'s and *you look nice*'s—and I can't help the ache in the pit of my stomach, the reminder that this is what it will probably be like from now on. Tentative smiles and detached conversation.

"Thanks again for your help," I say after a beat.

He nods. "Anytime."

"Well, maybe not anytime," I say. "Hopefully it doesn't happen again."

Jack laughs and I let my gaze drift back to Collin, who's practically bouncing out of his tux, hands flexing and curling.

"He looks nervous," I whisper.

"He is," Jack agrees. "But in a good way. Promise," he adds, eyes latching to mine, and even now, after everything, the thump of my heart steadies under the pressure of his gaze.

"I'm happy for them," I say. "I think they're going to be good for each other."

"I think so too," he says, eyes holding mine.

I try to smile, but my mouth won't quite make the shape.

In a way, it's almost ironic. Allison and Collin are about to walk toward each other, toward their new life together. A life of love and partnership. Meanwhile, Jack and I are walking toward a different kind of finish line. One of final goodbyes and increasing distance.

Right on cue, the music starts, and the bridesmaids and groomsmen proceed down the aisle.

"Ready?" Jack asks, holding his tuxedo-clad arm out to me.

"Ready," I say back, looping my arm through his.

He forces a tight smile, and I can feel him trying and hesitating to say something, but whatever it is he doesn't get the chance because the music swells and the event coordinator gives us the signal.

At the end of the aisle, Jack holds my arm a beat too long, eyes meeting mine in one last lingering look. It's not quite regret, but something adjacent.

I wish I could parse it out. That I could untangle each crease of skin and ridge of muscle, but the look lasts just a second before we break away and Jack takes his place beside Collin. They thump one another on the back in a bro-ish hug just as the music changes for the bride's arrival.

Everyone stands up as Allison and Bill come into view. She is absolutely radiant and my heart swells.

I don't realize I've also started to cry until a tear makes its way down my cheek. I wipe it away and reach out to accept her bouquet—white roses and baby's breath. Our eyes meet and she gives me a big, toothy grin before turning to face Collin, who's frantically banishing his own tears, which only makes me more weepy.

But it's not the tears, or even the gentle murmurs of *oooh* and *aww* as Jack hands Collin a handkerchief, that get me. It's the look on Collin's face. Like Allison is the only one here. The only one who matters.

As I watch Allison and Collin's first kiss as husband and wife through the cloudy blur of tears, any lingering traces of fear recede. Instead, I'm filled with a sense of hope. Not just for Allison and Collin. But also for me.

If Allison can find her *Mr. Right*, then so can I.

Maybe not now, not today, but someday. Someday I want someone to look at me the way they are looking at one another. I want to look at someone and know that forever won't be easy. But we'll choose it anyway.

AFTER THE CEREMONY, EVERYONE HEADS TO A BIG WHITE TENT OVERLOOKING the lake for dinner, dancing, and the usual fanfare.

I croak my way through my maid of honor speech, trying (and failing) not to cry. Meanwhile, Jack leaves everyone in stitches with a story about how he and Collin once took Collin's dad's car for a joyride in the middle of the night when they were fourteen.

Everyone's still choking back laughter when Jack launches into the story of how Collin and Allison met, a story I realize I've never heard before.

"Everyone knows that a great meet-cute has two components," Jack says, eyes bouncing across the hall of candlelit tables. "Bad timing. And bad luck. And fortunately for Collin and Allison, they had both."

A chorus of chuckles echo around the tent.

"I still remember Collin texting me the night he met Allison at the Mariners game. The first thing he said to me was, 'I think I just spilled beer all over my future wife.' Followed by, 'Also, on an unrelated note, do you happen to know any good home remedies for stain removal?'" Jack pauses for titters and I watch out of the corner of my eye as Collin whispers something to Allison and she throws her head back with laughter.

"If you know Collin, then you know he's a romantic guy," Jack continues. "The type of guy to write love notes and buy flowers just because it's Wednesday. But I'd never seen him fall this hard. Or this fast," he adds, followed by more laughter.

"At first, I was dubious. I mean, how well did they know each other? What if they were rushing into things? But in the last two hundred and six days these two lovebirds have been together, they've shown me time and time again that real love doesn't have deadlines or timelines or expiration dates. That when it's real, when you've really found the one you want to be with, you don't let anything stand in the way." Jack pauses, eyes turning more serious. "They've shown me that real love isn't waiting for the right time. Or the perfect moment. That real love comes when you least expect it. And I can't help but think that the odds are better for all of us because they're together."

Jack lifts his champagne flute toward Allison and Collin, who both beam back at him. "Please join me in toasting the bride and groom."

Everyone raises their glasses in unison.

"To beating the odds," Jack says.

"To beating the odds," the rest of the room repeats.

As I lift my glass, Jack's eyes drift in my direction, hovering for just a second, before snapping back to Allison and Collin.

AFTER THE TOASTS, THE DJ ANNOUNCES IT'S TIME FOR THE BOUQUET TOSS and everyone turns their attention to the dance floor, where Allison stands, bouquet in hand. I can't think of anything I'd like to do less than broadcast my singleness to an entire tent of family and strangers, so I take advantage of the distraction and slip into the cool night air.

Gravel crunches under my feet as I follow the sound of tinkling water into a nearby rose garden. It's too dark and shadowy to see much until I reach a circle of raised hedges surrounding a stone fountain, the basin illuminated by stripes of moonlight falling across the inky water like yellow lines on a desolate highway.

My feet are totally killing me, so I remove my heels and dunk my bare feet in the dark water. The cold instantly calms the angry red blisters on my toes and the back of my heel.

"Hey." A familiar deep voice cuts through the quiet.

I look up and see Jack's tall frame casting long shadows along the water. His bow tie is loosened around his neck and his shirtsleeves are rolled up. In his hand is a bottle of whiskey.

"Hey," I say back.

He rakes a hand through his hair before he asks, "Is it okay if I join you?"

I nod and Jack sits down beside me and begins to untie his Oxfords. He dips his bare feet into the murky depths.

"Your speech was great," I tell him.

"Thanks. So was yours."

Jack offers me the whiskey bottle, but I shake my head, and he tilts it to his mouth, granting me a view of his forearm. My breath catches when I see it: the compass drawing.

"You didn't wash it off," I say.

He follows my gaze down to his arm. "No," he says after a beat. "I didn't."

Our eyes meet, and I can practically feel the heavy press of unspoken thoughts passing between us. Finally, he says, "I want you to know that I don't regret last night . . . or this morning."

"I don't regret it either." I hesitate, swallowing. "But I thought about what you said earlier. You were right."

His brow furrows, scrunching against the moonlight. "About what?"

"That I'm not ready to jump into something right now. And neither are you." My breath wavers as I reach for the next words. "It wasn't fair of me to expect things to work out between us."

A hot, heavy exhale rushes out between parted lips. "It's not a matter of not wanting you, Ada. Because I do. A lot." He pauses, eyes drawing me in like quicksand. "I'm just . . . not in a good place right now. And I swear to God that's not a line."

Maybe it's the pale moonlight, or the collage of shadows taking up residence across his features, but there's a weariness I didn't notice earlier.

He doesn't just look tired after a long day of wedding activities. He looks worn down, like a sculptor's taken a chisel and whittled away at him, piece by piece, and perhaps for the first time I see him clearly without the tint of lust or *what if* clouding my vision.

He's still devastatingly handsome, but the same features that once delighted and intrigued me now suggest something different.

Gone is the beaming best man who had the room hanging on his every word. Instead, he looks defeated. Miserable, even. A hollow, carved-out ghost of the person I've spent the last few days with. Or perhaps that's not true. Maybe this is the real Jack, the one hiding behind flirtatious smiles and teasing jokes. The one I've only seen pieces of until now.

Maybe it's the wrong thing to do, maybe I'm misreading things, but I take his hand and give it a squeeze. "It's okay," I tell him. "I understand."

His gaze softens, mouth turning up in the corners as he squeezes back. "I wish you knew how much the last few days meant to me. That before you, I was dreading this wedding. That I couldn't stand the thought of showing up and pretending to be happy when I was so fucking miserable. Then you came along, and you were beautiful and funny and smart and just so happened to need somewhere to stay. I thought it was fate."

Fate. There's that word again. But it doesn't feel the same way it did last night. Not when I know how the story ends.

"I knew there was nothing I could do about the wedding or the pretending to be happy part," he goes on. "But maybe sleeping with the hot girl from the hotel lobby would make it suck less."

Heavy eyes find mine through the darkness, and even now I can't help the way blood rises in my cheeks.

"I wasn't supposed to see you again. You were supposed to be a Band-Aid on a wound that wouldn't close. But suddenly we were thrust together in this ridiculous situation, and I got to know you, and being around you made me feel things I never thought I'd feel again.

"We might have been stranded for the night, or in a broken-down car. But it didn't matter because for the first time in a long time all the voices in my head telling me I'd never be happy again weren't so loud. For the first time in a long time, I felt like everything would be okay. Like *I* was okay." He shakes his head, fear and hope warring behind his gaze. "I guess what I'm trying to say is that when I'm with you, I feel a little less fucked up."

My eyes skitter up to meet his. "I feel that way too," I tell him, voice cracking.

The corners of Jack's mouth inch upward but don't quite make it into a smile.

For a long moment, he doesn't speak, and we stay there, holding hands in the dark until, finally, he says, "I wish I could be the guy who is all in. The guy willing to crawl over broken glass for you. I wish I could hold your hand on a crowded street and take you on dates and make plans with you. I wish I could be all the things you deserve."

My heart cracks under the weight of his words. Though I can't tell if it's because of what Jack's just said or because I can hear the *but* coming.

"But I can't," he says, voice fraying around the edges. "I can't crawl over broken glass for you because I fucking *am* broken glass. And I can't be *Mr. Right.*"

I search the heaviness of his expression, the deep lines bracketing his mouth. It's the second time he's brought up *Mr. Right.* The first time he said it, I figured he was making fun of me for being naive enough to want something akin to the hero in a Hallmark movie. But now, the wounded look in his eyes makes me think I was wrong. Maybe he sees himself as incurably flawed, unable to be the person he wishes he could be. Like he's somehow letting me down by not being *Mr. Right*.

The thought brings a fresh pang of hurt to my chest.

If this were a movie, I'd be able to fix him. My dazzling personality and quirky sense of humor would be enough to heal his trauma and show him he's worthy of love. That he doesn't need to be *Mr. Right*.

But this isn't a movie. This isn't something the love of a *good woman* can solve. And these aren't the types of issues we can look past because we have feelings for one another and the sex is good.

I can't save him. I can't fix him. And I can't make him be with me.

All I can do is let him go.

I hadn't wanted to cry, at least not more than I already had, but my eyes well with tears and the emotion I've been trying to keep at bay finally spills over.

He runs his thumb along my jaw, flicking away a tear. "Ada." The way he says my name, a little desperate, a little hungry, makes me feel like delicate glass cracked right down the center. "Please don't cry," he whispers.

But I can't stop.

I don't even really know what I'm crying for. Maybe it's the slow, steady release of the tension I've been holding in all this time. The relief of finally hearing how he feels. Or maybe it's because I know it's not enough. That we still have an expiration.

Jack pulls me into him, letting me bury my face in his chest.

"I'm sorry," I sob. "I'm getting your dress shirt all wet."

"It's okay," he says, stroking my hair. "It's not the first time I've had to change shirts today."

I make a noise that's somewhere between a sniffle and a laugh.

"I'm gonna miss you," I say.

Jack squeezes me tighter. "I already miss you."

He presses his lips to the top of my head, leaving a delicate kiss, and I feel the words behind the gesture, the hollow, carved-out goodbye that neither of us is saying.

I'm not ready to break away and neither is he.

His hands shift, sliding farther down my back. Not quite low enough for it to be like *that*, but low enough to remind me of last night. Of memories of tangled limbs and brushed lips and hungry murmurs whispered against damp skin.

I try to stockpile the moment. The way he smells. The breeze tickling the backs of our necks. The weight of his hands molding around my hips, grounding me to him. I try to memorize everything so that when it's over, when I'm back home, sleeping alone, I'll have something to revisit. A mental tattoo whose lines I can trace over and over.

The thought jogs a memory, and I pull back. "I have something for you," I tell him.

Jack's eyes flash with uncertainty as I reach into my clutch and pull out a folded piece of notepaper with the hotel logo on the top. Below the logo is the same drawing of a compass I'd drawn on Jack's arm, though this time with cleaner lines and shading.

I'm not sure what I mean by it. Maybe it's a peace offering. Or a thank-you gift for everything he did for me. Or maybe I'm hopeful he'll get the tattoo and prove that even if we have an expiration date, our memories don't. That they can live on in the ink on his skin.

Jack takes the paper, frowning. "What's this?"

"I don't know if this is weird, and if it is, please just throw it away or whatever, but in case you actually wanted to get the tattoo, I made you a sketch."

I brace myself, waiting to see if he'll tell me he doesn't want it, that he didn't mean what he said last night. Instead, his mouth slingshots into a smile. "Thank you, Ada. I love it."

"It's okay if you don't want—"

"I want it. Really," he adds.

Maybe it's the warmth in his eyes or the way the tightness in my chest unspools, but I feel brave enough to ask, "What about our pact?"

He blinks. "Our pact?"

"The pizza pact," I say, reminding him of the promise we'd made at Mrs. Poyevich's inn.

Understanding slogs through his features. "You mean us going to Italy together?"

"Is that still on the table?" I ask.

His mouth parts, eyes widening with surprise. "Do you want it to be?"

I'm not sure how to answer him. Of course it's what I want. I brought it up. But as my eyes skate from the crease between his brows to the tension held captive in his posture, I wonder if he thinks I'm asking to make him feel better, to dull the sting of goodbye, and now he's offering me an out, a way to leave him behind, free and clear. If he thinks I'm like Lexi. Or his dad. If he thinks I'm looking for an excuse to leave.

I take back his hand, threading his fingers through mine. "I know this is cheesy. Pun intended," I add, mouth creaking out a grin. "But what if in one year, if we're both single and we're still interested in *this*"—I gesture between us—"maybe we can meet there? At the pizza place you told me about?"

Slowly the tension drifts from his features and he dips his chin into a nod. "I'd like that."

I smile and he smiles too. It's not a promise or a guarantee. But it's filled with hope. And maybe, for right now, that's enough.

Silence swells between us, the moment filling with echoes of laughter and the clinking of glasses floating through the night air. The DJ starts to play a vaguely familiar melody I can't quite place. It's soft and a little melancholy, and we both turn our attention toward the tent, where dancing shadows stretch like ghosts across the lawn.

"We should go," I say, pulling my feet out of the water and shaking them dry before sliding them back into my heels. "Allison and Collin are probably wondering where we are."

I doubt they even remember who we are. Last I checked, they were so tightly wound around one another on the dance floor, they'll need to be surgically removed. But I need an excuse to end this moment before I no longer have the willpower to do so.

As we walk back to the tent, an indulgent silence filling the space between us, I can't help but feel lucky. Lucky that our paths crossed. That he picked up that stray tampon. That he asked to buy me that drink. That I said yes. That he invited me upstairs. And every wonderful and terrible thing that happened after that. Most of all, I feel lucky that we had last night, even if it was just a fleeting moment.

Maybe this is all it can ever be. But maybe that's okay.

THE REST OF THE RECEPTION GOES BY IN A FLURRY OF BAD DANCE MOVES and one too many pop remixes. Then Collin and Allison are given a sparkler send-off to a chorus of cheers, and just like that, the night is over.

After the last drink has been poured and the final candle blown out, Jack walks me to my room.

"Well, this is my stop," I say, leaning back against the door, but making no effort to open it.

His gaze lifts, eyes pulling mine. Then he leans in and places a gentle kiss on the side of my cheek. The gesture doesn't linger, as though he doesn't quite trust himself. And right now, neither do I.

"Good night, Ada," he whispers, face still close to mine.

"Good night," I tell him. But neither of us moves.

I grasp for something to say, something to stretch out this goodbye a little longer.

"Have fun in Italy," I tell him. "Eat some pizza for me."

His mouth wavers into an almost-smile. "I will."

My brain wants to skip ahead to what's next. To whether we'll see each other again a year from now. Whether we'll talk before then. But I push the thought aside, instead trying to focus on this moment right now, this final moment I can hold on to. If this is all I get, I want to savor it.

I focus on the hard lines of his jaw, and the way his mouth is soft in the dim light of the hallway. I focus on every beautiful inch, trying to draw him in the sketchbook of my mind, and based on the way he's looking at me, eyes sharp with a kind of intensity that feels almost indecent, I can guess he's doing the same. But hidden behind his blown-out pupils and the tick in his jaw, I see something I didn't see earlier. *Fear.*

I expect the realization to give me a sense of solidarity, a knowledge that we're both afraid to walk away, to find out what's next for our lives, to leave the bubble we've inhabited for the past few days. Instead, it makes me sad and honestly a little angry. Angry that the people he loved chewed him up and spit him out. Angry that he doesn't feel good enough. Angry that he doesn't see himself the way I do.

I reach out, letting the pad of my thumb trail down the side of his face, cupping his cheek. "You deserve someone who would crawl over broken glass for you too," I whisper.

Our eyes lock. He breathes. I swallow. Another beat passes. Then he lifts his hand, thumb catching the underside of my chin.

"Goodbye, Ada." He keeps his thumb there a second longer before pulling it back.

My eyes burn with tears, but I force them back, determined not to cry again. "Goodbye, Jack."

There's no passionate meeting of mouths, no slamming of doors and unbuttoning of clothes. Only quiet good nights and the kind of dull emptiness usually reserved for the day after Christmas. Then he steps back and gives me one last look before turning and disappearing down the hall.

We're doing the right thing, both of us, I remind myself. And yet, there's still a part of me that craves the happy ending—the glittering final scene, the grand gesture, the sweeping kiss right before the credits roll.

But I have to let that go. It's over now.

Instead, I have a whole new life ahead of me.

Maybe I'll go to Paris. Maybe I'll reopen Sleeve It to Me 2.0. Maybe I'll fall in love.

I don't know. But for the first time I feel okay not knowing.

Chapter 31

51 WEEKS AFTER THE WEDDING

I pull my paintbrush back, surveying the mural in front of me. Fuchsia flowers layer over cerulean water, framed by green seaweed and dancing dolphins. In the corner, a cartoonish mermaid with flowing purple hair swims toward the surface. Behind her, mischievous fish and assorted crustaceans juggle pink seashells.

It's certainly not in my usual repertoire. A far cry from the skulls and crossbones and pinup girls I'm used to inking into skin at Sleeve It to Me 2.0, but it's a good change of pace for me. And it feels good to hold a paintbrush again. Like putting on a well-worn coat that fits just right.

"How's it coming in here?" comes Allison's voice from outside the hall. I turn around just as she waddles in, one hand cradling her swollen belly.

"Pretty good. I just finished the mermaid. What do you think?" I ask, stepping aside so she can see the mural I've been working on since she announced she and Collin were expecting a baby four months ago.

Allison's face stretches into a wide smile. "She's beautiful. Like our tattoo."

Our eyes meet and a warm burst of tenderness flickers between us.

It's been hard finding time to work on the mural between reopening Sleeve It to Me, moving out of my parents' house, and working double shifts at a local coffee shop to help pay bills while I get the business up and running. But I've been over at Collin and Allison's house every spare chance I get.

Mostly I'm here to paint, but Allison and I have restarted our movie night tradition, meaning that every Tuesday we cuddle up on the couch with enough red dye 40 to send us to early graves and watch rom-coms until Allison falls asleep and Collin has to carry her to bed.

Collin always says he isn't going to watch the movie with us, but somehow, about ten minutes in, he magically appears and doesn't leave until the credits roll.

His presence is often accompanied by lengthy commentary about how the heroine barely knows the hero and they can't possibly be in love, to which Allison responds by throwing popcorn at his head and I remind him that he and Allison didn't know each other much longer.

Despite his different (read: *bad*) taste in movies, my feelings toward Collin have softened a lot in the past year. Not only is he a loving, supportive husband to Allison, he's also a good friend to me.

When Collin found out I was trying to reopen Sleeve It to Me, he helped get me in touch with some family friends who specialize in small-business loans and credit rehabilitation. He also offered himself up as the first customer and now has their wedding date permanently inked into his left bicep.

As if on cue, Collin appears in the doorway behind Allison.

He wraps his hands around her bump and gives her a peck on the cheek.

"Hey, looks good," he says, craning his neck to see past Allison. "I like the way the colors pop. Reminds me of trying acid in college."

I lift one eyebrow. "My mural reminds you of tripping on acid?"

Allison and I share a knowing look and she playfully smacks her husband's hand. "Babe, you can't say that. She's a sensitive *artist.*"

"Yeah, but I meant it in a good way," he says quickly. "Houghton and I only did acid once, but it was wild. Everything was so vivid. I could taste color."

I try to keep my expression neutral, but the skin on the back of my neck prickles. Even though Collin and Allison bring Jack up in passing every now and then—*I was on the phone with Houghton last night,* or *Houghton was telling me about so-and-so*—I still can't control the bodily response I have to the mere mention of his name.

For the first few weeks after the wedding, I thought about texting him. But every time I tried to compose a message, I'd realize I had no idea what to say. Eventually, enough time elapsed that it would definitely be weird if I texted him, so I didn't. Now it's been a whole year and neither one of us has reached out.

It's not that I don't want to talk to him—I do—it just feels like a lot of pressure. Like, what if it's awkward? What if we have nothing to talk about? What if whatever Jack and I were was just a blip on the horizon, there one second, gone the next?

I know we'll see each other eventually—Allison and Collin are asking him to be their baby's godfather—but for now I'm settling for vague, secondhand updates. And pretending like his name doesn't still spark goose bumps on the back of my neck.

I clear my throat, pretending to be absorbed in a nonexistent smudge on the wall. "Have you seen Jack recently?"

"Not in a while," Allison says. "He's been working nonstop since he took on that big oil company lawsuit. The last time we saw him must have been . . . ?" She scrunches up her face, giving her husband a questioning look.

"Thanksgiving, I think," Collin says. "I can't believe it's been that long."

True to his word, Jack had indeed come to our family's Thanksgiving, but I'd been in Paris last fall and hadn't been there, though Allison had told me later he'd asked about me.

I wonder how he'd responded when she'd told him that I'd finally gone to Paris. Or that I'd reopened the tattoo shop and moved out of my parents' place.

I wonder if he ever thinks about me the way I think about him.

"How's he doing?" I ask in what I hope is a diplomatic, casual, *I only just thought to ask* voice. I don't want Allison and Collin to think I still have a thing for him. Even if I do.

"He's doing a lot better," Collin says. "He's training for the Portland Marathon. Says it helps him deal with stress. And . . ." Collin pauses, catching Allison's eye. "He's in therapy."

"It's been good for him," Allison adds, giving me a meaningful look.

Something in me shifts into place. "That's great," I say. "I'm happy for him."

And I really mean it. Even though our paths only crossed for a few days, I never stopped caring about him. Or wanting him to be happy. Even if that's not with me.

"He sent us flowers the other day," Allison says. "Did you see the big bunch of roses in the kitchen?"

"He did?" I ask, thinking back to the mammoth bouquet I'd assumed were from Collin, who is always buying Allison flowers, *just because*. "What for?"

"For our anniversary," Allison says, giving me a look as

though she's hoping I didn't dare forget. "It's not until next week. But it was so sweet of him."

Allison and Collin launch into reminiscing about some wedding memory, but I'm not listening. I'm too busy thinking about how next week is Allison and Collin's first anniversary. Which means it will be one year since Jack and I made our pact.

I never told anyone about the pact. Mostly because it seemed too silly, too far-fetched. Too much like something Nora Ephron would write into a movie. Certainly not real life.

Still, I watched the date on the calendar move steadily closer, wondering what, if anything, might happen. If one of us would call. If, by some twist of fate, we'd actually meet in Italy.

But at this point it seems most likely that we'll let the day pass. Jack's probably already forgotten. Or will be too embarrassed to acknowledge we made the promise in the first place. And yet, knowing that Jack not only remembered their anniversary, but sent a thoughtful gift a week in advance, makes my insides feel like they've been set to a low-grade simmer. Does that mean something? A sign? Or am I merely overthinking this?

I decide to probe just a bit.

"Is Jack . . . uh . . ." I avert my eyes, pretending to be inspecting the mural. "Seeing anyone?"

Allison and Collin exchange looks. "Nope. He's single," Allison says. "Right, babe?"

Collin nods. "Yes, he's single. *Very* single."

Jack is single.

What if . . . ?

No, no, no. I stop myself. I'm being ridiculous. We haven't spoken in a year. He's probably moved on. Or forgotten entirely. Either way, Jack is an attractive, single guy who I'm sure has better things to do than fly to Italy to make good on a corny nineties rom-com-esque promise.

Besides, I'm at a good place in my life right now. Sleeve It to Me is doing better than ever. I'll be able to pay off my debts soon. I've even got my own place with an IKEA dining set I assembled all by myself.

I'm finally in a place where I feel good in my own skin. Where I feel perfectly whole and complete on my own. Which is exactly why I don't need to get worked up about this. About *him*.

"You know," Allison says, cutting through my thoughts, "Jack finalized his divorce."

I hate the way hope burns against my chest when I squeak out an unsteady, "Really?"

Collin and Allison swap not-so-subtle looks.

"They officially signed the papers a few months ago," Collin says. "Like I said, he's single."

"*Very*," Allison adds.

I cross my arms. "You two aren't exactly subtle, you know that, right?"

"I'm just saying. *You're* single. *He's* single. You're both doing well. Maybe now is a good time to"—Allison pauses to wiggle her eyebrows—"*rekindle* things."

"Don't get me wrong, I want to see him eventually," I admit. "I just don't know if now is the right time."

"But what are you waiting for? You're kicking ass right now! Your business is booming. You finally moved out of Mom and Bill's. And you're happier than I've seen you in a long time." Allison turns to Collin. "Babe, don't you think Ada and Jack should see each other?"

I can't help but search Collin's face, hungry for some kind of clue. If Jack still had feelings for me, would he have told Collin? Do guys even talk about stuff like that?

"I think Ada should see him if she wants to," he says diplomatically.

Allison rolls her eyes. "Not helping." She turns back to me. "You still like him, don't you?"

I pause, unsure how to answer her.

In a way, it feels silly to confess to still having feelings for him. He wasn't my boyfriend. We only knew each other a few days. We slept together once (twice?). For all I know, we merely got caught up in the gravitational pull of sheer proximity and heightened emotions.

But it's hard to pretend the thought of him doesn't still send heat to my cheeks. That his name alone isn't enough to inspire a visceral response. That every time I'm scrolling through photos on my phone and I see the selfie we took on Arthur's Seat my heart doesn't do a little flip-flop. Or that every time I hear a Donna Summer song, my mind doesn't wander back to that smoky nightclub in Belfast.

"Yes, I still care about him," I admit. "But it's not that simple. I mean, what if he isn't interested in me anymore?"

Allison's gaze hovers over mine, searching. "But you won't know until you see him, right?"

"Yes, but . . ." I let the rest of the sentence dangle, unsure how to finish the thought.

The safe choice is to wait for Jack to reach out to me. To hold out hope that one day our paths will cross in the right place at the right time. But maybe this *is* the right place and time, not because of timing or circumstances, but because I'm deciding it is.

I think about Allison and Collin. My mom and Bill. How they each had layers of baggage and heartbreak and disappointment between them. How there was no *right* time. But they chose each other, even when it was hard. Even when they were afraid.

And maybe that's what I need to do too.

I know it wasn't love between Jack and me. We only knew each other five days. But it wasn't nothing either. I wish there was a word for it. The space between longing for someone but not quite loving them. But also knowing that in another time, another place, under different circumstances, with more time, it could be love. Maybe it's potential. The potential of something great.

I'm not ready to give up on that potential. And maybe neither is he.

I look back at Allison and Collin. "I think I'm gonna head out," I tell them, reaching for the lid to the paint can.

Allison's expression deflates. "But I thought you were staying for dinner? I ordered pizza. With pineapple," she adds hopefully.

"I know, I'm sorry . . . there's just something I have to take care of. Rain check?" I shoot them both apologetic smiles, then toss my painting supplies into my canvas tote and rush toward the door. "I'll see you guys later," I shout over my shoulder.

"Ada . . . ?" Allison calls.

But I don't stop rushing until I'm home, in front of my computer, fingers poised over the mouse, staring at a screen telling me I have three minutes and forty-seven seconds left to make my purchase.

What if this is a terrible idea? What if he doesn't show? What if I waste a bunch of money only to end up embarrassed?

And yet, if I've learned anything this past year, it's that it's okay to be embarrassed, to fail, to take risks, even ones that don't work out.

I don't know if this will end in a passionate kiss or stinging disappointment, but I think I want to find out. I want to give this a chance.

At the very least, I think Jack and I deserve that.

I shut my eyes and click.

I'm going to Italy.

Chapter 32

52 WEEKS AFTER THE WEDDING

Naples hangs with a heavy heat, the kind that's thick and sticks in my throat, making it hard to swallow. Or maybe that's just nerves. Just like it was my nerves that made me awkwardly nudge the guy beside me on the plane so that I could get up and pee eleven times during the transatlantic flight.

But sixteen hours, one layover, and eleven in-flight trips to the bathroom later, I'm here. *In Italy.*

Sun pours down my back as I stand outside my hotel, waiting for my Uber. I wipe the tiny beads of sweat gathering at the base of my neck and pray I don't have pit stains. I bet Meg Ryan didn't have to worry about pit stains when she met Tom Hanks at the top of the Empire State Building.

I smooth down my lavender dress and check my hair—now back to its natural dirty blond—in the nearest window, hoping the curls I ironed in won't completely lose their shape in the heat.

Thankfully, my Uber doesn't take long and I'm able to climb

into the air-conditioned back seat before fully melting into the concrete.

"I need to get to a restaurant," I tell the driver, Leo, a young guy in his early twenties with olive skin and thick tendrils of curly black hair. "It's called Pizzeria Vergini. Do you know it?"

He taps his finger on the dashboard, brows creased in thought.

"I know the place," he says at last. "Near Palazzo dello Spagnolo. Good pizza, no?"

I bob my chin excitedly. *"Grazie mille!"*

I have no idea if this is the right place, but this is all the information I have, so I'm just gonna go with it and hope I'm right.

Twenty minutes later, I step out of the air-conditioned car and onto a street near Palazzo dello Spagnolo where the buildings are old and narrow as though time has squished them together.

I follow Leo's directions down a main road before turning into a romantic square lined with cafés and elegant shops. There's a fountain at one end and a tall spire at the other. Each of the buildings lining the square is a different hue of pink and orange and red except for a domed basilica casting long shadows across the cobblestone.

As I cross the square, following in the direction of the falling sunlight, a new thread of confidence weaves inside me.

Maybe there's nothing terribly risky about flying to Italy. Or telling a guy you like him—it's not slaying dragons or fighting crime—but maybe not all stakes in life are the big, flashy ones. Maybe the risks that change our lives are as simple as saying yes. Being honest. Putting ourselves out there. Unapologetically asking for what we want. Maybe the biggest risk we can take is remaining hopeful in a world that often feels hopeless.

At the edge of the street I spot a small eatery with big block letters over the door spelling out PIZZERIA VERGINI.

Hope flares in my chest.

This is it. I'm here.

The place isn't anything fancy, just a few small tables set on the street behind a chipped, orange stucco building. But apparently this is the best pizza in *the world* (according to Jack).

Hands slightly trembling, I approach the restaurant's front door and give it a tug, but it's locked.

Shit.

I tug again, but no luck.

It's five o'clock. Shouldn't they be open for dinner? I look up and down the street. There's another restaurant across the way. Also closed.

Why is everything closed? It's not a holiday or something, is it?

Nerves coil inside me, and I wonder if despite all my careful planning, I've still managed a massive oversight.

I lean against the shady side of the building, hoping for some relief from the sun as I try to figure out my next move.

I should call Jack. Let him know I'm here, waiting for him. Sure, it's not as romantic, but this is the twenty-first century. We're no longer living in the world of *You've Got Mail,* and I don't want to stand here for hours, wondering if he's going to show or not.

But just as I'm pulling out my phone, ready to call a number I haven't called in a year, I stop myself.

I've come all this way. I'm in a beautiful place, dressed in my best. I can wait a little longer.

I PEOPLE WATCH FOR A WHILE UNTIL I GET RESTLESS, THEN I PULL OUT MY sketchbook and graphite pencil, deciding that if I'm going to sit on a beautiful street in Italy, I might as well sketch it.

I start with the steeple across the street, shading the long shadows, then I add the buildings covered in bougainvillea, and the man walking his dog on the cobblestone, and the tiny cars all parallel parked within an inch of their lives. And slowly, the gaps close between the vision in my head and the scene on the page.

I haven't sketched for pleasure in a while, not since I've been busy with the business, but as my pencil moves across the paper, shading and blending, I remember how good it feels to create something that's just for me. Not for a customer or Allison, but just for me.

It's a quarter past eight when the sky begins to morph from bright blue to hazy purple. Behind me the pizzeria is in full swing as patrons clink glasses and chatter in Italian. Apparently, no one in Italy eats dinner before eight.

The scent of garlic and pizza dough waft in the still warm air, reminding me it's been hours since I last ate, and I can't help but feel a little sorry for myself, sitting here, all alone, watching people eat dinner while I wait for a man who is increasingly unlikely to show up.

I know it's my own doing. I'm the one who assumed the risk of showing up without any assurance he'd be here. But it still hurts knowing that he doesn't feel the same way I do. That the five days we spent together last year didn't impact him the way they did me.

Tears prick my eyes and I decide that's my sign to admit defeat. I'll go back to my hotel or find a little café where I can drink enough wine to make me forget Jack's name. Then tomorrow, I'll pick myself up and explore Italy. Just because Jack isn't here doesn't mean I can't still have a good time on my own.

I'm standing to go when I see something shiny on the ground. I lean closer, realizing that it's a penny. Face up. *A lucky penny.*

My heart rate ticks up.

I haven't looked for good luck symbols for a while now, but something magnetic draws me toward it. My hands are just closing around the sun-scorched metal when I hear my name.

"Ada?"

I jerk my head up.

Jack.

He's walking toward me, tall frame casting long shadows across the cobblestone, the hazy blur of the sunset bringing out golden flecks in his dark hair. It's like something from a dream, and it takes me a moment to fully process that this is real. *He's* real. And he's here.

His hair is disheveled, his clothes are wrinkled, and there's a bead of sweat running down his neck. But there's light in his eyes and the beginnings of a smile on his mouth. The sight of him makes my stomach swoop like I've just missed the last step on the stairs.

"Hi," I say, at the exact same time he says, "You came."

The familiarity of his voice hums inside me, making me realize how much I've ached to hear it again. How much I've missed him.

"I was worried I'd be too late," he confesses. "I would have come sooner, but my flight to Rome got canceled at the last minute, so I got on a flight to Venice instead. Then I had to take the train from there, which ended up taking five hours."

I think about saying, *I didn't think you'd come.* Or *I'm so glad you're here.* Or even *I missed you.* Instead, what comes out is, "You must have terrible luck with travel."

His face cracks into that slow, easy grin I remember so well. "I'd agree with you, but these things only seem to happen when you're involved."

"So you're saying I'm some kind of bad luck charm?" I tease.

He steps closer and gives me a simmering look that makes me feel like someone's vacuum-sealed all the air around us. "I'm not sure I believe in luck," he says. "I think everything happens for a reason."

"Like fate?"

"Like fate," he agrees.

I inch closer, eyes narrowed in mock suspicion. "Who are you and what have you done with Jack Houghton?"

"People change, you know. And clearly you have too." He looks me up and down, eyes scanning. "You look different. No more purple hair, I see."

I touch my hair. "I decided it was time for a new look."

"And you've got some new ink."

I follow his gaze down to my arms, now dotted in artwork. *My* artwork.

A nervous laugh rises out of me. "You like?"

His eyes catch the pinkish light of the setting sun at just the right angle, making his eyes shimmer as his mouth stretches into a wide smile. "I love it. It suits you."

"You look different too," I tell him.

"Don't tell me I could no longer be Ryan Gosling's body double?"

I laugh. "Don't worry, it's a good different." I squint, trying to discern what exactly is different about him. He's still handsome. With the same perfect five-o'clock shadow. And based on the way his shirt stretches across his broad chest and shoulders, he could definitely still be Ryan Gosling's body double. But there's something else. A lightness to him. Like whatever weight had once sat on his shoulders is now gone.

"You look happy," I say at last.

"I *am* happy."

He lets out a long sigh. But it's not sad or resigned. It's a hopeful sigh. Like he's taking one big, much-needed exhale.

"A few months ago, after the divorce was finalized, I decided it was finally time to do what I should have done a long time ago," he says. "I started seeing a therapist."

My heartbeat stumbles, a newfound levity in my chest. "How's it been?"

"Hard, but good," he says with a resolute nod. "The first few sessions were brutal. Like having my insides excavated. But it feels good to work through stuff. To see light at the end of the tunnel."

"I'm really happy for you," I tell him.

"Thanks. Me too."

There's fragility behind his eyes, but also hope. And before I can stop myself, hot tears are running down my face as I reach for him, wrapping my arms around his neck.

Slowly, he squeezes me back, running a hand up and down the length of my spine.

My body remembers his touch, the feel of his hands, the scent of him—tangy and musky with a hint of something sweet. All of it comes back with aching clarity.

"Hey, it's okay. Don't cry." He wipes a stray tear from my cheek, which only makes me cry harder.

"I'm sorry," I blubber, as a fresh wave of tears cascades down my cheeks. "I don't know why I'm crying. I just . . ." I choke on the words. "I'm so happy to see you. To know you're doing okay."

He squeezes me harder, grounding me to him. "I feel the same way," he says, stroking my hair.

"I can't believe you're here," I say, clutching him like I'm afraid he might evaporate from under my grip. "You came."

"Ada," he says, voice low like the purr of a car engine. "Of course I came. I haven't stopped thinking about you."

I pull back from him, my stomach churning like it's full of bouncy balls. "But . . . Why didn't you reach out?"

He rakes a hand through his hair. "There were so many times I wanted to call you. To text you. Just to see how you were doing, or to tell you when something funny happened. But every time I thought about it, I worried you wouldn't want to hear from me. That maybe it was too late."

"Jack, I—"

"No. Please. Let me say this," he says, holding out a hand to stop me. "A year ago, when we met, I was in a bad place. I was getting divorced. I was miserable and dead set on never being in a serious relationship again. Then I met you and I found myself wanting things I never thought I'd want again. I started wondering what it might be like to wake up with you. To run errands and watch movies and go on dates and plan trips together. But I knew I couldn't give you what you wanted, or needed," he adds with a knowing look. "I knew I had to let you go."

I nod, feeling the familiar memories rise inside me like acid.

"Then a year passed, and I figured you'd moved on. But I couldn't stop thinking about you." His eyes bounce over me, and I can't help the goose bumps that rise everywhere his gaze lands.

"I told my therapist how I was still harboring feelings for you even after all this time, and she asked me why I hadn't told you, so I told her I was scared. It turned into this whole conversation about my fear of rejection after my dad and my ex-wife left. God, I think I cried through the whole session," he admits, rubbing his temple with the heel of his palm. "The point being, I walked out of there knowing I had to tell you how I felt, even if it ended in rejection. I owed it to myself, and to you, to be honest about how I felt. Am still feeling."

He pauses, swallowing. When he speaks again, his voice comes out low and sturdy, like he's pulled a newfound confidence from somewhere deep inside. "I still don't believe in soulmates," he says. "But I do think we get to choose who we *want* to spend the rest of our lives with, and that we can grow together without growing apart. I know it won't be simple or easy, none of the good things in life ever are, but you challenge me and excite me more than anyone I've ever known, Ada.

"And it's okay if you don't feel the same way," he says quickly. "I don't expect you to. It's been a year. We haven't so much as exchanged a text. But I wanted to be honest with you about how I feel. To tell you that I've spent every day of the last year thinking about you, and to see if maybe I still had a chance with you."

When he finishes, his eyes are wide with anticipation like he's still waiting for the other shoe to drop. For me to tell him there's been some misunderstanding, that this is all a mistake.

I step toward him, taking his hands in mine. "Do you really think I'd fly across the world and wait three hours in this heat if you didn't still have a chance with me?" I ask.

Jack leans toward me, mouth slightly parted, and I get that same excited feeling of anticipation as when the lights go down and the movie is about to start. My breath catches and my stomach contracts. Then he tips his lips to meet mine, answering my question with a kiss.

The kiss is full of idiosyncrasies. Slow and urgent. Desperate and deliberate. And I kiss him back, fingers coiling in his hair, heat pooling in the nooks between our sticky limbs as our bodies say all the words we haven't yet spoken. *I missed you. Don't let go. I'm here. I'm here. I'm here.*

The pads of his thumbs trace my jaw, sliding lower until he's cupping my face. Then he tilts my chin back, deepening the kiss, and my chest lifts, every part of me levitating, humming with a new tune. *Him, him, him.*

When finally we break away, Jack's grinning, lips swollen, face flushed with heat. "You're really here," he says, voice a little breathless.

"I'm here," I say back, mouth parted in an uneven smile.

The life I have is a good one. A life of movie nights with Allison and solo trips to Paris and painting murals for beautiful babies who haven't yet been born. It's full and complete and happy, but right now, with Jack's arms around me, both of us slightly out of breath, I know it's possible to be even happier.

"I feel really lucky right now," I say into his chest.

"I don't."

I look up, confused. "What do you mean?"

His gaze narrows in thought. "When we met a year ago, maybe that was luck or fate or whatever you want to call it, but that's not the reason we're standing here right now. We're standing here because we want to be. Because we're choosing this. Both of us."

My breath stutters, pulse ramming against my sternum as his words excavate something deep inside me. He's choosing me, not just out of convenience or obligation or because it's easy, but because he wants me, *all* of me. No expiration date. No breaks. No reservations or hesitations.

They're words I've needed to hear. And maybe Jack needs to hear them too.

I lift my gaze, eyes finding his through the dim half-light of the setting sun. "Yes," I tell him.

"Yes?" he repeats.

"Yes," I say again, this time more confident. "I choose you."

He tucks an errant strand of hair behind my ear, eyes wavering across me. "I choose you too." Then he pulls me closer, this time tighter, like our confession is an invisible string tying us together. The cadence of his breath is steady and I feel his lungs expand and contract against mine as though each exhale were filling me up.

"I'm trying not to have regrets," he says. "It's something I've been talking about with my therapist, but I do have one."

"What's that?" I ask, playing with the cuff of his shirt.

"That I never got to dance with you at the wedding." He holds out his hand, eyes flickering with warmth. "Will you dance with me, Ada?"

I balk at him. "You want to dance? Here? Now? In the street?"

"When in Rome, right?" He takes my hand, drawing me into the landscape of his body. We're both hot and sticky, clinging to one another like wet pieces of paper.

"It's sort of hard to dance without music," I tease as we sway back and forth, totally off beat.

His hands find my waist, fingers digging into the fabric of my dress. "I know. But we can try, right?"

I smile. Somehow it feels like he's talking about more than just dancing.

As we sway to a nonexistent beat, I play with the hem of his sleeve, eyes scanning the length of his arm. It takes me a moment to realize what I'm looking for.

"You didn't get the compass tattoo," I say.

He follows my gaze. "No. I didn't."

"You changed your mind?"

He shakes his head. "I was hoping you'd be the one to do it."

My heart swells, growing two sizes too big for my chest. "Really?"

"If you have any availability, that is. I heard you're quite busy."

"I'm sure I could pencil you in for a private session," I say, mouth splitting into a grin.

Jack lifts one eyebrow, giving me an unscrupulous look. "A private session, huh?"

I playfully smack his chest. "I run a very professional business, Mr. Houghton."

"I hope it's not all business," he teases.

My mind begs to skip ahead, to what comes next, to where this moment leads. But I shake the thought free, focusing instead on right now. On the seconds I can still hold on to. The rhythmic tempo of his breathing. The scratch of his facial hair against my cheek. The fact that we're choosing each other, and no matter what happens next, it will be together.

"Ada?"

I tilt my chin up to face him. "Mm-hmm."

"Do you have any plans tonight?"

"Funny you should ask. I'm actually meeting another guy at the pizza place down the street in fifteen minutes, so if it's cool with you, can we wrap this thing up?" I twirl my index finger.

He shakes his head, grinning. "That's too bad. I was hoping to take you on a date."

"A date?" I repeat like I've never heard the word before. "Now?"

"Yes, Ada. Tonight. A real one," he adds.

His fingers trail along my waist, dipping in and out of the divots in my lower back.

"What exactly did you have in mind?" I ask.

His mouth lifts into that flirty grin I know so well. "Well, I was hoping you might join me for dinner. I know a great pizza place. Best in the world, in fact." He gestures to the buzzing pizzeria behind us.

I put a finger to my chin in thought. "Mm, do you think they'll let me put pineapple on it?"

"No chance."

"And what comes after this date?" I ask.

He steps toward me, closing the remaining distance between us. "You want to know my intentions?"

"Well, I gotta weigh my options here."

He laughs then takes my hands in his. "Well, I'm thinking dinner, then maybe a walk around the square, you know, to digest after we consume copious amounts of pizza," he adds.

"Then?"

"Then we can talk."

I raise one eyebrow. "*Just* talk?"

His eyes shimmer in the warm, yellow light. Then he leans in close enough that the scruff on his jaw snags my cheek. "There might be more than just talking," he says. "I'll have you know my intentions aren't purely wholesome," he murmurs against my ear.

"Were they ever?"

"No. No, they weren't."

My cheeks simmer, mind racing ahead to Jack and me, pressed against one another, clothes on the floor while he shows me exactly what his intentions are.

"I have a hotel room not far from here." I nod down the street. "I'm not sure if you booked anywhere to stay tonight, but I'd be happy to share my bed with a stranded traveler such as yourself."

He pulls me closer. "Stranded traveler, huh? And you're sure you don't have any ulterior motives?"

My bottom lip disappears between my teeth, the corners of my mouth arching upward. "I might have a few."

"So . . ." He gives me a conspiratorial look. "Just to clarify, so no one is mistaken this time, you mean sexual intercourse?"

"I could provide a chart and some diagrams if that would be helpful."

Jack's eyes flare as he lifts his thumb to my lips, gently brushing against the peak. "I love hearing you talk dirty," he whispers.

I laugh and the sound echoes between us, traveling all the way down the street.

His dark eyes, now awash in pink light, sweep over me, hands roaming the length of my back, scraping against the sweaty skin below my neck before traveling up into my hair. He holds me closer, neither of us in a hurry to be anywhere, to do anything, other than be here, in this moment. Just us.

The sun is starting to set, and the sky morphs from pink to

lavender. I close my eyes, basking in the final moments of sun before it finally dips beneath the surface.

Soon enough, this moment, *this perfect moment*, will end. We'll board flights and head back to real life, where jobs and commutes and the inherent messiness of life await us.

We'll have things to figure out. We'll argue and say things we wish we could take back. We'll hurt one another and make mistakes. There will be good days and bad days. Hard times and easy ones.

But I want that because I want him. Because I know that here, in a series of fleeting seconds, on a street corner in Naples, under the shadow of beautiful buildings in a beautiful place, I'm exactly where I want to be, with exactly the person I want to be with.

Epilogue

2 YEARS LATER

"Mom, they're here!" I hear my sister yell all the way from outside the house. It's already dark at five o'clock and warm yellow light shines through the windows, casting long shadows across the driveway.

I shoot Jack a look. "I can't believe you wanted to cut our trip short for this. We could still be in Edinburgh, having hotel sex."

"As much as I love hotel sex, you know I'd never miss Thanksgiving with your family," he says, pulling a hastily purchased bag of dinner rolls out of the back seat of the car. "Besides, aren't you excited to tell them the news?"

A jittery smile spins its way across my face. "You think they'll be happy?"

Jack leans over and plants a delicate kiss on my forehead before whispering, "Are you happy?"

"Deliriously."

"Then they'll have no choice but to be happy too."

He's probably right. But a flurry of nerves whips up inside me nonetheless.

"Do you think your mom made her berry cobbler again this year?" Jack asks, excitement dancing in his eyes as we ascend the front steps of Collin and Allison's house.

A smile tugs at the corners of my mouth. "Of course she did. You only told her you hoped she would make it thirty-seven times. And you know she can't resist you."

"Few women can," he says, giving me a rueful look.

I roll my eyes, trying—and failing—to pretend like even now, three years later, that look still doesn't come with a whoosh of heat and an increased heart rate.

Jack lifts his hand to knock on the front door and a second later Allison appears with Francesca in her arms and Collin behind her, grinning ear to ear.

"You made it!" Allison cries. "We didn't think your flight would land in time."

Collin and Jack exchange one of those bro-y slap-on-the-back hugs and I lean in to give Francesca a sloppy kiss on the cheek.

"How's my favorite girl?" I coo, taking hold of her chubby little wrists. She giggles, making me instantly forget what was so great about Scotland and hotel sex anyway. "How's it possible she got even more cute than when I last saw her?"

"That's because she takes after my wife," Collin says, kissing the top of Francesca's head. We all give an obligatory *aww* except Allison, who rolls her eyes, pretending to be embarrassed by her husband's flattery.

Mom and Bill come in and give us both hugs.

"We're so glad you could make it," Mom says. "I made two cobblers, just in case."

Bill wraps his arm around my mom's shoulders. "She's been baking all day."

Jack beams. "Thank you, Mrs. Gallman. That's really kind."

My mom shakes her head. "How many times have I told you, it's Christine."

"So? How was Scotland?" Allison asks, ushering us inside and out of the cold. "I can't believe you two wanted to go back there, especially this time of year. Wasn't it freezing?"

"We managed to stay warm," Jack says, catching my eye.

"We sure did." I lean against Jack, placing my left hand on his chest like it's on display.

Allison's gaze narrows in alert, like she's a police dog ready to sniff out a bomb. Her eyes dart suspiciously between us before landing on my left hand. As soon as she sees it, she screams.

"Oh my God! Shut up! Shut up!" Allison hands Francesca to her husband before snatching up my hand to examine the diamond on my ring finger. "You got engaged! I knew it!" She looks at Collin, hopping excitedly from foot to foot. "See? I told you Jack would propose in Scotland!"

"Well, not exactly," Jack says, fighting back a grin.

Allison frowns. "What do you mean *not exactly*?"

Jack takes my hand in his and gives it a squeeze. "We didn't get engaged."

Allison's frown deepens. "I don't get it. So that's not an engagement ring?"

I shake my head, heart thumping wildly inside my chest. "It's actually"—I pause, eyes dancing to Jack—"a wedding ring!"

"Surprise!" Jack yells as he and I burst into excited laughter.

Mom's, Allison's, Collin's, and Bill's mouths all fall open.

"You got married? In Scotland? Without telling us?" Mom asks at the same time Allison cries, "You *eloped*?"

"Well, you know Jack and me," I say, eyes finding Jack's. "We're not really into big weddings."

Acknowledgments

Whenever I start reading a new book, the very first thing I do is flip to the acknowledgments. There's something so special (and tear-jerking!) about seeing the pages and pages of people who spilled blood, sweat, and tears to get that book into the hands of readers like me. And now, as I write my own acknowledgments—oh boy, here come the waterworks!—I can't help but feel a swell of emotion thinking about all the people who supported and encouraged me, who spent HOURS on plot girl walks, talking out developmental edits and character arcs, who let me agonize and overthink and verbally process until I was blue in the face. You know exactly who you are, and this book truly wouldn't exist without you.

First, thank you to my dream editor, Sareer Khader. You have been, well, *a dream* to work with and I am endlessly thankful to have you as my creative partner. Thank you for loving Jack and Ada the way I always hoped an editor would.

Thank you to my amazing agent, Kim Lionetti. I am still pinching myself that I get to have you in my corner. Thank you for everything you've done to help get this book off my computer and into the hands of readers. Also, thank you to Maggie Nambot. I am so glad we slid into one another's DMs when I was in Orlando and that we got to meet. I hope our paths cross again soon!

Thank you to Vikki Chu for the gorgeous, action-packed cover that truly captures the spirit of *Wedding Dashers,* and to the whole team at Berkley for their support.

Thank you to my tough-as-nails CP, Kelli Moon, who always pushes me to be better even when I don't always want to be pushed (you know I love you). Your fingerprints are all over this manuscript and I am so thankful for all the hours—honestly, more like cumulative *days*—you spent helping me refine and hone this book into what I hope is the best version of itself. Most importantly, thank you for being the first person to tell me you thought this book was "the one." As usual, you were right.

Thank you to the board of directors aka "the plebs" aka the group chat that I consult before I quite literally do ANYTHING (including send this to my editor). Amy Buchanan, Kjersten Piper Gresk, and Ava Watson, y'all are the sisters I never had, and I love you so much. Writing is a very solitary endeavor, but y'all make it a team sport and I am endlessly thankful to have you on my team.

Thank you to Megan Oliver for your brilliant feedback and for always being one text away. I am so glad we met in the most unconventional way. Thank you to Ellie Palmer, who is much cleverer than I for thinking of the name Sleeve It to Me.

Thank you to my Smoochpit mentor, Meredith Schorr. I might be biased, but I'm pretty sure you're the best mentor ever. Thank you so much for your editorial insight, publishing wisdom, and always sage advice. This book is much, much better because of you.

Thank you to my OG writers group, Apheira, Erin, Hannah, and Malina, for being on the early parts of this journey with me. Special thank-you to Erin for your comment, "Where is the sex scene? Did I miss it?" thus prompting me to write my very first sex scene.

Thank you to Rachel Andeen for your thoughtful insight on a very, very early draft.

Ahhh I feel like this is the part of the Oscars speech where the music starts playing and I know I'm supposed to wrap things up!

Thank you to my best friend: my mom, Daphne. You haven't read the book, or idk, maybe by the time you read this you'll just have finished, and I'll be breathing down your neck, waiting to hear what you thought, but I literally wouldn't be writing this without your tireless support. I know rom-coms aren't exactly your cup of tea, but when I asked you to read just one to better understand the genre, you read ten, and nothing says *I support you* louder than that.

Thank you to my husband, Alex, for your love, support, and laughter, and also for that one time you slept wearing a zebra-print eye mask. No, for the last time, this book isn't a long-form fantasy about you.

Thank you to the closest thing I have to a sister: my best friend of twenty-five years, Demi of Demi Karina Custom Bridal fame. Thank you for making my wedding veil and transporting it to my own destination wedding, and then later explaining to me how to fix a small tear so I could write about it. Thank you for making sewing hot. I love you and I am beyond blessed to call you my lifelong best friend.

Thank you to all the dear friends who ever asked me how writing was going. The fact that you kept asking year after year, even when I had nothing to show for it, means so much to me.

Thank you to my in-laws, David and Susan, for hyping me up and always having a new book idea at the ready. I'll be sure to find a way to squeeze mermaids AND outer space into the next one.

Thank you to the Berkletes, SF2.0, and the Kitchen Party. I am so thankful to be part of such supportive, talented communities of writers.

And finally, thank you to everyone who has been a part of this journey. Like any good road trip, this journey had its share of hills, valleys, layovers, and detours, and I truly wouldn't have made it to this story's final destination (publication!!!) without you.

Wedding Dashers

HEATHER McBREEN

READERS GUIDE

Behind the Book

This story is a love letter to many things, but it is first and foremost a love letter to the year I lived in England. A year spent taking risks and saying *yes*. From 3 a.m. flights to Berlin and renting a terrifying apartment in Paris that didn't have a bathroom (my friend and I had to pee in the sink!), to working at a haunted opera house and meeting people I'm lucky enough to still call my best friends. It was a formative year that changed me, challenged me, and showed me just what I was capable of. And so, four years later when I started writing *Wedding Dashers,* it felt very natural to set Ada's story somewhere that played host to my own coming of age.

Anyone who's lived through their early twenties knows what a wonderfully chaotic and confusing time it is. A time of experimentation and self-discovery and all the extreme highs and lows that come with that. A time when it often feels like you're doing both too much and not enough, and like you'll never catch up to everyone around you. Which is exactly why when I was twenty-two, I decided that while my friends were starting careers and joining the "real world," I was going to move to London and complete a master's degree in art management despite having zero clue what on earth I was going to do with it (and quite frankly, still don't).

When I think back on that wing-stretching, horizon-expanding year, I think about how London wasn't just somewhere I lived, or a crowded, polluted city bursting with art and history and culture, or even the backdrop to my adventures—the city itself *was* the adventure. It was both the main character and the setting.

If you've ever spent any time in London you'll know that public transportation is as much a part of the experience as Buckingham Palace and fish and chips. Iconic red double-decker buses. A cool, robotic voice reminding you to mind the gap between the train and platform. The instantly recognizable circular Tube logo. And of course, the notorious train strikes that can turn navigating what is typically an incredibly user-friendly transportation network into a major headache.

Said headaches eventually became the spark for this book, one that would center around various modes of transportation, Murphy's Law, and loose reimaginings of my own misadventures.

Like the time my dad and I rented a car to drive from Edinburgh to St. Andrews and got flipped off every time we veered out of our lane because we were both too jet-lagged to stay awake at the wheel. Or the time I missed the last train from Windsor back to London and spent hours on a cold, lonely train platform frantically trying to figure out a way back home. Or the time my British friends showed me the dating show with the naked people, and I couldn't believe that was allowed on TV (though my friends reassured me, only after 9 p.m.).

I so clearly remember thinking, as I struggled to drag two massive suitcases through the London Underground on my way to a flat I was supposed to share with a stranger I met on the internet—unsure if I was about to have the best year of my life or get murdered—that *if I can do* this, *I can probably do anything.* And now, seven years later, as I type this out, I still think that's true. During that magical, sometimes woeful, ultimately wonderful year, I made lifelong friends, discovered new favorite places, and learned a lot about myself along the way.

I learned how to stand on my own and try new things and engage with other cultures and perspectives. Most importantly I learned how to be alone. So much of that year abroad was spent on my own: living alone, cooking alone, shopping alone, boarding planes and trains alone. But I was never lonely.

Well, sometimes I was, but I learned how to enjoy my own company, how to be my own best (and sometimes worst) travel partner. How to sit in silence and stillness. How to listen to, and wrestle with, my own thoughts.

And in many ways that's really what Ada's story is about too. About learning to be enough on her own. About discovering who she is and what she's capable of amidst failure and frustration. About finding empowerment in the vulnerable, the unknown, the scary, the difficult, and letting it mold her into a stronger, braver, more confident version of herself.

So much of this story is a tapestry of my own experiences—an interwoven collection of memories and love letters to places I've been and people I've met, and how the joys and heartaches of travel have shaped me. (I even have my own compass tattoo to prove it!) So whether you're reading this from the comfort of home, a plane, a train, or an automobile, I hope this story takes you somewhere new and fun, somewhere you can escape "real life" for a little bit and have your own adventure.

Discussion Questions

1. Have you ever told a stranger a secret thinking you'd never see them again? What happened?

2. Ada lost sight of her own wants and needs while in a relationship with Carter. What are ways someone could rediscover themselves after leaving that type of relationship?

3. Ada "failed" the first time she pursued her dream. Have you ever had a setback while pursuing a dream? How did you handle it?

4. At the end of Ada's relationship with Carter she remains optimistic that she will one day find the type of loving, supportive relationship she needs. Jack, after his breakup with Lexi, grows cynical and decides to give up on love entirely. Why do you think people often respond in such extremes when it comes to heartbreak? How do *you* respond to heartbreak? Are you more like Jack or Ada?

5. Prior to the wedding, Ada believes she knows better than Allison and therefore has a right to protect her from making "bad decisions," which Allison disagrees with. Do you think you can ever truly protect your loved ones from making a choice you disagree with? Or do you think it's up to them to make their choices and learn from them if they do end up being wrong?

6. Ada and Jack experience many travel setbacks on their journey from London to Northern Ireland. Have you ever had a travel setback? How did you handle it?

7. After the wedding, Jack and Ada decide to put their relationship on hold while they heal. In what situations do you think people should heal separately versus together?

8. At the beginning of the novel Ada is a firm believer in luck, while Jack is not. Do you believe in good luck and bad luck?

9. After Ada loses her business, she struggles to rediscover her creative spark. Have you ever gone through a period where you struggled with something like this? How did you rediscover your passion?

10. Ada has preconceived assumptions about both Collin and Jack, but later realizes she was wrong. Have you ever made an assumption or drawn a conclusion about someone before truly getting to know them and later realized you were wrong?

Heather's Forever Faves

- *Beach Read* by Emily Henry
- *When I Think of You* by Myah Ariel
- *Exes and O's* by Amy Lea
- *The Truth According to Ember* by Danica Nava
- *Sarah's Key* by Tatiana de Rosnay
- *Let's Call a Truce* by Amy Buchanan
- *Yours Truly* by Abby Jimenez
- *Water for Elephants* by Sara Gruen
- *How to Fake It in Hollywood* by Ava Wilder
- *Bend Toward the Sun* by Jen Devon
- *Anna and the French Kiss* by Stephanie Perkins
- *Before I Let Go* by Kennedy Ryan

Author photo: *Almodine Thompson*

HEATHER McBREEN currently lives in Seattle, Washington, but spent the best year of her life living in London, where she completed an MA degree in arts and cultural management. When she's not writing or reading books about kissing, she can be found surfing the web for travel deals and plotting her next adventure. *Wedding Dashers* is her debut novel.

VISIT HEATHER McBREEN ONLINE

X HeatherJoyMc

HeatherMcBreenWrites